ROOT
OF
DECEPTION

By

Jeff W. Temple

Root of Deception is a work of fiction. Names, characters, places, and incidents are a product of the author's imagination and any resemblance to actual locales, business establishments, events, or persons, living or dead, is entirely coincidental.

ISBN: 979-8-9875794-0-4

for the memory of

Allen "Buck" Plank
1951 – 2022

my friend

Thanks to the following people for invaluable assistance and advice:

Detective Joseph Centeno, Philadelphia Homicide

Salvatore J Canzoneri

William Greenleaf

A special thanks to my wife, Debra, who has always supported my creative pursuits. Her wit, savvy, and sense of humor inspired the character of Amy Lepone.

CHAPTER 1

Alvin Cruz clicked off three more photos and lowered the night vision camera. He glanced at his watch—12:19 A.M. The whole thing had taken less than twenty minutes. He watched for a moment as they left the gazebo. The man went one way and the mystery woman another. He didn't need to follow, at least not in any hurry—the man's 2019 Lexus LS 500 had a hidden GPS locator. Even if Mr. Bigshot didn't head home to his very pretty wife, tracking him would be easy.

Cruz stuffed his equipment in a leather bag, emerged from behind some hedges and quickly started across Tacony Creek Park. Loosely matching the path of the woman, he went just fast enough to catch up without attracting attention. She was on the sidewalk now about a hundred feet away and turned the corner past a long chain link fence. She slowed about halfway up the block and glanced around, looking a little nervous. *Interesting—was it routine caution or did she have reason to be edgy?* Turning the corner, he was closer now and stepped between two parked cars, crouching down. She came to a stop by a light green SUV across the street from some twin rowhomes. He pulled out the camera, twisted around for a better view and fired off a series of shots of her under the streetlights. She climbed in and drove right past him so he ducked down and leaned over to snap a few of the car and license plate. A Mazda, he was pretty sure, probably a CX something-or-other in good condition. He walked back down the street and took a moment to assess this odd little rendezvous, not knowing what to make of it.

Whoever she was, she knew her destination all along. And yet, she parked at least a block farther away than necessary. Unusual, since most women alone at night would park close as possible. He remembered watching as she approached—slowly, alert. She was wary and tense about the meeting. As well she should be since Mr. Bigshot had been lurking in the bushes for ten minutes before she arrived. *Idiot …*

Damn it! Now he wished he'd unpacked his long-range listening equipment so he could have heard and even recorded that conversation. From the start, it was obvious this guy never had a late oversees conference call. Expecting only kissing, hugging, and then a dash to the nearest motel, he hadn't thought to need it. When a suspected wayward husband lies to his wife and comes to an otherwise-deserted public park so late and a sexy young woman comes along—well, it's a natural assumption. Now at least it was safe to report that this gal wasn't a mistress. In the last few days, the guy seemed totally into phone calls, texting, fax-ing, fattening snacks, office meetings, and tending to business. He yelled a lot about stupid shit, needed to lose forty pounds, and liked three-martini lunches. So far, that was the extent of his vices.

One thing for sure: the babe from the gazebo was *hot*. Late twenties, around five seven, trim, but not thin. He hadn't picked up on the gorgeous tanned skin until seeing her under better light. Maybe of Latino heritage. The long dark hair pulled back in a French braid was sexy. If needed, he could track her down now easily.

The question on his mind: *what was this night's event all about? Industrial espionage? Payoff?* They obviously were not lovers. Not even ex-lovers or just-breaking-up lovers. Through the wonders of enhanced optics, he'd watched the exchange carefully but at a bad angle for lip-reading. The green and white image was satisfac-tory and he got a number of good shots. From their expressions, he knew the talk was serious in nature. They weren't allies, exactly, or even friends—more like strangers brought together by … *something*. Not necessarily criminal. Suspicious, to say the least.

Trying to come up with answers, he strolled back to his car, wondering how he ever stumbled into this line of work. Sure, it was fun—most of the time. Other times, boring. He did enjoy handing out business cards and introducing himself as a PI. The person's face often lit up with images of a livelihood that was all glamour, gunfights, and slick dialogue. That was

3

television. He was more likely to spend a day combing through dreary paperwork or handling a stakeout from behind a dumpster than anything even remotely exciting. At age 36, he wasn't getting rich but did all right. A few friends in Philly PD came in handy when he needed a peek at official records or found himself in trouble—which was more often than not. All he did in return was an occasional odd job or throw a little intel their way. Sometimes, sure, his methods might drift into the shadows of legality. But he never lied, manipulated, or manufactured evidence. His father, a newspaperman, had taught him that facts and truth would let justice prevail. Of course, sometimes one needed special equipment to find it. Besides night-vision binoculars, disguises, phone taps, listening devices, and well-placed spy cameras were his tools of the trade.

He climbed in his 20-year-old Pontiac Sunfire, pulled out a device hidden from under the seat and switched it on. He smiled—it looked like Mr. Fancy Car was heading home.

Why the hell would she think he was cheating on her?

CHAPTER 2

"Well, this is it here. On the right."

The man nodded and angled towards the curb, bringing the shiny convertible to a stop and flashed a smile. He didn't look like a dirtball. Not really. Sort of average with neither rugged nor handsome features. Average height, average build, but way above average in felony suspicion.

"I sure hope you're gonna invite me in for a nightcap," he said playfully.

"Hmmm," Amy said, pretending to consider the matter. She was definitely inviting him in. She just didn't want it coming across too easy. "It is late," she said. "And I'm suddenly a little tired."

"It's early and it would just be for a goodnight drink. I did drive you home."

She gave a dubious nod, so he pressed further. "And don't forget our dinner date … this Sunday."

When she asked earlier where they would go to dinner, he suggested Venita's in Chestnut Hill and she became appropriately gushy. Men like this figured that all you had to do was name a few of Philadelphia's classiest restaurants and the ladies would swoon. Sure—for actual hookups, it probably worked a lot of the time. Amy smiled. "Yes, of course, Dirk. I guess one drink will be fine."

Energized, he jumped out and ran around the car to open the passenger door. She nodded thanks and led the way, realizing that the profile on this guy was pretty darn accurate.

He'd given his name as Dirk, although it wasn't really his and he took great care to hide his true identity. She was pretty sure he'd have a phony driver's license with the name Dirk Allewelt and business cards with a non-existent company. His real dossier showed employment in the family's thriving business. She was sure this was a token position at best, since he'd flunked out of four colleges before the parents finally gave up. The flashy wheels were a rental. For tonight, he'd chosen a classic convertible. When they'd left the club and reached the parking lot, she'd said, 'Oh, wow. Is it a Corvette?' It seemed to be all he could do to keep from laughing out loud while politely explaining that it was a 1967 Austin-Healey.

"Nice place," he said, as she led him inside.

Which Amy knew was a load of bullshit. Dirk Allewelt was really Zachary Chastang, a thirty-one-year-old trust fund kid, party animal, druggie, and serial date-rapist. The decoy apartment was properly prepped in the Greys Ferry section, a small place next to an Italian market, a typical two-bedroom for a single woman of average means. So well prepared, in fact, she would swear to the lingering scent of leftover Chinese and stale beer in the air. There were knick-knacks on a shelf, some silly pictures on the fridge, and a living room set with a faux-leather sofa and recliner that might have been halfway-decent a few years back. Her cover would give the impression of an eager partier who got decked out to get her groove on in posh nightclubs, hoping to hook up with doctors, lawyers, and other high-rollers.

"There's beer in the fridge," she said. "I've got wine and hard stuff, too. I'm going to freshen up. Make yourself at home, Dirk."

"Take your time," he said to the closed door. "I'd be glad to fix you something. I make a mean Cuba Libre—how's that sound?"

Her reply was quick. "Just fine."

"Coming right up."

Amy stood by the bathtub, looking towards the door at the full-length mirror, and had to grin at the image looking back. The black knit skirt was a little daring, five inches above the knees and hugged her shape. The legs were fit from regular exercise and a pink blouse plunged just enough to preview the arrangement underneath. Amy Lepone, Homicide Detective. But tonight, on loan for an undercover op by a special task force. She assumed the offer was due to her good record, age, familiarity with the area, and physical description which matched Chastang's victim profile. She had been briefed late in the afternoon and gladly accepted the assignment. The only preparation thought necessary was some hair styling and glitzy clothes in her size.

Yes, she looked fabulously sexy but no way was she telling her mother about this.

"You're really doing great."

The sudden voice from an earbud startled her a little. It was Sergeant Amos, the task force commander. "Thanks," she whispered. A miniature microphone was sewn to the inside of her blouse.

"Chastang is looking over the apartment. Bedroom. Now the spare room."

Amy calmed herself. "Is he going for it?"

"Looks that way. In the kitchen now. Checking the fridge. He took out two glasses. Rum. Now he's slicing up pieces of lime. There it is. Yep. He just took a canister from an inside pocket. And a sugar packet. It's a go. I'm sure he'll hand you one of the glasses. Hang back by the kitchen. We're all in position. Good luck."

Of course, sugar. Amy knew that some of the common drugs used in date-rape were salty or had a peculiar flavor, so a sweet drink was best to disguise any shift in taste. Okay. The time had arrived. Give a great performance and reel in this sorry excuse for a human being.

Amy reappeared with a festive vibe. "Okay. Sorry to keep you waiting."

"Cheers." He said and handed her a glass.

Well, didn't waste any time, did he? She accepted it from him with a grateful nod. "Thanks. I've always liked—"

The knock on the door was startling and he looked up, alarmed. "Who's that?"

Amy shrugged with a look of ditzy. "I don't know."

"Expecting anyone?"

"Nope."

Chastang walked to the door and looked out the peephole. "What is it?"

"Delivery," came the reply.

He whipped opened the door so fast that the black man in a plaid shirt and baseball cap took a step back. It was Sergeant Amos, the one in charge. He had a pizza box with a 'Traditional Taste of Italy' logo. "We didn't order anything."

"Sorry, man. I got a call for this address."

Amy slipped behind the counter, grabbed an evidence jar from a cabinet, and poured in the contents from her glass. She quickly refilled it with plain Coke as Chastang got in the Sergeant's face. "It ain't here, I'm telling you, man."

"Isn't this two-oh-four?"

Amy stepped forward and pointed. "No, that's the one to the right. With the blue shutters."

Chastang slammed the door in the man's face. He turned around and she could see sheer delight in his expression as she sipped her drink. She accepted his courteous touch to the small of her back and followed his lead to the couch while talking about a promising job at her uncle's plumbing supply store. He made a pretense of listening as she droned on and tried her best not to lose sight of the objective.

"What do say we toast your uncle, "Chastang said. "He sounds like a great guy." He raised his glass, then took a big sip. She played along and took a healthy slug, watching the eager tell on his face. They chatted for a few more minutes and she kept sipping, then gently leaned back, beginning to slur her words. She sat quietly when he got up to dim the lights.

"I'm really fading." She giggled. "Sorry. kinda tired. I guess maybe you should go."

Chastang smiled. "I think I'll stay a while."

"I really need to sleep. Got an early day."

"Yes, I know. At your uncle's hardware store."

"Plumbi'g s'plies."

"Whatever."

Her glass was nearly empty. She clunked it down on the coffee table and said, "What's that buzzy fun?" She relaxed her body and sank deep into the cushions, keeping her eyes about three-quarters closed.

Chastang laughed and looked her over. She knew what he was doing. Sure, fantasizing. But he was relishing the silly expression, her vulnerability, helplessness. This was the time when his victim would start being very agreeable.

"I think we should get you out of these clothes," he said.

"Clothes?"

"Yes." He chuckled and reached over and ran his fingers across her shoulder and arm, then slowly slid down to caress her breast. "That material you have over your skin. It's in my way."

"Material?"

"You just relax. You won't remember this tomorrow, anyway."

"I got to turn in."

"We'll turn in together," he said, beginning to pop the buttons on her blouse. When he had them undone, he spread it open and stopped to admire the lacy black bra and its contents. "Wow. Perfect. These are *real*, right?"

Amy made a grunt. "Huh?"

"Never mind." He grabbed her by the shoulders, gave a little shake and smiled. "Definitely real," he said happily.

Chastang stood and Amy glimpsed his head slowly turning one way, then another. She knew exactly what he was doing—making a plan. He looked towards the bedroom, then the bathroom. His MO was to dump the woman in a tub afterwards to wash away trace evidence. Looking down, she was sure he was wondering how much she weighed and how hard it would be to move her. Finally, he sighed and sat down, content to begin right where they were. He leaned in and wrapped both hands around her, pulled forward, then yanked up the bottom of her blouse. She let her head bob around, then flopped against his shoulder as he reached around back and began fumbling with her bra strap. With her hair in his face, it seemed like he was getting frustrated, and she wouldn't be surprised if he started looking for a pair of scissors. In her ear, the voice of Sergeant Amos said, *"That'll do it."*

Enough was enough. Amy said, "In the front, Asshole."

"What?" The word came out as a high-pitched yelp. Chastang leaned back and looked at her with bewilderment.

"The bra, idiot!" Amy said. "The clasp for this kind is in the front." She pushed him away, stood up and began fastening her buttons.

He took a disbelieving look at her near-empty glass on the coffee table, probably wondering if he'd mixed them up.

As if reading his mind, she said, "I didn't drink it." She crossed the room, unlocked the front door, and pulled it open. "Meet Detective Sergeant Amos of the ninth district. These gentlemen are with the local FBI office."

Sergeant Amos stated that he was under arrest, then began with "You have the right to remain silent." Chastang jumped up and tried to run. Amy gripped his wrist, spun him around and shoved his face against the back of the couch. Amos handed her a set of handcuffs and she enjoyed placing them on and hearing the unmistakable click. Amos continued the Miranda warning over Chastang's objections.

"This chick invited me here," he screamed while twisting around. "I don't even know her."

Amy stood him up, then held him down on the couch. "Oh. Well, we can fix that now. Amy Lepone. Detective." She went to the kitchen and retrieved a small jar with a blue cap that contained brown liquid.

Taking a pen from one of the FBI agents, she wrote on the label and held it up. "This is the drink you poured me. When we analyze it, I wonder what we'll find?"

Chastang's expression went quickly from outrage to fear.

"Yes," she continued. "The pizza. When he knocked, I secured your little potion in here and put plain Coke in my glass."

Chastang screamed out. "Get these fucking handcuffs off right now. I don't know anything about this shit. And I don't know what she put in that fucking jar. It could be anything."

"It could be, but it's not," Amy said. "I'll bet it's midazolam—right, tough guy?"

"That's crazy. All of it is." He turned to the men. "That bitch was a slut and I don't know what she did that night. The cops already questioned me about the whole fucking thing last month. They let me go, right? It means I didn't do anything."

"No," Amos said. "It means there wasn't enough evidence to charge you. Now there is. Possession alone of such drugs is a Class B felony in the U.S. We'll have a warrant to search your home by morning."

Amy got in his face. "Remember the waitress at the club where we met? She's an investigator with the DA's office. She collected the drink I pretended to sip. I imagine that contains a little of the same concoction."

"I ... I don't—"

"You don't have to talk to us," Amos said. Amy liked his style. Before today she'd only heard of him.

13

He wasn't tall but thickly built. He had dark brown skin, large hands and a funny nose like he might have been a boxer. "You have the right to an attorney and I suggest you get one. We know that you're really Zachary Chastang. We know where you live and that your father is respected in the business community. Here's how it shapes up—ten weeks ago you slipped your magic drink to a woman and she experienced bleeding after you raped her. She did the right thing by going to the hospital right away. Her memories were vague and all we managed to find at the time was a security tape of you walking past an ATM with her. Then there was the incident last month when you were questioned. We've been tailing you and know about your purchases. There are five cameras in this room. Every move you made, everything you said and did since walking in here is recorded. After tonight— you're really in *the shitter*. Think it over."

Detective Amos walked Amy outside, thanking her for the cooperation. "You were great," he said.

"Ahh, thanks. He's not too bright."

"Bright enough. He's done this to at least four women. Probably more. And then there're the ones who were too scared or too confused to come in with a complaint. His MO and description fit enough cases that we got approval for this. We can take his DNA now and send him away. Thanks."

"My pleasure, Sarge. I was glad to help."

Amy hopped into the back of a delivery truck that was really a mobile crime van, and had the concealed wire taken off from under her sleeve by a female tech.

"You were amazing," she said. "Sounded pretty intense in there."

"I'm just glad we nailed the bastard."

"You did. I listened in, every word. Just great."

"Thanks."

"Can you believe that jerk didn't even realize it was a set-up apartment? He still thought he was at your place."

Amy nodded. "Yeah. It's easy to prey on unsuspecting women who are just out to have fun. He comes off smooth, but phony."

"Well, you did great." She paused, then said, "I heard you're partnered with Frank McGrail."

Amy detected a slight shift in speech pattern. The woman was probably mid-forties, attractive in what men called the girl-next-door way. No wedding ring. *Was this one of her partner's old flames?* There was no telling if she was Frank's type; no one had ever narrowed that down since he seemed to know half the eligible women in town. If rumors were true, he might know a few *ineligible* ones, too. "Yes," she said. "It's been an experience."

"I'll bet. Such a sharp dresser. Has he still got those broad shoulders and intense eyes?"

Amy laughed. "You forgot the cocky strut and arrogant delivery."

The tech laughed along with her. Amy changed her clothes and they did small talk for a few minutes. When leaving, Amy didn't mention that she was headed to Frank's place.

CHAPTER 3

Amy pulled into Frank McGrail's driveway and came to a stop in front of the garage. She turned down Liz Phair in mid-song and listened to her 1993 Mustang purr for a moment before shutting off the V8. Purchased used while in college, with a little help from mom and dad, this was her baby. Over the years, she added keyless entry, a 6-CD changer, aftermarket speakers, replaced the convertible top, and had the engine rebuilt in 2016. Original condition and collectible value were not real concerns since she had no plans to part with it.

It was cool and clear, 71 degrees: gorgeous for an early September night. On the drive she'd barely listened to the music, instead reflecting on the Chastang operation in detail. She felt good, since for once, things had gone smoothly like a textbook case. Undercover work was not her specialty but it was satisfying to be part of a team to bring down someone like Zachary Chastang. She had actually decided to volunteer before they even finished the briefing. The FBI's local office tracked Chastang's movements in cooperation with Philly PD and expected him to make a move. The profile suggested that the suspect would go for a single woman, roughly 25 to 35, average height or shorter, brunette or redhead, and a lean figure with accentuated shape. She assumed that was the politically correct way to say *curvy*.

Amy tapped the screen of her cell phone to hear voicemails. The first was from her mother, a reminder about dinner tomorrow evening, and she made a mental promise to call her back in the morning. The second was from Frank, who was in Carbon County visiting his parents on his day off. A well-liked couple in their little community, they still lived in the four-acre family home on the side of a mountain not far from Jim Thorpe, PA.

"Amy, it's me. Still here but I'll be back in the city tomorrow by eight. Don't forget to check on that damn dog. Thanks, by the way."

A man of few words … Grinning, she thought how amazing it was that their partnership had transformed so much in a reasonably short time. It had been tense in the beginning. They'd been placed together, the seasoned top banana with a rookie, by the Chief of Detectives, a decision never made lightly, and she'd begrudgingly decided to make the best of it. Getting up for work those first weeks had felt like she was going in for a root canal. Frank seemed to have the personality of a bulldozer. He was big, gruff, and stuck to business. She thought the problem could be her college degree or maybe he was just pissed off at having a newbie tagging along. Initially, she suspected it was the *woman* thing, like she was a token concession in a man's job. Did her gender have anything to do with the move into Homicide? Reasonably, yes—it could have. To take her, surely a number of men would have been turned down for the position. But life was a series of puzzle parts that were always finding a way to connect. One of her father's favorite lectures had been about never trying to outwit destiny. He'd say, "most of the time, you'll notice that life kicks you in the teeth. So, when you get a break, take the win. Accept it. No guilt. Somehow, fate made the decision. The next time, it'll be someone else's turn and you won't get a say in that, either." She believed his words and never looked back. So far, it had worked out. To this day, she still wasn't sure if Frank's antics were a routine act for any new partner or he really hated her guts back then.

Then on their fifteenth day together, they came upon a serious three-car accident, maybe a minute or so after it happened. Not part of their regular duties but no other help had yet arrived. Frank parked to effectively divert traffic and flicked on their emergency lights, all while concisely calling in to dispatch. He was methodical, assessing the scene, directing shaken people off the street and quickly calming others. One SUV had gotten the worst of it. From extensive damage to the front and smoke billowing from under the hood, Amy knew that they'd need to move fast. The driver, a woman in her twenties, was barely conscious.

The air bag was cumbersome but she was able to reach under it and slip the seat belt from around the woman's shoulder. The strap around her waist was impossible to move and the release was jammed. Just as Amy turned to go find a solution, Frank appeared alongside. He produced a knife, seemingly from nowhere, slashed the airbag, then reached down and with one swipe, cut the seatbelt. They were able to get the woman out of the car and just far enough away before something exploded in the engine compartment, sending up flames and debris. Before long, first responders and EMTs had the situation in hand. Frank leaned over at one point and said quietly, "Always have a knife. Always. A flashlight, too."

That was all. No judgement. No criticism. Just advice—which she took. That, for no reason she could conjure up, seemed like a turning point. The real Frank began peeking out after that, the jokester, rule bender, sly fox. A little cynical, a lot charming. A friendship with professional success had emerged and she hadn't seen it coming. They did each other favors now, had friends in common, occasionally got takeout and watched a movie together. She'd had a key to Frank's house for what … at least six months? They told each other when they were out of line, off base, or full of shit. Even shared personal things— sometimes, not always. And the sharing was more hers than his. But she could live with that. Upon reflection, the Chief of Detectives had apparently known exactly what he was doing.

Amy grabbed her backpack, locked up and headed inside. Frank lived in the northeast, a family-oriented area on Montague Street near a section of Pennypack Park. His house was small-to-average for the neighborhood, a three bedroom, one-bathroom rancher with a secluded backyard, fenced in, and big back porch. She went up the short flagstone walkway, took out the key and let herself in. On the panel, she punched in the code for Frank's security system and couldn't help smiling at the familiar scampering sound. His place was masculine and not the work of a decorator. The nice-sized living room was dominated by a large sectional sofa in dark gray with a matching smaller one against the opposite wall. An old area rug with a wooden coffee table that could be antique. The obligatory recliner looked worn and was in optimal position for viewing the wall-mounted big screen, probably a sixty inch.

She went straight for the kitchen, the doorway blocked by a two-foot safety gate. Layla, Frank's puppy, danced in circles and yapped lightly at her presence. The five-month-old Golden Retriever had been a gift a month ago from Frank's parents who thought the addition would brighten Frank's life. Unfortunately, Frank didn't agree. Amy assumed they were trying to domesticate him, or at least experiment to see if such transitions were possible. She remembered her own mother's advice from long ago: "You can trust a man with a dog. It means he's the type to come home every night." Amy had done some research and came up with the name from a popular song by Eric Clapton, her own not-too-subtle attempt to secure the canine's status. It was certainly better than "dog," which was what Frank called her for the first week and a half.

Despite good intentions, Frank swore he hadn't time or patience for care and training. To *pet* people, a puppy would be a positive addition for any household and worth the adjustments. Amy actually agreed, since their beloved black Lab, nearing twelve, still lived with her mother in the house where Amy grew up. Frank, unfortunately, had no such sentimentalities, preferring his carefree come-and-go existence. No decisions had emerged yet, but she figured Frank was secretly contemplating Layla's eviction in a way that wouldn't hurt his parents' feelings.

Amy stepped over the gate, glad that she had changed into sweatpants and a t-shirt, and greeted the puppy who energetically sprang up and hammered her with flapping front paws. She wasn't sure if this was a purebred but the dog was sturdy with big bones and a soft light, yellow coat. She bounded back and forth and showed her excitement by urinating across the floor and upsetting her water dish. After a few moments of vigorous petting, Amy opened the back door and watched her bolt happily across the porch and into the fenced yard. In such nice weather, she knew Layla would gladly run around for at least a half hour before wanting back inside.

After cleaning up the kitchen, Amy walked in the living room, eyed Frank's massive brown lounge chair, and then flopped into it. She leaned back while flipping the side lever, and the foot rest popped into place. To one side was a TV tray with three remote controls and an empty bottle of Blue Moon Belgian White. Amy smiled—now she knew why these things were so popular. She jumped up, went to the kitchen, and returned a minute later with a cold Blue Moon for herself and a bag of chips. She was still revved up from the operation and the big lounger felt so good, kind of enveloping her in comfort. If she ever found time to relax on a regular basis, she might consider getting one for herself.

Recalling Frank's extensive cable package, she thought about watching a show to unwind. His tastes were heavy on sports but he also had HBO, Netflix, Prime, and a few other movie channels. She studied the remote control for a moment, then turned on the set and flicked around for a few minutes, while taking swigs of beer and nibbling chips. Apparently, the last things Frank watched were The Invisible Man, Once Upon a Time in Hollywood, and Star Wars: The Rise of Skywalker. Just the thought made her realize she'd never make it through a half-hour tv show, much less, a movie.

She watched the news distractedly for a few minutes and felt herself unwinding with thoughts settling onto a plan. It was well after midnight. Awake since 6 A.M. and this was the first moment of peace she'd had all day. If not careful, she'd be asleep in the chair. Also, there were concerns about Layla's potty needs first thing in the morning. Frank said he'd be back from the mountains by 8 A.M. Would he go straight to work or home first? Considering that, staying put made the most sense. She had no reason to rush back to her apartment and this way, there was more time for sleep.

Amy clicked the TV past regular programming until she found music channels and stopped at *I Want You To Want Me* by Cheap Trick. Smiling, she realized Frank had really influenced her musical taste with a shift towards classic rock. She hummed along and went through the house to get her bearings since she'd never been further down the hall than the bathroom. Frank's bedroom was easy to spot and relatively neat with curiously rustic-brown walls and beige curtains. The effect was warm and subdued. There were two framed movie posters: The Outlaw Josey Wales and Star Wars—not surprising. She spotted two ticket stubs in a smaller frame and looked close. They read: The Rolling Stones, Steel Wheels Tour, August 31, 1989. Amy smiled, thinking Frank would have been around 15 or 16 then—probably a memorable concert. The room was clearly masculine, efficient, and sported a king-sized bed. It looked quite comfortable but for whatever reason, she just couldn't see herself sleeping there. It wasn't exactly wrong and yet, if someone asked if she'd ever spent the night in Frank's bed, then the answer would be *yes*. Maybe that's what they always meant by "it's the principle of the thing."

She and Frank had never been intimate—not that the notion hadn't crossed her mind more than once. They maintained an informal sparring with her jokes about his late-night poker, numerous lady friends, and loose interpretation of police procedure. He needled her about meticulous paperwork, rule-following, college degree, and figure. They often disagreed on aspects of a case while respecting each other's opinions. Frank had been right more often since they'd partnered, but that was okay. He was the senior officer. Overall, however, she knew she pulled her weight. It was the trust, confidence, and familiarity that offset the boy/girl issue and helped them rely on each other. Overall, she liked him. As a friend. Was there a physical attraction? Sure. At six two, he was impressive with broad shoulders and a flat stomach. He defied the late-forties label and the wavy black hair showed only a hint of gray at the temples. A wry sense of humor kept people amused and good instincts solved crimes. The man definitely knew his way around a kitchen and had several dinner specialties he could whip up to impress a date. However, casual affairs or even a one-night stand with a partner was just plain dumb and seriously unacceptable. The truth was—she really couldn't see them together in *that* way. Physically, yes. Romantically, no. Their friendship had taken hold and was too rewarding to screw up with anything more. But there was still no damn way she was sleeping in his bed.

Another room had been converted basically into a den with bookshelves and a desk. Frank never came across as an intellectual but seemed to have a broad scope of knowledge. She knew why—he had quite a collection of reading material, both fiction and non-fiction. Not surprisingly, there was no computer. Frank embraced technology on the job but wasn't the type for home-based IMing, texting, and paying bills on-line. With her help, she hoped he would soon accept life in the 21st century. The third room fit her needs. Kind of a junk and sleepover area with cartons, a few storage tubs, an old armoire, a bureau with a small clock on top, some folding chairs against the wall, and happily, a full-sized bed. Probably maintained for inebriated partiers, she noticed it had clean sheets and a folded blanket. *It'll do.*

She went to find her backpack, then returned to the spare room and rummaged to see what clothes were available in case she went straight from here to work. Finding an acceptable wrinkle-free tan pantsuit, she got an empty hanger and hung it on the closet door. According to established guidelines, detectives were to dress in business-casual attire, unless a particular situation called for something else. Always prepared, she kept an assortment on hand. She spread out cosmetics, facial scrub, brush, toothbrush, and deodorant on the bureau. Removing the Sig-Sauer automatic pistol from its waistband holster, she tucked it next to her backpack. With a clean towel from the hall closet, she undressed and headed to the bathroom.

The tub was old-fashioned, probably original, but had an add-on sliding door for showering. She just stood for a moment, glad for the feel of the warm water, then washed and conditioned her hair. It was a shame, she thought, since it had been professionally trimmed and styled for her earlier assignment. Sighing, she knew she'd never be able to get it looking that good again. Just as she was soaping up, the lights went out.

Peculiar, she thought of the near-blackness. Fortunately, pale moonlight crept in from the bathroom's small window that faced the backyard. She relaxed for a moment, hoping the power would come right back on. When it didn't, her cop instincts took hold. She rinsed quickly and got out, toweling herself dry and pushing back her wet hair. Standing completely still, there were no errant sounds.

Sliding the curtain aside, she stood on tiptoes to look out in the moonlit yard and smiled—Layla was still running around, clumsily leaping and trying to bite something, apparently chasing moths or lightning bugs. Various porch lights and indoor lights glowed—the neighborhood still had power. All at once, a shiver of alarm went through her. *Why would Frank's house go out by itself?* She hadn't turned on appliances, air conditioning, or anything that might cause a problem. And Frank had never mentioned trouble with the electric.

Okay, one thing at a time. She knew for sure the house was locked up tight and felt secure. Still, she preferred to err on the side of caution. Wrapping up with a towel, she figured to arm herself for a quick check—no sense taking chances. She peeked out of the bathroom and looked down the hall left and right; it was mostly darkness with faint illumination coming from the living room, probably the big front window. The walls were faint outlines, the doorjambs vaguely discernible, and there was no sign of movement. Everything quiet. No problem. The spare room was ten feet up the hall and she always kept a good LED flashlight in her backpack that might require a little rummaging.

Amy started down the hall, still feeling antsy. The gloved hand that clamped her mouth seemed to come from thin air. She twisted immediately away from the attack and aimed her elbow high, connecting with what felt like a jawbone. She heard a groan and the grip weakened just enough. Pivoting, she slipped away from a powerful arm and glimpsed her assailant in the dimness, making instant determinations. Tall, big, strong, serious. He'd been hiding in the den. Not Frank and not a joke. She'd stunned him and needed follow-through. Using an open-handed straight punch, she aimed for the neck and connected, not as solidly as she'd hoped. The man made a gagging noise and stumbled backwards, slamming against the wall. Her towel unraveled and she dismissed the urge to grab on as it swirled to the floor. Although the sudden starkness was unnerving and a blood rush was deafening, her inner resolve took over. She was no more vulnerable without clothes—it just seemed like it. With more room to maneuver, she used a reverse sidekick and aimed for the solar plexus, feeling her foot connect slightly lower against hard bone and muscle. He moaned in pain and crumbled slightly, then sprang forward with amazing speed, snagging Amy's arm with a powerful hand. Flailing wildly, Amy broke his grip and turned away, sprawling on the carpet. She managed to roll with the fall and scramble quickly to her feet, only to see a fuzzy shape disappearing down the hall. A second later, there was a sound of shattering glass. She ran to the spare room, fumbled for her Sig and dashed out to the living room. Moonlight came through the big front window that outlined jagged glass and splintered wood. Her attacker had jumped, or more likely dove, right out the window. Armed and naked, she considered her next move and decided that foot pursuit was *not* an option.

She tried to quell the ragged panting by forcing slow, controlled breaths. Beads of sweat were forming on her forehead. Her weapon at the ready, she listened carefully and did a slow turnaround, then when back to the room and felt around for her flashlight. Placing it face up to adequately light the area, she quickly redressed in the same sweatpants and t-shirt. With a sigh of relief, she cupped her breasts for a second, glad for the support. If there was ever a Round Two with that guy, she vowed to be wearing a sports bra. Methodically, she scoured the house, flashlight in the left hand, gun in the right, one cautious step at a time. Satisfied she was alone, for now, a series of shivers surprised her, even though it wasn't really cold. Unused adrenaline and welcome relief—an odd mix. Questions began to flood her mind. *How did the guy get in? Rapist? Burglar? Serial killer? Did he know a cop lived here? Was someone after Frank and simply attacked the only person in the house? An old enemy or a new one?*

The most frightening questions were the ones she didn't want to think about: *What would have happened if she'd already been asleep? Or if she hadn't been in good shape from regular runs and kickboxing?*

While trying to figure out what the hell just happened, she went to the back door to let in Layla and then called the police.

Frank was thinking about the visit to his boyhood home during the ride back to Philly. It had been just an overnighter, but well worth the drive for his parents' anniversary. His father, a retired County Sheriff, and his mother, formerly a nurse, were happy, reasonably healthy, and had married right out of high school. From all appearances, they were still in love after 59 years of marriage. Next year, he would take a few days off, rent a place and arrange a party for their big 6-0. Maybe he'd try to make it a surprise and contact their friends himself.

He imagined that he was feeling a little family closeness since this visit had been different than usual. It was actually a jolt—the first time in all these years they'd brought up their son's 'love' life. They had never previously said anything directly, but it was obvious they'd always hoped for grandchildren. Old fashioned and set in their ways, they had only gone to a flatscreen television when their previous console unit would no longer perform. They played in a bridge club, listened to big band records, and still watched reruns of The Dick Van Dyke Show, Bonanza, and Gunsmoke. Throughout his teenage years, they had never talked much about relationships, and never about sex, condoms, pregnancies, or any such topics— all seemingly taboo. Last night, the bomb dropped and they'd outright asked. Frank's mother had held his hand at the kitchen table and said out of the blue, "Frankie honey, do you think you'll ever settle down and have children?" The question had taken him by surprise, although he supposed it was long overdue.

In the end, he went with the truth. He wasn't against the idea but simply never found a woman he wanted to have children with. Now he was creeping ever closer to fifty. Not too late by modern standards, although certainly coming down the home stretch. He was always looking and considering prospects, but …

What the hell?

Frank pulled into his driveway behind Amy's Mustang. He glanced at his watch—7:22 A.M. Her presence wasn't strange by itself since she either stayed overnight or came along early to let out that simple-ass dog. The thing that piqued his curiosity was the black plastic garbage bags taped over his front window.

Frank climbed out of his 2017 Chrysler 300 and looked over the property closely. The garden along the front of his house had crushed flowers and snapped-off plants. The window was definitely shattered and someone had cleaned up. Even so, tiny pieces of glass still glittered in the dirt. The outlines under the taut bags said that some of his wood panels had been dislodged or broken off. Not from a kid's soccer ball, it looked as though some drunken idiot had thrown a beer keg right through his window—which actually happened once in the summer of '09. *What the hell had Amy been doing?* It would be a little insulting if she'd thrown a wild bash with him out of town.

Frank let himself in and was somewhat relieved that his living room didn't resemble the trashed-out frat in Animal House. *That* had happened before, too. Everything looked intact, sans the window, and he quickly tapped the code into his security panel. Layla was on her hind legs leaning on the gate and giving little yelps from the kitchen. The dog could wait—Frank felt a great story coming and was anxious to hear it.

The house seemed deserted. The only discrepancy was the locked door into his spare bedroom. He took the key from above the jam, opened it quietly and a broad grin spread across his face. Amy was lying on her side and sound asleep, facing the far wall. Her bare legs stretched out from under a tangled sheet that covered part of her torso. She was wearing a blue t-shirt, but the tush and lace panties made the view really interesting. Frank crept in, leaned down and gently slid his arm around her waist. He whispered in her ear, "Will you still respect me in the morning?"

Amy snapped awake and scooted across the bed. She turned and mumbled, "Damn it, Frank! That's not funny."

"Neither is my picture window."

She sat up and pushed hair away from her face. "It's a long story."

"It always is. Want me to put on some coffee?"

"You hate coffee."

Frank grinned. "I have a coffee pot for guest emergencies."

"Oh, thank God."

Before long, Amy was nursing her second cup as they sat around Frank's kitchen table. Layla had been let out and back in, fussed over, scratched behind the ears, and was now applying her attention to a bone-shaped chew-toy. Amy had given a nutshell version of last evening, starting with the operation to snare a date-rapist and ending with the police response to the break-in and assault. They'd been here taking her statement, securing the area, and helping her cover the shattered window for more than two hours. She'd finally trudged exhausted into bed around 4:30 A.M.

"You won't believe," Amy said, "what this smart-mouthed uniform asked me. Obviously, I went all through the usual. You and I are detectives, partners, etcetera. First off, he asked me three times if you were around somewhere. When I told him you were at your folks' place, he asked me if that's what I wanted him to put in the report. Shit! Like I made it up on the spot and might want to think of something better. *Jesus!*"

"I see your frustration." Frank grinned. "What about this night stalker? How'd he get in?"

"I looked around pretty close. So did the patrol guys. The best I can come up with—he picked your front door. We'll need a check to be sure. I found it unlocked and I know I locked up."

"And my security system?"

Amy rolled her eyes. "Forgot to arm it."

"It was on when I got here."

"I armed it before I went to sleep."

Frank grinned. "This was *after* you were attacked?"

"Can we focus on something else, please?"

"Okay. So, this guy left by the *express* route."

Amy laughed a little. "Yeah. He must have shut off your breaker when he came in. I turned it back on."

"Okay. What'd he look like?"

"My image of him is a blur, more like a vague outline. It was pretty dark so I wouldn't be able to pick him out from mug shots. He might have a bruise or two."

"Gave him good ones, did ya?"

"Yeah. My elbow nailed the bastard's face. I got some distance between us and used a sidekick. I gave everything I had. It hurt my foot, Frank. Felt like I hit a wall instead of a stomach."

"So pretty fit. And you said he had on gloves. Then this wasn't like a junkie looking for a quick score. How tall?"

"Well over six foot. As big or bigger than you. Dark, long sleeve shirt and dark pants. Caucasian. He wasn't bald … or at least his head was dark like he had hair."

"Weapons?"

"I didn't see any. Didn't see him reach."

"He say anything?"

"Not one word."

Frank let it gel for a moment. "All right. He's prepared to get in quiet. Ditches the lights. He takes you from behind—or tries to—didn't have a blade for a quick kill. Didn't draw a gun when he met resistance. Sounds like he was pretty tough. Why didn't he continue to fight?"

Amy shrugged. Tough, and then some. That was the question needling her since it all happened. He'd run off—why? It all unfolded so fast, the memory was jumbled like some crazy nightmare. There'd been no time to think, to second guess options. On instinct, she'd met the challenge head on and controlled her fear. Police training had kicked in; she felt good about that. But now, looking back, she could see the truth. In her mind there'd been a fleeting sense of being overwhelmed, outmatched. And then suddenly, it was over. She'd won the battle—by forfeit. "I ... I don't really know."

"Who knew you were here?"

"Nobody." Amy didn't need to think about it. "*I* didn't even know I'd be here. That special assignment came up and went late. Came straight here to let out Layla. I planned to go home, then decided it made more sense to stay."

"Okay. Planned out.. I guess it could be a dirtbag has it in for me. Somebody I pissed off."

Amy had to smile. "Sure. Angry fathers, jilted lovers, jealous husbands. We'll need help with *that* list."

Frank scowled. "Thanks a bunch. I actually meant, you know, *criminals*. But let's think of it like a regular case. We have to narrow down what he had in mind. Either the guy was a burglar and thought the place was empty. Or he was after me. Or he *followed you* here. Think this could have something to do with your little sting last night?"

"Umm ... I'm not sure." The undercover thing? Oddly, the thought hadn't occurred to her. The break-in was so different, so detached from the earlier operation. "How could it be that fast?"

Frank said, "Just an idea. According to everything so far, this wasn't a garden-variety lowlife. He broke in for a reason. Could you have been tailed?"

"Well ... Maybe, I guess. Sergeant Amos didn't want to take chances. Our cars were in a business lot with an attendant a few blocks away on South 34th Street. After the arrest, I had the wire removed and changed clothes in the van, then walked to get my car. Nothing suspicious. I should have noticed another car behind me, especially that time of night. Thinking back … I guess I really wasn't looking."

"So—possible. Now, I hate to ask this. Could it have been a rape attempt? Like maybe some dirtball was out looking for trouble and saw you pull in here alone."

"You know, that crossed my mind—a *little*. But in this neighborhood, I doubt it. And from the perp, I have to say I didn't get that impression."

"Okay." Frank leaned back. "Not likely. Let's look at it this way. That asshole came here because he thought I'd be in bed asleep—or knew I wasn't home. Or because *you* were here."

Amy nodded. "Maybe. Let's go onto a different track. I'm figuring if that guy came in expecting to confront *you*, he would have been better prepared. You're big, well trained. He'd have a gun ready or maybe a Taser."

"I'll buy that. So maybe he expected the place to be empty."

"Or he might have thought I was someone else."

"Like who?"

"Well, you have quite a number of lady friends."

Frank frowned. "Me?"

"Ha. Yeah, *you*. Maybe Patricia."

"Nah. She's four inches taller than you and skinny with long, dark hair."

Amy looked at him aghast. "So, I'm not skinny?"

37

Frank raised an eyebrow. "Well, you're certainly not *fat*."

Amy laughed. "How about Angie?"

"Haven't seen her in a couple weeks."

"What happened?"

Frank looked puzzled. "With what?"

"Well, what I mean is—if a woman you date isn't around for … You know what? Forget it. How about Sharon?"

"Took off on tour."

"On tour?"

Frank nodded. "Yeah. Eighties and nineties tribute band. They're playing the Midwest."

"So," Amy said, tilting her head. "You date a woman who's in a touring rock band?"

"Yep. Plays guitar. Pretty cool, huh?"

She gave him a squint. "I suppose."

"Look. Let's assume just for a minute he was after *you*. We need to ask a couple of questions. Did he run off and do a Peter Pan out my window because he didn't think he could handle you? Or because he didn't want to try?"

Amy took a deep breath and exhaled slowly. "I've been wondering about that. You're asking what would have happened if it kept going?" Frank nodded. "I don't know for sure. I think I surprised the hell out of him and that gave me an edge. He seemed fast and very strong but didn't throw a punch. I never saw specific fighting skills so I just can't say."

"That makes sense." Frank grinned. "One thing does puzzle me. You'd just had a shower. Wrapped a towel around yourself, right?"

"Yeah."

"It's lucky the towel stayed on in the ruckus."

Amy shrugged. "I guess." She hoped her expression didn't give anything away. Frank didn't need to know the towel ended up on the floor. She just didn't want the squad room buzzing with tales of her in a nude karate battle.

"Anyway, you done good." He held up his palm and Amy responded with a lackluster high five. "I gotta say—it must have been a hell of a fight."

"Thanks." Amy looked down and back up again, speaking more solemnly. "Frank, I ... I was *so ... fucking ... lucky.*"

Frank reached for the coffee pot and topped off her mug, then shook his head. "Nope. It wasn't luck. Obi Wan has taught you well."

CHAPTER 4

"What's this thing?" Frank asked.

Goggles looked up from his microscope. "That's for isopycnic centrifugation. Uses a cesium chloride solution to isolate and separate DNA."

Frank was standing near a workstation that featured a collection of test tubes and a shiny metal device. "Yeah. That's what I thought."

Amy laughed, despite her distraction. Although Frank had glossed over the incident at his home, she knew he was bothered more than he'd let on. Frank's basic analysis was correct—that guy didn't break in on a whim. He was after something or someone. She'd made the report and turned it in but no one seemed overly interested. As far as their supervisor, Lt. Trainer, was concerned, she'd simply foiled a random burglary attempt, off duty. He'd actually seemed more interested in the reasons she was at Frank's home late at night. She'd explained—completely the truth—for all the good it did. She thanked God that Frank wasn't in town at the time. Otherwise, the rumor mill would have the two of them shacking up, a juicy misconception she didn't need floating around.

Amy brought her attention back to the matter at hand. They were at Goggles' lab in the Forensics building, for what amounted to a favor. Frank had removed his front door lock and replaced it with a newer and tougher unit. Goggles took the old one apart to determine if that was the way the intruder had entered. It was unofficial, just for Frank and Amy's enlightenment. No one wanted something entered into evidence for an attempted burglary with no leads, no stolen property, and no way to ID a suspect. Goggles was a good friend and possessed a strong knowledge of all the physical sciences. Mostly considered a Biological Sciences Tech, he was equally proficient in Forensic ID and Trace Evidence. The-30 year-old genius was a lanky five ten with short springy black hair and Buddy Holly-style glasses. The formerly thick lenses from his youth had been replaced some years back after laser surgery. His real name was Shawn DeLuca but his old nickname just stuck and wouldn't go away. One thing was sure—they were all glad to have him. Despite the grand portrayal on television, most actual police labs were underfunded, outdated, and often staffed with the passably qualified who couldn't find higher-paying jobs elsewhere. Fortunately, these facilities were a cut above most with varied sections that could handle latent fingerprints, DNA, toxicology, microscopic analysis, firearms, and photographic and video enhancement with relative efficiency. She wasn't sure exactly who was in charge of what or how the departments were structured, but they usually got solid reports and the answers they needed.

Goggles looked up and said, "Well, I can't be positive, but I'd say so."

Amy slid off the table and walked over. "No to be a pest, but why can't you be sure?"

"Well, it's an older lock with a lot of wear. Plus, there are two sets of inconsistent lateral scratches, some older and some look new."

Frank cleared his throat. "I, uh, had to break in myself a few years ago. Got dropped off and left my keys someplace."

"No keys … But you happened to have picking tools?" Goggles frowned. "Forget I asked. In that case, I believe a cogent theory is possible. There's a strong chance this was manipulated recently by someone skilled."

Frank and Amy looked at each other. Frank shrugged and said, "That's about what we thought. You can toss that lockset; I doubt I'll need it. Thanks, my friend."

"Don't mention it. How's that new addition?"

"A pain in my ass. Gotta let her out all the time and she still pisses on my floor. If you need a dog for some experiments, she's yours for ten bucks."

Amy backhanded Frank on the arm. "He doesn't mean it."

Goggles laughed and turned to Amy. "How are you doing? Okay?"

"It was a little tense. Yeah, I'm good."

"I heard you effectively subdued the intruder."

"Well," Amy said, while rolling her eyes. "I wouldn't say *that*, exactly." This was actually a good development. If people focused on the action, they wouldn't be thinking about anything else. She really wished she could have taken the guy into custody and brought him in to answer some hard questions. "The guy was big," she added. "I took him off balance and didn't let him use his size."

"That's great. I'm really glad you're all right." Goggles started to tidy up as Frank and Amy prepared to leave. "By the way, where was Frank when all this was going on? Asleep?"

Amy froze in mid-step and her eyes opened wide. She turned and glared at Goggles. "What the hell is *that* supposed to mean?"

Goggles looked at her strangely. "Why? I'm not following you?"

Omigod. Amy studied Goggles for only a second and realized that he wasn't clowning around or acting innocent—he really *didn't know*. The story was circulating rapidly without—to Amy's way of thinking—the pivotal factor. "Frank wasn't home, dammit. I was there to let out his new dog."

Goggles was a little startled. "Oh, okay. My apologies. I didn't know."

"Seriously. Frank was at his parents' place in another county."

"That's fine. Really. I did not hear that."

Amy looked at Frank. "This is just *great*. Everyone around here is in fucking law enforcement. So why can't anybody get a story straight?"

Frank seemed to restrain a laugh, barely succeeded, and held up his hands. "Hey! Don't blame me. I wasn't there, remember?"

His phone starting playing Kashmir by Led Zeppelin, a ringtone that Amy showed him how to download more than a year ago. He answered and she noticed his expression change after only a few seconds.

Frank ended the call and said, "A body awaits.

Amy looked over the neighborhood as Frank pulled their unmarked car, a beige 2003 Dodge Stratus, to a stop on McCallum Street in West Mount Airy. An impressive home of cut stone had landscaping that featured many varieties of shrubs that were immaculately trimmed and included a gorgeous canopy of tall trees. A handful of hovering onlookers ranged from old to young. Unknown to them, they'd all be discreetly photographed in the hope of finding their bad guy among them, checking out his handiwork. She knew it didn't happen often—but it happened. Official police vehicles stood out on the nice block— three patrol cars, an unusual white van with CRIME SCENE UNIT on the side, and a black van that read MEDICAL EXAMINER'S OFFICE. After signing them on the Crime Scene log, she donned the required rubber booties and latex gloves, then followed Frank inside a large home with a modern open floor plan and two-story living level. The ambient smell was sour and unpleasant—not really the owner's fault.

According to information they had so far, the deceased was resident, Marcus Jarrett, age 35, single, and lived alone. Seated on a gorgeous, deep brown, sectional sofa that looked like a Parker Living, she figured it would retail around four grand. Mr. Jarrett was dressed in neat Dockers slacks, sandals, and a tan pullover. He looked to be of average height and weight with neatly-trimmed dark hair and a bullet wound in his chest. His current coloring was like wet cement, the eyes and mouth open in an expression of surprise. A photographer was finishing up with stills and video while evidence technicians were starting to collect trace. Walt Danby, the Deputy Assistant Medical Examiner, was studying the corpse and making preliminary determinations as to the cause and time of death.

Amy looked over the scene and immediately nodded to Frank. A half-full bottle of Killian's Irish Red sat directly in front of the deceased on a fine glass cocktail table with leather upholstery around the edges. At the far end, another full bottle sat in front of a love seat that matched the couch. If no forced entry was apparent, it was likely that Jarrett knew his killer and that he or she had been sitting in the chair before the murder. Any prints on the bottle would be top priority, although lucky breaks were rare and obvious conclusions were not always correct. Initial hunches would be shelved until a thorough check of the premises was complete. Any and every detail could be important and a good detective never started out by leaning towards a pet theory.

Danby nodded hello to Frank. They'd been together on many such occasions over a span of years. He was tall and lean with thick white hair and piercing eyes, a combination that gave off an aura of wisdom, like a favorite uncle. "Been about eleven to thirteen," he said, saving Frank from asking. "I'll know more in a bit."

"Surprises?"

"Not yet."

Amy took that to mean the cause of death was just how it looked—so far. Danby was shrewd and didn't miss much. As always, these were just cursory findings—the actual autopsy would yield the complete story and final determinations.

"Who called it in?" Frank asked.

A uniformed officer standing nearby looked at a clipboard. "Anonymous. Female, adult. 10:04 A.M."

"Do you know what was said?"

"Yes, sir. I was given the call accession code by the dispatcher and listened through twice about fifteen minutes ago. It was short. A woman claimed to have heard shouting and gunshots. Was afraid her neighbor was in danger. She gave Jarrett's name and address. A unit responded and found the front door unlocked."

"At ten this morning? That's bullshit! The guy's been dead since last night. You sure she said *gunshots*—plural?"

The officer nodded. "Yes, sir. To me, the woman caller sounded agitated, sincere. There were typical traffic sounds in the background, nothing else. I checked with Communications. They believe the call was from a burner phone in the immediate area."

"Good work. I doubt it was really a neighbor. It's someone who didn't know when he really died. I'm guessing she walked in here this morning and found the body."

"And we'll need to find *her*," Amy said, and took off slowly through the house. They did their walk-throughs separately to get individual impressions. As always, she moved carefully, avoiding the little plastic evidence markers and any contact with surfaces until given the okay from technical services. She sniffed the air as she went, mindful of lingering scents. The place was enormous. There was no disarray anywhere. No evidence of a fight, burglary, or an intruder's search through the victim's belongings. The place had a solarium and three wood-burning fireplaces. A huge oak-paneled den, complete with pool table. Everything looked neat, tasteful, and organized. Mostly top-end furniture. On a high shelf were a few photographs that would likely be a younger Jarrett with family. She thought one man, probably the father, seemed familiar. Three small tennis trophies from amateur club tournaments with dates in 2009, 2012, and 2013.

She walked through the bedroom and peeked in the gorgeous walk-in closet. Nice dress shirts in 15 ½ / 33 and suits in a size 40R. The good stuff. She lifted the lid of a hamper that was only about half full of mixed clothing. She rummaged through predominantly men's items and noticed pink sweatpants in size medium and a purple 34B bra. The room was obsessively neat—no jackets hanging on chairs and no socks on the floor. The bureau drawers held typical men's wear in four of the drawers. In the other two, she noted several pairs of size 6 jeans, a pink V-neck T-shirt, three blouses, two more bras, panties, black exercise pants, women's socks, and a few sleek negligees. The large bathroom had digital panel controls with an oversized tub plus a shower. The medicine cabinet held the usual array of men's toiletries and a few common prescriptions that Amy wrote down. There was also perfume, facial cream, nail polish, various other cosmetics and women's deodorant. A home-office had an L-shaped desk that looked like fine oak with a modern laptop and all-in-one printer. There were shelves, trays, and cabinets that all looked remarkably uncluttered. Amy went further on and came to a back room with only a washer, dryer, three empty clothes baskets and a DeWalt toolbox. She went through a doorway that took her into a three-car garage with a 2019 BMW X4 sedan and a Nissan Titan pickup truck; both were registered to the deceased.

Nice wheels, Amy thought, and wrote in her notes. They probably wouldn't relate to the murder, but she was ever aware of Frank's rule of thumb that vehicles were number one among physical evidence. Cars and trucks were collectors—the grill, the tires, the carpet, the air filter. Many cases hinged on something left behind or gathered by a vehicle. If there were any concerns about the victim's recent movements, they would be searched and possibly impounded.

Amy went back to the living room where two orderlies had the body bagged and were readying it for transport. Frank was still taking in the scene, looking up and down, under and over.

Regina Kirkner, a top-notch CSI tech was in full crime scene gear, making her look like a puffy tan blob. The long blond hair was tucked under a stretchy cap. She knelt in the corner of the room, checking the floor through magnifiers. Amy called out, "Any prints on that other beer bottle?"

"Jarrett's, that's all." The woman sat up and slid the glasses off her face. "He twisted off the cap and sat it right where it is. Your perp never touched it. Did you get a look at his hands?"

Amy grinned. Regina had the nickname Gigi bestowed within the department. With a degree in forensic science and a minor in chemistry, she was a wizard when it came to crime scenes and made the jobs of many detectives a lot easier. "No."

"Professional manicure. Also, his right arm looks a little better toned than his left. I saw a few tennis racquets in the front closet. I'll bet he was a pretty good player. Mostly healthy food in the fridge."

Amy jotted notes. "What else?"

"My guess: a small caliber. Definitely no bigger than a .38. Bullet's still inside him. Pretty sure your shooter was sitting in that chair."

"What height do you figure?"

Gigi smiled. "You're putting me on the spot. I'll plug all the variables into our Virtual Re-enactment program once I get the wound tract."

Amy rolled her eyes. "Can you give me a hint?"

"Detectives—they're always in a big rush. Okay. I'm only guessing at the angle of entry. That said, it's likely someone no taller than me. I'm five seven."

Amy thanked her and stood out of the way while jotting down a few final thoughts When Frank seemed satisfied and ready to leave, she said, "Anything strike you as odd?"

"Not really." Frank thought for a moment. "Very ritzy, glad I don't have to pay the mortgage. This guy was neater than most. A handful of books and magazines around. Decent DVD collection. My hunch is that he worked a lot."

"That's what I thought, too. A huge place for a single man. Out of five bedrooms, only two have furniture. A lot of stuff in boxes. Seems like he hadn't lived here long. I can't wait for our techs to go over his computer. If he had a secret hobby or a vice, that's where it'll be. Also, I suppose you noticed he had a girlfriend."

"Or some weird fetishes."

Amy scribbled more notes. "He sat down with the shooter. Someone he knew. The person came to kill him and didn't drink from the beer bottle."

"Could be a friend or business associate who likes beer. Jarrett thought so."

Amy pointed at Frank. "What's the one rule you always tell me?"

"Never trust a man who hasn't seen Star Wars."

"No. Well, yes. What's the other thing?"

"Beware of the obvious."

Amy harrumphed. "Right! The shooter hates beer—asked for it to throw us off. Or he killed Jarrett, then got the beer and placed it on the table. He could've squeezed Jarrett's hand on it first."

"Nah." Frank grinned. "I like my way better. Beer drinker. I heard Gigi say it's somebody shorter than average. Let's go over his appointments and day planner. We can pick up our killer and have a confession before lunch. It happens, right?"

Amy shook her head and sighed. "Not often enough."

Amy was glad to be back at the Roundhouse to dig in. Police Headquarters was a peculiar building on Race Street whose interior reflected the rounded shape with curving corridors and walls. The PPD was divided into regional operational command north and

south, then into twenty-one districts, each headed
by a captain. There were more than 7,500 members
and 800 civilian personnel. Each handled the crimes
occurring in their respective jurisdictions from their
own district headquarters—except for murders. All
of those, city-wide, came to one of the three homicide squads in this building. A mugging across town
was handled in the district it occurred. If the victim should die, it became Homicide's case and came
straight to the Roundhouse.

It had taken Amy only a matter of minutes on the
internet before she knew why the man in the photo
with their victim had looked familiar. It was Bradley
C. Jarrett, a businessman who'd been well known in
the tri-state area. She'd called ahead to Nancy, their
researcher, who'd prepared a quick dossier. The man
had an impressive list of accolades: Vietnam vet with
two Bronze Stars, a degree in engineering from Brown
University on the G.I. Bill, started an excavating company in 1978 that soon branched into construction
and development. Had a reputation as tough, fair, and
donated to worthy causes. Died of heart failure a few
years back and the ensuing battle over the will made
interesting reading. Marcus Jarrett, his son and their
victim, had expected to inherit, but was unpleasantly
surprised by stipulations that provided a respectable
trust fund but no control over the company. From
what she could piece together, Bradley was a tireless
success and Marcus, an underachiever in his teenage years. He'd straightened out, earned a degree

from Clarkson University, and for years held a position of responsibility. Bradley remarried sometime after his first wife's death from cancer. His widow, Sylvia Stremmel Jarrett, now held the company reigns and was apparently of no mind to veer from her late husband's wishes. Marcus, with no further legal options, had finally moved from the family home only five months ago.

They'd need to interview Sylvia Jarrett, by all accounts a respectable force in the business world. Amy looked over the numbers and did a few calculations. By Sylvia's age now, she'd have been in her early twenties when she married the wealthy Bradley Jarrett, age 46. *Interesting* … Marcus would have been a young teenager. It couldn't have set well, particularly as he grew, who'd expected to gain control of a financial empire upon his father's death. Instead, he'd battled and lost, forced on the sidelines with a conciliatory allowance.

Frank appeared alongside Amy's desk. "Got big news," he said.

"Good or bad?"

"Well, more like some interesting and some weird."

"I'll take *interesting* first."

"Okay. Check this out: After we left, Gigi pulled up some prints at Jarrett's house belonging to your pal from last night, Zachary Chastang."

Amy was surprised. "Chastang?"

"Yep. Beer bottle. An empty in the kitchen. Plus a few others on the counter."

"So—they must have been friends. Let's see … *Damn it!* Chastang can't be our killer. He was under surveillance. Plus, can you believe it? *I'm* his damn alibi. He was with *me* getting arrested around Jarrett's TOD. I still want to talk to him."

"Oh, yeah." Frank turned grim. "Sorry, that's the weird news. Chastang's *dead.*" Amy's eyes widened and he continued. "His father's Cameron Chastang and has a lot of clout. Found a judge to sign off and had him released on bail earlier. A shot took him out less than an hour later in front of his house."

Amy stood up, too stunned to speak as she processed the information. "I can't believe this."

"Yeah. I just got it from Lt. Trainer. Sergeant Amos called a few minutes ago for a heads up. Once the press gets wind of that arrest, they'll go apeshit. He wanted you to know."

"What about the shooter?"

"Nothing yet. They said it had to come from a distance. Witnesses are a few neighbors. Heard the shot and found his body in the driveway. Not much else."

Amy flopped back down in her chair. "This is bizarre. We've got two dead gunshot victims about the same age. Who's on Chastang?"

"Good question. For now, Turk and Kristi. Amos and the DA's office need to be in the loop."

"There almost has to be a connection. Don't you think?"

"I wouldn't bet against it. If so, it'll turn into a task force. We can't say squat to the press and can't lean on Cameron Chastang. The word is: he plays golf with half the VIPs in town."

Amy's mind was swimming with activity. She'd already pushed thoughts of Zachary Chastang to the side. Except for a final report and testimony at trial, she'd chalked it up as a done deal. Now a strange chain of events linked Chastang to their newest murder case. "Jarrett and Chastang, both dead within twelve hours of each other. Incredible."

Frank picked up a file folder and turned a page. "There's only one connection I can think of—two local boys from big money who knew each other. Otherwise, Zachary Chastang was a total shit-for-brains. Two arrests for pot, two for cocaine. Three car accidents in five years. Ran over a stop sign while texting in 2017. Twice questioned in relation to date-rape, no charges. Drunk & Disorderly arrests here and there, the most recent in March. Arrested in 2018 for being naked in a bowling alley. On the other hand, Marcus Jarrett has one possession charge for marijuana at sixteen—paid a $400 fine. And one underage DUI when he was eighteen. Nothing else since."

"So those are what got Marcus's father mad. But he's nowhere near the same league as Zach Chastang." Amy flipped open her notebook and started jotting ideas. "We need to see how else Chastang and Jarrett cross paths."

"We know there's a tie-in. We *don't* know if they're both dead for the same reason. Chastang was gunned down in front of his home. The rifle slug is in ballistics now. If you and Amos hadn't arrested him last night, he'd just be a regular victim now, the same as Jarrett."

"Or he might not be dead at all."

"Good point. The thing I'm wondering—did the same killer nail them both?"

"It fits. Obviously different weapons. Both bold, quick, efficient. But let's not get ahead of ourselves."

Frank nodded. "Exactly. We can't assume anything so let's forget Chastang for now. Like with any other case, we shake Marcus Jarrett's tree and see what falls off."

"According to what I've been reading, Sylvia Jarrett is running the show. It's a multi-million-dollar company but Marcus only got a trust fund. Since his father died, he's been fighting the terms of the will. Ongoing, but it looks like he recently gave up."

Frank grinned. "I get it. You're saying we have a great place to start—the evil step-mom at the top of the heap."

CHAPTER 5

In one of their first late-night chats over a few beers, Amy remembered Frank telling her that detective work was like looking into the night sky. A true astronomer, he'd said, could pick out the constellations while still experiencing the whole thing. There were lots and lots of stars, clusters, galaxies, planets, and the moon. Everything was far away—and yet by comparison, some objects were deceptively close. Some moved in respect to others and some remained fixed. Because of the earth's rotation, the view constantly changed. The detective, much like an astronomer, had to consider the data, bide his time, focus on the important points, but never lose touch with how it all fit together.

Of course, that was her recap of a discussion that took place over the course of an hour or more, fueled by exhaustion, frustration, and alcohol at the end of a long day. Somehow it really made sense and she'd never forgotten the gist. Despite a penchant for watching football, playing poker, and juggling dates, Frank could be unusually deep at times.

Amy sat reading her notes as Frank drove them up Germantown Avenue and onto Bethlehem Pike for a trek into Chestnut Hill, a ritzy section of Northwestern Philly that featured big properties, lush landscaping, and many old homes built by famous local architects of the late 19th and early 20th centuries. From what they could gather, Bradley Jarrett's widow lived there alone except for a typical staff of maids, security personnel, chefs, and groundskeepers. Records showed that Bradley Jarrett married Sylvia Stremmel shortly after she graduated from college with a degree in computer science and a 4.0 GPA. She got a master's degree in business from the University of Pennsylvania after that. At some point, she'd apparently gained substantial clout to be left in control of the family's enterprises in the event of Bradley's death. Marcus, contesting the will, had continued to live in the huge house until taking up his own residence in April. None of it was suspicious by itself, but all sounding juicy enough to leave a long trail of gossip—interesting, however useful.

This case she knew, would be the one to require more discriminating eyes and concentration. For starters, big money and corporate power always complicated things. The police hierarchy would want a strong show of effort to solve the murder of a prominent citizen, while wary of what they'd uncover in doing so. Political pressure, lawsuits, and unfavorable press were always a concern. Reporters would snoop and ask loaded questions, looking for that big story involving newsworthy subjects. By birthright, Marcus Jarrett was rich, yet he'd been living on a budget dictated by a piece of paper. His death was brutal, fast, and deliberate, yet there was no clear or implied motive. There were no defensive wounds. Marcus saw it coming, too late to react. The murder of Zachary Chastang was another issue and quite possibly related. Zachary too, was from a wealthy family, but with a father who was very much alive and would be screaming for answers. Unfortunately, they had none. And yet, the evidence showed only that Zachary knew Marcus Jarrett. Close friends? Casual acquaintances? *Were the crimes like dominos, each leading to the next? Or unrelated and obscuring the real truth?*

Conceivably, Zachary's arrest could be a matter of coincidental timing and nothing more. The case was solid and the evidence irrefutable—but a jury would never hear it. The whole sordid story would be rendered an enigma or a fabrication, depending on what leaked out and who heard it. Zachary would be seen as a victim now, instead of the lowly, date-rapist he was. One thing for sure: a rifle shot was definitive action—someone really wanted him dead. The same could be said for Marcus Jarrett.

Unfortunately, the house-to-house check had yielded no leads and no witnesses in the hours around Jarrett's time of death. Every close neighbor had been questioned. The best vantage point, directly across the street, was unoccupied, the owners away on vacation.

Frank always said motive was usually the key element. Not always. In the case of a serial killer, for instance, a motive was extrinsic. Such investigations relied on a different paradigm. However, most murders could be boiled down to three motives: love, hate, and money. *Who hated enough? Whose love would be spared or bestowed? Who would gain or lose?* A killer could manipulate timing, find opportunity, and acquire the means—if he or she was properly motivated. The WHY + HOW + WHEN = WHO. They'd need to find out for sure pretty fast.

When Amy looked up, she knew they had arrived where the *other half* lived. A cobblestone walkway led to a large stone house secluded by beautiful shrubs and trees with tiny flowers in blue and red. A double-pitched roof, a portico with four columns, and she could see at least three chimneys. Something in her memory told her the home was Georgian Revival design—in fact, she recalled an article about homes from the very neighborhood in Philadelphia Magazine.

"Christ," Frank said as he pulled to a stop. "I wonder what they paid for these digs."

"Not sure," Amy answered, "The current value is six and a half million."

"You looked it up online?"

Amy shrugged. "Yep."

"And you said this woman already knows about the murder?"

"The police commissioner came over himself earlier with a few others. They drove her to ID him."

"Talk about *special treatment.* The thing is—I don't see her being all broken up about it. They can't have gotten along too well. If she'd been the one who got whacked, Marcus Jarrett would be our top pick."

"I still can't see why she'd have a motive for wanting him dead. He'd run out of options for fighting the terms of his father's will."

Frank grinned. "There could be other motives. As I recall, she's a serious babe and only seven or eight years older than Marcus."

Amy nodded. Leave it to Frank to zero in on the sordid angle—although, in this instance, he could be right.

The flawless lawn was impressive, as was the stone-enclosed fountain, complete with a nifty angel statue. The whole design was like a work of art in and off itself. They went up fifteen stone steps to the portico and came to a huge oak door.

Frank knocked, whispering, "Doctor Frankenstein, please."

Amy said, "Shhh."

The door swung open and both detectives were startled by the familiar man in jeans, Sketchers, and a Hawaiian shirt. "Hi guys," he said, seeming equally surprised. "You're on the Marcus Jarrett case?"

Amy glanced at Frank who was at a loss for words. Alvin Cruz, local private investigator, was a longtime friend of Frank's and hung out in the same crowd. Amy knew him as well, especially since he'd inadvertently worked with them on a few cases, always under odd circumstances and with mixed results. A vague reputation preceded him for unofficially helping the police by dubious means. He was mid-thirties, a ropey six-footer with lean muscles, and medium-length brown hair reminiscent of the '70s. She knew he was basically a *good guy* but his casual attitude and illicit skills placed him as an odd blip on her radar—sort of a cross between Inspector Clouseau and Sam Spade. Frank liked him and yes, so did she. There'd been occasional flirting and coy remarks, but he'd never actually asked her out. If he did, she'd consider it. Maybe. Not that she was holding her breath.

"Yes, we are," she said. "May I ask what you're doing here?"

Cruz shrugged. "I think I work for Sylvia Jarrett."

"You think? Since when?"

"About twenty minutes ago."

Amy and Frank stepped in to an elegant entry hall with a marble floor, impressive wainscoting, and a decorative balustrade. It spoke of old-world charm and modern upkeep.

"Nice place." Frank grinned approvingly. "So, I take it you're the new butler?"

Cruz laughed. "Not hardly. It's a long story."

"It always is. Give us the short version."

Cruz led them slowly through a huge living room with an immense white sectional sofa, four matching chairs, magnificent hardwood floors, a giant fireplace, grandfather clock, and high beamed ceiling. "I didn't get the whole deal yet but Sylvia Jarrett wants her own investigator on the murder."

"No offense," Amy said. "How'd she find *you*?"

"Recommendation. I've been doing some work for a friend of hers recently. Believe me, I told her the police would be thorough. She wants someone she trusts to look into it."

"And that's you?"

Cruz laughed. "Why do you pick on me?"

"I'm ... not. It just seems odd that she'd hire you before even talking to *us.*"

"Well, I think she's just overwhelmed. She's pretty broken up about it."

Frank raised an eyebrow. "Seriously?"

"Yeah. Hey, I heard about the ruckus last night. You two okay?"

"Fine," Amy said. "Frank wasn't even there. He was at ... Oh, forget it."

A huge sunroom came into view that was obviously a newer addition designed to complement the warmth and elegance of the home itself. It was patio-themed with outdoor tables and chairs in fine wood with white cushions. Sylvia Jarrett was seated next to a handsome 50-ish black man who seemed familiar. Cruz was right—the woman was without makeup, her eyes rimmed in red, and had shiny tears on her cheeks. Otherwise, stunningly beautiful.

Frank introduced them; both detectives produced identification. Sylvia nodded and remained seated.

The man stood and formally shook Frank's hand, then Amy's.

"I'm Warren E. Hamilton," he said.

Amy nodded. "I thought so. Pleased to meet you." She knew the name well and had seen him around the courthouse many times. More often, she'd seen him on the nightly news. Hamilton was Philadelphia's premiere choice of attorney for the rich and famous. He mostly handled business law these days but had done his share of criminal work in years past. He had silvery hints in his short dark hair, a deep resonant voice, and easygoing charm. About five ten with a strong build, the impeccably tailored suit made him stand out. Unless he was present as a family friend, she wondered why Sylvia Jarrett felt the need for legal representation.

"You're the detectives in charge of Marcus's case?"

"Yes, ma'am," Frank said. "This is a difficult time and we're sorry to intrude on your grief. It's very important we quickly get a complete understanding of Marcus's activities."

"Excuse me," Cruz said to Sylvia. "Should I let you have some time alone with these detectives?"

"No, that's quite all right. You should know what is said. Besides, I'd really appreciate it if you'd stay for lunch so we can talk further." Turning to Frank, she added, "I don't know what help I could be, but ask me anything."

"Just to get our facts straight, Marcus lived here until April of this year. Is that correct?"

"Yes. He was, of course, welcome to remain as long as he wished. He recently chose to draw money allowed by his trust for his own home."

"Must have been a nice amount."

Sylvia nodded. "Yes, the terms did not specify a limit. I actually thought he went a little overboard. I told him he should start with a townhouse, something less pricey. But he went ahead and bought a very nice house."

"Why did you object?"

"Well, it wasn't an objection, not really. It seemed rather sudden. I just wanted him to think it through."

"Could there be something specific? Romantic reasons, maybe?"

Sylvia looked thoughtful, then said, "He's a young man, so that may be a part of it. I really can't say. Marcus dated of course, but no one special. Ultimately, I supported his decision."

Very slick … Amy watched in fascination as Frank took her through the usual barrage of questions, some bland and routine, but others with an edge that might rattle a person with something to hide. Sylvia Jarrett spent the next fifteen minutes answering smoothly and confidently. Amy thought the woman's pain seemed genuine but doubted her own assessment. She and Marcus were embroiled in a battle over the will for several years—some lingering resentment had to have caused a rift. Strangely, Sylvia didn't defer to her attorney or even glance over for a nod of approval on leading questions. Hamilton, for all his big fees and reputation, never butted in, told her not to answer, or so much as coughed. *Peculiar* … If her response to the interview was based on the attorney's prep work, then he was damned good.

Amy thought back a few years and recalled that Bradley and Sylvia Jarrett had been a local icon. Despite the difference in age, they came across as a happy couple. There'd been no steamy articles or damning photos. There'd been no rumors of affairs, domestic disturbances, reckless squandering, or public bickering. They'd been marginally into social events, mostly shunning the limelight, and seemed content to concentrate on business matters, quiet family vacations, and quality time. When Bradley passed away unexpectedly from heart failure, Sylvia had quietly grieved and effectively taken control of an enormous corporation—much to Marcus's dismay. On her own, she now seemed to favor some media attention and delved into charities, fundraisers, and local politics.

Amy studied the woman as she responded to Frank's questions. How the subject answered, voice inflections, nervous twitches, confusion, fear, hesitations—it was all about trying to get a feel for truth, lies, and uncertainty. Sylvia Jarrett was—in a word— delightful. Maintaining control, while overcome with emotion. Regal, but vulnerable. She came up short of breath once in a while, then stopped to inhale slowly as if holding back tears. Simply clad in a flared beige skirt and black blouse, she seemed genuinely *nice* and not someone who'd hit people over the head with her wealth and status. Though she'd been seated the whole time, Amy knew she was around five eight. Slender, firm, and the delicate features combined with great cheekbones could place her on the cover of Vogue. A late summer tan looked like the real thing and not from a bottle or tanning booth. And if Amy wasn't mistaken, the woman's brown hair with nice highlights was all natural.

Brains, beauty, personality, and money. Life definitely wasn't fair.

According to Sylvia, Marcus had no enemies and a few friends that Amy jotted down. He was not into drugs or gambling and drank only socially. His position in the company was stable and he was well liked. Sylvia admitted to running the show but said that Marcus held the title of Vice President and was in charge of equipment rental, leasing, and purchases, a considerable responsibility that required continuity with all departments. Although, yes, he disliked the terms of his father's will, he still had a respectable trust fund and earned a substantial yearly income with full benefits. His office was in their main complex uptown and the police were more than welcome to question his staff. They could also have access to his computers, mail, and email once she'd spoken to her legal department about concerns for customer privacy. *Smooth, very smooth, like a milkshake on a hot day. Was this care, cooperation and grief? Or was her down-to-earth manner a façade?*

Frank looked like he was wrapping it up. There was a real rapport going—not like opponents squaring off—more like new friends deciding if they trusted each other. He seemed to be going a little easy on her and Amy wondered if it was caution from her attorney's presence, the Jarrett name, or because she was simply bewitching. This woman could charm any man on the planet.

"May I ask an ungracious question?" Amy said.

Their eyes met, really for the first time. Sylvia looked at her with sincerity. "If you honestly feel it will help find Marcus's killer, then by all means."

"It seems a bit unusual that you were left in total control of a very large company. Obviously, your abilities speak for themselves. However, an understanding of Marcus's interests, ambitions, and even limitations, might be helpful to us. Why do you suppose your late husband did that?"

"Detective," Sylvia said, "you are very direct. I appreciate that so I will answer as best I can. By the time Marcus was five or six, the family was well off. He was an only child, you know. According to Bradley, Marcus's mother was attentive but also very indulgent. Bradley felt that Marcus grew up spoiled. He was complacent, and as a teen, just didn't want to apply himself or work hard for anything. It was Bradley's intention to give more and more responsibility to Marcus if and when he proved himself. As it turned out, he'd been doing just that."

"His father was pleased with the improvement?"

"Yes. I recall a number of such discussions. Marcus changed as he got older. Focused, determined, and even more so since his father's death."

"Although Bradley never altered his will."

"Regrettably, no. But I believe I understood his intentions. In a few more years, I would have honored Bradley's ultimate wishes and turned control over to Marcus."

"Thank you. Did you have a key to his new home?"

"No. He never offered me one."

"Also, a woman called in about a disturbance at his home but didn't leave a name. That's what brought the police. Do have any idea who that could have been?"

Sylvia smiled sadly. "No, I really wouldn't have any idea."

Amy smiled back. "Of course. And again, our condolences. Thanks so much for your time."

"So," Amy said, "what'd you think of *that* shifty performance."

Frank paused with the key halfway to the ignition. "What? You think she killed Marcus?"

Amy shook her head. "Well, no. I hoped *you* did. She's just too perfect."

Frank laughed, then started the car and turned around in the driveway. "She's not *that* perfect."

"Oh, is that so? What's wrong with her? I mean, as a man, what would you say are her major flaws?"

Frank drove in silence for thirty seconds. "Okay. She doesn't have any."

"No kidding. I noticed you two getting along."

"Yep. I played her just right. You might say she was under my spell."

"Yeah, yeah, right. She had you eating out of her hand."

"Now that's *bullshit*."

"Sure it is." Amy made a mock laugh while flipping through notes. "Don't underestimate the former Sylvia Stremmel. Born in Hanover, Pennsylvania. Her mother is a retired history professor and author of four historical novels. Father deceased, but before that, a dentist. Sylvia was valedictorian of her high school class. Full scholarship."

Frank shrugged. "Okay. I get it—she's smart."

"Yes. Something to keep in mind. And what's with Cruz being there?"

"That, I don't know. What he said rang true. He gets around, you've got to give him that."

"It's just a little odd that Sylvia Jarrett has her attorney and a private investigator there before she even spoke to the case detectives."

"She knew about Marcus hours ago so maybe not that odd. And I'm sure you noticed that Hamilton didn't make a peep."

"Yeah. He didn't introduce himself as her attorney, either. Maybe that was all for show, like she doesn't need legal counsel and he just happened to be there.

What do you suppose Sylvia Jarrett, Cruz, and the esteemed Warren E. Hamilton are discussing now?"

"It's anybody's guess. We need to do a lot of background checks. Like talk to Marcus's co-workers and friends and get their impressions of Sylvia and Marcus's relationship. We might also want to see if any of them knew Zachary Chastang. And we need to find out who the female caller was. It might have been the owner of those clothes in Marcus's bureau drawers. I want Marcus's social calendar, squeezes, friends, appointments, business contacts. Who knows? Maybe he was banging a married neighbor. Or a worker he fired came by to give him payback. It's a lot of ground to cover. When you look at all this closely, some things could be in our favor."

"You mean Cruz, right? You're suggesting he might throw some help our way?"

"At least indirectly."

"Yeah. Which means he'll be breaking the rules. Or, excuse me—*bending* the rules. Those items that fall into a gray area of legalities—if there *is* such a place."

Frank grinned. "You know, you're really getting the hang of this detective stuff."

CHAPTER 6

Alvin Cruz reached into an envelope, removed a selection of reports and photographs, and sat down at the kitchen table. "You sure it's okay to do this here? I've been at my office for a while and haven't been keeping tabs on your husband. Is there any chance he could come strolling in?"

Joyce Kyser made a small hoot of contempt. "Not hardly. He's always working. I haven't seen him this time of day on a Friday in years. Unless it was during one of our few and far-between vacations." She placed a plate of jumbo shrimp and cocktail sauce, plus an assortment of expensive cheeses on the table. "Please have a snack."

"Sounds good." Cruz studied the woman as she sat down next to him. She was petite—a pixie, a lot of men would say. Her long blond hair—honey blond, he thought it was called—was straight and fell to the middle of her back. She was about five one and very pretty with a nice shape—105 pounds, maybe. Some women achieved a similar look by replacing meals with celery stalks and doing an hour a day on a Stairmaster. He was fairly sure Joyce came by it naturally.

"I think you impressed Sylvia Jarrett. She called to thank me for suggesting you."

"I appreciate the referral." He really did. Three hours ago, he'd been hired to privately supplement the police investigation into Marcus Jarrett's murder. In truth, his efforts would probably be a waste of time; Frank and Amy were as good a detective team as he'd ever known. He supposed it was piece of mind for the rich Ms. Jarrett, utilizing her vast resources to do something helpful.

Joyce Kyser, and now Sylvia Jarrett, were probably the most upscale clients of his career. The Kyser townhouse in no way compared with the luxurious Jarrett mansion, but was recent construction, tasteful and modern, in a nice area on Corinthian Avenue near Poplar Street. The best news: his latest clients were both stunning ladies. The pay was good and the scenery pleasing. He dabbed a large shrimp into some gourmet cocktail sauce and savored the flavor. Contrary to their portrayal on television, P.I.'s rarely had it this good.

Cruz spread out the documents on a kitchen table that he recognized as Grand Cayman styling with intricate leaf detailing on the legs. Joyce immediately snatched up some photos and scrutinized the strange greenish images. "I can tell that's Gilbert." Bitterly, she said, "So who's the tart?"

"That's the good news. No one important." Cruz took out his notes and broke it down for her. "You were right. He didn't go to the office for a conference call on Monday night. He met this woman in a park. They talked for seventeen minutes, never touched, and went their separate ways."

Joyce was still looking from one photo to the next as though she had to be missing something. "Really? Is that the truth?"

"Absolutely."

"What was it all about?"

"I couldn't hear their conversation so I can only guess. It seemed to be business related. Industrial spying is common and he may have been getting information from this woman. I can tell you for sure it didn't come across as a girlfriend or even an ex-girlfriend."

Joyce's eyes lit up. "Oh, my. All right. He's been so distant in the last few years. Or maybe I just started noticing it. Also, kind of … short-tempered. I was sure he'd found someone. Why would he lie about something innocent?"

Cruz smiled gently. "Well, he might not have wanted to tell you … I don't know. Maybe because he thought you'd be jealous."

She smiled slightly at that. "What about the rest of the week?"

"All very tame. Lunches with colleagues, mostly male. No women alone. He does have a few drinks with his meals. One day I put on a disguise and applied for a job—with a phony resume of course. I didn't speak to your husband but I saw him coming and going. Talked to his own secretary and two others while I waited. He's very businesslike in the office. No suspicious chatter."

"And you followed him?"

"Yes. Routine stuff. One stop at a men's store on Wednesday afternoon. Tried on some sport coats. Had a hoagie at a sub shop."

"I'll bet it was Italian with hot peppers and extra meat." Joyce sighed. "He's never going to lose weight."

"Yes, it did, and probably not. The upshot is—no other woman in his life. I have the whole timetable laid out and some other photographs. Believe me, this is all good news."

Joyce touched his shoulder and lightly ran her hand down his arm—Cruz felt a little jolt of pleasure, accepting it as a gesture of thanks. Then she stood up and looked out the window. "Can you continue with this case?"

"Do you want me to?"

"Frankly, yes." She turned and came back to her seat. "Something's not right, Mr. Cruz. I feel it. I know my husband works in a high-pressure job. He's changed in the last few years. I just assumed it could be another woman. He said I could get a new car a few months ago. Then he had a meltdown when I got one."

"Would that be the Challenger?"

Joyce nodded.

"Very nice," he said.

"He called is a *man's* car. Thinks I should have gotten a Z4 or a Jaguar or something like that. He says a *muscle* car isn't dignified enough for an executive's wife."

Cruz saw the woman's pain, a deep anguish that he'd missed before. When they'd met last week, he'd expected this to be a simple case of a wayward husband nailing his secretary. Or quite possibly a paranoid wife with an overactive imagination. Either way, his fee wasn't going to cramp their lifestyle.

"I realize," she continued, "that you've now got this murder investigation to deal with."

"Don't worry about that. If you want me to take this further, no problem. Often, different cases coincide. I promise to budget my time and bill you fairly."

"It's not that. You understand, don't you?"

"I think so. You want to be sure—so let me be honest with you. Your husband seems to be a businessman to the core. It's likely that there's nothing going on. It is at least possible there's something I didn't pick up on yet. Not in a week of surveillance."

"Yes, of course. Please continue. I just … I just want to be sure he's the man I married."

Cruz appraised her for a moment, then said: "Is there something you're not telling me?"

Joyce looked stunned, then quickly regained her composure. "Oh, no," she said with a smile and the wave of her hand. "Nothing like that."

Cruz nodded, as though he were satisfied. He wasn't. Something else was in play here and a few things went through his mind. *Was her husband into rough stuff? Or actually beating her? Or some type of psychological thing? Or did she think he was into something crazy like selling secrets to North Korea?* She seemed jumpy and more nervous than he'd normally expect. If the man's a cheater, she should be indignant, ready to pack his bags and stick them out by the curb. But not that—he was sensing something else altogether. It wasn't hard to imagine that a person might make up a routine story about suspected infidelity because they didn't want to say out loud what was *really* on their mind. *Gilbert Kyser, what are you up to?* Cruz knew he might need to turn up the heat a little by using some of his electronic toys. "That's fine then, Mrs. Kyser. I'll be glad to keep an eye on him for as long as you like."

"I really appreciate that. And please call me Joyce." She reached out, squeezed his hand and gave a wink.

CHAPTER 7

Amy moved the mouse, clicked the arrow and listened intently for the third time.

FEMALE VOICE: "I just heard shouts and some loud bangs from my neighbor's house. It might have been gunfire. I'm really worried. It's on McCallum Street. The man who lives there is Marcus Jarrett. Please hurry."

911 OPERATOR: "Ma'am, can you ... Hello? Hello?

Amy removed the headphones. "Where'd the call originate?"

Frank was just returning from the break room with a Coke for himself and a cup of coffee for Amy. He took a seat and slid over next to her. Their desks were side by side so they could share data and refer to each other's monitors. "Burner phone. Not operating now."

"I wonder if that's luck—or planned. Okay. So even if the timing wasn't way off, it doesn't fit. Most callers can't say it fast enough. This woman speaks clearly and pronounces her words, as if she doesn't want to be misheard. Plus, she's hurting—like just reporting it causes her pain."

"What her age?"

"Thirties, I'd say. Educated. Which makes sense."

"Did she kill him?"

Amy shook her head. "No way. He died last night and her call came in around ten in the morning. Plus, she says 'loud bangs'—plural. He was shot once."

"Right. This lady's got no clue what happened or when. She came across the body, freaked out, and wanted us to find it sooner rather than later. Could be a girlfriend."

"Maybe."

"Let me ask you something seriously. Even a hunch. What do you really think about Zachary Chastang and Marcus Jarrett? Are the murders connected or not?"

Amy considered it. "There's no logical reason to think so, at least on the surface. The fingerprints in his house only suggest they knew each other."

"Tell me more about Chastang. It sounds like you nailed him good. How'd they get on to him in the first place?"

"I only got the basics. They wanted to get me in position so I was briefed in a hurry. Sergeant Amos said that Zachary had been questioned twice about cases involving drug-assisted date-rape over the last year. No hard evidence. But then a few months ago a woman went directly to a hospital, certain she'd been assaulted. Woke up alone, naked and wet. She'd been bathed, couldn't remember anything about what happened. Zachary Chastang was seen with her earlier in the evening on a hazy security camera image, but they couldn't find a witness or a way to place him with her. He was questioned, not enough for an arrest, and they started keeping loose tabs on him."

"I'm with ya. What was he like in person?"

Amy thought for only a moment. "A schlub."

Frank laughed. "A schlub? Can you be a little more specific?"

"Okay. He was … mediocre."

"Interesting. Go on."

"Well, he came across as a putz. I mean, I know he's from money. Self-indulgent, but he didn't seem like someone who'd put a lot of effort into anything. The profile they had on this type of perpetrator was pretty close. It said he'd have a low opinion of women and think he was above any wrongdoings. He really seemed shocked when we arrested him. Didn't start out by demanding a lawyer. Didn't play it cool like a wealthy professional. First, he denied knowing anything and then he started screaming to get the cuffs off. Honestly, I think he expected to make a fuss and complain his way out of it like a bratty eight-year-old."

Frank took a few swigs of Coke and thought it over. "Okay. Let's shift tactics, at least for now. Zachary Chastang sounds like a real player. We should know where he hung out, understand his workplace. And we should know who the other men were at that party. A little leg work. Let's check the reports on the women who made those other complaints. See what happened to them and where. And also, let's check other prints in Jarrett's place and see who connects to Chastang."

"You think Jarrett and Chastang were in something together?"

"Possibly. Two rich boys who knew each other got blown away eleven hours apart. I want to look at Zachary close up and see if any trails lead to Marcus Jarrett."

"My guess is there will be."

Frank grinned. "Then we'll just solve *both*."

"Oh sure." Amy wasn't convinced this was a good idea but trusted Frank's instincts. She'd rather be concentrating on Marcus Jarrett, interviewing his friends and co-workers, then looking over his recent activities, dates, appointments, purchases, trips, and meetings. How people talked about the deceased and what they said—and didn't say—was often crucial. Sometimes one version didn't match the others which set off alarm bells. Under scrutiny, that anomaly would sometimes break the case. Maybe she could get to that chore in a few hours if nothing turned up to further connect Chastang with Jarrett.

The truth was that she found Zachary Chastang to be a vile, reprehensible human being. Obviously, no one should be gunned down with a shot to the back, but she had no doubt of his guilt. In her pretense of semi-consciousness, she recalled watching him decide how to proceed with a rape like a homeowner starting to clean the garage. It was clear what he'd been thinking as he'd looked around, checking for comfort and convenience—a feasibility study for assaulting his drugged victim. Such barbaric behavior for brief pleasure, only to leave the victim violated, confused, frightened, and ashamed ... Just thinking about it made her skin crawl.

The experience provided insight only to what women must go through, left to the whims of immoral deviants. For Amy, it had been different. In the apartment last night, she'd known how it would play out. She was trained, under video surveillance, and discreetly surrounded by other officers the entire time. Plus, even one-on-one and unarmed, she could've kick Chastang's pitiful ass.

Drug-assisted date-rape was defined by the use of any physical or mind-altering substances to aid the attacker. Alcohol was most common, but as with Zachary Chastang, many assailants added their own sedatives or hallucinogens. Unlike other rapes, those women rarely remembered details, and in many cases, not much at all. The drugs of choice were mostly undetectable in liquid, odorless and sometimes tasteless. Even the ones with an odd taste could be disguised. The results were relaxation, sleepiness, loss of inhibitions, loss of willpower, hallucinations, and amnesia. Side effects ranged from mild to critical: spike in blood pressure, seizures, strokes, anaphylaxis, blackout, and even death. The main problem was that the charges were hard to prove and complicated because the victims were left confused and unsure of a course of action. Their memories of the incident were vague at

best. If she'd been drinking, a woman could mistakenly assume overindulgence and not come forward.
A time factor also was also involved since many of the
drugs left the system after as little as eight hours. In
1996, President Clinton signed The Drug-Induced
Rape Prevention and Punishment Act which was a big
step forward. Other legislation followed with further
stipulations and newer drugs defined. Most people
didn't know that unauthorized possession of such
drugs came with a sentence of up to three years, regardless of intent to use.

Amy couldn't help but wonder which was prefer-
able—seeing the attack clearly and knowing exactly
what happened. Or the haunting blur of the unknown. To Amy's way of thinking, though a different
kind of pain, both were equally heinous. If she could
put perpetrators behind bars and prevent more such
crimes, it made her glad to be a detective.

Beginning the task methodically, Amy reviewed
the information she had, listed her questions and
made a to-do list. By the time Frank returned from
a trip to the lab, Amy had spoken to Sergeant Amos,
two other detectives, a rape councilor, and a civilian
profiler working for a nearby district. A pattern had
definitely emerged.

"Got news," Frank said as he slid into his chair.
"Mostly Jarrett's prints. Two prints on the coffee table
that don't match anything on file."

"Why aren't I surprised?"

"Because lucky breaks don't come our way very often. Also, a few cloth fibers that didn't come from anything in Jarrett's house—but nothing out of the ordinary. Some long brown hairs that might have enough follicle for DNA, but they were upstairs in his bedroom. Here's the big shocker: They found some goodies hidden in the back of a bureau drawer. They're testing it and so far: rohypnol, GHB, ketamine, scopolamine, others. A nice variety that would've been more than enough to land the guy in prison for years."

Amy brightened and slid around to face him. "Finally, a connection. Marcus's drugs. He and Zachary were in it together. It might have been a game to them."

"Or a competition."

"That's gross, Frank. Although I guess it's possible in a sick, perverted way."

"That's why you keep me around, for the sick, perverted angles. None of his prints on the bag—he might have worn gloves to handle it. However, one partial print that's not Jarrett's. It doesn't match anything on file, either."

"Uh-huh. Well, at least we have our link between the murders—plus I found another one. There was a rape victim last month at a party. Want to guess where it was?"

Frank shrugged. "At Marcus Jarrett's place?"

"Nope. At *Sylvia* Jarrett's place—the mansion on Meadowbrook Avenue where we interviewed her. That weekend she was in Ocean City at their beach house. It was Marcus's thirty-fifth birthday. Since he doesn't have a lot of furniture yet, he had the party at the mansion."

"Great place for a party."

"Yeah. Except for a woman named Dixie Newberry. She claims to have had only one glass of punch. She woke up in one of the eight bedrooms, naked, about 4 A.M. She was sore and certain she'd been assaulted. Get this—she was wet."

"Wet?"

"Yes. Well, damp. Her hair was wet. As if she'd bathed and didn't dry off. The sheets were wet, too. She found her clothes on the floor, got dressed and went straight to the hospital on her own and demanded a blood test."

Frank grunted. "She should have called 911 from the house right away."

"Yes. That was a mistake on her part. One thing of interest—her cell phone was missing and never found. The party had ended and the living room deserted. She said at least one couple was still having sex in a bedroom she passed by. By then, she just wanted to get out of there."

"Okay. She'd be disoriented. I understand that. Some asshole tossed her phone. Made it tougher for her to contact anyone when she woke up. So where does Zachary Chastang fit in?"

"Not a big surprise—he was at the party. Dixie fits his victim profile. Age, figure, height."

"And why *you* were picked to reel him in."

Amy shrugged. "Anyway, the doctor in the ER did the standard rape kit. He called it in, got the police interested, and they interviewed her. It was almost nine in the morning by the time the police got to the house. Marcus wasn't around. Three guests still there, all sound asleep—in the same bed. None of them knew anything useful. The household staff was cleaning up. All the empty bedrooms had been stripped and everything washed together."

"That's rotten luck. The timing makes me curious. And I wish we'd known this when we talked to Sylvia Jarrett earlier. I'd love to hear her thoughts on it."

"Me too," Amy agreed. "Anyway, since Dixie had scopolamine still in her system, they started an investigation."

"And I'll bet it was hell getting a guest list."

"Yeah. Until they tracked down Marcus Jarrett. According to detectives, Marcus was cooperative."

"Where'd they find him?"

"At his place with a woman from the party." Amy paused to look over reports. "Okay. They left shortly after midnight, according to statements. Besides Zackary Chastang, nine other men, ages twenty-three to forty-four were in attendance at some point, all acquainted with Marcus, all interviewed. Approximately eight females. Dixie plus six others are known, ages nineteen to forty-three, all interviewed. And yes, everyone backed up Marcus. He and a woman left there together, although no one verified the exact time."

"Which makes sense, a big party like that. Would Marcus team up with Zachary to drug one woman when he was leaving with another?"

"Doubtful. But he must have provided the drug."

"True." Frank took the report from Amy and flipped through it for a moment. "Who invited Dixie?"

"She drove a friend, Vonda Cantu, then decided to stay. That checks out. Vonda, incidentally, is the woman who went home with Marcus."

"Marcus may have still been at the party when Dixie was assaulted. We can't be sure with what we have so far. Zachary or Marcus drugged Dixie. At some point, he dumped the drug in Dixie's drink then shuffled her off to a bedroom when she started to drift. A party like that, nobody would even blink. It says here there's a private bathroom where she woke up. That means afterwards it was easy for him to get her in the tub to wash away evidence."

Amy nodded. "And then he just put her on the bed dripping wet and left. What a slimy fucking useless *pig*."

"Yes indeed." Frank raised an eyebrow. "No more caffeine for you today. One thing I'm curious about— you figure, it's been a month. By now it's pretty clear that no one's going to be charged for what happened to Dixie. It seems like Marcus has been a bad boy, too. It makes me wonder if Dixie has any close male relatives, boyfriends, or a high school sweetheart."

"Like one with a hot temper, shooting skill, maybe a military background?"

Frank nodded. "Something like that."

CHAPTER 8

Discreetly a block behind, Alvin Cruz watched the display of a GPS device that represented Gilbert Kyser's Lexus. Kyser, for some strange reason, had slipped out of work an hour ago, stopped at a Wawa on the corner of Christian and South 2nd Streets, came out with a milk shake, then continued through town just west of I-95. Cruz couldn't imagine why—there'd be no stores he would normally frequent and no real clients to visit. After a few more blocks, Kyser made a left turn, then another, and headed back the way he'd come. The area changed complexion as he went along. It never ceased to amaze him how Philadelphia could go from rundown, to comfy, and then to high-end fancy in a relatively short distance.

Cruz watched the display as Kyser turned right on 3rd Street, went up to Gaskill, then came back down 4th Street and turned onto South Street. *Conforming to an abundance of one-way streets … But driving in circles?* As the reading showed a decrease in speed, Cruz slowed the borrowed van and eased further along until he could see Kyser pulling into a small lot with $15 all-day parking. He smiled, realizing what Kyser had been up to. It was all to make sure he wasn't followed. He'd gone east, far out of his way, and taken a roundabout route to end up just twelve or so blocks from where he'd started at 4th and Market. That technique might have shaken off your average tail—unless your pursuer had modern electronics on his side. *Very interesting.*

Going on by, Cruz figured to circle the block, then opted for an open spot on the left. The area looked typically busy for this time of day and he was glad to get a parking place. He three-pointed quickly and checked on Kyser who was now out of his car and heading up the sidewalk. Dressed in an expensive suit, he looked slightly out of place. He was carrying what looked like a small plastic bag that Cruz didn't remember seeing earlier.

Cruz slipped into the back of the 1997 Chevy Astro Van, a marvel of electronics and specialized equipment. Originally owned by pimps who preferred discretion for delivering their operatives, it had been refurbished with a computer system, recording and video equipment, and a nearly impregnable compartment with weapons, tactical gear, assorted bugging devices, GPS trackers in various sizes, and enough fast-entry and lock picking tools to make a cat burglar jealous. The vehicle didn't belong to Cruz but he had a few friends in the department that owed him a favor or two. At the moment, Cruz's only interest was his trusty camera and the tinted side window with one-way viewing.

Sliding onto a bench-type seat, Cruz watched as Kyser stopped in front of a popular lunch shop called Sam's and Herb's Deli and acknowledged a man coming towards him from the other direction. Zooming in and firing off a series of pictures, he pegged the guy to be around forty, average build, and maybe six foot. Judging by the scraggly brown hair, worn flannel shirt and ratty jeans, this wasn't a big client or Wall Street investor. He seemed jittery, looking right and left, as he and Kyser entered the building together. Cruz zoomed closer using a polarizing filter to cut glare on the front window, but lost them somewhere near the counter. He shifted around and scanned all visible areas but still couldn't pick them out. Donning a Phillies blue cap, he then quickly added a goatee and bushy eyebrows from a small kit under the front seat. It wasn't much of a disguise but a few changes in facial hair really altered a person's look.

The interior was no surprise since he'd eaten here before. They had good subs and burgers but their claim to fame was Philly-style, mouth-watering cheese steaks. It was only 11:25 and the place was half full already—the take-out line about twelve deep. Not surprisingly, Kyscr and thc othcr man had taken a secluded booth all the way against the far wall. He considered one of the surrounding empties, deciding that might be a little obvious and chose a seat at the counter. It was too noisy to hear anything at that distance so he settled for observing. A waitress came along, brought two drinks and wrote some things on a pad as Kyser read from the menu. It seemed like this would take a while. A tall friendly guy leaned over the sneeze-guard and asked what he'd like so Cruz ordered a Dr. Pepper and a cheeseburger with the works.

Cruz snuck a glance from time to time as the men conversed. The discussion was one-sided with Kyser doing the majority of the talking. It was completely subdued, unanimated, and of a serious nature from their expressions. Both of them seemed unusually alert, watching for passers-by or anyone's approach. They were purposely isolated, secretive. This was definitely not two boyhood chums hashing over old times. First had been the midnight rendezvous with the hot babe. Now lunch with a scruffy character that had 'hoodlum' written all over him. *What was this uptight businessman doing?* He didn't appear to be cheating. *But up to no good? Maybe.*

About the time Kyser's order came, the other man got up to leave. They both seemed grim but satisfied and didn't smile or shake hands like two friends might. Cruz feigned disinterest and kept his eyes on the grille and sandwich-making as the man came past on his way towards the exit. With his peripheral vision he glimpsed a few simplistic tattoos on the guy's forearms and fingers, figuring him for an ex-con. Interestingly, he carried the same bag that Gilbert had brought along. It didn't seem like it held anything heavy, maybe something the size and weight of a small paperback. Cruz thought about following him since it could be useful to take down a license plate and a make of vehicle. To leave right now would also look strange and maybe cause a disturbance since he'd already ordered. He couldn't draw that kind of attention to himself in front of Kyser.

After the man had gone, Cruz took a look as Kyser heartily devoured a large cheese steak. He couldn't be certain, but thought it had sliced pepperoni and hot sauce, looking really tasty. When his own burger came, he decided to relax and enjoy. In any case, Kyser's very cute wife was right about two things. One, her husband was up to something. And two, he was never going to lose weight.

Earlier, Amy had taken the time to watch a press conference by Cameron Chastang. He expressed his love of the city but denounced its violent tendencies. He listed his son Zachary's accolades, spirited existence, creative nature, and love of life. Naturally, he didn't mention Zachary's colorful arrests or his recent troubles, and alluded to police harassment and general wasting of time when good citizens needed protection. Sometime later, a clip aired with the Chief doing a short statement from right outside near the entrance on North 7th Street. He looked intense and promised a thorough investigation into the shooting and swift justice.

An interview with Marcus Jarrett's staff had yielded informative, if surprising, results. According to his secretary, accounting clerk, and two research assistants, Marcus was fair, dedicated, and a good strategist in their marketplace. Yes, they'd heard stories that he'd been a party-dude in his younger years, but that was before any of them worked there. Since they'd known him, he'd been a great boss who gave incentive bonuses and reasonable time off for personal problems. Last year he'd treated his immediate staff of eighteen to box seats at a Phillies game. The rumor mill said he was dating someone special—much to the obvious dismay of a few single ladies—but no one knew for sure. Since his father's death, he'd been concentrating even harder on raising his department's standards and expanding their role within the company. He was popular and well respected. To Amy, he sounded nothing like an empty-souled, drug-peddling date-rapist—but that was often how it went.

Oddly, although the staff knew the Chastang name, none knew of any friendship with Marcus. His own secretary didn't remember any calls, messages, or emails to or from Zachary Chastang.

As Frank drove along, Amy read from the report they'd pulled up before leaving the Roundhouse. "Sorry to say, Dixie has no close male relatives. Father died in 2011. Mother moved to Edgewater, Florida in 2015. One married older sister lives in Portland, Maine."

"She a local girl?"

"Yep. In fact, she graduated from Roxborough High like me."

Frank grinned. "But about ten years later."

"Five," Amy snapped. "Okay, *six.* I guess the vigilante angle doesn't seem likely."

"She could have a boyfriend. Or even an ex-boyfriend."

"We'll ask her. I'm still not sure about this. Lt. Trainer might not be wowed by the connection with Jarrett."

"We'll sway him. We've got too many little threads for us not to tug on one or two and see what happens. Both of them into date-rape. Both were at that party and both end up shot to death. I want to hear Dixie's version of that party firsthand and see how well she knew Marcus Jarrett. If it doesn't go anywhere, fine."

Frank drove past the Belair Shopping Center and pulled into Birch Tree Apartments on Haldeman Avenue. Amy noted it was a stylish, two-story group of buildings with nice landscaping. The sign out front cited vacancies, a pool, and sundecks for each unit. Frank turned towards the first building which featured a large gold A. Dixie's apartment was A-114 which would likely be on the first floor. They hadn't called ahead, preferring the informal approach. It was around dinnertime and Amy was hoping they'd catch her at home.

They found the first-floor apartment easily and Frank knocked on the door. It was opened by a woman with light brown skin and exotic features. She was slender and a few inches taller than Amy with long thick brown hair that flowed past her shoulders. Even in jeans and green ruffle t-shirt, she was stunning. The right age but all-wrong description.

"We're looking for Dixie Newberry," Amy said.

The woman looked them over curiously. "I'm her friend. Why?"

Amy produced her ID and introduced them. The woman turned a little antsy which often happened.

"There's no problem. We're just following up on an incident that involved her. She does live here, correct?"

"Oh, yes," she answered, visibly relaxing. "She'll be along soon. Would you care to wait?"

Frank and Amy looked at each other. Frank said, "Sure, that sounds fine. Who are you?"

"I'm Vonda Cantu. Dixie's my best friend."

Vonda led them inside a tidy living room. She offered refreshments which they declined and took seats on a beige sectional couch. There was a glass-topped coffee table that held a vase with fresh-cut flowers. A large framed oil painting of a waterfall dominated one wall. There were a few personal 8 by 10 photos. One of them featured Vonda and Dixie in a posed shot near a gazebo. Dixie, she recognized from her DMV photo, had a pleasant heart-shaped face with curtain bangs and a medium-length, wavy hairstyle.

Amy recalled Vonda's name from her notes and was sure Frank did, too. She figured this turnabout could be quite helpful since Dixie had gone with

Root of Deception

Vonda to the fateful party. Also, Vonda was the one who left with the birthday boy, their dead victim, Marcus Jarrett. Vonda was, in fact, one of the key people they'd been planning to track down. Suddenly it occurred to Amy that they really didn't know how close Vonda was to Marcus. Did they have a fling that night? Or did the women's clothing at Marcus's place belong to Vonda? By her affable mood, Vonda didn't know about his death or just didn't care much. She suspected the former. Sylvia Jarrett found out officially this morning but the name hadn't been given out yet. Unless Sylvia had called Vonda, which Amy seriously doubted, this would catch the young woman unprepared. Unfortunately, the Jarrett name was well known in the area. It could be any moment that the press got hold of the information.

Amy glanced at Frank and knew he was thinking the same thing. Turning to Vonda, she mentally searched for a tactful approach and decided to come from left field. "How long have you known Dixie?"

Vonda smiled. "Oh, many years. We met in eighth grade."

"That's great. Vonda, how well do you know Marcus Jarrett?"

She frowned. "Marcus? I ... I don't understand. Dixie was assaulted. I mean, yes, it was at his family's home. But Marcus wasn't there. Neither was I."

"I understand. We just need to get all our facts straight. How did you get to that party?"

101

"Well, Dixie drove me there. My car was getting inspected. She decided to stay and I"—Vonda lowered her eyes with a wince of discomfort—"left with Marcus. I had no idea something terrible would happen to her. It's been awful."

"Do you live here?"

"I have my own apartment in this complex, the next building over. I've been staying here with Dixie a lot since, well … the *incident*."

"I understand. So, you know Marcus well?"

Vonda smiled a little. "Yes. I actually do. He's very sweet. And he was horrified about what happened to Dixie at his own party. He offered to pay for therapy or anything at all she needs."

Amy nodded. *Okay—it was worse than she thought.*

Vonda continued with a confidential tone. "You see, I'm a junior accountant for the Jarrett Corporation. Marcus dated someone in the company a while back and it caused some tension. So, we've been keeping it quiet. Not many know about Marcus and me. I don't work directly for him, but you know how the rumor-mill is."

Do I ever? Amy thought. "How long have you been dating?"

"About eight months. At first, it was casual. I wasn't even sure I should go out with him. I was me who actually asked Marcus if we could keep it to ourselves. Things have changed. We're going to make it all public knowledge very soon."

"I see." Amy noticed the sheer joy in that explanation and it gave her a sting of heartbreak for the poor woman. In all likelihood, Vonda was the reason Marcus moved from the family mansion and got his own place so they could spend more time together. Their relationship was kept discreet for business reasons, so Sylvia Jarrett and most others wouldn't know about it. From Vonda's tone, she was in love with him. It complicated matters that Marcus Jarrett was connected to date-raping and may have directly or indirectly participated in the attack on Dixie. "And does Dixie know about you and Marcus?"

"Oh sure. She likes him a lot. She doesn't blame him at all for what happened."

"I understand that." Amy stopped and drew a breath, steadying herself for what was to come. "I have some very bad—"

A sound of footsteps drew Amy's attention and then the front door burst open. She recognized Dixie from her photograph as rushed in with her eyes wide in panic.

"Vonda, oh Vonda," she cried out. "Did you hear?"

Vonda jumped up and ran to her. "What? What is it?"

They hugged briefly and then Dixie noticed Amy and Frank. "You're police?" she asked. "Then it's true. Oh, my God!"

Amy and Frank stood up. "We're so very sorry," Amy said. *The story had gotten out.* "We were just about to explain."

"Marcus is dead," Dixie blurted. "It was on the news. They had his photo and everything."

"Marcus?" Vonda's eyes widened in terror. "It … can't be."

"We're sorry," Amy said. "Yes, it's true."

"It can't be true. It can't be . . ." As Vonda collapsed, the three of them caught her awkwardly and got her to the couch. She sobbed in deep gasps and Amy feared she might lose consciousness. After a few minutes, the grieving woman settled down and stared straight ahead as her mind searched for solace and answers that would never truly come. Frank went to the kitchen, found a glass and brought Vonda some water. She took a few sips and seemed content to stay still in Dixie's embrace. Frank and Amy stepped quietly to the small foyer so they could keep the women in sight while talking privately.

"You did fine," Frank whispered. "Bad timing is all."

"I know. It's just … We'll have to take it easy on her."

"Yeah. Nothing about Marcus's nice drug collection."

"You realize that Vonda probably knew him as well as anyone."

"Or thought she did."

Amy sighed. "Yeah."

It was several minutes later when Vonda calmed down enough so that they would attempt some questions. Vonda said she felt able to answer and Dixie remained by her side. Amy apologized for the way Vonda had been informed. They had no idea that Vonda would be at Dixie's apartment, nor the seriousness of her relationship with Marcus Jarrett. As expected, she'd asked what happened to him and Amy admitted he'd been murdered at his home but couldn't tell her more details. The last time Vonda had seen or talked to Marcus had been a phone call around dinnertime last evening that was about twenty minutes long. They'd discussed ideas for the weekend and planned to take in a movie. Amy knew the timing was correct and matched up with Marcus's call log.

The questions got tougher now and she readied herself. "Where were you between 9 P.M. and midnight last night?"

"Is that . . .? You think it's me? Really, I loved him. I cared—"

"Please understand," Frank said, standing off to the side. Amy didn't mind him jumping in—it was how they always worked to divide people's attention, a little like good-cop/bad-cop. "This is just a formality. We ask everyone we interview in these cases."

"All right. I was here. So was Dixie. We watched an episode of Grey's Anatomy together. Dixie's mother called right around ten o'clock."

"That's right," Dixie said.

A little iffy for an alibi, but Amy wouldn't dwell on it. "Where were you all day today?"

"I was working, same as every weekday, from eight-thirty to five."

It rang true and much easier to verify. Vonda probably wouldn't be their mystery caller who phoned in erroneous reports of gunshots. She didn't think it was Dixie, either. A voice analysis would clear it up. "Did Marcus ever seem like he was into anything that was suspicious?"

Vonda seemed offended. "Like what?"

"I don't know. Was he secretive about anything?"

"Of course not."

"Afraid of anyone?"

"No. Why would he be?"

"We have no idea," Frank said. "You were close and we never met him. It's our job to find out what happened and who did it. We don't know yet what might be important."

"Fine. Then put this in your little notebook. He was the sweetest, kindest man I ever met. He got along with people. Everyone liked him. Except that *bitch* Sylvia Jarrett."

CHAPTER 9

Amy sat at her mom's kitchen table mindlessly petting the family's beloved black Labrador while wondering how soon the husband-family-kids inquiries would begin. Not that she held it against her mother for bringing it up. Amy, nearing 34, figured it was inevitable. Thankfully, her mom seemed to come up with a tacit arrangement and only brought it up every *other* visit. The latest bomb to drop—two visits ago—was her idea for Amy to take over the house. The mortgage long gone, she would only have to pay the taxes, which would be less than the rent she paid now. Her mother's possible plans included buying an over-55 condo, going to live with her brother in Allentown, or possibly her niece in Jacksonville, who interestingly needed help with two spirited children, ages five and three.

"Some ice cream, Honey? It's your favorite: Double Fudge Brownie."

Amy tried not to smile. Her mother insisted she was too thin, although at a shade under five foot six, Amy weighed 138. A good part of that was hard-earned muscle from high school sports and these days, regular workouts. Clara Lepone was taller than Amy by two inches on a similar frame, although hers was now giving in to the soft acceptance of middle age. Her parents had been very conventional—the old-fashioned homemaker and the 12-hour-workday provider. The two of them had been a truly happy couple for their 35 years together or at least they had found a partner in each other who meshed with what they believed married life should be. Now her father was years gone and her mother still carried on much as she always had. Financially, she was doing fine—Howard Lepone had seen to that with insurance and wise investments. Amy felt her mother was still attractive at sixty-nine with a nice smile and reddish-brown hair streaked in gray. Strangely, as far as Amy knew, her mother hadn't dated anyone or expressed a desire for romance since her father's passing.

"No thanks, Mom," Amy said. "I shouldn't eat that this late."

Clara made a tsk-tsk face, let it pass and busied herself with the dishes and cleaning. Amy knew the real problem. Action-packed, crime-solving life versus nurturing, conventional, home maker. Her mom thought a single woman of thirty-four should be out diligently husband-hunting with fluttering eyelashes and cooking skills, not tracking criminals. Amy had already offered to help twice but was turned down. She'd been nearly an hour late for a dinner consisting of a delicious ham with a pineapple glaze, a potato casserole, and assorted mixed vegetables. The lateness didn't seem to be a factor in either temperature or taste—in fact, Amy was sure Mom had expected tardiness and adjusted her cooking accordingly. In lieu of chores, Amy decided to take a few more minutes lavishing attention on the needy, ten-year old lab Spock, so named by her father, a big fan of Star Trek, after the noteworthy Vulcan. Her father was a real 'dog' person and she had been raised accordingly. Spock was their third. The first, acquired before she was born, was in Amy's earliest memories and had died when she was eight; its decline and death an experience she could even now recall. The second died when she was twenty and away at college. Just seeing Spock now seemed to bring an odd mixture of joy and sadness since he was two when her father died.

She'd gotten so much from her mother and father, a couple who'd had their one child at the ages of 33 and 40, respectively. Her mother, of course, had contributed more of the actual work involved with raising a daughter: the ultimate homemaker. She had changed most of the diapers, comforted Amy in sickness, eased her sorrows and shared her triumphs. During those rebellious teenage years, her mom had dutifully baked cookies and made pitchers of iced tea, welcoming all her friends. This, Amy had always assumed, was her mom's attempt at enticing the whole gang to stick around so she could keep an eye on them. It worked, for the most part, and Amy had grown up relatively trouble-free. Her father, a notorious workaholic, had been in the restaurant business all his adult life. For many years prior to his death, he'd managed a popular eatery with elegant dining, separate banquet rooms, and a brisk trade. Nights and weekends were always the busiest time, and vacations were rare, yet he'd somehow attended nearly every major event in Amy's life. When she'd dress as a princess for Halloween or in a gown for the prom, her father had been right there with his trusty old 35mm. He never missed a parent-teacher conference or graduation ceremony and attended many of Amy's high school gymnastics meets.

The more focused family discussions began in her sophomore year when she'd switched her major from political science to criminal justice. *Career path? Financial considerations? Dangers?* Her mother had the strongest and most vocal objections. Her father had been more neutral but she remembered the concern in his eyes. She also remembered his look, beaming with pride, when he'd first seen her as a uniformed officer. He was worried, as any parent would be. But excited for her, too. A big crime fiction fan, he loved Raymond Chandler and Dashiell Hammett novels and they'd had some great discussions during her first years on patrol. Fate would have been kinder if he'd lived to see her become a detective. She suddenly found herself absent-mindedly rubbing Spock vigorously behind the ears, so much that the delighted canine rolled to his back, helpless from an overdose of attention.

Clara went on chattering in generalities about various family members, both near and far. Amy enjoyed the banter and thought how much she'd have loved the chance to discuss real-life crime solving with her father.

Alvin Cruz pulled his blue 2001 Pontic Sunfire next to a red, white, and blue pick-up truck with oversized tires and stepped out into the cooler evening air. The lot was barely half full—everything from clunky old sedans to minivans to customized Porches—but it was still early yet. The serious partiers wouldn't start arriving until 10 PM or later. He walked around and opened his trunk, rummaging through the contents. Finding only two rumpled black t-shirts in his gym bag, one MOTORHEAD and the other AC/DC, he decided to just go with the loud Hawaiian shirt he was already wearing. A few blocks from Marconi Plaza on West Oregon Avenue, The Odyssey Club was a well-known Italian-American hangout in South Philly.

He stepped inside the foyer to a blast of slightly cooler air. A general rattle of chatter and music drifted from the main room. A burly bouncer on a stool looked him over and said, "five bucks."

Cruz paid the man and went in to find a sea of bobbing heads bouncing wildly on the dance floor. From his estimation, the place was less than half full. Couples nuzzling in booths and singles on the prowl.

Had it really been more than fifteen years ago when he'd be slipping in as a teenager and trying to get served? How some things changed, Cruz considered, while others stayed the same. The building was legendary. In thirty plus years the place had paralleled every phase of American culture with commensurate remodeling. The first transition he recalled hearing about was from a simple working man's bar to something very *Saturday Night Fever*-like with flashing silver balls and a lighted dance floor. After the fall of disco, it had been a sports bar, an oldies club, a glitter-rock palace, a hard-rocking biker hangout, all with intermittent attempts at livening up, playing down, more and less light, louder, softer, strict dress codes, no dress codes, and one valiant attempt at using bikini-clad waitresses. The latter—Cruz's admitted favorite—had been effectively scuttled due to picketing efforts by a group of relentless conservatives and religious zealots. As far as he was concerned, freedom meant free choice. The crybabies could just stay home if they don't enjoy it.

A Black-Eyed Peas song was playing over a respectable sound system as Cruz ambled in, surveying the crowd more closely. It was lively, but not outrageous. The men wore neat jeans and pullovers, t-shirts, a few do-rags and one cowboy hat. A scant few businessmen wore jackets and ties. The women were in stirrup pants or skinny-jeans, some designer-types in tight skirts. He spotted a noteworthy leather mini with lots of leg. Some couples, more singles. Slightly more men than women. Mainly twenty-five to late thirties, though a few older. At first glance no one seemed underage.

Cruz decided that the most recent change met with his approval, at least on the surface. Whatever this new configuration might be deemed, he had no idea. The crowd was pleasantly varied, though normal—by today's standards. The waitresses were cute, albeit clothed, and the obligatory neon beer signs covered the walls as in the old days. Some names seemed new: Victory, Leinenkugal's, Bullfrog, Heartland. But the standards were still there: Budweiser, Coors, Rolling Rock. After a few, they all tasted the same anyway. A large wooden sign with a beer mug declared happy hour to be from 5 to 7 o'clock but some irreverent patron with a marking pen had altered the seven to a nine.

Cruz made his way towards the back room. It would be quieter there, with some measure of seclusion. Plus, he'd hopefully find the guy he wanted. Two women in their twenties strolled by, giggling and swaying their hips to the beat. One was clad in a yellow halter-top; her breasts struggled against the flimsy fabric. The other wore a red T-shirt with a drawing of a frothy mug and the words: *SAVE THE ALES*. Both smiled openly and gave a friendly wave.

Cruz nodded in reply and kept moving. "Got to get out more," he muttered to himself.

The adjoining room had changed the least, though it had been a while. Set up for 'old-style' bar games, it featured foosball, darts, shuffleboard, slide bowling, and pool—sort of a hands-on, *anti*-videogame theme that Cruz appreciated. His own gaming memories consisted of Big Nose and Super Mario Brothers and he'd never been very good. There was no dancing but the muffled hum of music made its way from the main room. This area's noise consisted solely of soft chatter, assorted thumps, slaps, and pops from competition followed by an occasional yelp of victory or groan of defeat. Table service was provided by a several waitresses wearing white shorts or skirts and Odyssey T's in a variety of colors. After a dance or two, this was where you brought the girl to buy her a drink and chat—several such operations seemed to be in progress. One pool table was vacant; the other occupied by a large man with a gray ponytail and a heavy-set woman in a Harley jacket. Two average-Joes played Strike-90 on the slide-bowling machine; the familiar *ching-ching* sound repeated annoyingly.

A bartender washed glasses and mugs as Cruz's eyes moved along the barstools. A young couple, two empty, old guy with a beer belly, another empty, two college-types matching shots. At the end was a thin fellow slumped over and sound asleep on his own arm.

Cruz pointed. "That Woody?" he asked.

The bartender chuckled slightly and nodded. His expression changed quickly to concern and added, "he ain't drivin'," as though sensing this may be the heat. Cruz waved the man off, figuring his Hawaiian shirt wasn't cutting it—should've gone with the rock band T-shirt to blend in. He put his hand on the sleeping man's shoulder and shook lightly until he came around. Willard Woodland was thinner than he remembered, the hair longer and more snarled with added streaks of gray. It had been maybe a year and a half. Nobody called him Willard and most people wouldn't know his real first name.

"Cruzie," the groggy one muttered through his self-induced haze.

"Yeah, Woody, it's me." He thought the man looked like shit and twenty years older than he should but tried not to let it show. "C'mon," he said and helped the quivering man to his feet.

Cruz negotiated Woody to a booth and was quickly greeted by a mid-forties waitress with dark hair in a ponytail that ran halfway down her back. The round face had some mileage, the eyes bright, and skin with the glow of faithfully-applied creams. Her purple T-shirt was cinched in a knot revealing a soft but narrow waist. Cruz remembered her from a while back in his partying days. She hadn't come with the plumbing but had been around at least ten years. He ordered a chicken sandwich, fries, and a cup of coffee—all for Woody—and a Leinenkugel's Northwoods Amber for himself.

"You with me?" Cruz asked.

"Yeah, man," Woody said, slurring the words. "I'm jazzed, man, really. Great, jus fuckin' great to see ya." He blinked a few times and rolled his tongue around as though fighting with a mouthful of cotton balls. "Ya still a gumshoe, Cruzie?"

"Nobody talks like that these days. But, yeah."

Cruz knew the man had once been a mover and shaker in the underworld though more for penny-ante gophering than anything else. Through the eighties and nineties, Woody dabbled in running numbers and then found occasional work in their legitimate enterprises. After the old-timers died off, the next generation had no real need for a washout and he'd quickly gone downhill with drugs and alcohol. Out of respect for their departed kin, the new bosses threw him occasional odd jobs to keep him alive. He'd always had a great memory despite his lifestyle. Cruz was counting on those contacts and hoped the man still knew everyone on the streets.

"Can I bum a smoke from ya, Cruzie?"

"Sorry, don't smoke. Where's yours?"

"I quit so's I stopped carryin' 'em."

"Of course."

The waitress brought their drinks and Woody obliged by starting to sip the coffee. Cruz knew he wouldn't rat out any big-timers, partly from loyalty and mostly from fear. However, he would gladly spill what he knew about the little guys for a fee. Cruz slid two fifties across the table and placed photographs in front of Woody. Both were respectably sharp. One showed Gilbert Kyser and the other man, a wide shot that had sidewalk at the bottom and the Sam's and Herb's Deli sign at the top. The second was a similar view but closer, more of a torso and head shot of the two men. The faces were at an angle but identifiable. "Know this guy?"

Woody nodded and reached for the money, placing it in his shirt pocket. "Dunno the fat dude. The other one, yeah. Let's see … Yeah, that's Corky Buck."

"He done time?"

Woody dipped his head and sat motionless for so long that Cruz thought he might have fallen asleep. Then he looked up and said, "Yeah. Once, maybe twice. Beef in Jersey. Did a couple years."

"What's he do for a living?"

"Anything for money."

"Got that. Who's he work for?"

"Nobody special. Up for grabs."

"All right. Think about this. Let's say, the other guy there has a thick wallet. He's a married, smart businessman, fancy car, nice house. He met with Buck in secret. Slipped him a small bag, probably money. Got nothing in return. So, what's it about? What's going on? Just give me your best guess."

"Dunno, man." Woody shrugged his bony shoulders. "I'm thinkin' fat boy wants somethin' done. Buck knows locks and cars and like, you know, machines real good. Nothin' much 'bout computers. He does okay with electronical shit—you know, wiretaps, alarms, shit like that. He likes guns, don't do explosives. I heard he sliced up a guy in a knife fight once. Don't do drugs no more but wouldn't mind selling."

"He tough?"

"He's crazy. Worse'n tough."

Their waitress brought a basket with sandwich and fries. She set it down in front of Woody and gave Cruz a sympathetic wink before heading off to the kitchen.

"Eat up," Cruz said.

"Really?"

"Yeah."

Woody picked up the sandwich and looked it over as though he'd never seen one before. After a minute he began taking tiny bites. Cruz took a few swigs of his beer and thought about this new information. *Why would a living-large, big-earning, exec be talking to a thug like Buck?* Woody stated the obvious answer: to hire him. *But for what?* Kyser wouldn't use Buck as a bodyguard. With no computer skills, he'd be a lousy choice to mop up if Kyser was skimming the company. Couldn't be any type of infiltration or industrial espionage—the skills might be there but Buck wouldn't fit into the corporate world. Kyser wouldn't need a car hijacked or money collected. Maybe to scare someone or threaten them—that was reasonable. Cruz shook a little as a strange sensation suddenly passed through him. *Could Kyser be planning to have Joyce killed?* His very sexy wife. *Was that even possible?* He couldn't imagine why Kyser would want her dead but stranger things happened. *Big insurance policy?* He also recalled how Kyser had looked at the deli—jittery, secretive. Statistically, 70% of murdered women were killed by someone they knew, often a husband, boyfriend, co-worker, or an ex. If a hotshot with no criminal connections started planning his wife's demise, Corky Buck was exactly the type of lowlife hoodlum he'd come across by greasing a few palms on the street. He sounded unprincipled, available, and would be happy to make it look like a mugging or burglary while Gilbert Kyser conveniently attended a board meeting or was away on business.

Not jumping to conclusions, he at least had to factor all this into his thinking. Just do it one step at a time. Suspicions were one thing. What were his ethical and professional responsibilities? Joyce Kyser was his client. He rolled the possible ramifications around in his mind along with the legalities and thought: *Fuck it!* He needed to get his priorities straight. Joyce was a major babe. He'd do whatever it took protect her and that included the use of some specialized equipment.

"Just out of curiosity, would Buck get nasty? Like maybe do a hit?"

Woody paused. "Sure. He'd want it *his* way. And a nice paycheck. Yeah, he'd do it."

"Okay." Cruz took out another fifty and slid it across the table. "You never saw me, right?"

"Sure, man."

"And eat the rest of your sandwich."

Cruz found their waitress clearing a table. "Take care of my friend," he said, handing her a fifty and a twenty. "This should cover it and you keep the change. Give him anything else he wants—except booze."

"You got it." She paused in her work, drawing her order pad." You're a cop, right?"

"Private."

She smiled. "Oh, cool. Been a while since I seen you in here, Sugar."

"Yeah," he said. "I must have forgot how hot the waitresses are."

She rolled her eyes but broke into a hundred-watt smile and gave Cruz a mock punch in the arm. "I forgot how cute the private eyes are, too. I, um, get off in an hour. You heading home to a wife or something?"

"No," Cruz said sadly. "I'm kinda . . ."

"On a big case?"

"That's about it."

"Too bad."

Cruz sighed, thinking of hot waitresses, sexy clients, dangerous killers, and wishing he wasn't such a devoted servant of the people. "I'll be back in."

"I'll be here." As she jotted something down, they both turned in time to watch Woody stirring his coffee with a French fry. "Poor old guy," she said, chuckling. "That man's brain cells washed down the drain years ago." She held out a slip of paper with her phone number. "You're a cute one but you sure keep strange company."

Cruz sighed. "Don't I know it."

CHAPTER 10

Frank pulled into his driveway behind Cruz's dilapidated old Pontiac. He sat for a moment reflecting on the evening's second interview with Sylvia Jarrett—necessary, if only marginally helpful. She'd been gracious once again and agreed to a chat without legal representation. Despite Amy's reservations, the woman definitely acted like she had nothing to hide. Yes, she'd known about the rape accusation by Dixie Newberry and was shocked and dismayed by it. At the time, she'd been interviewed by detectives on the case and had no pertinent input since she was away at the time. The facts, as Sylvia understood them from discussions with police, Marcus, and his friends, were accurate, as far as they went. Her impressions were that the woman was not lying, though possibly confused, or misinterpreting events. An argument would have been pointless, although the facts were clear—there was no *misinterpretation* of a date-rape drug in Dixie Newberry's system. Without a doubt, someone put it there. Sylvia claimed that she hadn't mentioned the month-past incident in the previous interview because it was unrelated. Her reasoning was that since Marcus had left the party with a woman, an alleged rape that occurred later had no bearing on his death now. Yes, a reasonable point. Except that Marcus may have been there late enough to have participated or could have helped cover it up. A strong possibility existed that he may have gotten Vonda out of there so she wouldn't find Dixie incapacitated and raise the alarm.

Marcus may look uninvolved to Sylvia, who didn't have all the facts. To a cop, every detail was considered vital and part of the search for relevance until deemed otherwise. There was indeed a connection, one not shared with Sylvia Jarrett since they'd suppressed the discovery of date-rape drugs in Marcus's home. Zachary Chastang may have done the deed with supplies from Marcus; Marcus may or may not have joined in. Neither, however, would ever be held accountable. The job at hand now was to solve Marcus Jarrett's murder. If Zachary Chastang's crimes, his own murder, or their date-raping was involved, those links needed to be explored. Per orders from above, they would continue treading lightly with Sylvia Jarrett.

Frank got out, locked his car, and ambled inside; faint aromas were suddenly sending messages to his stomach, reminding him that he hadn't had a bite in hours. Cruz was sitting at his kitchen table drinking a beer with one hand and scratching Layla's head with the other. At least there was a large pizza box on the table.

"Pepperoni and green peppers?"

"And onions. Tell me a little more about this attack on Amy. Sounds off the hook."

"Yeah. A big guy according to her. It was dark."

"Do you think he was after you?"

"Can't be sure, my gut says no. I called a few sources. Doesn't seem to be anybody after me or nosing around my life. A handful of likely candidates are all in the can or accounted for. It's weird. Could have been a half-ass burglary, I guess."

Cruz frowned. "But you don't think so."

Frank shook his head. "Doesn't have the right feel. The guy came in with precision. Also, went in the basement to cut the power off."

"Okay. Kills the lights—*after* he was already inside. So, he definitely knew somebody was here."

Frank nodded. "Right. It would be to keep his actions in the dark, maybe add some confusion. The real question—was it because *Amy* was inside—or just that *somebody* was?"

"Tough to say. But then when she fought back, he took off like a jackrabbit."

"That's about it. I'm at a loss."

They sat in silence for a few minutes, enjoying pizza with occasional swallows of beer.

Cruz finally asked, "What have you got on the Marcus Jarrett murder?"

Frank said, "Is this a trade?"

"I haven't got anything yet. You know I'll share."

"Fair enough. How'd you get onto the very rich Ms. Jarrett?"

"Friend of hers hired me. Deficient husband thing. I'm not even sure he's cheating."

"Anything I need to know about?"

"Not really. Anyway, she told Sylvia Jarrett about me. I got there right ahead of you and Amy, just like I said."

"She legit?"

"I'd say so. She wants me to nose around. Thinks she owes the family a personal look. She's really hurting from his death. I guess it's just catching up with her."

"What do you mean?"

"We first talked on the phone. She was concerned, but very … controlled. When I first got to the house, she was different. Agitated. You know the dude in the fancy threads?"

"Sure. Warren Hamilton. Big-time attorney."

"Right. Well, when the maid first brought me out to that sunroom, they shut up quick. This would have been maybe twenty minutes before you and Amy got there. Sylvia and that guy were talking about something pretty intense—I could tell. They covered well. Hamilton tucked some papers in a briefcase, very smooth. Sylvia greeted me and we got down to business. We had a completely normal talk."

"What's your take?"

"Mmm." Cruz had to think it over. "My guess: the attorney brought her paperwork, maybe bad news. Or unexpected news. Something she didn't like hearing. But hell, remember this is just my feel for what I saw, maybe a few seconds. By the time I walked up and introduced myself, Sylvia Jarrett was all class and poise."

"Okay, good. I'll roll that around. Did you know Marcus had a serious girl friend?"

"Sylvia never mentioned it."

"She probably doesn't know. Hush-hush. Name's Vonda Cantu, works for the company. Nice girl. Remember—all this is off the record. I mean it. I'll shoot you in the foot. Nothing we talk about here is for Sylvia Jarrett's ears or this could turn into a real goatfuck." Cruz nodded, so he continued. "For the murder we got no real suspects yet. Clean shot, no witnesses, no nothing. Somebody was having a beer with Jarrett before he died. Bottle was full, not even a sip missing. And before you ask—no prints."

"That says something. Like maybe a pro."

"Yeah. And this next kicker is not for *anyone's* ears, at least not from you. Especially not the press."

"I'm cool with that."

"Okay. We found a variety-pack of roofies hidden at Jarrett's place. Enough to tranquilize a sorority house."

Cruz frowned. "Didn't see that coming. Marcus Jarrett was a hard-worker, from all I've heard. Sylvia even praised his work for the company."

"There's another weird connection. We found prints on beer bottles in the kitchen belonging to Zachary Chastang."

"Chastang? I heard about him on the news. The guy who got shot this morning."

"Yep. They don't have any suspects yet. Get this—he'd been under investigation for drug-assisted date-rape. Amy was on an undercover op, busted him just last night."

"Last night? The story I heard—she was shacked up here with you when she kicked a burglar's ass."

Frank grumbled. "Geez, don't let Amy hear that shit! I wasn't even home. I was up north at mom and dad's place. Amy came by to put out this crazy dog."

Cruz was ginning. "Whatever you say, Frank."

"I'm telling you straight up. Friend to friend. There's nothing there."

"Seriously?"

"Completely. And she's the best partner I've ever had. I want to keep it that way." Frank shrugged. "Just don't, you know, tell her I said that."

Cruz laughed. "Okay. Sure. I've heard of Chastang, a real nutjob. So, Marcus Jarrett and him were partners in the date-raping stuff?"

"That's how it looks. Goes back to a complaint from a woman who was assaulted at a party a month ago—at the mansion. Zach Chastang was there for sure. Marcus left with the girlfriend at some point. Other than the fact both these guys are dead, I can't imagine what the hell's going on. The exact timing of the rape is in question since the victim's memory is lemon meringue. Don't forget—all this is on the down-low. And I'm ordered to go easy on Sylvia Jarrett."

Cruz stood and nodded, the wheels apparently turning. "I'll be in touch."

Frank finished off his beer, got undressed, and tried to forget all about crime in the city—for the moment. Climbing in bed, Frank wondered what Cruz was into and what he might find out.

CHAPTER 11

Amy hated it when things didn't make sense. Just about the time that you'd honed a vague notion into a brilliant hypothesis, new facts emerged that just didn't fit. Sometimes the line separating the good guys and the bad guys was vague, making it tough to get a fix on their intentions. It was much nicer when the perpetrators had a long arrest record, stolen property, illegal firearms, and the whole crime had been recorded on a security tape—although, admittedly, that rarely happened. In law enforcement, the proverbial *smoking gun* was almost a myth, like a unicorn or bigfoot.

Mostly on her mind were the events of last evening—it had been rough. Not only had Vonda Cantu been unaware of Marcus Jarrett's death, but the two of them were an item, albeit secretly, and she took the tragedy extremely hard. The part that stuck with Amy was the way Vonda adamantly stood by Marcus and extolled his character. They seemed to spend a lot of time together, particularly for a clandestine relationship, and the proof was right before her now—the last months of Vonda's life in her own handwriting. When they'd finally been able to calm her down and gently get some information, Vonda had gratefully offered up her diary if they thought it might help find his killer. Vonda was sporadic in her notations but had many useful entries about Marcus. Unfortunately, most of those were about thoughts and feelings with fewer times and places.

Amy read quickly, slowed up in spots, but tried to cover all the material before going back over it to make notes. Vonda's first date with Marcus was December 19th, almost ten months ago. At the time, she'd already known him for nearly a year, crossing paths for business reasons from time to time. At several places, she'd mentioned him—he was cute and thought he might ask her out—apparently her instincts were good. After they began dating, there were a few short references to "the other woman," but no actual name was listed. Vonda wrote that she was pleased the woman had backed off and hadn't bothered Marcus lately. Amy put in her note that at least one ex-girlfriend had been in Marcus's life until late last year. She then made a chart and wrote down some observations while flipping though and picking out specifics. During the rest of December and January, Marcus and Vonda had gotten together six more times—dinner, drinks, one movie and one night of dancing at a jazz club. They'd also been together for New Year's Eve, staying at Vonda's place, sipping champagne and playing monopoly. Maybe not hot and heavy yet, but more than casual. It wasn't hard to see that Vonda was falling for him—she was dotting her i's with little hearts and describing him with words like 'sweet' and 'cuddly.' They'd become intimate on February 13th, the evening before Valentine's Day. From that time until the final entry just over a month ago, they'd been together at least a few nights a week and spent nearly every weekend together. There was no shortage of flowery language as Vonda talked about their romance.

Amy read one passage through:

Marcus is so cute sometimes when he's excited about something. They cinched a new contract today and he brought a big bouquet of gorgeous flowers. For no reason of course. Me and my department had very little to do with the deal but he just wanted to celebrate. I really like his enthusiasm for the job. He has a real passion. He almost reminds me a little of dad – is that weird? I guess not. Marcus is organized, smart and has a good heart. He's not a tough macho guy and was never in the military, but I still think dad would have liked him. Can't wait to see him tomorrow, we're going to that new Italian Restaurant for dinner and afterwards … It's so HOT between us.

Okay—Vonda was over the top, no doubt about it. It made Amy's heart ache for the women; she just couldn't help it.

Marcus is getting his own house – it's huge and so beautiful. I think I'm the reason, but also to get away from that awful bitch. Marcus is so smart. I understand why he believes Sylvia tampered with his father's will. Or maybe she got rid of the updated one somehow. His father decided Marcus would be the one to run the company before he died. Marcus is taking his time but will figure it out. He can do it, I know he can.

In all likelihood, Marcus moved out of the Chestnut Hill mansion and got his own place to expand the relationship. Clearly, Vonda didn't care much for Sylvia Jarrett. However, for the first time, a motive had surfaced. Although, that could be just what Marcus told Vonda—it wasn't necessarily true. Amy was hoping for more to go on and wondered why Vonda stopped writing suddenly. The reason became clear in the final few entries: the assault on her friend, Dixie. The romantic reflections stopped completely. Understandably, Vonda switched topics to Dixie's shock and outrage and the fleeting attempts to comfort her. She praised Marcus and his profound sorrow, offers of help, and promises of action. Vonda took days off work, spending more time with Dixie, missing Marcus. Concern about Dixie and some gradual improvement. Disappointment when the police investigation stalled. Unfortunately, the last entry was more than a week ago.

All things considered, the diary was interesting and painted a picture of Marcus Jarrett's last months of life. It wasn't much help as far as the investigation. If anything, it showed a caring, professional businessman, a man in love. Vonda didn't know the real Marcus. The one with perverted obsessions and a bag full of nasty drugs. Maybe, in fact, Bradley Jarrett suspected Marcus's transgressions or actually knew about it. That could be the reason Bradley left control of the company to Sylvia. It made sense. Vonda didn't know about any of that yet. They hadn't brought up the drugs or any connection to Zachary Chastang. It would be pointless to do so—she'd just say it was all a lie or a mistake.

Very curious, Cruz thought, while reaching for his Nikon D5500 camera with a 55-300mm zoom lens. My, my. Who is this? From an unassuming Chevy Astro van down the street, Alvin Cruz readied the camera and leaned towards the tinted side window. He clicked off five shots as she stepped out of her car and then one of her license plate. The big silver Volvo SUV was a bold and snazzy touch of class. She was pretty, stylish, and quite tall, with one of those curly hairstyles that definitely came from a trendy salon. Business-casual in a black and white dress with a straight neckline and cut just above the knee. *Nice stuff.*

He watched as Gilbert Kyser greeted her at the front door and led her inside. There was scattered small talk and footsteps. Moments later, he heard a door close and their voices coming from the den. He was very glad that he'd placed a hidden bug in there as well as the kitchen and living room.

"Hello Mindy. What brings you around?"

"Sorry to intrude."

"*Don't give it a thought. I guess this is about the meeting this morning.*"

"*Yes. Cameron is hurting for his son. I understand that. But you heard what our lawyers said. The police seemed to have a solid case against Zachary this time.*"

"*Sure. Although, none of that really matters now.*"

"*Gilbert, I think he was really guilty of those charges. Or at least a similar thing he did before.*"

"*That's hard to believe, Mindy. What makes you think that?*"

"*I overheard Zachary and Mr. Einsohn talking. It's not like I eavesdrop. But they stepped into the supply room and I happened to be in the back. They didn't see me.*"

"*Even so, the man is dead. Say, would you care for a drink?*"

"*Um … Well, I guess so.*"

Cruz heard the hesitation in her voice. Mindy was focused but didn't want to appear unfriendly. The scrapes and clinks would be Gilbert at his fancy fully-stocked bar.

"*Here you go.*"

"*Thank you. I know he's dead. Of course. But listen. Zachary was worried. Really worried. He said somebody accused him of slipping a drug in a woman's drink at a party last month. He called her Dixie. He told Mr. Einsohn that she's a slut and wanted sex. But … I don't know. I've heard rumors about Zachary and know he's been in trouble. Maybe he really did give her a drug and raped her while she was unconscious. Someone was insisting he confess but he didn't*" *want to. Zachary said it would embarrass his father and the company. He said that Kurt Waldo should take care of it."*

"Why does it matter now? Mindy, you know I'm loyal to the company and Cameron Chastang. Zach is dead. You don't want to stir up—"

"Marcus Jarrett."

"What? Jarrett! I … I heard on the news that he was murdered."

"Yes, I know. That's the problem. He's the one who was insisting Zachary turn himself in. Zachary was telling all this to Einsohn and now Marcus Jarrett has been killed."

"Okay, Mindy. We've got to keep calm. Maybe it's something else. It could be unrelated. Marcus may have got into problems with drugs. Or some jealous husband nailed him."

"No! No! He wasn't like that. He was sweet. Gilbert, you must understand. Zachary was afraid Marcus would turn him in. Einsohn may have assigned Kurt Waldo to remove the problem—and he took it seriously."

"Yes. Okay. I understand what you're saying. Kurt is a security expert. Which means he might do that sort of thing. So maybe Waldo killed both of them."

"I didn't say … that. I mean … not exactly. Marcus, for sure. Why would Waldo kill Zachary?"

"Maybe he thought it was the right thing. Mindy, Zachary was a drain on the company. Eliminating both of them might make sense to a guy like that."

"Well, that's certainly true. Kurt Waldo is, well, I've heard things. Frankly, he frightens me. I know Zachary was a public relations nightmare. But killing him? I mean, my goodness . . ."

Things were quiet for a moment and Cruz imagined they were both sipping on drinks. For now, a fresh clue and maybe a suspect: Kurt Waldo. He was unfamiliar. But clearly these two knew the guy. They spoke his name with awe and a hint of wariness. Maybe the company had a hatchet man on the payroll.

"Okay, Mindy. Remember, Zach was arrested Thursday night and the charges were really serious. You may have something here. Marcus must have thought Zachary was into that dreadful stuff. With Zachary and Marcus dead, it all goes away."

"I ... I just can't imagine. I've always been a little afraid of Kurt Waldo. Yes. I suppose it makes sense, doesn't it?"

"Absolutely. It's classic. You figured it out."

"But what can we do?"

"Nothing. We shouldn't do anything. We'll honor the memory of Cameron's son. We grieve. I think we should leave everything else to the police."

"I ... I don't know if I can handle that. Marcus didn't do anything wrong ... He was a nice man."

"Mindy, we have to think of the greater good here. If Waldo did this, the police will find clues. I'm sure of it. We just shouldn't go stirring up trouble—for Cameron's sake. He's lost a son, and frankly, I'm worried about him."

"All right. For Cameron Chastang and his family. I suppose I can remain silent and let things work themselves out."

"That's good. For now, we can—"

"But Kurt Waldo should be charged for his crimes. Zachary was, well, Zachary. He was a horrible person. Marcus was a good man."

"I'm sure he was. We just need to let the police do their jobs now. Please relax and go get some rest. This ordeal has been tough on all of us."

So—keeping an eye on this asshole husband had brought about an odd turn of events. His two cases were linked. Not only was he earning his keep with Joyce, but his surveillance had produced a lead on the Marcus Jarrett murder. The very cute Mindy thought this Kurt Waldo may be involved. Obviously, the guy worked for Pierce Brothers—he'd check it out fast. From the dynamic, Mindy also worked for the company. She referred to Zachary Chastang as a 'public relations nightmare' which put her in some upper-management capacity. She didn't come across as Gilbert's boss, but not really his subordinate, either. Educated and in her 30s. He'd find a last name and check her out, too.

Zachary Chastang was well known in the area. Basically, an infamous mini-celebrity for always being in trouble: cocaine possession, disorderly conduct, fender-benders. Mindy's version made it sound like Marcus was leaning on Zachary to tell the truth about a rape. Although why would a guy with shitload of roofies make his buddy admit to a crime? Something was way off here.

Gilbert Kyser was the other oddity. Although Mindy came to Gilbert's house and initiated their talk, Gilbert seemed to gently steer the woman toward some conclusions. *Why was that? Did Gilbert believe this Waldo killed both men or did he conjure up the notion for other reasons? Who is this Kurt Waldo and what's his story? Were Zachary and Marcus really contemptible pals or was something else going on?*

This wasn't adding up and it was time for answers. Cruz flicked open his cell phone and punched a speed dial. It answered in three rings.

"McGrail."

"It's me. You ever heard of Kurt Waldo?"

"Don't think so. Should I have?"

"He works for Pierce Brothers, maybe some kind of arm-twister."

"What else?"

"A little bird overheard Zachary Chastang talking to someone named Einsohn. I remember on the company website it lists a Klaus Einsohn as a senior VP. Zachary was worried because Marcus Jarrett wanted him to confess to raping a woman. He wanted this Einsohn to get Kurt Waldo to handle the problem."

"You've got my interest."

"The name *Dixie* mean anything?"

"Yeah, it does. That would be the rape victim from the party I told you about. Jarrett mansion, last month."

"Mentioned by name."

"I like Zachary Chastang for it. Nice girl, too; I met her. The case went south."

"He was never charged?"

"No. Like I said, Dixie's memory was fuzzy and she was bathed afterwards—no usable evidence. But Amy nailed Chastang good on a special assignment.

His ass would've been dogshit. So, yeah, he was a slimeball. This other thing—*Jarrett* wanting him to confess—doesn't gel. Why would Marcus Jarrett want to pull on that thread? If he supplied the drugs, that would put him in the searchlights, too."

"When I figure it out, I'll tell you. Get me whatever you can on Waldo."

"I will. He's now my number one suspect. Who's the little bird?"

"I'm working on that."

Frank paused, then said. "All right. Don't fuck me on this. We've got two rich families with dead kids and we can't piss on their graves."

CHAPTER 12

Amy frowned at her ringing phone and tapped the screen. "This can't be good."

"Busy?"

"Well, obviously. It's Saturday night. I'm out on a date."

Frank scoffed. "Seriously?"

"Of course."

"Okay. Then, where are you?"

"I'm salsa dancing at GoSway."

"Dancing ... Fancy nightclub ... Really? How come I don't hear crowd noise or music?"

"Well, that's because I just slipped in to the rest room for club sex. That's right. With a tall Brazilian banker." She lowered her voice. "Just hold on, Enrico. My partner is a pest. I'll get rid of him."

Frank grinned. "It seems awfully quiet for a night-club. I think you're sprawled on your couch watching Dirty Dancing."

"Hey, watch that kind of talk, Mister. I'm a *cop!* If I'm home with a Patrick Swayze movie, it'll be *Roadhouse.*"

"Okay, I stand corrected."

"Actually, I just got in. Early night."

"Good. I'm on my way. Pick you up in two."

"Do I have time to change?"

"No."

"What's up?"

Frank exhaled. "Nothing good."

Amy had been planning to slip into her comfies and watch *Weekend at Bernie's*, although she'd never admit that to Frank. After a pleasant dinner date earlier, they'd gone to a piano bar before the orthopedic surgeon got an emergency call to consult after a serious two-vehicle traffic accident. Single, late-thirties, drove a Mercedes E-class—a little intimidated by her profession—which was standard for most of her dates. *Would it have ended with something hot and steamy?* Maybe, she hadn't decided. If he called again, she'd give him another chance.

So here she was, still in her cocktail dress, yet considering a movie that came out while she was in grade school—funny, though it was. She glanced at the clock—11:50—much too late for anything routine. This couldn't be good. Two minutes and twenty seconds later, Frank pulled his charcoal Chrysler into the complex on Ridge Avenue. The main buildings were restructured from an old stone manufacturing plant with several newer additions designed to match. She got in the passenger side and Frank started to laugh as he pulled away.

"What?"

"That getup." He looked her up and down. "It's shorter and tighter than anything I ever see you in. Makeup and heels, too." He gave her a broad grin. "So, what did I interrupt?"

Amy just glared at him. "Nothing! I literally just came in the door when you called."

"Ah. He hadn't put the moves on you yet?"

"That's not it."

"Perfume, too. Is that Burberry Weekend I detect?"

"Christ! How can you know *that*?"

"I know women's scents."

"I'll just bet you do. For your information, I was on a date tonight. Seriously. He was called away on an emergency and dropped me off. I just didn't change yet."

"You look great, I have to admit. I understand completely now. This Mexican baker you were out with had a taco crisis."

Amy continued to stare, then said, "Fuck you, Frank." He finished laughing and drove in silence for a minute. She added, "Besides, it wasn't a baker; he's a Brazilian *banker*. Tall, handsome, and *very* wealthy." Then they both laughed.

"Just trying to lighten the mood," Frank said. "We're going to check out a body in Bustleton."

"New case?"

"Not ours. Schoen and Cunningham. I'm taking a peek and thought you'd want to come along. The vic is a young woman, probably Latino, at Birch Tree Apartments."

Amy was stunned. "Oh shit! Not *Vonda Cantu?*"

"That's the word. Don't know for sure. No ID on her. Ever hear of a guy named Kurt Waldo?"

"Don't think so."

"I just had him checked out. Works for Pierce Brothers. Ex-Delta Force and does security these days. Big guy. Tough. I'm sure he eats thumb tacks for breakfast."

"Is he our suspect?"

"Could be. Someone heard Zachary Chastang talking to a senior executive at Pierce Brothers recently. Zachary was worried. The gist of it: Marcus Jarrett wanted Chastang to confess to raping Dixie at the party. It doesn't make sense, but I can see how it would be a shitstorm for the company. This Kurt Waldo may have been told to clean up the mess."

"How'd you get on to this Waldo guy?"

"Tip."

Amy laughed without humor. "Tip? That's the best you can do?"

"I have it in my notes as an anonymous tip. Cruz told me. He heard someone talking."

"Oh, I see. Like at a dinner party, I guess. He just overheard this revelation."

"Right."

Amy turned in the seat. "That's bullshit, Frank. Is he bugging someone illegally?"

"I don't know that for a fact."

"Then he is, dammit." Amy took a breath. Frank had a penchant for cutting corners like this. She was aware he had some kind of arrangement with Cruz. Frank was like a sponge when it came to street-talk and seemed to have a network of people throwing scraps his way. A lecture on the 4th Amendment would be pointless since Frank's methods rarely came back to bite him. Clearly, he was smart enough not to let anything end up in court that couldn't be substantiated. She decided to let it drop, for now. "Never mind. Assuming it's true, that would make Waldo a viable suspect in Jarrett's murder. Marcus started leaning on Zachary Chastang to admit to a felony. Waldo eliminates Marcus, a big favor to the Chastang family."

"True. But it doesn't follow. Our theory all along has been that Marcus was supplying the drugs."

"Ah, maybe not."

Frank turned to give her a quick look. "What's that supposed to mean?"

"Just this. I called Detective Amos earlier today to clarify a few things. Chastang was under surveillance for a few days prior to the bust. Remember I told you that Thursday morning Chastang visited a suspected dealer?"

"Yeah."

"That's why they set the whole thing up with me right away—their profiler said a guy like Zachary with his MO would be anxious to find a victim. They were right. Then they went in and busted the dealer yesterday. His stash matches what Zachary used exactly."

Frank thought it over for a few seconds. "All right. From the fingerprints we know he had beers with

Marcus Jarrett recently. It seems an odd coincidence that Marcus has a load of date-rape drugs, but Zachary bought his someplace else. Why is that?"

"Good question. Guilty conscience? His spare time, at least for the last five months, was all spent with Vonda Cantu. He lived in the Jarrett mansion all his life but only moved out in April, possibly to be with Vonda. Before that, he could have purchased his own home at any time and never did."

"I suppose you're factoring in Vonda's *feelings.*"

"To a point. She *adored* the guy. What's the big rule you always tell me?"

"Never trust a man who hates football."

Amy shook her head. "Not *that* rule. The love, hate, and money thing. Your all-time big motivators. Didn't need money. Didn't hate anybody. The man fell in love."

"Okay. I think I get your drift. Maybe he was … *stuck.* Like he reformed or something."

"Exactly." Amy nodded. "Maybe he stopped or at least refused to continue supplying. Doesn't excuse his previous actions, but we need to consider the possibility if it factors into both cases. And going back to when I arrested Chastang: Sergeant Amos mentioned a GPS tracker was found on the Austin-Healey Zachary rented for the night. Seems he never took his own car on his little adventures. Hidden below. Like someone was keeping tabs on the car."

"Could be our killer. They have any idea who put it there?"

"No. Top of the line, a commercially available unit. And admittedly, it might not mean anything. Also, Vonda's diary has an interesting tidbit. She mentions that Bradley Jarrett had amended his will so that Marcus would control the company in the event of his death. Sylvia Jarrett supposedly tampered with that somehow."

"Mmm." Frank grunted. "Worth considering. Although that could be just what Marcus told Vonda."

"Sure. But apparently, Marcus was compiling data. I don't think we've come across anything like that."

"Now that the possibility has come up, maybe we look closer for it—just in case."

"Okay. Some things to think about."

Frank shrugged. "This brings to mind an old joke. It goes like this: How do you sculpt an elephant? You get a big block of marble and chip away everything that doesn't look like an elephant."

Amy was staring at him, then grinned. "Okay . . ."

"Maybe not that funny. Basically, it's saying there's an elephant in there someplace. You have to get rid of all the extra marble to find it."

"So, what, then?"

"It means we need to find out if Marcus Jarrett and Chastang's connection is part of the elephant—or part of the *extra.*"

The Klieg lights were visible between the second and third buildings. Frank pulled alongside a patrol unit and flashed his badge to a uniformed officer who was sipping coffee. "I'm going to leave our car here." The man nodded and both detectives hopped out and headed towards the activity.

A perimeter had been set up with yellow crime scene tape that stretched from the building on the right to nearby trees that blocked roughly a sixty by ninety-foot section of lawn. Patrol officers kept the area secure. Onlookers were watching from porches and windows; the obligatory crowd of residents hovered around, whispering and sharing their curiosity and distress. Every one of them would be discreetly photographed in the hope that the perpetrator stuck around for the show.

The victim was close to an apartment rear entrance. A police photographer was snapping pictures of the surroundings and the accompanying flashes lit the building like tiny bolts of lightning. Amy showed her ID to an officer and Frank graciously lifted the tape for her. Once inside they watched their footing and were approached by Jerry Cunningham, a plainclothes detective on another squad. Amy didn't know him well, other than from typical wisecracks and general razzing. He was bald, short and stocky, in his early fifties, and had just gone through his third divorce. She'd heard he had two children with each of the first two wives.

"Jerry," Frank said.

A big grin formed on the detective's face. "Well, well. You two out on the town?"

"No," Amy said more forcefully than she intended. "I got home right before Frank called."

"Sure, sure. Hey, you should dress like that all the time, Lepone. It'd distract the criminals."

Jerry was laughing at his own joke as Derek Schoen walked up to join them. He was a lean six-footer in his late thirties with a military buzz. Derek checked Amy top to bottom—the elevator look—and said, "All right. Homicide's power couple has arrived. Sorry you had to leave the prom early. Love the dress."

"Listen," Amy said. "I just got home from a date when Frank called."

Derek shook his head. "No explanation needed. What you two do off the clock is nobody's business. Besides, I heard about the ruckus the other night. You two pummeled a burglar."

"No. Just me. Frank wasn't home. I was letting out the dog."

"You two got a dog?"

"Dammit, no," Amy said, then paused for a deep breath. The razzing never ended with these two. "It's Frank's dog. Frank was away. And tonight, I was out with someone earlier, someone else. Frank came and picked me up."

"Yeah," Frank said. "It's true. She's dating a Portuguese boxer. Nice guy."

"Uh-huh." Jerry looked quizzical. "Sure, she is. Anyway, I heard you might want a look. Our vic was stabbed … maybe. Large round puncture between the ribs, but ME says not a GSW. There's no ID on her but we think the name is Vonda Cantu. She was going in her back door no more than two hours ago. The manager knows her and lives on site. He's on his way here now."

"The work of a professional?"

"Hell, yeah." Derek nodded towards the body. "If this was the guy's first kill, I'll resign. That's her apartment, B-109. Dispatch says you talked to her yesterday afternoon?"

Frank nodded. "Yes. But at another resident's place in the next building over."

Jerry led them forward and pointed to the left of the porch. "She was behind the bushes right there. A couple walked by and noticed her feet sticking out. One lives in B building, the other in C. They often cut through the back to each other's place. They didn't touch her and called it in right away. Good thing. Otherwise, she might have been there til morning."

"Just a head's up," Frank said. "You do know Marcus Jarrett is our case, right? This woman dated him."

"Yeah. We'll compare notes. I'll talk to Lieutenant Trainer, see how he wants to play it. If you take point, whatever."

Amy took it all in. Two steps led up to the tiny porch with a sliding glass door; a single key stuck out of the lock. To the left was a row of neat hedges. Although the body was now being prepared for transport, she could reconstruct the scene. Vonda must have come home and started to unlock the door while her assailant came up behind her. He would have clamped his hand around her mouth, made the kill, dragged her backwards a few feet, and let her limp body fall off to the left. Conveniently hidden from view and could have easily gone unnoticed until daylight. Sometimes this job really sucked—Vonda seemed like a real nice person. Her friend was raped last month. Then her lover was shot to death. And now Vonda stabbed to death. Remaining detached and impersonal was part of all investigations, a necessary component for detectives. But it didn't come easy and she hoped it never did. It took an effort to hold back sobs—they would have to come later.

Amy took a deep breath and did a slow turn to study the layout. B and C buildings faced away from each other and shared a common backyard. *Why would Vonda be coming in her back door?* Neighbors visited each other this way—otherwise there'd be little foot traffic, particularly late. The perp would have made sure it was clear and moved quickly. The assault was far enough from the opposite building, especially in the dark. Unless someone was at a window or on their porch and looking this way … "Just the one key in the door?" she asked.

"Yeah, Jerry said. "She had a small key ring in her pocket."

Amy thought that over and said, "Odd."

"Yeah. Two on the ring that look like house keys, one that looks like maybe a desk key, and one modern car key. There's a 2019 Mazda CX-9 registered to Vonda Cantu. The lot for this building is around in front but it's not there from what we can tell."

"So where was she coming from?" Frank asked, rhetorically. "Did you check for her car in the A and C building lots?"

Jerry frowned. "No. Should we?"

"Worth a shot. Anything else?"

Jerry lowered his voice. "This is not for the press. We found five grand in hundreds. Bureau drawer, one stack, wrapped with rubber bands."

Frank shrugged. "Suspicious. Although, she was an accountant. Made decent money, I think."

Derek blocked the view of prying eyes by turning his back to the crowd and reached in his pocket. He slid out an evidence bag, then withdrew a clear plastic bag that contained large caliber rifle cartridges. In a quiet voice, he said, "These were next to the money. Normally not used for *accounting*. Six .32 Winchester Specials and one empty shell casing. No prints on them and no idea what it all means right now."

"Can't even hazard a guess on that one," Frank said. "Mind if we have a look?"

Derek shrugged. "Be my guest."

Two orderlies were fitting the corpse into a black bag and stepped aside. Amy looked over at the body, shot a quick glance at Frank, and then focused again on the dead woman. Frank reached down and pulled away the plastic to afford a better view. Amy stared at the woman's pretty face and thick beautiful hair. Full lips that would never speak or smile again. So very sad. Although, one thing was certain . . .

She said, "It's *not* Vonda Cantu."

Jerry was surprised. "It's *not?*"

"No chance."

Derek grunted. "Are you fucking with us? She was going in Cantu's apartment."

"This woman has a similar look," Frank said. "But we're serious—*not* the woman we met. We'll be back. I want to check Dixie's place."

"Dixie?"

The detectives left their puzzled colleagues and ducked under the tape. They wedged through the crowd of people milling around and then started across the grounds.

Amy said, "I couldn't believe it wasn't Vonda when I looked down."

"Me, either. We've got a Jane Doe who was letting herself in Vonda's apartment with a key. And inside there's cash and rifle cartridges."

"Not sure what this all might mean. But I have a hunch that victim lives on the premises."

"I'll buy that. Back door. If she came in a car, she'd use the front."

"Yeah." They walked in silence for a moment and Amy added, "Everybody thinks were living together now."

"Don't worry about those meatheads."

"It's not worry. Not exactly. It's an image thing. You know, it's just—"

"Tougher for a woman." Frank shrugged. "I know. But you're solid. You do the job and that's what counts. Besides, those two are like a Roundhouse scandal sheet. Jerry's first wife dumped him for sleeping with her cousin. His second wife left him for a scooter salesman. Derek Schoen gambled away an inheritance right after he turned twenty-one. He's in love with a zoology professor from Nova Scotia—sees her like three times a year. Lives with his mother, his girl-friend's pet snake and six cats."

Amy smirked. "I feel guilty saying this, but that actually makes me feel a little better. It's just that the lieutenant might hear this chatter and think I stay at your house sometimes. I know he's not going to fire me or anything. But like you said—*image*. I don't think you're taking it seriously."

"Of course, I am. That would be shocking behavior. A rumor like that could make people think less of me."

Amy scoffed. "Yeah, right. Nothing short of an orgy in Fairmount Park on family day would hurt *your* reputation."

They walked up to apartment A114 and looked around. No one nearby and no noise from inside. "This is the one, right?" Amy nodded. Frank stood off to the left and knocked once with no result and then a second time, a little harder. "What do you think?"

Amy crouched down, leaned left, and put her ear to the door—not easy in the tight dress. Like Frank, she was always mindful of hidden threats. If bullets were fired from inside, they usually came through a door in the center around four feet high. "No TV. I don't hear the shower or a blow dryer. Seems vacant." She stood up and looked over the lot. "Vonda mentioned she's been staying here with Dixie a lot since the rape. A CX-9 is a sporty-looking SUV. Don't see one anywhere close by."

Frank glanced around and slid a small case from his pants pocket. "Keep watch." He withdrew two picking tools and bent down, starting to manipulate the lock.

"You just love an excuse to use those things, don't you? I'm surprised you didn't become a cat burglar."

"Don't sweat it. If there's evidence inside or more dead bodies, we'll just say it was unlocked and we feared for Dixie's safety."

"Uh-huh. You say that like a joke. But I think you'd do it."

Frank looked up at her and winked. The lock gave up and he twisted the knob. Instinctively, both detectives kept their hands near their weapons as they stepped inside. Amy noted the living room was much the same as on Thursday, with no apparent disarray. No unusual smells. They split up, made a practiced search of the premises and met back in the living room moments later.

"All clear," Amy said.

"Same. No sign of trouble." Frank pulled out his cell phone and called in, asking for DMV information on Dixie Newberry and Vonda Cantu. He waited until the police operator came back on. Shutting it off, he said, "Just the Mazda for Vonda. A 2016 Honda Civic for Dixie."

"There's a blue Civic out front."

Frank walked outside, checked the tag and came back in. "That's it."

"Dixie's car is here, Vonda's is gone. Chances are—they're together."

Frank locked up. On the way back to the crime scene, they tossed out theories, both agreeing that Vonda and Dixie were basically law-abiding citizens. Yet, like all cops, Amy knew average people gave in to temptation or were coaxed into criminal activities every day. Nothing made sense yet. She had a hunch that it all started with the assault on Dixie just over one month ago. Zachary Chastang's arrest and then death, Marcus Jarrett's death, and now a Jane Doe. Gut instinct told her Dixie wasn't doing anything but healing. Vonda and now their Jane Doe were pivotal elements. She also had a feeling there was more than one bad guy in the mix. It wasn't a single conspiracy and nothing so simple as revenge. However, there was a link—down deep, she knew it.

Some of the crowd had dispersed by the time Frank and Amy got back to the crime scene. Jerry came over to them immediately.

"You were right," he said. "The manager IDed her. Name's Dolores Griego, lived here almost three years. Good tenant, so he says. Her place is right there— C-106." Jerry pointed directly across the lawn and slightly to the left. A uniformed officer stood on her back porch. "Derek just started going over it; I'm headed in there now."

"Were Dolores and Vonda friends?"

"The manager doesn't know, but says *probably*. Vonda Cantu has been right across from her for a year and a half so it's likely they at least knew each other."

Frank nodded. "Let me know if there's anything of interest in the Griego place. My hunch says no. We'll put out an Attempt-To-Locate for both Vonda Cantu and Dixie Newberry." He turned to Amy. "Got any other ideas?"

"I'm lost."

Frank sighed. "Yeah. Me too."

Cruz was about to give up and call it a day. Actually, a long day since it was almost midnight. Once again in the Astro van, he'd been listening in on the Kyser home, wondering what was going through Gilbert's head. They'd had a late dinner of salad, baked salmon, and asparagus tips. Gilbert seemed to respect his wife's wishes when it came to home-cooked meals, but there wasn't much doubt he'd rather be feasting on steak, lasagna, fried chicken, or any of the other dishes that she adamantly refused to serve. Still—he was never going to lose weight. Despite her good intentions and solid efforts, Joyce couldn't win that battle since Gilbert ate enough to choke a whale whenever he left the house.

One thing for sure, Gilbert was distracted tonight. Whenever Joyce made a comment or asked a question, she'd needed to repeat herself nearly every time. To a bachelor, it seemed odd that a wife who looked like her would have difficulty claiming attention from any man under eighty. Yet Gilbert said little and hadn't initiated any conversations. Joyce went to bed alone nearly an hour ago with Gilbert declining due to important paperwork. He'd been in the living room ever since, now eating something that sounded a lot like pretzels and watching Fast Times At Ridgemont High.

Cruz heard a faint jingle that he knew was Gilbert's cell phone set on very low volume. The television muted and Gilbert answered in a whisper.

"Yeah … Any problems? … You will … Sounds good. Text me a time and place. Yeah."

Cruz listened carefully and heard what he thought was one of those big exhales that signify everything will now be all right. The television stayed silent and was replaced by routine sounds of cleaning up: walking, plates clinking, refrigerator door, water running. Moments later, all became quiet, at least in the kitchen, living room, and den. Since he hadn't placed a bug anywhere else, Cruz could only guess that Gilbert was in the bathroom or had more likely turned in for the night.

Well, it didn't take any brilliant deductive reasoning to figure this one out: Expecting that phone call—surely the reason Kyser stayed up late and his earlier distractions. It didn't sound like any top-level venture landing the company a fat new contract. That call was *personal*. Not a friend, not even an acquaintance. Just business. Private business. He could only imagine what was said on the other end but at least he knew it held some importance. Kyser was probably meeting the caller and definitely soon. *What was this dickhead up to?* As Cruz started the van and headed home, he had the sneaking suspicion that the call came from Corky Buck, the all-purpose hoodlum. One thing was certain: Cruz would be keeping tabs on Kyser as much as possible tomorrow and every day forward until he found out for sure.

CHAPTER 13

"Just tell me one thing, Frank." Lieutenant Trainer said. "Are the Marcus Jarrett and Zachary Chastang killings linked?"

Amy remained silent. It was protocol; he was the senior detective. This was touchy since the Jarrett and Chastang families were both formidable and respected with business interests and influence throughout the Delaware Valley. If the murders were connected, and especially if further danger could be anticipated, a task force would be set up and additional manpower assigned. If the cases were isolated and could be resolved quickly—by far, the preferred scenario— Lieutenant Trainer and his superiors would be very pleased. No one wanted a huge mobilization where none was needed. Neither would the department want to appear slow to respond if definitive action was indicated. She was learning to accept that such administrative maneuvering was simply the way the wheels turned. Sadly, huge cases became a cat and mouse game that defined careers and dictated promotions. News feeds, bloggers, and television would grab on, create heroes and villains, spinning the story for their own agendas. As always, the more controversial the news, the greater the lingering interest.

"Somehow," Frank finally said. "I was with Danby for part of the autopsy. No surprises. We've got the prelim now. Blood pooling shows he was killed right there, never moved. No defensive wounds, nothing. TOD roughly ten o'clock Thursday evening."

Lieutenant Norman Trainer was a tall, lean man with chocolate brown skin, short gray hair, and a tough-but-fair reputation. Amy was intrigued by how he commanded respect simply by walking into a room. Contrary to the stats of most officers, he had a successful marriage, four children, and nine grandchildren. They were rarely in his office at the Roundhouse on a Sunday morning, but all duty officers were expected to apply their efforts as needed, particularly on tougher cases.

Amy looked at Frank as he formulated an answer. She knew the truth—that in all likelihood, the murders were committed by different UNSUBS, but with common elements to both. Frank thought Vonda killed Chastang, but Amy wasn't sure she agreed. They both knew she hadn't killed Marcus. Although Lieutenant Trainer respected the hunches or his detectives, right now he would want to hear about facts, hard evidence, and solid suspects. A top investigator with good instincts, he had climbed the ladder of success in the police department by not bending rules or taking chances on suppositions. He had the look, the background, and the charisma that impressed the brass and was favored in the press. Frank, on the other hand, had no political aspirations, prevailing with guile and creative methods, although his official reprimands were surprisingly minimal. He had a love of the job and his own code of conduct that didn't always conform to established guidelines. She believed he had integrity, though occasionally stepping over the edge. When that time came, the important thing was knowing where to plant his feet. Overall, Frank would have a higher clearance rate—slightly—than someone like Trainer, but would trade favors and lean hard on informants in the process. There'd be more firefights, car wrecks, controversies, and disputes, as well. Amy respected his abilities while sometimes resisting his methods.

Trainer stretched his arms and placed his hands flat on the desk. "And no clues, as well. I realize that Zachary Chastang is not your case. And yes, Sylvia Jarrett's press release was reasonably fair to the department. However, Cameron Chastang is another story. His son was arrested, released, and then gunned down fifty feet from his own door step in a normally safe neighborhood. *His* press conference was less than kind. I meet with the Mayor, the Police Commissioner, the Deputy Commissioner of Operations, and the District Attorney tomorrow morning. If this is all part of a single plot, I need to know now. What exactly do you have?"

"I won't bullshit you, Lieutenant. It's not much so far because there's a lot going on. I don't think Chastang and Jarrett are part of one big scheme. First, Marcus Jarrett didn't supply the drug that Chastang used Thursday night."

Trainer nodded. "He bought from a dealer; I read that in the report. And Detective Lepone, your work on that operation was exceptional, from what I've heard. Congratulations." Amy nodded a thanks and Trainer turned immediately back to Frank. "Go on."

"About a month ago, on Marcus Jarrett's birthday, he had a bash at the family mansion. A woman named Dixie Newberry was drugged and raped, we're pretty sure by Zachary Chastang. The timetable is questionable because Dixie doesn't remember much. Marcus Jarrett left at some point with Dixie's close friend, Vonda Cantu. He may have helped Chastang with the rape and left with Vonda to keep her from finding Dixie unconscious—we can't be sure. No evidence because the damned maids came along first thing and did everything but sandblast the place. Last night, Dolores Griego was murdered on her way into Vonda Cantu's apartment. Incidentally, Vonda and Dixie have vanished. No one knows where they are."

"Where are you going with this, Frank?"

"There's just too damn much happening for there not to be a connection. You know what Jerry found in Vonda's apartment, right?"

"Of course. Cash. Plus, five cartridges and one expended shell—all .32 Winchester Special."

Frank nodded. "Sound familiar?"

"The caliber used on Zachary Chastang."

"Yes. A powerful and *unusual* caliber, too. No ballistics since we don't have a weapon but will likely be an older Winchester hunting rifle. They're comparing the slug with those cartridges, definitely the same brand and composition. One thing we just found out—Vonda Cantu's father served four years in the army. Corporal Hector Cantu, honorable discharge. Good Conduct ribbon and Sharpshooter Badge. Also, he was a deputy sheriff in Crockett County, Texas. Died of cancer a few years back."

"Damn, Frank. You're suggesting he taught his daughter to shoot?"

"Verified. Parents divorced in 2007, but stayed in touch. Mother is local. According to her, Vonda's father took her hunting, fishing, and camping. Got her first deer at sixteen. She came with mom in 2012 to live in Philly and attend Drexel University. After that, Vonda settled down here."

"Looks like revenge! Jesus, what a story." Trainer sat quietly for a moment. "This Cantu woman and the rape victim are good friends. If she thought Zachary and Marcus Jarrett were in collusion, she may have killed them both."

"No, sir," Amy said. "Not Marcus. Thursday night, Vonda's alibi is Dixie Newberry. Dixie talked to her mother on the house phone starting at 10:01 PM. Vonda was there and also spoke to the mother. I checked phone records. Verified and the call lasted for twenty-eight minutes."

"That's a tenuous alibi, considering Dixie would be the one avenged by our killer's actions. What about Zachary?"

"It's possible, but the window is tight. Vonda is an accountant for Jarrett Enterprises and had typical business appointments all day. Between sites when Chastang was shot. His house is in East Falls. Vonda met with clients in Rising Sun Plaza to present a prospectus shortly after the time of death. Allowing for daytime traffic, she could have had time—barely."

"You like her for it?"

"I'd like to keep digging."

Turning to Frank, he said, "How about you?"

"Good motive and the pieces fit. I'd like to check the layout, make a tactical study."

"All right, get to it. Did you see the newspaper this morning?"

Frank nodded. "Yeah. It reads like Vonda Cantu was killed going into her own place—which is how it looked. Jerry didn't release any victim's name so it's not his fault. He told the manager not to say anything but there must have been twenty residents standing around who would know it's Vonda's apartment."

"Just find her fast. We need Vonda Cantu alive and in custody ten minutes ago."

"Her car hasn't turned up. Her cell phone is off or out of range. Same with Dixie's."

"Keep on it. Who's this Griego woman? And why was she killed?"

"Just a neighbor. We have no idea—yet."

"Are there risk factors?"

"None that we can find. Clean, no criminal record."

"Maybe she's the shooter."

Frank shook his head. "Jerry already ruled her out for Zachary. And we checked the TOD for Jarrett. She was at work both times, part owner of a donut shop."

Trainer let out a low grumble. "This sounds like a big pile of nothing, considering we have three dead citizens. You've eliminated suspects but not found others."

"Give us time," Frank said. "There's a trail somewhere leading back to Marcus Jarrett's party. We'll find it."

Narrowing his gaze, Trainer looked him in the eye. "You know a few things you're not telling me. Right?"

Frank didn't flinch. "Yes, I do."

Trainer grunted. "Just hurry up and connect the damn dots."

Cruz was lost in thought as he drove along on the way to the Kyser residence. It was time to give Joyce an update but he didn't know exactly what or how much to tell her. He'd originally hoped to finish up with Gilbert Kyser and start concentrating on the Marcus Jarrett murder, but that just wasn't possible yet. Gilbert's behavior was just too secretive and erratic for him not to be up to something. Joyce thought Gilbert had been cheating on her. But so far, boffing some leggy secretary was about the only thing Cruz was sure her husband *wasn't* doing.

At least there'd been progress of sorts on Jarrett. First, he'd been able to get a profile of Kurt Waldo. The big man looked like a strong possibility. He was ex-military with combat training and had been making a comfortable living in the private sector since 2014. Employed in recent years by Pierce Brothers, he was apparently Cameron Chastang's top dog and all-around security wiz. One arrest in 2015 for aggravated assault, charges dropped. Cruz suspected that Waldo had leaned a little too hard on someone who caused a beef and a quiet payoff made the problem go away.

Mindy O. Lyons, age 30, the woman who'd met with Gilbert in his den, had checked out as expected. The O stood for O'Brien, her mother's maiden name—cute. Top college, excellent grades—smart, skilled, and headed up Public Relations for the company. Damn nice looking, too. She'd sounded sincere in her concerns. Zachary had complained about problems with Marcus Jarrett to a top VP, asking that Kurt Waldo handle the problem—then Marcus ends up dead. In anyone's book, that indicated Waldo as a plausible suspect. Although a third-hand conversation from illegal eavesdropping wasn't any kind of usable evidence, at least now Frank and Amy had a head's up. They could take a close look and see what shakes loose.

Right now, Gilbert's actions were what gave him immediate concern. Joyce had called early and whispered that Gilbert was up at 7 A.M.—unusual for a Sunday—and then locked himself in his den for a few minutes. He'd then gotten quickly dressed and said he was going out for a while to a business meeting. Joyce had been more nervous than mad, apparently sensing that her husband was involved in something risky. Cruz had leaped up and used his GPS tracker to catch up with Gilbert just as he arrived at a Starbuck's at Broadway and Arch. As before, Gilbert had carried a small disposable plastic bag with something small inside, possibly an envelope. He had gone directly to a booth and met once again with the unmistakable Corky Buck. Cruz hadn't even bothered going inside since he could see them clearly through the window. Their conversation took just over six minutes and Gilbert left without the bag, heading for home. Buck waited about five minutes and left cautiously, climbing into a beat-up beige Buick Skylark—with the bag.

That was nearly four hours ago. It was now almost noon and Joyce was expecting an explanation that hadn't gelled yet. Gilbert had come home, claimed his morning had consisted only of a client meeting, and then left a little while ago with friends who had great Phillies tickets. In this case, Gilbert was telling the truth. He met up with two friends, dressed in lots of red and white, and headed to Citizen's Bank Park.

So, what the hell was going on? He knew for certain that Gilbert met with Buck twice in three days for some kind of delivery. Logic said it had to be money. *But for what?* A guy like Gilbert Kyser, in his capacity with a big, profitable company, had all sorts of underlings for errands, chores, and research. Any college kid on an internship would be thrilled to assist an executive, even for unofficial assignments not in the usual job description. Since Gilbert would have gone out of his way to find Buck, there had to be a strong reason. Something that required illicit skills, secret meetings and quick payoffs. Something that he didn't want anyone to know about.

What should he tell Joyce?

Ten minutes later he pulled up to the Kyser's splendid townhouse with only a vague idea of what to say. First of all, there really wasn't proof that Gilbert had done anything illegal and he sure as hell hadn't been screwing any strange women. Second, Cruz knew he couldn't make a comment or ask questions based on any discussions he'd overheard from within their home. He hadn't told Joyce about his access to high-tech equipment and never even hinted that he might plant bugs. It was better if she didn't know because then she wouldn't adjust her own conversations or chose subject matter based on someone listening in. Her apprehension would affect Gilbert and it was better to have husband *and* wife talking naturally.

Joyce opened the door just before he rang the bell and his breath caught in his throat. She was barefoot and wearing tight pink gym shorts. Covering her tor-so—barely—was a frilly tank top of somewhat diaphanous fabric with spaghetti straps. About six inches of trim waist was exposed below the lacey bottom edge. Cruz thought it actually might be a nightie but then casual fashions these days were often quite risqué.

"Hi, Mr. Cruz," she said brightly and gave him a hundred-watt smile. Running her hand up and down his arm, she added, "I'm so glad you came by. Gilbert will be gone all afternoon and they'll all probably stop for dinner after the game. C'mon in."

Cruz stepped through the foyer and went inside thinking that her greeting could easily be misinterpreted. *Was that a whiff of some expensive perfume?* Following a few paces behind, he couldn't help running his gaze over the sleek form that was short and slender, but by no means, scrawny. The wavy blonde hair, natural, he thought, complimented her sensuous stride as it shifted across her shoulders and back. *Wow!*

Joyce led him into the plush living room and stopped in front of a beige leather sectional sofa that Cruz knew would retail at around eight grand. The walls were dark, kind of mahogany, which gave the room a subdued but warm ambiance. The coffee table was big and unusual. The surface, padded in a dark material, held a vase of fresh cut flowers, a couple of remote controls, and a laptop computer. A handy and expensive all-purpose surface—you could put up your feet or spill a beer with no worries.

"Would you like anything?"

The way she said it made Cruz a little uneasy. "Whatever you're having."

She winked. "Give me a few minutes."

He watched her leave and berated himself for it. Lusting after a client was never a good idea. Checking out her laptop, he noticed she was on the Philadelphia Daily News website. For many people, it was the 21st century equivalent of reading an actual newspaper. The headline on the familiar opening page read: WILL PHILLIES SWEEP THE MARLINS? Below that, the big story was more from the White House on healthcare reform. The Top Local Stories section: DELCO ADMINISTRATOR ACCUSED OF TAKING $1 MILLION FROM ORPHANAGE, PHONY DOCTOR GETS NINE YEAR SENTENCE, and BUSTLETON WOMAN KILLED OUTSIDE HER APARTMENT. He clicked on each and quickly scanned the articles. The third was about an accountant, Vonda Cantu, age 27, who had been stabbed to death outside her residence at Birch Tree Apartments. Cruz knew the area but the name or the complex didn't ring any bells. Interestingly, she was employed by Jarrett Enterprises. He scrolled down to the photo and froze. There was no doubt in his mind—it was the woman from the gazebo. This pretty lady had met Gilbert Kyser secretly for a midnight rendezvous less than a week ago and was now dead.

"Everything all right?"

Cruz jumped a little in surprise as Joyce handed him a fancy glass. "Oh, just lots of bad news on this thing. What do we have here?"

Joyce grinned. "I made us Apple-tinis."

Cruz took a sip and savored the flavor. He knew a call to Frank was mandatory about the dead girl at Birch Tree Apartments. The fact that she met with Gilbert Kyser could be crucial to the current case. No one else knew that.

Joyce filled her own glass from a small pitcher. "Are you all right?" she asked.

"Fine. Just checking my, um, service." Okay, so he didn't have a service. He had a no-frills agency and handled all his own business from voicemails—but she didn't need to know that. "I've got a few things to report."

"Good! I'd really like to talk about all this. I'm so stressed out." She sat down the pitcher, slid onto the sofa and crossed her legs, tucking one under the other. Patting the spot next to her, she added, "Please have a seat."

Well, he figured the call to Frank could wait a few minutes. "Okay, sure. That'll be fine." Maintaining a respectable distance, Cruz eased down and savored the feel of elegant furniture. Getting on to business, he slid one of the telephoto shots of Gilbert and Buck from an envelope and held it up for her inspection. "Recognize the guy with your husband?"

Joyce studied it for only a moment and frowned. "No. Who is he?"

"To be honest—he's a local scumbag. This is from Friday afternoon when Gilbert met up with him on South Street. They went in a place for a few minutes and Gilbert gave him a plastic bag, like a small grocery bag. I don't know for sure what was in it. He met the same guy this morning—that's where he was going when you called me. They met up at a coffee shop, talked for a few minutes. Gilbert walked in with another plastic bag and this guy left with it." Joyce looked puzzled and he added, "I've got the feeling it was money."

"What are you saying, Mr. Cruz? That he's paying this man for something?"

"Yes, I think so. Drugs are a possibility."

"No." Joyce shook her head. Gilbert is totally against drugs. Although, he drinks too much. Go figure."

"Okay. It's a complicated business world out there. It could be industrial espionage of some kind. Or he may have hired this guy to cause problems for the competition. I really don't know yet."

Joyce huffed. "I really wouldn't know if he's been overspending or making big withdrawals. Gilbert handles all our finances and he wants it that way. You see, I have an Associate's Degree in secretarial services. When we met, I was working for a company in Upper Darby. That was 2010 and I was making about twenty-two thousand a year. Not much, I know, and nothing like the kind of money Gilbert earns. I really liked working and continued my job after we got married in 2012. I kept it up for the next few years but Gilbert acted like it was ... I don't know, a hobby or something. Like it was a waste of time to go to work every day for such a small paycheck. If I had to work late or go in for inventory on a Saturday, he'd get upset." She paused and let out a long breath. "Two years ago—I finally just quit. It was okay at first, then things changed. Or more like the way I saw things. That was back when I thought that Gilbert was ... Well, when he . . ."

Cruz studied his client's pained expression as she seemed to search within for the right words. She needed to get an issue out in the open but he couldn't imagine exactly what it was. There'd been something bothering her, something she hadn't said out loud since the first day they'd met almost a month ago. At first, he'd thought it was all part of the reason he was hired—a woman who simply thought her husband was screwing around. Now he felt it was more than that. He really wanted to know the truth and was telling himself that it was all part of his duties—that Gilbert's actions and Joyce's feelings were integral to resolving the case, especially if Gilbert had crossed a line. Maybe he had problems that hadn't revealed themselves yet, owed money to the wrong people, or was planning to have someone killed. Just an association with a thug like Buck was suspicious. Joyce could be in legitimate danger or, at the very least, be greatly affected by her husband's transgressions. She deserved to know in advance. In truth, none of that mattered right now. The woman outright intrigued him. Not just her looks, but the entire package. She was beautiful and a little insecure. She was smart, bored, and felt unaccomplished. She wanted to be independent and had trouble accepting the vulnerability of it. Regardless of his responsibilities, one thing was certain: He would be sitting right here on this couch, hanging on her every word, even if she was giving a step-by-step explanation of how to fold laundry.

"What?" Cruz said. "Tell me. I want to hear it." He hoped that didn't come out sappy.

"Well . . ." Joyce was apparently wrestling with the idea of baring her soul. "I guess back then I didn't notice how preoccupied Gilbert always is. When I worked, I had a schedule, more friends, and more responsibility. I was busy every day and I'd come home tired. Like other couples, we didn't really spend a whole lot of time together. At least then I didn't seem like a pet, like his goldfish or something. I still hardly see him, but … I guess I don't feel like I'm getting anywhere. When I told that to Gilbert a while back, he just said, 'Where do you want to go?' Like I expect a trip to Paris or something. I mean, is he dense? He just doesn't understand."

"I get it." Cruz nodded. "You're not the type to sit around the house eating bon-bons and watching soap operas."

Joyce brightened. "Yes! That's it. You and I really relate." She looked down and then back up slowly. "You know, Gilbert and I hardly ever have sex anymore."

Cruz was a little stunned, then said, "That's hard to believe."

She laughed. "Is that a compliment?"

"Sure is."

Joyce stared at him for a moment and said, "Three times."

"Excuse me?"

"Three times. That's the sum total we've done it this year so far. I mean, sure, we're getting older. I'm thirty-six; Gilbert is forty-two. That still doesn't seem like very much sex."

Cruz cleared his throat, both stimulated and uncomfortable with the direction this conversation had taken. "No, I guess not," he said, for lack of anything better. It could be that this woman was feeling neglected, a little lonely, and needed reassurance from a male perspective. Either that or he'd just been hit a pop-up and all he had to do was raise his glove … But no. That was improper.

Joyce reached out to a fancy coffee table and picked up a device that resembled a TV remote controller. With the push of a few buttons, she shut off the lights, and then closed both sets of curtains. The room became very dim, faint illumination coming only from the adjoining corridors. She knelt beside Cruz, bent over him and brushed her lips lightly across his, then came back to plant a solid kiss. From a pocket in her shorts, she placed something in his hand. Cruz looked down, squinting in the darkness, and saw one, two, three condoms. *Was she an optimist or just really horny?* He tensed, lost for a course of action. Sometimes women got a little too caught up in the mystique of being around a private investigator.

"I'm not sure this is a—"

Joyce silenced him by fluffing her hair, pulling off her tank top, and tossing it on a chair. She wasn't wearing a bra and her breasts were firm, real, and a little bigger than he'd realized. "Don't bullshit me, Mr. Cruz. I'm attracted to you and I think you're attracted to me. Believe me, you're not interfering with a happy marriage. I really need you right now."

When Cruz caught his breath, he reached for her and their bodies locked, their mouths colliding. She ran her hands under his shirt, exploring the muscles of his chest and abdomen. They kissed again, then toppled over while groping and fondling. Bouncing into a new position, Joyce straddled Cruz's stomach while he squeezed her breasts and ran his tongue over the nipples. After a few breathless moments, she led him quickly down the hall and to a king-size bed where they would stay for the next two hours. On the way, he said, "Please just call me Al."

CHAPTER 14

Amy was distressed when Monday morning came with no new information on the whereabouts of Vonda Cantu or Dixie Newberry. Both their cell phones were still off or beyond the range of a tower. None of their credit cards had been active. Vonda's SUV had not been spotted, no local hospitals had admitted them, and no new Jane Does had turned up matching either of their descriptions.

The Dolores Griego homicide was still a mystery and the autopsy, scheduled early, yielded no big surprises. The COD was as it seemed, a puncture wound between the 6th and 7th ribs that penetrated through the lung and all the way into the right ventricle; death would have been immediate. The murder weapon was determined by the medical examiner to be round and tapered, possibly homemade and approximately nine inches long. He described it as 'kind of a big ice pick.' A search of her apartment revealed no disarray or signs of criminal activity. Jerry Cunningham found several informal photographs on Griego's computer that showed the victim with two other women, now identified as Vonda Cantu and Dixie Newberry. The three women were acquainted, for sure. Although no specific reason was known for Dolores to be entering Vonda's apartment, Jerry speculated they may be close enough that she had a key and such visits were routine.

"You know, Cruz called me this morning."

Amy turned. "Uh-huh. Do I want to know what he said?"

"Nothing bad. More like weird. He asked about our victim at Birch Tree Apartments. Saw it on the news. Thought he might know her."

"What? He knows Vonda?"

Frank shook his head. "Turns out no. I told him the dead woman wasn't Vonda. That it was just somebody who looked a little like her."

Amy was silent for a moment. "And that was it? Doesn't make any sense. Either he recognized her or he didn't."

"That's what I was thinking."

Amy grumbled loudly. "He's up to something."

"Probably. I'll find out. For now, let's concentrate on Waldo."

Amy nodded and refocused her thoughts. On today's agenda was a visit to the Pierce Brothers main office building at 4th and Market. Although Cruz's audio surveillance was illegal and his meddling unofficial, a combat-trained security expert demanded their attention in relation to the Jarrett homicide. No accusations could be made and they would conflate their inquiries with talk of Zachary Chastang, but his reactions to questions, and most importantly, the ones he evaded, would be noted.

"Just make sure you don't get into a pissing contest with this guy."

Frank glanced over at his partner. "Me? C'mon. You know better than that."

"I do, huh?"

"We got nothing on him. Besides, I'm sure Pierce Brothers has a stable of high-priced lawyers. We'll just squeeze him a little and see what leaks out."

Frank and Amy continued across town and left their unmarked Stratus in the company's parking structure. Once inside the building they were greeted with polite regard and assumed it was due to the routine of police presence since Zachary's murder. They were escorted by a uniformed security guard to a reception area on the twelfth floor. Plaques, awards, and photos of Little Leaguers covered the walls. The floor was carpeted in a lush dark blue with the gold and red Pierce Brothers logo at the center. Two corridors branched off to a series of offices and a young receptionist sat at large L-shaped desk talking on a headset while simultaneously staring at a monitor and tapping away at a keyboard.

"You're here about Zachary Chastang's murder?" the guard asked, a short and nondescript sixty-something.

"In part," Frank said.

"That's good. Cameron Chastang is a great man. He's really hurting."

"I've never met him, but I know he's quite a guy. How long have you worked here?"

"Almost four years."

"Good job?"

"Not bad. They treat us pretty well. Usually it's just following procedures, not really much trouble."

"So, Kurt Waldo is your boss?"

"No. Mr. Waldo works directly with the senior staff. I've only talked to him a handful of times."

The man went on his way so Frank and Amy took a seat on black leather chairs that were stylish, comfortable, and meant to impress visitors. Except for the busy receptionist, they were alone. After a few minutes, a portly man in a nicely tailored suit walked by and studied them momentarily, then continued towards the elevators. It wasn't surprising—everyone was curious about visits from police.

"Very interesting," Frank whispered. "That guard's been here for years and hardly knows Waldo. That means he doesn't handle internal security."

"Makes me wonder what he *does* handle."

Two minutes later, the receptionist stopped typing, came over with a warm welcome and then led them to a back office. The inside was large and modern but surprisingly uncluttered. There were no photos, certificates or other expected décor that suggested personal life or qualifications. The desk held a laptop computer, a few files folders, and some stationery items, but little else. Kurt Waldo sat as his desk and came around to greet them, glancing briefly at their

IDs. Oddly, he was dressed in jeans, boots, and a neat black t-shirt that hid none of his powerful frame. Amy shook his hand, feeling typical male firmness but sensing controlled strength below the surface. He was slightly taller than Frank, carried himself well and had little bodyfat. This was a man who kept himself in top shape. He wasn't conventionally handsome but had a rugged look that many women found appealing. He probably had a surplus of testosterone and a five-o'clock shadow that showed up around two-thirty.

"Have a seat," he said. "I've been over everything with the other detectives. How can I help you?"

"Thanks," Frank said affably. He sat down and Amy did the same. "We're here because we're checking into the relationship between Zachary Chastang and Marcus Jarrett. We're hoping there's something you might be able to tell us."

Amy scrutinized the man as he digested her partner's words. She saw a flash of thought and calculations run across his otherwise stoic face. In an instant it was gone. He was surely a think-on-his-feet type, one who'd been in countless jams and usually prevailed. It suddenly crossed her mind that Waldo could have been the man who broke into Frank's house on Thursday night. His height and strong build matched her general impressions of the attacker, which certainly could be coincidence. There were no links to connect up those events to Waldo unless you count Zachary Chastang—and she'd never even heard of him until four o'clock that afternoon when the assignment came along.

"I know about Jarrett's death," Waldo said. "Tragic. I don't really know that he and Zachary were friends."

"Friends or something else," Frank said. "We found Zachary's fingerprints at Jarrett's home. And before you ask—no, he's not suspected of the murder. That particular night he was working on his little hobby. When Marcus Jarrett was killed, Zachary was busy getting arrested for attempted date-rape. I'm sure you know all about that, too."

Waldo sat impassively, and then said, "I only know that Zachary was released."

Frank grinned. "Yeah, true. Damn lawyers really make things happen. But believe me, Zachary wouldn't have weaseled out of this one. Soon enough, guys with big arms and tattoos would've been bending him over the sink."

Waldo sat quietly for a moment and then leaned back in his chair. "That's a smart mouth you've got there."

"I get that a lot."

"What the hell is it you're *really* after?"

"Where were you this past Friday morning, say around eleven o'clock?"

"Let's see … Wilmington. Big meeting, job related."

"Fine. That can be checked. Where were you late Thursday evening between midnight and 1 AM?"

"Am I under arrest?"

"Not at all. We're just eliminating possible suspects. When we check one off, then we can concentrate on others."

"Fine. I was home watching television."

"Alone?"

"Yep."

"Did you murder Marcus Jarrett?"

"Nope."

"Did you know Marcus Jarrett?"

"Nope."

Amy said suddenly, "Ever been in the Lexington Park area?"

Waldo turned to her. "Is that where Marcus Jarrett was killed?"

"No," Amy said. "Possibly a related matter. Again, we're eliminating suspects."

"You'll have to be more specific."

"Montague Street, just west of Pennypack Park."

"Now why would I be up there?"

"It's just a simple question."

Waldo leaned forward. "What's this all about?"

Amy couldn't decide if she liked the man's voice. He was articulate but spoke with a low, clear rumble that reminded her a little of Darth Vader. She found herself looking over his face and couldn't be sure if a faint discoloration was really there or wishful thinking. She decided to try a different path on a hunch. "I was there where a break-in occurred shortly after Zachary Chastang was arrested. Would you know anything about it?"

"A break-in, you say. My, the crime rate is staggering. Was anything stolen?"

"Actually, no.

"Not much of a break-in then."

"I overpowered him and he ran off."

"Oh. Well, nice work. This was at your place?"

"No."

Waldo's lips curled into a tight smile. "Boyfriend, I'm guessing."

"It's not your concern."

Waldo fixed Amy with a challenging gaze. "Of course not. And I'm not judging. You can stay anywhere you like in a free country."

Amy refused to look away but couldn't think of a good comeback. She needed to control the questioning and wouldn't get into some kind of half-baked explanation or how she'd stopped by to let out a dog. She just held his stare.

"It's not really important." Frank shrugged. "She's right. Couldn't have been you. She said the guy was slow and clumsy."

Waldo leaned back in his chair again. "Why do I get the feeling that you two are trying to piss me off?"

"That's certainly not our intention," Amy said, showing more bravado than she actually felt. She stood up and placed her business card on Waldo's desk. "There's a connection between Zachary Chastang's activities and Marcus Jarrett's death. We're going to figure out what it is. If you can think of anything to help, please give us a call."

Waldo stood as both detectives headed for the door. His brow was creased and his poker-face slipped a little. She wasn't sure how to read this guy. Arrogant, no doubt. *A killer?* She just wasn't sure.

"I'll do that," Waldo said. "I hope you catch the guy. Oh, Detective Lepone."

Amy turned. "Yes?"

"This slow and clumsy fellow you tangled with—I gather you didn't arrest him. How'd he manage to get away?"

"I'm not at liberty to discuss an open case."

Waldo grinned. "I thought you *came here* to discuss open cases."

Amy exhaled in frustration. "If you must know, he jumped out a window."

"Really?" Waldo stood up and walked slowly forward, stopping right in front of her. "Right out a window, you say." Looking down, he added, "I'm just a little curious. Why didn't you give chase and bring him in?"

Amy swallowed hard and held her place, refusing to retreat from a man who clearly wanted to intimidate her. "It wasn't feasible at the time."

Waldo leaned against the wall. "Well, I'm sure you had your reasons. You know, for slow and clumsy, this person sounds pretty agile to me."

Amy summoned all her resolve to form a smile. "I suppose he was really scared. Then people can do amazing things."

Cruz pulled into the cobblestone driveway of the Jarrett home, finished off a small bag of peanut M&Ms and washed them down with a cup of Wawa coffee. He gathered a few folders and checked his appearance in the mirror, readying himself for an update of progress he'd made—little as it was. Actually, he was stalling because there was a lot going on and worries branched in all directions. Recapping the last few days, he could hardly justify all the money he was making by conducting illegal surveillance. He knew very little about the murder and had begun a torrid affair with a married client. A few non-stop hours of wild feats in Joyce Kyser's bed made yesterday one of the most fabulous and memorable afternoons of his life. A shower together afterwards had been an adventure that was more about wet orgasms than cleanliness. A refueling snack morphed into an hour of sitting around stark naked and talking about everything from God and the universe to favorite foods and vacation spots. Then they did it one more time, making her original estimate of three condoms in error—they'd actually used four. The physical aspect was outrageous but they'd also connected somewhere a lot deeper. He really enjoyed her company, was wishing she was single, and couldn't wait to see her again. He had no idea where this would go but the possibilities for disaster were immense.

Cruz rang the bell and was greeted by a sad-faced Sylvia Jarrett, looking gaunt and still reeling from Marcus's death. In gray sweatpants and blue V-neck t-shirt, she seemed very earthy and more like a typical housewife than a rich widow. She led him through the mansion to the big sunroom. On the table was a fancy plate of rare roast beef, a silver bowl of au jus, a basket of fresh rolls, and an impressive selection of fresh fruit along with fine silverware. In a champagne bucket were four Heineken bottles packed in ice. Sylvia excused herself to freshen up but told Cruz to please help himself with whatever he'd like. It looked great and he was actually hungry. If this kept going, he'd need to up his workouts.

Cruz ate a sandwich, drank half a beer, and had gone over his files by the time his hostess returned. She did look better in a beige pantsuit, but still aching from within.

"I'm so sorry, Mr. Cruz," she said. "I guess it's just starting to hit me now. Marcus had really been developing into quite a businessman these last few years. His father would be proud." She took a seat and drew a long breath. "The medical examiner's office said his body would be released soon. I was thinking of having the funeral Saturday."

For lack of anything else, Cruz said, "That sounds fine." He understood it now. At first, this very elegant and educated woman had been maintaining her composure, preserving the visible role of leader. Now the buildup of emotions had caught up with her. She was alone at the top and really feeling the emptiness of it.

"Tell me—was he really shot?"

"Yes. You told me to be honest with you, so I will. Gunshot to the chest. He wouldn't have suffered. And it was absolutely *not* a suicide. I've spoken to the police and they've heard nothing but good things about him from friends and employees."

"Thank you for that."

"His toxicology was negative, meaning there were no drugs, poisons, or unusual compounds." Cruz withdrew several photographs from a folder and held up the first. "Recognize her?"

"She looks familiar."

"That's Vonda Cantu, Marcus's girlfriend." Sylvia looked skeptical. "More than a girlfriend, actually. I think he purchased his home so they could spend more time together. Possibly … something long term. She works for your company as an accountant."

Sylvia looked flustered. "I do know her. Well, this is a lot to take in. I had no idea there was anyone serious. Why wouldn't Marcus have said something? I mean if he cared . . ." She paused, as if a thought came to her. "Oh, of course." Smiling faintly, she said, "Obviously he could have broken his father's rules about executives in relationships with employees. Marcus … Well, he wouldn't want to appear inappropriate."

"I think you're right. I'm telling you this because I thought you should know. I guess you haven't seen this picture on the news?"

"News?"

"The newspapers reported that Vonda Cantu was murdered." To Sylvia's frantic look, he said quickly, "they're wrong, though. It was a mix-up. A different woman outside Vonda's apartment. Vonda is missing and the police can't locate her."

"Oh, my. This is all such a shock. And it has something to do with why Marcus was killed?"

"I'd say it's likely. There might have a connection to Zachary Chastang's death."

Sylvia looked puzzled. "I know about Zachary being killed. Cameron Chastang does a good deal of business with us."

"I can't explain it all yet. Zachary's fingerprints were found in Marcus's place."

"That could be. They knew each other but I couldn't say if they were close friends."

Cruz withdrew another photo—the one of Mindy Lyons that he'd snapped when she left the Kyser home. "How about her?"

Sylvia looked it over and shrugged. "Yes. A friend. She worked for our company a few years back and I see her socially. She left to take a position at Pierce Brothers and there are no hard feelings. Is she a suspect or something?"

"Again, no. She's of little or no concern. I'm just trying to be thorough."

"None of this makes sense. What could a prominent construction firm have to do with Marcus's murder?"

"I don't know—not yet. We can't jump to conclusions and I can't interfere with the police. I do have some useful contacts and I'll keep digging if you want me to. There's just a lot going on that I'm trying to make sense of."

Sylvia leaned forward in her chair, an odd intensity replacing the fragile look of loss and outrage. "Mr. Cruz, I want to explain something. I've been doing a lot of soul-searching these past few days. I don't think I realized the depth of my feelings for Jarrett Enterprises or about how much I saw of my husband in Marcus. This family's legacy is very, very important to me. I hate it that Marcus won't be able to follow in his father's footsteps and I regret our legal problems. Marcus didn't agree with his father's will and thinking about it now, I guess I don't blame him. I do want Marcus's killer brought to justice. I'm telling you right now to stay on this and spare no expense. Find the mother fucker and see that he rots in jail or in the ground, I don't care *which*."

Cruz reached for his beer and took a long slug. He was just now realizing that this was possibly his biggest case ever. Sylvia Jarrett loved her late husband and his son. She didn't know about the drugs found in Marcus's place and he hoped she never found out. This brave woman wanted justice and he wanted to deliver. Not just for the paycheck, but because it was important, like Karma or fate, or one of those cosmic things that had deep significance. He just hoped to do it without Sylvia finding out about his affair with Joyce, her married friend.

CHAPTER 15

On Amy's cell phone, the earlier text message had read: *Dinner my place 6 PM.*

Frank was a man of few words and his texts were more so. Just past his mailbox was Gigi's Nissan Maxima, Goggles' Subaru Outback and beyond that, a very familiar green Chevy Astro van that was PPD owned and operated. Alvin Cruz seemed to have connections to rate a loan of the nicely equipped unit—baffling as that was. Amy checked her appearance in the rear-view mirror and then noticed that full repairs had been done to the front window. It looked good as new, but the encounter was seared in her memory, an unforgettable blur of high-intensity action.

Disturbing as it had been, from a legal standpoint, pursuing the matter as a B&E or attempted assault was pointless. The cost of damages was only a tiny blip on a homeowner's policy. Nothing was stolen, no one was injured, and no real evidence was likely to turn up. If the incident was related to either murder case—and she felt sure it was—then there was an obligation to make sense of it. *Why didn't you give chase and bring him in?"*

A reasonable question. Or did Waldo ask it as a taunt—because he already knew the answer? Through instinct or police training, she'd somehow been prepared for the fight. Even in faint light, her attacker would have noticed a white towel falling off in the struggle. For her, the remaining battle had been all nude. And yes, it was the main reason she hadn't darted out the door after him. *Did Kurt Waldo know that because he was there?* The thought gave her chills.

Frank had been alongside when Waldo spoke and, despite his flippant attitude, didn't miss much. He hadn't asked about it—not yet, anyway. She'd expected some silly comment by now or for Frank to at least ask why she'd tensed up. However, he was biding his time, waiting for maximum embarrassment potential.

Amy cleared her mind and headed inside. The atmosphere was festive, the aromas delicious, and ZZ Top's Eliminator album was playing on the stereo. She enjoyed such a diverse group of friends, and looking them over, she knew it felt good to be there. Cruz was flopped in a chair and swigging a Miller Lite. Layla was using her nose to get attention by nudging his free hand on the armrest. In warmer weather, Cruz mostly wore those damn Hawaiian shirts. She wondered if there was a story behind the odd fashion choice and would get around to asking about it one of these days. Today's was red and yellow with parrots and palm trees, along with cargo shorts, and a pair of flip-flops.

Frank had on a faded cut-off blue sweatshirt with the PPD emblem, his brawny arms and part of a Marine Corps tattoo showing. Goggles wore a tan pullover, looked up briefly and nodded hello, then went back to doing something on a tablet. Gigi was sipping from a wine glass, wearing tan sandals, jeans and an orange Syracuse University t-shirt. Amy had to smile since she was so used to seeing her in facemasks, scrunchy caps, and the bulky laminate suits used at crime scenes. It was easy to forget she had long blond hair and, at five seven, probably weighed 120 pounds. Amy sat down and everyone dug into pizzas for a few minutes until Frank reached over and turned the music off. Time for business—they'd been down this road before.

Cruz finished chewing and said, "I had a nice chat with Sylvia Jarrett today."

Frank asked, "Still think she's on the level?"

"I do, yeah. She wants me to stay on the case and find the mother fucker that killed Marcus."

"She said *that*?"

"Word for word."

"You didn't mention the drugs, right?"

"Nope. I did ask about Zach Chastang in general. She said Marcus knew him but they weren't really chummy. If it turns out that Marcus was killed by some pissed-off date he drugged, all the dirty shit will come out anyway. Any news on Vonda Cantu or Dixie Newberry?"

Frank shook his head. "Still among the missing. Vonda's supervisor got a text message that said she was taking some emergency time off. Nothing else."

"You don't even know for sure if it really came from Vonda?"

"Nope. The phone's not on now."

"The ammo is a match," Goggles said. "I can say conclusively that the rounds from Vonda Cantu's apartment are the same make and consistency as the slug that killed Chastang."

Amy nodded. "I expected that. Vonda may have had time and still make her appointment across town, even in Friday traffic. They'll want us to go by the evidence itself. No way we'll charge her with what we've got. Considering she was taught hunting by an expert, the brass thinks she looks guilty."

"The thinking is," Goggles asked, "that Vonda Cantu shot Chastang because he attacked her friend?"

"That, plus he wasn't charged. No evidence. Dixie was bathed while she was out. And the staff cleaned up in the morning before the police got there."

"Chastang was a real dickhead," Cruz said. "I get the reasoning. Why in God's name would she be smart enough to pull it off and ditch the gun, but dumb enough to keep bullets around?"

Everyone was silent until Amy spoke up. "He's right. Doesn't add up."

Cruz laughed. "You're agreeing with me? Quick! Mark this day on the calendar."

The comment sent chuckles around the room. Amy realized he was correct—she and Cruz didn't often see eye to eye. She'd known him for a more than a year and he often seemed to be on the periphery of their cases. A few times, directly involved. On those occasions, he'd been both help and hindrance. Regardless of qualifications or intent, he shouldn't be present for what they were about to discuss, but Frank seemed intent on allowing it. She would bow to Frank's judgment this time. Since Cruz was getting the benefit of tonight's brainstorming, he'd better contribute something back. "Credit where credit's due, that's all."

"You know, we could get a hold of Vonda's recent texts from her cell provider," Gigi said. "Goggles or I could analyze speech patterns, see if it's likely someone else reported her off."

"Not a bad idea." Frank waved a hand through the air. "We'll do that. Also, I heard back from tech services about that stuff from Vonda's diary."

Amy perked up. "Really! What did they find out?"

"Nothing. Nada. They combed through his home computer and his work computer. No files or internet searches that had to do with Bradley Jarrett's death or his will."

Goggles asked, "Marcus suspected subterfuge of some kind?"

Amy nodded. "Well, yes. But that's only according to Vonda's diary."

"Disappointing, I know," Frank added. "He definitely protested in court a few years back. That's a matter of public record. But nothing since. I didn't get all the techno-crap. Basically, they looked really close. It didn't seem like he'd been researching his father's will, digging into Sylvia Jarrett, or making any kind of notes."

"So, he may have made up the story for Vonda's sake."

Frank nodded. "Could be."

"Okay. Got something a little better." Cruz grabbed a manila envelope and spread photos out on the coffee table. "Check this."

Amy studied the first photo and its unmistakable night-vision enhancement. She recognized Vonda Cantu next to a stocky man on a bench-style seat. He looked familiar. After making a few mental notes she passed it around.

"We saw this guy," Frank said. "At Pierce Brothers. He walked past us before we met Waldo."

Amy nodded, looking over a second photo that showed Vonda on foot in the street near a row of parked cars.

"That was all last Monday around midnight," Cruz said, "exactly one week ago. Vonda met this guy in Tacony Creek Park. She parked far away and walked in slowly, looking nervous. They talked but I couldn't hear what was said."

"So that's where you knew her from." Amy gave Cruz a fierce look. "Frank said you called to ask about her. So that was bullshit?"

Cruz raised his hands. "Uh, yeah. I'm sorry about that. When I saw her photo and the murder story, I flipped out. I needed to know—"

"Never mind excuses. I knew you were full of it. Why were you tailing her last week?"

"I wasn't. This doesn't leave the room but I've been checking out the guy with her. He's Gilbert Kyser. You'll know the name—an exec at Pierce Brothers. His wife thinks he's been screwing around. Vonda didn't seem like his squeeze so I didn't take it further. Didn't even know who she was til I saw the news." He held up a third photo. "That's Kyser again on the right. Anybody know the other guy?"

Amy looked it over, a street she recognized. The man was around forty and had wild eyes like someone who'd been on the edge all his life. Next to the well-fed man in an expensive suit, he seemed sadly out of place. She held it up and everyone shook their head.

"He's an ex-con named Corky Buck," Cruz said. "I asked around to see what he's up to these days. The way I hear it, he's a dirtbag-for-sale. Not dumb, real tough, does anything for money."

Goggles said, "Why would Kyser be meeting a fellow like that?"

"Don't know. Kyser earns a bundle—great job, pretty wife, big home. He's way outside his zone with

Corky Buck. He's met him twice that I saw, gave him a small package both times."

"Nothing in return?"

"Nope."

Frank said, "Then it's *money*. He's got to be paying Buck for something."

"That's the way I see it. There's no sign that Kyser has a mistress, but he's suspicious as all hell. At first, I had this notion he might want to get rid of his wife. Now I'm not so sure." Cruz took out a fourth photograph of a tall blonde. "This is Mindy Lyons on her way into Kyser's place. She's head of Public Relations at Pierce Brothers. Good credentials and reputation. This is the woman I overheard talking to Gilbert Kyser. And yes, I'm bugging the Kyser home, part of my case and keeping the client safe. According to Mindy, Chastang was worried because Marcus Jarrett wanted him to confess to the rape—mentioned Dixie by name. Zachary wanted Kurt Waldo assigned to take care of the problem. Then Jarrett was killed, and Mindy freaked out." Cruz passed the photo to Amy and held up his hands. "You have everything I know. That's it, I swear."

"I believe you," Amy said.

"Really?"

She switched to a frown. "No."

"Hey! It's true."

Amy ignored him and took out her notes. "I'm sure I know that name." After a minute, she said, "Gilbert Kyser was at the party when Dixie Newberry was raped. He was interviewed the next day but didn't know anything."

"Or so he *said*." Frank studied Mindy Lyons's photo for a moment. "Quite a babe." Drawing a breath, he said, "Okay. We know that Vonda Cantu was Marcus Jarrett's lover. This woman in the picture heard Zachary Chastang complain about Jarrett—who was then shot in his living room. Right before Zach Chastang is shot on his front lawn."

"I'm just a little lost," Goggles said.

"You're not the *only one*."

"It's a puzzler," Cruz said, "but I like Waldo for killing Marcus Jarrett. Tough, knows weapons. Maybe he thinks he's helping save the company's image."

"Could be," Frank agreed. "He's an arrogant prick. For some reason—we don't know why—but Marcus Jarrett may have turned on Zack Chastang. Makes sense that Waldo might take care of the problem."

"I want to mention something," Gigi said. "Waldo is big, right?"

"Real big."

"Okay. Well, I finally had time to run that crime scene re-enactment program. By my calculations, your shooter is most likely shorter than average."

"How short?"

"Well, my results say between five feet and five four."

Everyone paused for a moment. "Damn," Frank said. "That's a monkey wrench in the gears. Could that be, well … *wrong?*"

Gigi laughed. "Of course, it could. The computer gives results from established standards. The bullet came from the direction of the chair. Based on trajectory from the angle of entry in the wound—that estimate would be accurate."

"But that's not evidence, right?" Cruz asked.

Gigi nodded. "Correct. These are conclusions *drawn* from the evidence. What the police use as tools and what is presented at trial are different things. The killer could have been kneeling. Or standing behind the chair and bent over. Or Marcus could have been leaning back."

"Or," Frank said, "a tall perp could have reached down, drawn from an ankle holster and fired as he brought it up."

"Exactly right. Any one variable could throw the projection off. Our assessment is assuming your shooter was seated normally, and the weapon was held conventionally, and the victim was exactly where we found him when the shot was fired."

Everyone present, Amy knew, understood the scope of forensic sciences to be different than the imaginary version portrayed on TV shows. It wasn't so quick and easy to access satellite surveillance, view security recordings, tap phones, track cell signals, or call up detailed records from limitless databases as it was made to seem. The feds had the best toys, but not the majority of local PDs. Sadly, tight budgets kept technology limited or out of reach. Even so, the instant results from infallible, glittering, laser-powered devices used by tv and movie cops were only available on 23rd century starships. It made things tougher for prosecutors who faced jurors expecting a level of intricacy that didn't actually exist. "The point being," she said, "this is a guideline, but it doesn't exonerate Kurt Waldo. Or anyone else."

Gigi gave a thumbs up. "For sure. If it was an amateur, like a first-timer ... or someone seated in that chair was holding a gun on him and fired, then I'd stand by my numbers. But a pro, not so much. This Waldo guy might be aware of crime scene analysis techniques and tried to trip us up on purpose."

"I'd say so."

"Let's go back to drugs found in Jarrett's place," Goggles said. "He's an offender himself. His interference seems counter-intuitive."

"For that, I have one idea," Amy said. "The night of the party, I thought that Marcus hustled Vonda out of there to protect Zachary and keep her from finding Dixie unconscious. Now I'm on another track. Maybe something changed. Or Marcus may have had his own, sort of, principles—as weird as that sounds. Maybe Marcus was really furious that Zack did that in his family home. At least we need to consider the possibility. Gilbert Kyser probably saw something or knows what really happened. I'll bet he lied to the police to stay out of the mess. Vonda could have met him last week to ask about it. If Kyser confirmed that Chastang raped Dixie, it could be what pushed Vonda over the edge."

Cruz said, "That explains where Vonda and Dixie are. They split and went on the run before Vonda gets charged for Chastang's murder."

Amy took a swallow of beer while she thought it over, and then said, "It works—two separate scenarios. Kurt Waldo killed Marcus. With him gone, the threat of scandal goes away. Had nothing to do with Vonda Cantu's plans. Acting on her own, she took out Zachary Chastang—revenge for Dixie. Neither knew about the other."

Frank shook his head. "That all makes sense. But looking at the crime scene, Vonda's a wash. Remember, Chastang was in lockup all night. Got released and headed home, thanks to his father pulling strings. The shooter had to take position for a clear shot in good cover. This is right around the park, a wooded area just east of Wissahickon Creek. No quick access to or from. Plus, Chastang's house in on a road that ends in a cul-de-sac."

"But," Amy said, "Vonda's the daughter of a vet. She might know how to handle that level of difficulty."

Frank grunted. "Nah. I planned it out, soup to nuts. Took time and patience. The shooter would need to park somewhere safe—but there's nowhere really close. Then come in with a rifle on foot through the brush. Took the shot and disappeared, got away clean. At my best, it'd take half a day to scope out the area and thirty-five minutes to pull it off. To cut it that close, I'd need to know exactly when Chastang would come along—and no one did."

"So," Cruz said, "it had to be someone who had time to lie in wait."

Frank nodded. "Exactly right."

They all sat in silent contemplation for a moment. Amy finally said, "Well, fuck! It was *your* damn theory."

Everyone laughed and Frank said, "I know. That was before I worked it out. The shooter could have been tipped off about Chastang's release. Vonda wouldn't have those kinds of connections. We're *close* but still missing something."

"Like maybe the dead girl at Birch Tree Apartments."

"Yeah," Cruz said. "What's the story with her?"

"She's a wild card," Frank said. "Dolores Griego. Owns a donut shop. No enemies, no criminal record. She had a key to Vonda's apartment and was killed right outside her door."

After a moment of silence, Gigi suddenly said, "What if this Kurt Waldo killed all three—Marcus Jarrett, Vonda Cantu, and the donut shop lady?" Everyone froze like they were in a movie and some-one hit *pause*. Gigi's eyes widened and she said more quietly, "Well, you know, it's possible."

Frank's head bobbed around from side to side. "Crazier shit happens."

"Obviously," Goggles said, "such a pattern of variables suggests a sentential function could be established."

Cruz groaned. "Does that mean, like, it all fits?"

A round of chuckles went around as Googles answered. "Yes."

"Okay. So that would explain a lot." Cruz grabbed his beer and took a swig. "How's this Kurt Waldo seem in person?"

Frank looked over at Amy and grinned. "Very good question. What would you say, Partner?"

"What's that supposed to mean?"

"Just asking for your assessment of a suspect."

"Sure, you are." Amy frowned. Frank was goading her but she wasn't going to go there, especially with the others around. "If we can believe what this Mindy Lyons said about Chastang being pressured, then Marcus Jarrett would be a threat to his family and Pierce Brothers in general. Chastang was habitual so maybe Kurt Waldo cleans up after him a lot." Turning to Cruz, she said, "The conversation between Gilbert Kyser and Mindy Lyons isn't admissible. It's third hand information, obtained illegally, I might add."

"I know that." Cruz rolled his eyes. "Okay, I get it. You need a close look at Waldo. And maybe to find out more about Mindy Lyons's suspicions. Also, we need to find out what Kyser told Vonda Cantu and what he knows about that party. A smooth operator with special skills and tact could handle that easily."

Amy gave him a deadpan stare. "You know anyone like that?"

CHAPTER 16

Amy began her day by going over background checks and then making calls to a few semi-offenders who owed her a favor. It didn't take long to find out that Cruz was right about the ex-con. Corky Buck was a local hoodlum, known to police with a solid rep as a skilled loner on the streets. Considered pretty slick and knew the law with its limitations. Only a few arrests. One conviction in '96 for possession of cocaine. One conviction for aggravated assault in New Jersey and did eighteen months at Rahway. Made a living now as an ASME certified welder, mostly as a part-timer for small outfits. She suspected that was just his cover to appear legitimate on paper. He also had a mortgage on a house. Undoubtedly, he committed far more crimes than he ever got charged with because he excelled at keeping a low profile. Whatever the reason Gilbert Kyser was paying him couldn't be anything good.

Amy dressed and left for work but then veered off Ridge Avenue onto North 33rd Street and headed in the direction of Corky Buck's place in the Wynnefield area. It wasn't far, just over the river near the Mann Music Center, and wouldn't take long to check out. Buck sounded exactly like the kind of efficient all-purpose hoodlum that would hover in the shadows and swoop in when needed. She really wanted to get a better idea of his involvement. At least she knew what he looked like from his mug shots and the more recent photos taken by Cruz. Amy drove on Lancaster, turned on Girard Avenue and then pulled into a gas station with a large lot that ran adjacent to an under-pass. She parked at the far end, hopped out and went around to the trunk of her Mustang. She rummaged around in her extras bag and found a few items of clothing that were appropriate to the task. Buck might be a seasoned criminal, but from all accounts, he wasn't stupid. Her instincts said not to let him know the cops were checking him out. She needed him relaxed and roaming his turf so she could pick up his trail.

With a small bundle of clothes, she walked inside, headed through the candy aisle and found the ladies' room. Surprisingly, it was reasonably clean and she locked the door for a few minutes of privacy. Slipping out of a lightweight pantsuit, she donned tight denim shorts with ragged edges and a few rips that showed plenty of leg and a pair of brown sandals. She pulled on a snug black AC/DC t-shirt that was snipped at the neck to allow a deep V, then tied a small knot at the waist so it rode above her naval. She checked herself in the mirror, decided she looked pretty sleazy, and topped off the package by pulling her hair through the back of a faded Phillies baseball cap. She folded up her work clothes and walked out past a clerk at the register who gave her a lingering gaze and broad smile. Okay, she'd call the outfit a success. In some instances, her figure favored police work much the same as height or a rugged physique did for men. There seemed to be an equation for female skin: The more showing, the less a man staring at it could think straight.

She folded her good clothes, piled them on the passenger seat and continued, taking the scenic route through Fairmount Park, an immense system of public grounds that included lush gardens, art exhibits, museums, arboretums, old mansions, and wide-open spaces with a rich history dating back to one of the signers of The Declaration of Independence. It was among Amy's favorite places and she jogged the trails throughout whenever time allowed.

Eventually coming through to a residential section, she turned off North 54th onto North Wilton, a narrow street with row homes on either side. They were mostly two-story and similar in design, with a few steps leading to a small porch. Some were neat and tended; some were in disrepair with peeling paint and saggy roofs. She thought she actually caught a whiff of rotting wood. Slowing by Buck's address, she looked it over, saw nothing of interest, and thought the house seemed better maintained than some others. There was no parking on the street, so Amy went further along, turned right and pulled to a space along the curb. She slung a small paisley satchel purse over her shoulder that contained only car keys, her badge, a 9mm Sig Sauer P320 XCompact, and two spare magazines.

She got out and looked around, trying to formulate a plan. If nothing else came to mind, she'd just knock on the door of the closest neighbor, ask for a made-up name, act disappointed, and strike up a conversation. The weather was nice, a sunny day in the seventies at 8:20 in the morning. The sidewalks were narrow with plenty of chips and cracks. Unfortunately, there weren't any stores on the street, nor any hot dog vendors or newsstands that would provide a reason to linger. She decided to just take a stroll down Wilton and see what happened.

A few people were scattered around, walking, talking, and looking to be in no particular hurry. Most workers had already gone off to their jobs. Across the street, three teenaged boys slowed to check her out; one let go with a loud whistle. Amy grinned and kept moving.

As she got closer, a man with long hair came out the door, turned and locked up. He was sturdy and tall, probably in his thirties, and definitely not Corky Buck. He was moving routinely but not in a big rush so Amy made some quick assessments. The guy was heading off to a job but wasn't running late. Since he took the time to carefully lock up, Buck probably wasn't inside. This may actually be to her advantage.

"Hey there," Amy called out. Nice and sultry.

The man came down the steps while giving Amy the once-over and abruptly stopped at the bottom, breaking into a friendly grin. His seventies-style hair was clean and brushed, and the eyes, sharp and focused. Her impression was that of a working man, not a criminal posing as one. She'd been wrong before.

"Hello to you," he said.

Amy decided to go all out and get herself into character: hard-edged, with a hint of ditzy. "I'm looking for Corky. He here?"

"Corky?" The man frowned. "Oh, right. Mr. Buck. No. Well, he's the owner. Not here now, just rents it out."

She let out a huff and put her arms akimbo. "Damn. That bites. How long have you lived here?"

"Just since March. Got offered a job, moved from Lehighton. Lucky to find this place. Mr. Buck lets me go month to month."

"Where's he living now?"

For the first time, he paused, apparently deciding what and how much to say. "You a friend?"

Amy nodded and gave a helpless shrug. "Well ... His ex-girlfriend—that was a while back. Now he just owes me six hundred bucks."

The man laughed and relaxed a little so Amy introduced herself as Roxy. He told her that Mr. Buck lived somewhere in town and stopped by once a month to get the rent in cash. He didn't feel comfortable giving out his landlord's phone number and Amy said she understood perfectly. With a few minutes of chatter, she decided the man was on the level and really didn't know anything else. He had to get going to work but not before asking Amy on a date. Amy told him she was flattered but moving to a commune in California with a boyfriend to work on an apricot farm. The man smiled with a shrug and went on his way.

It wasn't unusual to own rental property, but Amy suspected that Buck did it to add a few extra steps toward tracking him down. The tenant might feel obligated to tell him about Roxy's visit but that was the least of her concerns. There would almost certainly be various pissed-off people trying to track down Corky Buck for one reason or another. Amy went back to her car and drove to work wondering what the hell he was up to.

CHAPTER 17

Amy sat at her desk going over files of the Zachary Chastang crime scene that included photos of his home and immediate area from various angles. Based on the evidence collected and using the latest software, a virtual reconstruction had been rendered to place a shooter outline, weapon, and bullet trajectory over simulated photographs with the body where it was at the moment of impact. The kill shot had traveled seventy-two yards from a thickly wooded area. The shooter would have needed the skill and accuracy of an average sportsman at that range and level of difficulty. Good cover and isolation, although no one knew the exact spot until investigators established it. Three witnesses heard the gunshot—two of those were nearby and outside. One neighbor near his mailbox only a few houses away, saw Zachary fall. No one noticed any strangers or heard a car pulling away. No suspicious tire marks or footprints had been recorded. There were no cigarette butts, papers, buttons, fibers, or other helpful clues left behind. Vonda Cantu was being actively considered, due to evidence and motive.

But Frank declared that impossible, and she would go with his expertise on the matter. Only if Vonda had known precisely when Zachary would arrive home, could she have been in position. Even then, it would be a stroke of sheer luck that the correct timing fell exactly into her day's schedule—a routine that had been pre-arranged by several secretaries through a series of phone calls. *No.* Either the shooter had time to wait around, or more likely, had inside information and got tipped off when Zachary was released. That's the person they needed to find. Amy knew that a $50,000 reward already had been established by the Chastang family for information leading to an arrest and conviction. Unless that offer produced more than the usual crackpots and habitual confessions, a strong effort and a bit of luck would be needed to break the case. Maybe that luck would turn out to be Vonda Cantu—if she was still alive. Vonda and Dixie were part of the puzzle and their statements paramount, but neither was likely to be the killer.

The new information from Alvin Cruz was also on her mind. It was as baffling as it was interesting. Vonda Cantu met Gilbert Kyser last Monday night in a park and both of them were at the party where Dixie was assaulted. Since then, a series of indirectly re-lated events had taken place. An employee overheard Chastang asking to have Kurt Waldo intervene with Marcus Jarrett. Then came Chastang's arrest. Marcus Jarrett's murder. The break-in at Frank's house. Zachary Chastang's murder. Gilbert Kyser meets with an ex-con twice, possibly paying him money. A donut shop owner is murdered on the back porch of Vonda's apartment. Incriminating evidence is found in Vonda's apartment, linking her to Chastang's murder. Vonda and Dixie completely vanish. Vonda, incidentally, just happens to have a strong motive for killing Chastang. Cameron Chastang, in turn, would have a strong reason for killing Vonda.

Amy reached in a bag for the soft pretzel she'd purchased earlier and broke off a small piece. Taking a few bites and washing it down with lukewarm coffee, she returned to business.

The Marcus Jarrett murder—their actual case—was still going nowhere. Marcus had been sitting on his couch—a .32 caliber shot to the chest from a revolver at a distance of approximately seven feet. The shooter wouldn't have been there very long, making a move soon after arriving. Kill shot. The heart, nearly dead center, severing the aortic arch. Precise, planned in advance. For Marcus—unexpected. No movement, no reaction, no defensive wounds. That, in itself, was one of their meager clues. No forced entry and no signs of struggle meant that Marcus let the person in. Nice and relaxed, no cause for alarm. *Who did a person normally sit across from in their living room?* A person who then killed him … A man? Statistically, yes.

Amy pictured her own living room sofa and chairs and then posed the question: *Who has sat there recently?* She wrote down names in the order they came to her. Okay. Neighbors, friends, relatives, co-workers, a woman on the reunion committee from high school, a college friend who was now her insurance agent. Social interaction, a little business. At 10 PM on a work night? This was a home he'd recently bought for $989,000. That narrowed the list since any wealthy homeowner would be wary of atypical visits at late hours. Maybe a friend or colleague. Someone Marcus felt comfortable with. *We need to talk. May I come in?* Marcus agrees. *Would you like a beer?* Not everyone drinks beer. Amy thought back to her own list and knew at least several of them disliked it, preferring wine, coffee, sodas, or iced tea. Marcus would only get his guest a beer on request or if he just assumed they'd drink it—knowing in advance that the person liked it. Something she'd learned from Frank was that, first, most cases had oddities that were never fully explained or resolved. If a button from the shirt of a victim turned up in the suspect's trunk, it might break the case. Unfortunately, it was almost never that simple. Since the victim was dead, much of their private activities, thought processes, and intentions would never be known. In all likelihood, the victim didn't notice the button pop off weeks ago when he last wore the shirt. It would never be seen again or have any bearing on the murder. And second, people usually didn't reveal much once arrested. Despite the "wrap-up" interview by TV cops as they unveiled solid evidence, a suspect was far more likely to lawyer up than break down and confess. She'd never seen a case where the guilty person caved in upon questioning, admitted to everything, outlined his original plan, and conveniently tied up all the loose ends. That worked fine on episodes of Columbo—just not in real life. It could be someone who asked for a beer to confuse things. Or to distract the intended victim.

Shifting focus for a moment, Amy considered the victim himself. Like every individual, the person was unique with his own traits, skills, and ambitions. *Who exactly was Marcus Jarrett?* A hard worker in recent years. A boyfriend who was clearly on a pedestal from Vonda Cantu's perspective. Unhappy with a will that left him subordinate in his own company. Otherwise, secure, wealthy, and well-provided for. Handsome. Popular. Respected by his peers. And yet, he had a dirty secret. Or did he? There was a new twist on that premise and she was anxious to bounce her ideas off Frank.

Maybe she needed to get past the beer thing. After all, that could be a fluke. A good detective would never hinge an investigation on a single random variable. Marcus may have grabbed the second beer out of habit for a killer who never drank a beer in his life. Or a neighbor or old friend could have stopped by briefly, never got around to drinking his beer, and then left before the killer arrived. Nothing like that turned up in the house-to-house but it was still conceivable. And then there was another possibility— Marcus never went for the second beer at all. The killer, wearing gloves, shot Marcus and then placed a beer where they found it to throw things off track.

It shifted her thoughts to Kurt Waldo. *Was he a man who could orchestrate such an elaborate plan to cover two, or even, three murders?*

A part of her really wanted to zero in on Kurt Waldo. From her first impressions, he seemed like a focused, efficient, and thorough henchman. A security expert who valued his reputation and would practice, and expect, loyalty. Marcus Jarrett's pressure for Zachary Chastang to confess would have represented a threat to the company. By eliminating Marcus, the problem would go away with no direct connection to Pierce Brothers or the Chastang family. Waldo could have eliminated Zachary the next day for the same reason. If Waldo killed Marcus, but not Zachary, then he would have had no idea Zachary would die the following day.

However, as nice as it would be to have one perpetrator and wrap the cases together is a single bow, she would stick to procedure. Another wrinkle was that Kurt Waldo seemed to be a longshot candidate for the mystery intruder at Frank's house. Zachary Chastang was the link. Until Thursday afternoon, she'd only heard of him through a few fleeting news stories here and there—those local 'bad boy' features that seemed to fuel gossip and attract readers. Thursday evening she'd pulled off the 'sting' and arrested Zachary at roughly the same time Marcus Jarrett was being murdered across town. An hour later, she'd found herself in a battle with a large and skilled assailant in Frank's house. The timing meant one thing: Zach Chastang didn't kill Marcus. Although, Kurt Waldo *could have.* She'd checked it herself. At that time of night, Waldo could have killed Marcus Jarrett at his home and still easily been the intruder at Frank's place in Fox Chase if he went directly there.

Frank arrived with a deli bag and slid onto his seat, spinning it around and rolling a little towards Amy. "Any word on Vonda and Dixie?"

"Not a thing. I can't imagine what happened to them. I did get hold of the report from the ER doctor who examined Dixie last month."

"Anything there?"

"No usable evidence—at least nothing that points to a particular suspect. Not only was she bathed, but he estimates that she slept for at least two hours after the rape. I did pick up one thing of interest. It says here he noticed slight bruising on her upper arms— particularly the medial heads of both triceps and the anterior biceps. So—I called him up. He said it indicates that she was picked up there—sort of lifted up with hands holding her on both sides."

Frank frowned. "That must mean—"

"Two people. Yes. She wasn't dragged by one person because that would have left other distinguishing marks. The doctor thinks it's likely she was carried by someone holding her under the armpits and someone else at her legs."

"Then Chastang had help."

"Right. And yet no one came forward."

Frank thought a moment. "That fits. Two people may have assaulted her. Since Vonda was at the party, I seriously doubt it was Jarrett. It also could be that Chastang did it by himself. He could have picked her up afterwards and dumped her in the tub, but needed help to get her out. Wet, unconscious, hard to handle. Did he seem strong enough to lift a slippery woman out of a tub?"

"He was a fucking wimp. Not to speak ill of the dead."

Frank raised an eyebrow. "No, of course not. Okay then. It was a pretty wild night. Chastang could have told some bonehead that she just got drunk and passed out. The guy might be half blitzed himself."

"All the men were interviewed within the next few days. Why wouldn't he have said something?"

Frank shrugged. "Probably afraid. You help carry an unconscious naked woman at a party and find out later she's claiming rape—believe me, all guys would clam up."

Amy thought it over. "We have a likely candidate."

"Gilbert Kyser?"

"That's what I'm thinking. Or he could have seen Chastang and some other guy carrying her. Maybe he was afraid to speak up but then told Vonda the truth about it."

"I hope we get to ask her. In the meantime, we might squeeze Kyser. By the way, did you come straight to work today from a big bash or something?"

"No. Why?"

Frank grinned. "Well, Turk said you showed up earlier in … *casual attire.* Then changed right away."

"Oh, right. I had to run a little errand. Wore something less businesslike."

"Uh-huh, sounds good. So, it was what—like jeans and a t-shirt?"

Amy scrutinized him. "What's with questions about my clothes? Out of curiosity, Turk used those exact words: '*casual attire?*'"

"I sort of paraphrased."

"Oh, did you really? C'mon. What'd he say?"

"Okay, fine. He mentioned shorts that barely covered your ass. And something about tits hanging out of a skimpy t-shirt."

"He did, huh?" Amy shook her head. "*Men,* Jesus. What is this obsession with women's bodies?"

"We like 'em. So, it's true?"

"Well—yeah."

"Wow. Sorry I missed it. Then I presume this errand had to do with getting information, probably out of a spellbound man."

Amy grinned. "Yeah. I went by Corky Buck's place. Dead end. I did find out from a tenant that he doesn't live there. No address, picks up the rent. My guess is that Buck likes being hard to find."

"That figures. Want some lunch?"

"Anything I'll like?"

"Roast beef sandwiches with au jus gravy and steak fries with Old Bay seasoning."

"Did you bring me a Diet Dr. Pepper?"

"Yep."

"Sounds good." Amy reached for the bag. "I called Ben Amos and asked for a favor. Remember how Chastang had been questioned a few times after a woman was raped? Also, he was at Jarrett's party. Then, when he visited a suspected drug dealer, they put two and two together. That's how they got onto him."

"I'm with you so far."

"Okay, here's the thing. It ties in to something my dad said."

Frank grunted. "Um, I thought your father passed away."

"He did. Years ago. But I just had dinner with my mom on Friday night and I got to thinking about him. My father read crime novels and true crime, kind of his hobby. He was smart, intuitive. Also, he had this way of reading people, I mean, really seeing a person for who they are. I remember when I was in my teen years. He would meet the boys I hung out with and size them up. He wasn't fooled by a clean-cut guy who had his shirt tucked in. That didn't matter. Dad could see past the superficial. He'd always tell me who the good guys were and the not-so-good. And when I got to know them better, I realized dad was always right."

Frank let out a whistle. "Well, I kinda wish I'd gotten to meet him. And it has to do with our case?"

"Yes. Follow me on this. Amos got back to me a while ago. There is no existing field intelligence on Marcus Jarrett. *None at all.* He was never questioned or investigated, certainly not about anything remotely like date-rape. The FBI, State Police, and Crimes Against Persons never heard of him. He was never even a guest at a party where a complaint was filed. Not observed going back five years. And no known association with sellers or buyers of any drugs whatsoever."

"Okay. I get it. Uptown dude with money and a sweet ride. He should have popped up on the radar someplace."

Amy nodded. "Yet he *didn't*. So, let's think about it this. Everything we've found about Jarrett suggests neatness, efficiency, even kindness. Paperwork, his home, handling employees. Nothing suspicious on his computer. All around guy, college degree, won some amateur tennis tournaments. I think he recently bought that big house with thoughts of having a family with Vonda. The only negative thing we've got is incriminating drugs tucked behind some socks. Doesn't that strike you as odd?"

"Well … Obviously, not the best place for it."

Amy nodded again. "Uh-huh. Maybe all right for porn. But that house is huge with extra rooms, a garage, a wall safe in the den, and a hidden floor safe in the master bedroom. I think a smart man would find a more creative place to keep something like date-rape drugs. Especially with a steady girlfriend using drawers in the same bureau."

Frank exhaled. "Point taken. He's not the brightest bulb on the tree. Or—you think he's really Mr. Nice Guy and someone *planted* the drugs."

"Yes. My dad would say an elaborate collection of drugs in that sock drawer—a really dumb hiding place—doesn't fit with everything else we know about Marcus Jarrett. That's the angle we need to pursue. Very possibly, the killer used the drugs to throw suspicion on Jarrett—and it did. Zachary Chastang's fingerprints were at Marcus's place which doesn't necessarily mean they were friends. He may have stopped to see Marcus to explain himself. Remember, I arrested Chastang so I know what he was like. I can see him trying to weasel out of it or even lying through his teeth. Marcus might not have been convinced and was still blaming him for Dixie's ordeal. Maybe Kurt Waldo took care of the problem."

"Possible. Waldo killed him and planted the party favors, making it look like Jarrett was into that shit."

"Yeah. That's about it."

"That would eighty-six his concern with Jarrett. The problem is—your arrest was solid. It wouldn't have helped Chastang against the new charges."

"Think of the timing. Whoever killed Jarrett wouldn't have known about that yet. The murder took place at the same time I was arresting Chastang. But going back to what Gigi said—Waldo could have killed Zachary, too. Two unrelated murders. All those issues down the drain, the company is protected, and Vonda is the one who looks guilty."

"True." Frank was quiet for a moment, then said, "Waldo definitely tops our suspect list. Let me roll it around."

Amy went back to her lunch, glad to relax and let Frank go over the pros and cons. He was a real nuts-and-bolts kind of investigator, a trait she admired. Big on common sense, logic, and evidence but never one to sit around with profilers deciding if the guy they were after hated his mother or still wet the bed. She could tell Frank was ever so slowly coming on board, giving her idea its due. She was lost in thought and taking a long sip of Dr. Pepper when the phone on her desk rang.

"Detective Lepone," she answered.

"Hello Detective. You gave me your card earlier today. Glad I was able to reach you.."

The resonant voice was unmistakable. She glanced over at Frank who was tearing into his sandwich. "I … What do you want? Did you want to make a statement?"

"Not really. I was hoping we could talk. Maybe have drinks or … dinner."

Drinks? Dinner? What's he up to? "Oh. Well, that wouldn't be appropriate. But you could come into the station."

"I'd rather make it something a little more relaxing. I'm not involved in any of what's going on. But I could give you insight on the victim. He was … shall we say, a troubled individual."

Is that a carrot he's dangling, trying to lure me somewhere? This guy was very likely the corporate equivalent of a hired killer. Frank was still chewing, but his eyes were on her, clearly starting to show a little interest in the conversation. "No, that wouldn't work."

"C'mon. How bad could it be? At least have one drink with me later."

"I can't. As I said, it wouldn't be within proper procedure."

"All right then. This is my cell phone so you have my number—in case you change your mind."

"I won't. Um, goodbye."

She hung up the phone and jotted in her notebook. Not many things took her by complete surprise, but *this* she hadn't seen coming. Looking up, Frank had a quizzical expression as he finished off the last of his sandwich.

Finally, he said, "Okay. I give up. What was all that about?"

"I sort of … think I just got asked out."

"So?"

"You know, for a drink. Tonight."

Frank laughed. "Well, don't look so shocked. Remember, you did come to work half-naked. Who called? Was it that Jamaican bowler you were dreaming about?"

Amy shook her head. "No. It was our main suspect in two murders."

CHAPTER 18

Cruz held her in his arms and winced. What started out to be a client update had quickly spiraled into something quite different. Not only that, it was the second time in a matter of days. Well, the second time they'd been together. Technically, today was really the fourth and fifth time. Having sex with a married client was totally against protocol and his own personal code of conduct. He had betrayed his profession. And yet, the tingles from such a memorable bedroom feat were like a thousand ants that tickled and massaged at the same time. With great effort, he said, "You realize, your husband could come along any minute."

"No. I don't think … Not any minute." Joyce, up on her tiptoes, paused from nibbling his trap muscle. "But, you're right." She released her hold on him—slightly, and then exhaled. "I don't know what to say … I'm just … still processing all this."

"I know. Me, too." Cruz leaned back to look her over and was glad she'd taken the time to pull on a pair of denim shorts that were way too short—and unbuttoned—with a plain sleeveless top that was way too tight. The lips were a little swollen and her matted hair flipped in all directions. He needed to get out of here fast.

Leaning in, he gave a quick hug, and said "I'll call you," before slipping out the door and closing it behind him. A fast exit or he wasn't sure he'd leave at all.

Cruz jumped in the Astro van and tried to displace the beaming smile from his face. This was wrong on so many levels. Finally, high profile cases had come along and he immediately screwed things up with an illicit affair.

Turning the ignition, he then slipped it in gear and pulled away from the curb. With a glance in the mirror, he noticed what was almost surely Gilbert's Lexus. Charcoal grey, the right model. *Damn! Why would he be parked down the street?*

Cruz kept going down the block, then turned right on Parrish Street and pulled off along the curb. He climbed in the back and into the seat, then slipped on headphones and activated the surveillance equipment. Admitting to himself this was more damage control than working on the case, he needed to know what happens next. Some faint footfalls with swishes and clunks could be heard, Joyce obviously tidying up. Gilbert hadn't yet arrived.

Could this have something to do with today's earlier visit to Pierce Brothers? Pretending to be a representative of the insurance carrier, he'd donned a business suit and nosed around asking some key questions while successfully working Kurt Waldo into the conversation a few times. The staff were mostly guarded when it came to Zachary Chastang, the way-ward son of their owner. No one claimed any knowledge of who might want to shoot such a fine young man in the prime of life. Mostly, it was an offering of thinly veiled sentiments for a person they clearly didn't know well and didn't care to. Kurt Waldo was more of a mystery to the bulk of employees, some aware of him, but many knowing him by sight only and having never actually spoken to him. Cruz had purposely steered clear of Gilbert Kyser, only catching a glimpse of him a few times and quickly moving on in other directions. By the time he left, he had no better assessment of Kurt Waldo than when got there.

So, what prompted Gilbert to park half a block from his home and sit in the car? *Did Gilbert suspect the affair? Did the even know Alvin Cruz existed? Hopefully, he was on a business call and just wanted to finish up.*

Suddenly the sound in the earphones jarred Cruz from his thoughts—a door opening, then slamming shut. Kyser had finally come in.

"Oh, hi Gil. You're home really early. Umm, everything okay?"

"Yeah, sure. Fine. I left work. Something I ate didn't agree with me, I guess."

"I'm sorry to hear that. Do you want some Tums?"

"No. Well, yes. Say are you all right? You look flushed and like, even a little sweaty. Have you been exercising?"

"Yes! Yes, I was. I was doing yoga."

"*Fine. Say when I pulled up, I was finishing up a call. Saw that insurance guy leaving*"

"*What did he want?*"

"*Insurance guy?*"

"*Yes. He just left and got into an old green van. What did he ask about?*"

"*Ask about?*"

"*What is this nonsense of evading my questions with more questions? I saw that guy earlier nosing around Pierce Brothers. I know he's an insurance investigator. I just want to know what he's up to. Was it about Zachary Chastang?*"

"*Zachary Chastang?*"

Cruz cringed, knowing he'd unwittingly set this train of events in motion. Obviously, Kyser had noticed Cruz earlier interviewing the staff at work, then probably asked around to find out what it was all about.

"*Oww, Gil, you're hurting my arm.*"

"*Just tell me what he wanted. What do they think happened? Why would they be talking to you?*"

Joyce grunted loudly. "*Let me go.*"

"*Tell me exactly—oooohhhhh.*" Cruz heard serious groans, then a thud.

"*You're scaring me, Gil. Now leave me alone.*"

Footfalls, then a door slamming.

"*Joyce … Honey, I … I might puke . . .*"

Joyce's voice had turned shrill and agitated. Kyser's voice had taken on a weak, hollow rasp. Cruz's best guess: Joyce had kneed her husband in the balls, then went to the bedroom and slammed the door. Kyser would now be lying on the floor, feeling as though his man parts were turned inside out.

The faint rhythmic thumping of music appeared, though Cruz could barely make it out. Much closer were some grunts and shuffling. After several minutes of quiet, Kyser's voice was a little stronger.

"Hey, it's me … We got more problems … A nosy insurance man … Yeah. And my wife is fucking insane … I can't. She locked herself in the bedroom, listening to Bon Jovi … How should I know? I told you she's fucking nuts … Also, you screwed up … Yeah, wrong woman … I saw the news, too. Well, you should be … Okay, later."

Cruz flopped back in his seat and ran a hand across his head. What a class-A mess on his part. A troubled marriage, a suspicious husband, and now he'd left Joyce to squirm in the spotlight of her husband's confusion. But regardless of his indiscretions, Kyser was still up to no good. Somehow he needed to figure it out and make it right.

Amy's first-floor apartment was a nice size two-bedroom on Ridge Avenue. She'd moved in with it mostly furnished since the previous tenant, also a single woman, was getting married and moving out of state. A modest sum got all the basics which was fine for the time being. Since then, she'd tinkered around and added a few personal touches but hadn't had the time nor inclination to upgrade since. The living room-dining area was painted a kind of a pale lavender with a curved beige sofa and matching armchair, a circular coffee table and smaller end table, with oak cabinetry and brown curtains.

Amy sat at an older wood dining room table, donated by her aunt, eating an apple, nursing a cup of coffee, and processing her day. Earlier it had been determined that the bodies of Marcus Jarrett and Zachary Chastang would be released tomorrow by the Medical Examiner's Office. Current information said that Chastang's funeral would be Friday and Jarrett's was scheduled for Saturday. Both would be grandiose, expensive, and of interest to Philly PD since, often times, the killer was in attendance. Not only that, such events were loaded with emotion, tension, duplicity, and usually brimming with secrets. In the case of murder, detectives always went on the notion that *somebody* knew *something*. The crowd would be observed, photographed, even videotaped and then carefully studied for anomalies, odd reactions, heated discussions—usually you didn't know what you were looking for until you saw it.

She'd gone to visit Gilbert Kyser at his office to see what might be uncovered but the man had gone home sick shortly before she got there. Bad timing—it happened when you tried to surprise suspects and not let them prepare for a visit by police. She'd go again tomorrow or track him down at home.

She continued to sip coffee and pondered her lack of any thriving social life. On Saturday night, the orthopedic surgeon had been called away—so not her fault. Before that, nearly a month ago—a lukewarm dinner and drinks with a timid county restaurant inspector. He'd asked about her life and each detail seemed to freak him out more than the last. Detective, Homicide squad, multiple felony arrests, kickboxer, and yes, had a gun in her purse. That date had gone nowhere fast. And the last time for any actual sex? Mmmm. *Oh geez, had it been that long?*

For now, she figured on achieving professional success and that meant reeling in Kurt Waldo. At Frank's insistence, she had called him up and casually withdrew her earlier rejection. She'd tried her best at being flirty and arranged a date for the evening. Frank, in the meantime, used his military connections to find out the scoop with some carefully placed calls to prior associates. Command Sergeant Major Kurt Waldo was formerly of Delta Force in the Aviation Squadron, an elite and versatile unit that specialized in counter-terrorism and counter-insurgency. According to his former commander, now part of Joint Special Operations Command at Fort Bragg, Kurt Waldo was a man of honor, of the finest character, and a tribute to the U.S. Armed Forces. From her understanding, that was high praise for a man with already-impressive credentials. Not the sort of data she usually liked to hear about a suspect. And in a little while, she'd be meeting him over drinks while wearing a wire, trying to finagle an admission to a few felony murders.

Glancing at the clock, she noted the time—6:04. Frank would be along to pick her up soon and she had much to do—like preparing for a phony date that might be more interesting than her real ones.

Thirty-two minutes later, Amy opened the door and Frank broke into a huge grin.

"Don't start that shit," she said.

Not that she hadn't expected to hear a load of crap—again—about her wardrobe. She'd gone slightly overboard, choosing to play the part in an orange A-line sleeveless shift dress that used retro elements from the sixties. The salesgirl, who couldn't have been long out of high school, said it would be a righteous hit—hopefully, she was correct. The hem was a little high and the neckline a little low, showing her shape to advantage and giving off the right sexy appeal. Purchased months ago, she wondered about a suitable occasion, never figuring its debut would be for a fake date. A few minutes with a curling iron had produced a flip at the ends, giving her strawberry hair a bit of helpful pizzazz. At Friar Tuck's Pub, she would fit right in. Besides, the idea was to get Kurt Waldo to relax and start talking. Everything had been chosen to that end and she vowed to keep her mind on business. Walking to the counter to get her purse, she could feel Frank's eyes on her. "Do you mind?"

"What?"

"You're checking me out." She turned and faced him. "I can tell."

Frank waved it away. "Only in a professional capacity."

"Yeah, right."

"Seriously. It's my job to evaluate your clothes. You're undercover, all part of the assignment. Besides, I've seen our harassment video. It would be inappropriate for me to mention, say, your great legs or killer body."

"Thanks for not bringing it up."

"You're welcome." Frank grinned. "By the way, I may as well tell you now. We're headed to Cruz's place first."

Amy stopped in her tracks. "What? Why?"

"We're using the Astro van Cruz has. Besides, he's good with this stuff."

"You mean Cruz is going along? You've got to be shitting me."

"Suck it up. You just need to decide if you want me or Cruz to fit the wire under that dress."

"I've got a gun, Frank."

He held up his hands. "Just kidding. Female techie coming along."

Amy shook her head and herded him out the door. This was going to be a strange night, she could tell already.

CHAPTER 19

Cruz lived in a nice stone house on West Coulter Street about a half mile due north of her own apartment. Cruz's mother had left it in his care while living with elderly relatives on Long Island. To his credit, Amy heard that Cruz kept it in good shape and the wild parties to a minimum. The trip there took only a few minutes and they arrived with enough time to get ready and be at the pub by eight o'clock. It was another gorgeous evening with clear skies and a temperature of 75 degrees. There was a new maroon Dodge Challenger off to one side in Cruz's driveway and she wondered if he'd just bought it. The last few years he'd been driving a Pontiac Sunfire that was past its prime.

Cruz let them inside and Amy leveled him with a glare to squash any onset of cute comments about her attire.

She'd been to the house once or twice before, a family home with distinct feminine touches and conservative charm, clearly not a bachelor pad for a thirty-something. The living room was spacious, kind of an ivory color, with hardwood floors, a fireplace, and decorative arched windows with deep sills. Beyond the formal dining room, she saw a cute breakfast nook with a countertop and four stools.

A petite blonde in bright blue shorts, sandals, and a white tube top stood off to one side, apparently their technician to operate the covert recording equipment. It was a fairly risqué outfit for support services. Amy went over and introduced them as detectives, then tugged on her straps. "Do you think this is okay for placing the wire?"

The blonde looked momentarily confused and Cruz stepped beside her.

"Oh, sorry," he said. "This isn't our tech. She's, um, a friend."

Amy felt embarrassed. "I'm very sorry."

The woman smiled. "That's all right," she said and extended her hand. "Joyce Kyser."

As Amy shook, something sounded very familiar. "Pleased to meet you."

"Joyce," Cruz said. "Um, we have to go soon. Could you give us a few minutes? We need to talk over some classified matters."

"Oh, sure. I'll head on home, anyway. Maybe that jerk will show up. Nice meeting you." Joyce disappeared down the hall after giving a little wave.

"Kyser?" Amy whispered.

Cruz said, "I know you remember the name. Yes, that's ... Gilbert Kyser's *wife.*"

Frank came alongside Amy. "His wife? Jesus. Who was she talking about—the jerk?"

"I think she means her husband."

"May I ask," Amy said, "what she's doing here?"

"Long story. Besides, she's my client."

"I'll just bet. Where's our female tech?"

"Picking her up on the way."

"Fine." Amy pointed towards the door. "We'll drive slow. Until we get there, you start talking."

Frank drove the van and Amy rode shotgun while Cruz told the story of Gilbert's odd behavior and how he'd yelled at his wife on Sunday. Since then, they'd barely spoken. Gilbert came home ill from the office earlier today, then received a strange call and had raced off with no explanation of where he was going. Joyce waited for several hours and then tried his cell phone multiple times. At that point she'd asked to come and visit Cruz.

Amy digested his words and looked over at Frank, who shrugged. She turned around to face Cruz who sat at a secured swivel chair near a component workstation. Finally, she said, "Why is *that?*"

"Why is *what?*"

"Why did she come to see *you?* Do you moonlight as a marriage counselor?"

"Ha. Not hardly. You see … We've become friends … Sort of."

Amy rolled her eyes. "Please don't tell me you're sleeping with her."

Cruz sat still like a deer in headlights. "Okay."

"Jesus. You're sleeping with a married client and she's linked to our case. Gilbert Kyser could be involved. You said yourself he's up to something."

"He *is*. Look, I'm not proud of it. She's going through a tough time. It just kind of happened."

"Yeah, sure! Frank," Amy said. "What are we going to do about this?"

"Let's put a sock in it for now. The tech is meeting us right up ahead. You jump in the back and let her set you up. Later on, we'll tackle Cruz's love life."

Their tech turned out to be Adrienne Barlow, who they picked up a few blocks from their destination. A six-footer with long brown hair, she kept it pulled back in a ponytail. Amy had met her a few times, thought she was competent, and figured her to be about thirty-five or forty. Frank appeared to know her, too, and she wouldn't be surprised if they'd dated. Adrienne affixed the wire to Amy's strap and then checked it for concealment while Amy moved from side to side. Adrienne would hear everything that transpired and could communicate with Amy via a small earpiece that was easily hidden by her hair. Frank drove down Walnut Street past Friar Tuck's, spotted Waldo's car and parked the van further up towards 18th Street. Adrienne would remain behind, monitor the situation, and operate the recording equipment. Cruz would enter shortly after Amy as a random customer and pick a seat to keep them in sight. Since Waldo would know Frank, he would go around the long way and slip in the other entrance. He'd choose a position out of sight and wait as backup, although they didn't expect real trouble. After a while, the plan was for Amy to depart, revelations or not, with Waldo still inside. If Waldo walked her out, she would claim to have arrived by Uber.

Amy was pleased at the choice of venue. Friar Tuck's Pub was situated about half a block from the quiet beauty of Rittenhouse Square. The fashionable hangout for trendy professionals had good drinks, snappy decor, attractive help, and tasty deli-style sandwiches. Like similar establishments in the area, most occupied the ground floor of tall buildings such as the Rittenhouse Hotel and had outdoor service in suitable weather with tables and chairs on the sidewalk. The inside offered a choice of secluded booths, front-row barstools, or hardwood tables with living-room type chairs. Paintings by local artists graced the walls and were available for sale in the $300 to $700 range. The music was soft jazz and the atmosphere generally dignified. If Kurt Waldo was going to loosen up, this was the place to get it done.

"You're all set," Adrienne said. "Give me a keyword to let me know if there's a problem."

Amy shrugged. "How about Sloe Gin Fizz?"

"Perfect. Just say it to the waitress or tell the suspect that you're going to order one, something like that. Everyone remember, Amy is the one with a microphone. I'll only be able to hear things in her vicinity. I've got Frank's cell number and I'll call if there's something he needs to know."

"When we're all inside and set up," Cruz said, "be sure to order a glass of water. I'll have eyes on you. If you want me to interrupt things and pretend to be an old friend, take a long slow sip. If you need serious help, knock it over. I'll be there in a flash."

Amy nodded. "I can't see this turning violent— or him admitting to something so soon. I guess you never know."

Cruz stood and popped open the side door. "Good luck."

Once he was gone, Frank pulled open a floor lay-out of Friar Tucks and pointed to the exits. "Be ready for anything. Give it an hour or so at the most. Make goo-goo eyes and see what happens. If he doesn't spill his guts, we can always try again."

Amy frowned. "Goo-goo eyes, right. Glad they taught that at the academy. Where will you be?"

"Won't know til I see where you end up. Waldo's probably in one of the big booths over near the back against the wall."

"Why is that?"

Frank shrugged. "More romantic. Because that's where I'd be. Don't worry. I'll be close by." He turned stern and looked directly ay Amy. "There is also one very important consideration."

"What's that?"

"I know Waldo is a big, swarthy, ex-military type like me. Keep in mind this is a work-related operation. Don't even *think* about getting laid tonight."

Frank laughed and Adrienne did her best not to join in. Amy looked out the rear window, saw it was all clear, and got on her way without another word.

CHAPTER 20

The pub was typically slow on a Tuesday and Amy spotted Kurt Waldo right away. She noticed he'd chosen a secluded spot over against the wall—just as Frank predicted. Nice and cozy. The light was subdued and there were no patrons in the adjacent booths. He stood up as she approached and greeted her with a big smile of approval, taking in her outfit with a long sweeping gaze and not trying to hide it. His oddly informal office wear had been replaced by a brown sport coat, ivory shirt, and gold tie with tan chinos. *Good God*, she thought. *Why did he look so effing good?* With his build and short-cropped hair, it was as if a professional wrestler had been groomed for the cover of GQ.

"Thanks for accepting my invitation," he said and remained standing until Amy took a seat.

"My pleasure," she said with a strangled breath.

"Great dress. You all right?"

"Fine. Thanks."

"Would you like a drink?"

"Sure. Yuengling Premium, on tap. Oh, and a glass of water."

"Ah," Waldo grinned. "A woman who drinks beer. I like that."

Amy tried to get her mind back on track as she slid into a chair that Waldo leaned over and held for her. She took notice where Cruz had taken up sentry duty on a barstool at an angle to Waldo's left. Cruz was playing the part well and looked to already be in an animated conversation with a few other men. She couldn't see Frank at all, knowing he'd keep out of sight.

The waitress appeared and Waldo ordered for them, also choosing a beer. Seated across, she tried to avoid studying the masculine features, but found herself doing it anyway. He had a large head and strong jaw, no fat under the chin. In fact, she noticed a few veins on the man's neck. Power seemed to emanate from the large hands. She remembered the forearms from their meeting yesterday morning when he'd been wearing a t-shirt. He was like a lumberjack or blacksmith with sinewy bands of muscle. Suddenly, she got hold of her thoughts. *It's not a real date, dammit. And he's probably a killer. Stop checking him out.*

For a several minutes they talked about Friar Tuck's and a few other local hangouts. She was surprised to learn he came in sporadically and knew local artists and some of the paintings on the wall by name. He also expressed a fondness for a song by Pat Metheny as it rolled smoothly from a nearby speaker. Amy brought up the subject of his job and he gave a rundown on his employment history that sounded truthful. He was originally an independent security consultant after retiring from military service, still moving around a lot. He only accepted a long-term contract with Pierce Brothers so he could live in town and be near his parents, two married sisters, and their children. He sometimes had to travel to job sites, mostly only overnighters. By the time their drinks arrived, Amy was impressed. It wasn't just his rugged features. She had to admit than in many other ways, he was … *appealing.*

"Tell me something," he said. "How long have you been a police officer?"

"I've been on the force for nearly eleven years. A detective for one and a half."

"Has it been rewarding?"

Amy nodded. "Yes, I think so. The job has its ups and downs. Overall … Yes, rewarding."

"Makes you feel like you're accomplishing something?"

"I suppose that's it."

"I have to say I respect that. I felt the same when I joined the army. I don't know—maybe like a feeling you can make a difference. I think people should have a goal to leave the world a little better than they found it. You're a lovely woman and intelligent. I'll be surprised if you don't have a college degree."

"Well, yes," Amy said and hoped like hell she wasn't blushing. *How could he be this charming? It wasn't fair!* "Penn State."

"Very nice. See, you obviously could have gone into a more lucrative profession. You chose something with substance. That's a good thing."

Amy was a little stunned and didn't know quite how to respond. Most men she went out with were put off by her job. Kurt Waldo thought it was just fine. *Was he being sincere? What did he really want?* He was thoughtful and philosophical, traits she hadn't expected. WTF? *This was the murder suspect they hoped would incriminate himself?*

"Are you all right?" he asked.

"Oh, fine." She reached over and grabbed her mug, hoping a sip of beer would clear her head.

"Can you tell me something honestly?"

"Yes," Amy said. "If I can."

"Why'd you agree to meet me tonight?"

Amy's insides clenched although she forced a look of pure confidence. *What should she tell him?* This wasn't the macho soldier-of-fortune type she'd been expecting. The man across the table from her was insightful and sharp. *What was his angle? And did he know the effect he was having on her? Was that his strategy?* Although she'd never been in the armed services, she understood the military mind and the use of distractions. It was like a magic trick—while focused on something snazzy and trivial, your opponent missed the telltale maneuver. That thought left her with important questions to answer. *Was this a distraction? And what was she missing?*

"You're really putting a lot of thought into this conversation," he said.

"Oh, sorry."

"How about if I put all my cards on the table? Would it help if you could see my hand before you place a bet?"

Wow. This guy was like a runaway train and she was all but climbing on board for a ride. "Fine," Amy said, for lack of a better idea. "Let's see it."

"You got it." Waldo took a long swig of beer, sat the mug down with a clunk, and leaned back in the seat. "Here goes. At first when I called, it was a flat *no*—our getting together was inappropriate. Then you call to say you changed your mind. And show up ready to break hearts. You look terrific, by the way. Now I have to ask myself, what's she up to?"

Amy was stunned once again. "What am—*I*—up to?"

"Sure. I saw the tail you had on me."

"Tail? I didn't have you followed."

"You positive? White sedan. A Kia Optima, I think. Didn't get very close, but I spotted it."

"Not us."

"Well, I'd swear it picked me up right after I left my place and followed me all the way here. Two up front, probably males. Never got so close that I could make out details. The driver was good." He stopped to give off an infectious smile. "Just not good enough."

Amy was truly baffled. "I'm telling you—that *wasn't* my people. Why would I have you tailed when I knew we were meeting here?"

Waldo seemed to mull that over. "All right. Could be something unrelated, I suppose. Makes me curious. But you figure I know something. That's it, right? I've been around Zach Chastang for more than a year. You want his killer and think I might lead you to him. Either that or you think I killed him. Or you're looking at me for Marcus Jarrett's murder and hope to get me to slip up and confess."

Dammit. Now things had gone from bad to worse. He was too smart for her to claim that this was just a regular old date. She needed to keep her cool—all right, *regain* her cool—and try to salvage the situation as best she could. Adrienne could hear everything that transpired and was recording it. Frank, and even Cruz, might be listening to it all later. If there was anything usable, Lieutenant Trainer and reps from the DA's office would soon hear it, too. And here she was, behaving like a lovestruck teenager with the school's star quarterback. *Would they hear the quakes in her voice?* For lack of anything that would come off sounding lame, Amy said, "Yeah. It's about like that."

"Amazing." Waldo laughed out loud. "I hate to disappoint you. I don't know a damn thing that would help. I wouldn't want Cameron Chastang to hear me say it, but his son was a real turd. I tell you straight up—I didn't kill him. And if there's a connection between Zachary and Jarrett's murders, I have no idea what it could be."

"I'm not on the Chastang case—it's in our squad, though. We're pretty certain there's a link between the two."

"I can't see that. Marcus Jarrett had his shit together from all I've heard. I'm sure, in that social circle, there could be a few friends in common. Not much else. Zach Chastang was a pissant. Now don't get me wrong—I have a lot of respect for Cameron Chastang. He's a great guy and I kept tabs on Zachary as best I could. I've been looking into his shooting myself and I'm telling you like it is. There's no word on the street about who did it."

Amy knew the last part was true. Thank goodness, they were getting back to basics. *A murderer?* The man was so suave, so forceful. Maybe the right word was … *captivating*, "Okay. Ever hear of Dixie Newberry?"

Waldo raised an eyebrow. "Sure. Claimed rape after a party at the Jarrett place about a month ago. The police were all over Zach. No charges got filed."

"*Claimed* isn't the operative word. She went directly to the hospital. I personally spoke to the examining doctor. She was drugged—and raped."

Waldo nodded. "I stand corrected."

"Did you know she's missing?"

Waldo exhaled and turned solemn. "Truthfully, I did hear that. Zachary has always been one problem after another. The company has ears on the situation—I was briefed."

"Fair enough. Since Saturday. Her friend, too. Vonda Cantu, who just happens to be Marcus Jarrett's girlfriend." Amy watched as he processed the information. "Ever hear of Dolores Griego?"

"Mmm. Not sure."

"Murdered on Saturday night at Birch Tree Apartments."

"And it's connected to all this?"

Nothing. She knew what to watch for as she tossed out the name. No sign, not even a hint of recognition or alarm. Unless this man was made of ice-cold indifference, there should have been something, even if he was able to cover it up quickly. "Somehow it is. There's no obvious motive and no robbery. All we know for sure is that this woman lived in the same complex as Vonda Cantu. In fact, Dolores Griego was on Vonda's porch when she was killed. Thirty-four years old."

"I can't imagine what *that's* all about. Zachary and Marcus were both dead days before. However, I see your point. Three murders, two missing women. This can't all be coincidence. Plus," he added with a grin, "I'm sure there's plenty you're not telling me—not that I blame you."

Amy smiled at his insight. "True. And true. Do you think Zachary could have raped Dixie at the party?"

"I wouldn't bet against it. Like I said, the guy was a shithead. And *you* know for sure. You're the undercover cop that arrested him on Thursday."

It wasn't a question and Amy considered denying it. Since the man was now deceased, that case was essentially closed. Finally, she nodded. "Yes. They assigned me earlier in the day. Before that, I'd never even heard of him. The truth is, they were watching Zachary long before and expected him to make a move."

Waldo nodded sadly. "I knew he was up to something, just didn't know what it was. Date-raping is real low-life shit. I wouldn't have put up with that, not even to spare his family or the business. Friday morning, there was a preliminary meeting by company lawyers on the situation. They glossed it over for Cameron's sake. When I got back to Philly later in the day, they gave me the real facts. The bust was solid, according to them. Zach was in a world of trouble."

"Yes, he was." Amy digested that and put the brakes on. *Dammit!* Time to take back control of this wacko date from her hormones which apparently, had run amok. No matter the circumstances, she couldn't reveal certain things about the connected cases, even in trying to solve them. Keep playing by the rules was the way, now with serious doubts that Kurt Waldo had killed anyone. "Let me ask you something—off the record. Seriously. I understand your loyalty to Cameron Chastang. If he knew, or thought he knew, who killed his son, would he be likely to retaliate?"

"Loaded question." Waldo studied her for a moment then smiled. "No pun intended. Okay. I do know Cameron. He's a gentle sort and down deep, I think he realizes his son was a lost cause. Do I think he's capable? Possibly. That is, if the guilty person was going to get away with it. Maybe … And that's a big *maybe*. But Cameron is thoughtful, a smart, natural-born businessman. Not a reckless bone in his body. Right now, he's coming to grips with what happened. He's still wrapping his head around it, searching for peace. I'm telling you he would *never* want one of the people with answers to die. I'm sure of it."

"Okay. So, if at some point he *did* want to, you know, take revenge, would he come to you for something like that?"

"Honestly, yes. I can see it. He's not a street person and would have no idea where to begin. If he decided on that course, which I think is unlikely, I'm almost certain he would ask for advice, recommendations. He *didn't*—I give you my word. And I'd bet a year's pay that Cameron Chastang isn't behind anything that's happened this soon."

Wow. If this was true, and she felt that it was, then they needed to rethink the motives. "All right. Since we're on a roll with all this honesty, tell me one more thing."

Waldo nodded, pleased. "I absolutely will."

"We got a tip from someone connected to this case. You know Klaus Einsohn?"

"Sure. Senior exec, electrical engineering his specialty. I heard his family came to America in the fifties. Overall, a decent guy."

"The tip we got was that Zachary talked to him about Marcus Jarrett. Overheard by someone in the office. Zachary told Einsohn that Marcus Jarrett wanted him to confess to the rape. He was worried and wanted you assigned to handle Marcus."

Waldo looked stunned for several seconds, then turned grim and said, "No way. First off, Klaus Einsohn would not come to me with a bullshit assignment like that. He knows I wasn't too fond of Zachary."

"So, you're saying Einsohn or even Zachary Chastang never approached you at all about Marcus Jarrett?"

"That's what I'm saying. Never happened."

"Do you think maybe Einsohn did have the conversation, told Zachary yes, then blew it off?"

Waldo shrugged. "Sure, I could see Klaus placating him. We all knew Zach and his ways. And for the record, I didn't kill Marcus, either."

"Okay, fine." She felt it was the truth. "I accept that. Now, one more thing. You know I agreed to this date because I thought you'd have information I want. Or that you might be guilty of something. There's one thing that's not clear—why'd you ask me out in the first place?"

Waldo stared at her for a moment. "Are you being serious?"

"Yes, of course."

"I suppose it comes as a shock that a man's attracted to you."

Amy looked at him askance. "We only met when I was in your office trying to push you for information. Now I'm supposed to believe that you called up and asked me out because you *like* me?"

Waldo laughed. "Hell, *yes!* Did you bother to look in the mirror before you left home? You're a knock-out. And if you don't mind the observation, built like a centerfold."

"Well, thank you. It's just that—"

"It's more than that, though. You're smart but didn't slip into a quiet nine to five. I like a woman who accepts challenges. So, yeah, there's attraction coming from my side. I know I'm a little older than you, maybe … *ten years?* I don't see that as a problem. Besides, my family is from this area. I make a decent living. Why *shouldn't* I ask you out?"

Definitely a runaway train. This was bad … So bad it could be good … But horrible timing. Waldo's voice was deep and soothing and he sounded so damned sincere. He claimed not to know of any link between the two murders. An innocent man wouldn't know. *Did Waldo? Did he know because he set it up and was pretending not to? Was this guy for real or was it a game?* All she could say was, "Six."

"What?"

Amy smiled. "You're *six* years older than me."

"Oh." Waldo laughed again. "Even better."

Amy cringed, thinking about all this being recorded. It had definitely moved into *flirting* mode. This man had a lot of testosterone that seemed to radiate in his gaze. She'd never hear the end of it from Frank and Cruz. Her professional instincts told her to just cut her losses and get up to leave. Yet, she knew there was more to it. Had to be. On one hand, he'd killed Marcus Jarrett and planted roofies to throw the cops off his scent. On the other hand, he was telling the truth—leaving one thing out.

"I think there could be something else," Amy said. "I mean, since we're being honest with each other. Maybe something you aren't telling me . . ."

Waldo paused and seemed to consider her words. "I *am* being truthful. I asked you out because I really want to get to know you." After a moment, he leaned in and spoke a little quieter. "All right. There *is* another reason. You caught my attention and I haven't stopped thinking of you from the first moment I saw you." He shrugged. "I don't know … Maybe because you're smart, but tough as nails. And, well … another part of it is because I have *excellent* night vision."

Amy frowned at first and then her eyes widened. "Are you saying what I think you're saying?"

Waldo broke into a grin. "In the hall at McGrail's house when your towel fell off—I almost *shit myself.*"

CHAPTER 21

Frank sat in a corner booth nursing his third O'Doul's. From his vantage point, Amy and Waldo were blocked, so he'd snuck up by the bar a few times for a quick peek. There didn't seem to be any shortage of conversation so perhaps progress was being made. Also, if Adrienne heard any bad indicators, she would call. The last time he checked, Cruz was chatting with a couple of guys while keeping one eye on the action. Looking around the pub, there were two waitresses he'd slept with at some point in the past, both attractive, though younger than him. Without trying too hard, he could also count up a few regular barflies that he'd had sexual encounters with over the years. Some would come home with him tonight if he asked. Somehow those thoughts didn't seem as gratifying as they once had. Was he in some sort of rut? Or was it his parents' influence that had him questioning life choices? It had occurred to him recently that among his over-30 friends and colleagues, he was not the only single man. He was also not the only one without children. However, every man from his in-crowd was married or divorced. He was indeed the only man who'd never been married even once.

Frank came out of his reverie and looked up when he realized someone was standing next to him. It was Cruz … and Amy. She slid into the booth across from him and Cruz sat alongside.

"What happened?" Frank said. "Where's Waldo?"

Amy frowned. "Is that a *joke?*"

"No, dammit. What the hell happened?"

"It was ridiculous. He knew exactly what we were doing."

"So? That doesn't mean you should bail out."

"In this case, it made sense. I sent him on his way and told him I was calling an Uber. Christ, he knows it's all a ruse, anyway. Besides, he didn't kill Marcus Jarrett."

"Why not?"

"Okay. First off, he's been checking out Zachary Chastang for a while. Chastang rented cars sporadically for no obvious reason. Oh, and remember they found a GPS tracker on the one he used?"

"Yeah . . ."

"Uh-huh." Amy exhaled loudly. "Waldo put it there."

"Really?" Frank was interested. "Just to see what the dirtball was up to?"

"Yep."

"Why'd he admit that?"

"Because right before, he admitted something else. He … Well, he's the one who broke in your house."

262

"He is?" Frank smacked his hand on the table. "Then we can tie him to the murders."

Amy shook her head. "No, we can't! He left at seven that morning with two engineers for a meeting. He was in Wilmington when Chastang was shot."

"I know that. He still could've ordered it. So why the hell did he break in my place and assault a police detective?"

"He didn't know who I was. He was tracking Chastang that night, trying to figure out what he was up to. He followed the signal from the nightclub to the apartment we had ready. I went in with Chastang, then a van pulls up. A pizza delivery and two men in suits show up. I came out and got in the van to change. Waldo was watching—had no idea who we were or what was happening. The Chastang family being wealthy, he thought it was some kind of shake-down. Waldo saw me leave and followed, planned on questioning me."

"And you messed up his plans."

Amy smiled. "Yes, I did—Waldo was impressed. He had no idea I was a cop. Shortly after he got back to his car, he got a text alert telling him to contact the family's attorneys. Then all the pieces made sense."

Cruz spoke for the first time. "Not to interrupt, but Waldo could still have killed Marcus Jarrett, right?"

Amy shook her head. "No. Timing's off. Waldo was definitely watching me and the op; he described what happened. This was down just off Grey's Ferry Avenue. It means Waldo would've been following me up to Frank's place—probably took thirty minutes—right around the time of Jarrett's death."

"Shit," Frank said. "Jarrett's house is over in West Mount Airy. So—no way. This is nuts. We solved my B&E, but nothing else. I don't suppose you want to arrest Waldo for manhandling you?"

A slight grin formed on Amy's lips. "Not really."

"That's what I thought. Lieutenant Trainer is going to hear this whole fucking thing and he's not going to like it. Especially your fight with Waldo. You'll need to lay it all out."

"Yeah," she said reluctantly, "I thought of that. The recording will be analyzed, but based on our conversation, I don't see Waldo's involvement. He's as confused about both murders as we are."

"I hear ya," Frank said. "I get that he couldn't have killed Marcus. But now he's implicated in Chastang's death, even if he couldn't have pulled the trigger. It could have been on company orders, behind Cameron Chastang's back. What happens won't be our call."

"I know, I know." Amy sighed. "We've got to turn it all over to Trainer. It'll be a mess. He'll make the decision to approach the district attorney."

Amy waited with Cruz by the door while Frank paid his tab. She noticed a pretty forty-ish woman in a tight dress sipping a cocktail who scooted right over as he passed by. Frank paused and they spoke briefly, the woman beaming some come-hither smiles.

Amy grinned. "You figure she's asking for directions?"

"Ha." Cruz shook his head. "Not likely. That's Carly Davenport, party gal. A regular around these parts since her husband flew the coup three years ago. She got an apartment in University City, nice cottage in Stone Harbor, and a Lexus LC in the divorce."

"Who'd the husband run off with? Let me guess—his secretary?"

"Yoga instructor."

"Ha. Figures. What's her place at the beach like?"

Cruz raised his eyebrows. "What makes you think I'd know?"

Amy watched Carly run her hand up and down Frank's arm. Next came an amused giggle, followed by a standard hair flip. Frank looked flattered but there was something else. His posture was more re-laxed, his expression more aloof than she would have expected. She turned back to Cruz with a roll of her eyes. "Educated guess. So, c'mon. What's it like?"

"Okay, fine." Cruz shrugged. "Pretty sweet. Bayside on 3rd Avenue, private parking, three bedrooms."

"Sounds nice."

"It is. I've only been there twice, I think. You know, for parties. Carly tends to, you know, invite small groups down some weekends. She's sad. I think it just her—"

"Never mind that. Actually … This has been a weird night all around. I really just want to get out of here."

Frank walked up. "Well, we ready to go?"

Amy smiled. This was too juicy to pass up. "That depends. Are you leaving with us?"

Frank laughed. "Good one. That's my insurance agent. There were some questions."

"She doesn't care about insurance. Probably wanted to invite you down to her crib in Stone Harbor."

Frank froze. "You know Carly?"

Amy and Cruz broke out laughing. "Not hardly," she said and patted Frank on the back. "Let's get out of here. I'm anxious to go get yelled at. Maybe disciplined for breaking protocol. Not to mention embarrassed when that recording goes on record."

Frank let go an amused grin. "Don't sweat it. I get in that much trouble every few weeks."

"I know. You're rubbing off on me."

On the way outside, Amy could sense the wheels turning in Frank's head. Detective partnerships were intimate—not on a sexual level. There was bond, almost psychic, in that they sensed what the other would think or do in a given situation. She figured a big part of it came from constantly comparing the results of so much observation and analysis. It was amazing the variety of conclusions, theories, suspicions, and even vague hunches, that came out of raw data. Right now, Frank was still fixated on Kurt Waldo's involvement—she could feel it. He'd be willing to ride it out for now, keep all that to himself and let things unfold naturally. Even so, he'd be expecting to arrest Waldo for something before this was over.

"That's odd," Amy said, squinting into the setting sun directly ahead. Things were quieter on the street than a little while ago. But the Astro van … Something wasn't right. They were about forty feet away with no cars in the way. The door wasn't closed which set off Amy's alarm bells. "The door is ajar. Adrienne, come back!"

Frank said, "Anything?"

"No. She should be hearing us talk. And my ear-bud's still in place. Adrienne, come back. I say again, Adrienne, come back." After a moment, she shook her head.

"Damn." Frank raised his hand to a fist and they all came to a halt. Amy watched him study the layout. No one in close proximity. The nearest pedestrians were further up the sidewalk heading away from them.

Frank spoke quickly and clearly. "Flank the van, Amy left, then to me. Cruz right, then front. Watch for civilians. I'll draw—you two, hands on weapons. I'll get the door. Go!"

Amy swung wide into the street, took a glance in the van's driver-side window. Nothing. Frank crouched down, moved fast, and flipped open the rear door with his left hand, completely blocking her view.

Amy quickly came around from the side to see Frank holstering his Glock. Adrienne was right where they'd left her in the operations chair, except now her arms and legs were duct-taped to it. She was gagged and her eyes frantic. Apart from that, she seemed okay. "Oh, fuck," Amy blurted.

Frank let out a sigh and leaned in, gently starting to peel the tape from Adrienne's cheek. "Yeah. I was thinking that, too."

"I believe I gave you two days to come up with something." Lieutenant Trainer looked at the clock and then returned a critical gaze to his detectives. "That was *sixty-one* hours ago by my calculations. Now I have an assault on support personnel and theft of police equipment to deal with. I was here all day and now I'm back in my office nearing eleven PM. Maybe one of you could do me the courtesy of an explanation."

Amy hadn't had time to change from the showy orange outfit she'd worn to meet Waldo. Yes, it had been chosen for practical reasons in the line of duty … At present time, however, that rationale didn't make her feel better about it. She wiggled backwards and subtly tugged on the hem in an effort to show a little less thigh. Frank was alongside her in deep thought, apparently trying to come up with a way to ward off their superior's wrath. Fortunately, Adrienne Barlow was only shaken up and not injured. Her attacker had made off with a digital recorder, laptop computer, and a bag of accessories from the Astro van. Fortunately, no weapons.

"There was no reason to expect trouble," Frank said. "It's a low-crime area."

"Any ID?"

"Nothing. Adrienne says he wore gloves and his face was covered. She just opened the door for some air and there he was. Slipped inside and closed the door. Pulled out a revolver. She's not sure of the make. White, average build, maybe six foot."

"Which fits about one-third of the adult male population. And you're telling me there are no witnesses for a man in a mask half a block from Rittenhouse Square Park?"

"We're working that angle. So far—nothing. He was pretty slick, moved fast."

"Do you have any theories, however remote, that you'd care to share?"

"We have one lead, sir," Amy said. "In our discussion, Kurt Waldo said he was followed on the way to Friar Tuck's Pub. He thought it was ours. A white Kia Optima."

Trainer nodded. "Thin. But you figure that could be our thief?"

"Possible, sir."

"All right, then. Follow up on it. Keep in mind, we can't be sure that Waldo knows cars well. Optimas share the same body style with the Hyundai Sonata and are similar to other models. See if anyone connected with either case owns one. Then all employees of both Pierce Brothers and Jarrett Enterprises. Check stolen vehicles, too."

"Right away, sir."

"Unless we recover the recordings made of the operation, we'll have to rely on your memory. You say that Kurt Waldo made no admissions to implicate himself in these murders?"

"No. He'd been watching Zachary Chastang because he often used rental cars when he wasn't going out of town. Waldo did say that he's the one who placed the GPS device they found on the Austin-Healey."

"That puts him on our list of players."

"It's exculpatory in a way, sir. He was looking out for his company's interests by keeping track of Zachary Chastang, a known troublemaker. Besides that, he was in Wilmington when Chastang was killed."

"I see that. There's another possibility. What if Waldo is lying? Maybe he made up the story about being followed by one of the most common automobiles on the road. Kurt Waldo has many resources. Did it occur to you that one of his operatives may be the man in the mask? And the one who shot Chastang?"

"There'd be no reason to have the recording stolen. He didn't even have to meet me. It was *his* idea."

"He could be toying with us. Don't look at reasoning before you first consider *facts* and *evidence*. A motive may not be clear, then will come to light later in an investigation. Possibly, Chastang's arrest was the last straw and his murder was sanctioned within the company. Why don't you try bringing Waldo in?"

Frank spoke up before Amy could answer. "If Waldo has something cooking, I'd rather he thinks he got away with it, at least for now. In the meantime, Kristi and Turk will help us check up and down Walnut for security cameras and interview shop owners. We may come up with video or a witness. We'll also run down the white Kia angle, see if it flies."

Trainer regarded Frank, then Amy, with a suspicious glare. "Come up with something fast."

Alvin Cruz turned off Henry Street and followed the directions he'd pulled off the net to Shawmont Avenue. It turned into a very rural-looking section with big secluded homes amidst old trees. Spotting the right mailbox, he glanced at his watch—11:09 PM. There wasn't much of a shoulder on the two-lane road so he drove past his destination by a few hundred feet. He then eased into the mouth of a wide driveway, glad that he'd taken the time to plot a basic route from satellite view on Google Maps. There was no house in view so he hoped his weathered Pontiac would remain unobtrusive while he left to do a little reconnaissance. Grabbing a leather case off the seat, he set off on foot.

Klaus Einsohn was originally an engineer and had moved up the ladder at Pierce Brothers, becoming a VP and one of Cameron Chastang's top advisors. Since Zachary Chastang was overheard requesting help from Einsohn, it wouldn't hurt to check the guy out.

It was a clear and cool night, about 69 degrees. He had a powerful flashlight in his pack, choosing not to use it unless necessary. The moonlight would have to do. Mostly tall oak and dogwood trees, some weeping willow and assorted evergreens. The underbrush wasn't too thick and with short, careful steps, he was able to slip through far enough to see twinkling lights that would be Einsohn's house up ahead. He came to the driveway and eased along its edge until coming to a detached three-car garage. Slipping around back, he crossed the yard to a point about sixty feet from the house. Two-story colonial, old, in pristine condition. A few huge Silver Maples would provide shade on sunny days. Cruz knew Einsohn bought the place in 1984. With five bedrooms on 1.7 acres, it appraised in the 1.3M range. Probably built in the fifties, now with extensive remodeling and restoration. A wrap-around porch that covered the back and one side was wide and dotted with nice outdoor furniture. Although he couldn't see it, he knew from research there was a big in-ground pool out back. The man lived well. He had grown kids who must have enjoyed their childhood here.

Cruz settled in next to a Colorado Spruce that was meticulously trimmed in a nice cone shape. He was in darkness, comfortably away from the porch lights, and on a slight hill which improved his perspective. Two vague forms could be seen on the back porch—and in a moment, he'd see them better. Reaching for his night-vision binoculars, he raised them up and smiled as the green-tinted imaged formed. The unmistakable Kurt Waldo was seated next to Klaus Einsohn, both engaged in conversation. Einsohn at 65, had a head of neat steel gray hair, and at five-eight, looked tiny next to Waldo, who wore the same sport coat he'd had on at Friar Tuck's. Cruz quickly set up a compact listening device and aimed the small parabolic microphone. The unit could easily pick up sounds through unprotected windows across an open area of 250 feet. Cruz stretched out on the grass, clicked it on and stuck in a wireless earpiece. Although the image was merely serviceable, the audio was crisp and clear.

Waldo exhaled. "So, it's true then?"

"Yes. Zach cornered me at work. Told some crazy story that Marcus Jarrett was trying to get him in trouble. Said he didn't do anything wrong. Had sex with a woman at Marcus's party, then later she claimed it was rape. He said it was to squeeze him for money."

"And you told him I'd handle it?"

"No. Not at all. He did bring your name up. He said 'It's Kurt's job, protecting the company.' Something like that. I wasn't about to stand there and argue with him in the supply room. I told him I'd see what I could do. That's all there was. We both know Zach was full of shit. The arrest came and then he died. That's it—the whole story."

"All right. That checks with what I heard. We're good. So, what else? The cops have no idea where Vonda Cantu is?"

"No. They're definitely looking. So far, nothing."

"Damned odd."

"Got what else you wanted," Einsohn said. *"I've had our resources working on this non-stop since yesterday afternoon."*

"Good work. Any skeletons?"

"Sorry. Not really. Frank McGrail, raised on the family ranch near Jim Thorpe, PA. His father is a retired sheriff up there, well respected, and does some amateur blacksmithing for locals. McGrail's got a few reprimands, just about the twenty-year mark. Four officer-involved shootings— all cleared by the board. Doesn't go after promotions. He's popular in the DA's office because his cases hold up and he's smooth on the witness stand. Got a small house in the Northeast. Single, no kids. Dates around, no one seriously."

"Military background, right?"

"Yep. Marines. Honorable discharge in '99. Incidentally, his older brother died in Afghanistan, 1994."

"Yeah. McGrail carries himself like a soldier. I'm more interested in Amy Lepone."

Einsohn's shoulders sagged as he let out a grunt. *"Yeah. She's the one who nailed Zach in that police setup. Would have been a nightmare for us all. But no red flags. Sorry. Lepone seems solid."*

"That's all right. What do we know?"

"Local girl, never married. Graduated from Roxborough High, decent grades. Bachelor's degree from Penn State, 3.21 GPA. Started out as a political science major, then switched to criminal justice. Went right into the Academy. Apartment on Ridge Avenue, has lived there three years."

"She got a Mustang?"

"Older one. A 1993."

"Hobbies?"

"Kind of an athlete. She runs, at least a few times per week. Played soccer as a kid, then varsity gymnastics in high school. Cheerleader, too."

"Intriguing."

"For sure. She's also into karate and kickboxing now."

"I had a hunch about that."

"What?"

Waldo grinned. "Never mind. What else?"

"She's had instruction but works out mostly on her own—doesn't compete. People who've seen her train say she's got the proficiency of a brown belt."

"I believe it. How long a detective?"

"Seventeen months. Partnered with McGrail all that time."

"They lovers?"

"Our people can't be sure. Not much chatter about it until recently. Last week she was at McGrail's place, middle of the night. There was a break-in. So, a possibility."

Waldo shrugged. "I think I'll let her slide on that one. What else?"

"Financials look okay. She dates, no one special. Got a few friends from childhood, no heavy social life. Father deceased, mother alive and well in the family home." Einsohn cleared his throat. "I'm sorry, Kurt. I realize this isn't what you wanted to hear."

Waldo shook his head. "It's fine. Just need to know who I'm dealing with."

"Well, that's the basics. Both seem clean. We can keep at it. If Lepone is sleeping with her partner, that might be useful. Other than that, there's no real leverage here."

"Not so much leverage, I need. It's just a matter of tactics. If they're closet alcoholics, involved in lawsuits, own big yachts, whatever—that tells me one thing. If they seem like stand-up, honest cops—that tells me something, too. It's not good or bad. I just deal accordingly."

"Understood." He removed something from a file folder and handed it across the desk. "There's one other thing. This man's name is Alvin Cruz."

Waldo looked it over. "Heard of him, I think."

"Local private investigator and Frank McGrail's close friend. Age thirty-six. His father was a popular newspaper man, killed by a drunk driver. Cruz had dinner at McGrail's place last night. He was driving an old van that's supposedly a special undercover police vehicle."

Waldo frowned. "Why would this guy have access to it?"

"That's a mystery. In fact, so is Cruz. Very sketchy livelihood."

"Must be doing leg work for the cops."

"It would be unofficial—but yes, that's our thought, too. Waldo stood up. Thanks, Klaus. You're thorough. Appreciate it."

Cruz was smiling as he packed up, then headed back to his car. He came through the brush and was happy to see no police cars or irate homeowners around. He jumped in his car and drove away thinking that Kurt Waldo was just a little too nosy for his liking.

CHAPTER 22

Amy began her Wednesday morning with an early chat about the Dolores Griego homicide. Jerry Cunningham had run aground after a thorough check of her current boyfriend, ex-boyfriends, co-workers, neighbors, relatives, and financial matters. No viable suspects had been uncovered. Even more frustrating was the lack of any reasonable motive for her to meet a violent death. She wasn't robbed. She had no mounting debts, no criminal ties, no jealous exes, no big life insurance policies, and her part-ownership of a donut shop produced an average income. Nothing out of the ordinary was found in her apartment. She was in good health and her tox screen showed no recent drug use. They shared info on the related cases and not surprisingly, Jerry brought up Kurt Waldo as a possible suspect. Amy played down the notion and was basically Waldo's alibi, anyway, a fact she wasn't anxious to reveal in detail.

Amy fused those facts with their current situation and it generated some interesting possibilities. Sometimes, the lack of apparent motive was a clue in itself. First, Vonda Cantu and Dixie Newberry were still missing and it was likely that they both knew Dolores. So why would Dolores have Vonda's key and why was she going in her apartment? Maybe the same reason anyone goes into someone else's residence. To borrow a book or a DVD. To drop something off. To check on the place. To water the plants. Amy concluded it might not be coincidence that those women disappeared the around the same time Dolores Griego was murdered. Amy remembered it well, particularly the initial mistaken identity, discovered only after she and Frank arrived on the scene. Both attractive, similar complexions. According to their information, Vonda Cantu was 27, 5-foot-8 and 136 pounds. Dolores Griego was 34, 5-foot-7 and 128 pounds. They both had long dark brown hair, just styled differently. Close up in good light, easily distinguishable. In the dark, coming from behind … not so much.

Had someone killed Dolores, thinking it was Vonda Cantu? If the killer spotted Dolores from a distance and moved in quickly when she got to the rear door of Vonda's place … At night in a relatively low-crime area, Dolores wouldn't be expecting trouble. Yes, it made sense. It might also explain what happened to Vonda and Dixie and why they hadn't been found. The killer could have realized his error, maybe even as Dolores fell to the ground. After that, he would have gone after the correct target. With Dixie's car in the apartment lot, it was assumed that she and

Vonda were together—which meant that Dixie was probably dead, too.

It also meant they'd never find a motive for Dolores Griego—there wasn't one since her death was incidental. They needed to focus on reasons to kill Vonda Cantu. It all fit together—but dammit, she really hoped she was wrong.

The big questions: *Who would want Vonda dead? What was it all about? And who was pulling the strings? What was the story behind ammo and cash in Vonda's drawer?* The money was only moderately suspicious on its own. Sitting next to rifle cartridges, the same type used to kill Zach Chastang ... They'd tested all of Vonda's dirty clothes for gunshot residue and found none, nor a rifle. They did come up with a Springfield Armory 1911 Range Officer in .45 caliber. According to Vonda's mother, that was a gift from dad on her twenty-first birthday. Besides, owning handguns was not uncommon—this was Pennsylvania. Most people had guns and, statewide, there were nearly 1.8 million concealed carry permits. All things considered, they had no irrefutable evidence, but a lot of things pointed to her guilt. Only her work schedule that day along with Zachary's movements produced an unfavorable timetable.

Adding it up: A military father. Hunting experience. Reasonable, although rushed, opportunity. Powerful motive for the rape of a friend. Winchester Special cartridges in her drawer. If Vonda had been killed at her back door instead of Dolores Griego, then investigators would have found the money and ammo just the same. Maybe Vonda got careless, not expecting a search of her apartment. It looked like Vonda killed Chastang out of revenge, and then someone targeted her in retaliation—but got the wrong person. It all added up. Yet for some reason, it didn't feel right.

"Hey there," a voice called out.

Amy turned and smiled. Nancy Bringham was a civilian police researcher in her mid-fifties. She'd been at the job for many years and could handle the jumble of requests from a busy squad of detectives with subtle efficiency. "Well, hello," Amy said eagerly. "Tell me you have something good."

"Possible." Nancy shrugged. "On that Kia you were interested in. We're still running down employees from Jarrett Enterprises and Pierce Brothers. Fourteen white Kias between the two companies— five of them the Optima model—nothing stands out so far. A call came in earlier on a missing car up on Algon Avenue. A man swears there should be a Kia Optima behind his neighbor's place."

"Did they send someone by?"

"Sure did," she said, and handed Amy the report. "The family is vacationing in the Poconos and can't be reached so far. A neighbor is taking care of the house and is sure the car should be there. Says it disappeared while he was at work, sometime between 8 A.M. and 4 P.M. yesterday."

"Thanks, Nancy. You're the best. Can you run this against our reports on both the Chastang and Jarrett murders? I'm looking for any commonalities you can find."

"Right away."

Amy skimmed the report and put it in the case folder. It could be just a mix-up—the missing Kia was simply sent in for servicing or borrowed by a brother-in-law. On the other hand, it could very well be the car that followed Kurt Waldo to Friar Tuck's. Vacationers were often targeted for burglaries and auto-theft since the loss wouldn't be discovered right away. Such vehicles would be used for a few days or a week, probably in the commission of felonies, and then sold to a chop shop or abandoned in a parking lot someplace. None of the information was really much help unless the car could be located.

"I saw your new boyfriend," Frank said from alongside her desk, appearing as he always did from out of nowhere. He was like a damned stealth fighter. For a large man he seemed to move without disturbing the air around him, probably a result of his military training.

Amy shook her head and cursed silently. She'd kind of expected this. Declining a trip to Pierce Brothers, it allowed Frank to go there alone for the purpose of leaning on Gilbert Kyser. It was something that needed done. She knew Kurt Waldo would likely be hovering around but she didn't want to cross his path again so soon. Avoiding the little chore carried advantages and disadvantages. She didn't really want to let Frank and Waldo do the male-bonding thing— God only knew what was said. In truth, she hadn't sorted out her feelings and just didn't want to talk to him yet. He'd admitted to breaking in Frank's house and attacking her—albeit with palliating circumstances. Which meant he'd already seen her naked, sort of. In the dark. Very briefly. The thought made her irritated—and tingly. At the pub, he'd been charming and sincere, viewing their meeting as an honest-to-goodness date, or at least it seemed that way. If they had met under different circumstances, she knew there'd be no denying a real interest on her part. Okay—if she was being honest with herself, there was already a real interest on her part. Amy enjoyed the exchange, accepted his explanations, found herself aroused, and gave him her cell number. An early morning text message had come in from Waldo that read: *Had a great time on our first date – or was that technically our second? Can we do it again?*

Some renegade hormones were saying *yes.*

"What about Kyser?" Amy said, not going for the bait. "Anything useful?"

Frank flopped into his chair. "Not directly. Kyser didn't come to work. Called in to his secretary and took off the rest of the week as personal days."

"That's interesting."

"For sure. I ended up speaking to a V.P. Okay guy, a real brain. He said Kyser has been acting a little squirrelly for the last few weeks. Kyser's secretary says the same. She called Kyser's home this morning, kind of a courtesy thing, to see if he was okay. No answer. She called Kyser's cell number and then also Joyce Kyser's cell number. Both went directly to voicemail."

"That's not a surprise," Amy said with an irritated frown. "Cruz and Joyce are probably sleeping late."

"Now, now. That isn't nice."

"True, right?"

"Well . . ." Frank shrugged. "Yeah, probably. Although, Cruz did throw us a bone."

Amy looked at him quizzically. "What?"

"Two bones in fact. Cruz did some snooping last night. Says that—"

"Snooping? The illegal kind?"

Frank shrugged. "Depends on your interpretation."

"Christ! You both drive me crazy with this stuff."

"Do you want to hear it or not?"

"Fine. Go ahead."

"Klaus Einsohn and Kurt Waldo were talking. Seems Kurt is very interested in you and me. Einsohn used the company's clout and had us checked out. You'll be happy to know there's no indication you and I are sleeping together."

Amy was stunned for a second. "Well, dammit. We're *not* sleeping together."

"I know. That's *why* it's good news."

"Very funny. What else?"

"Nothing incriminating. Waldo is really sniffing around this case. They talked about Vonda Cantu.

And Cruz. They know Cruz uses the police Astro van sometimes and wonder how he rates."

"I wonder that myself."

Frank laughed. "Give the guy a break, will you? He's useful. Remember he followed Kyser's car to Tacony Creek Park last week? Still got a GPS on it. Kyser's Lexus was parked in the Northeast Shopping Center on Roosevelt Boulevard. Didn't budge all day yesterday, according to Cruz."

"So, Kyser never went back to his car and called off work the rest of the week. Very odd. Will Cruz tell us if it moves?"

"It already did. Got towed."

"Good. Now you want my thoughts on a few things?"

"Sure."

Amy sat back and offered her theory that Dolores Griego was mistakenly killed instead of Vonda Cantu. Even though their investigation showed Vonda as, chronologically, an unlikely suspect, her shooting experience and strong motive would seem convincing to an outsider. Even if it wasn't ordered by the grieving father, a loyal friend or colleague might be quick to take action. The likely scenario was that someone believed Vonda fired the shot to kill Zachary Chastang.

"That'll be a tough road to go down," Frank said. "It'd mean a strategy meeting between us, the brass, and the DA if we're going to take on people connected to a VIP."

"True." Amy noticed he didn't say out loud what he was surely thinking. The investigation would look closely at Cameron Chastang's staff, colleagues, and associates, in a search for possible assets. Kurt Waldo, as head of the company's security and a known weapon's expert, could become a major focus. Such a complex case would involve a task force that would turn over every possible rock. Waldo was in the clear for actually killing Chastang and Marcus Jarrett. But he still could be involved. And what about Dolores Griego? Would he have a solid alibi for Saturday night when she was stabbed on Vonda Cantu's porch? Hopefully. Her instincts, or maybe it was hormones, were saying he wasn't involved at all.

"You think," Frank asked, "that Vonda is all right?"

Amy shook her head sadly. "At first, maybe. Now I don't hold out hope for that. Too much time has passed. No credit card activity and no sign of her. Whoever killed Dolores Griego realized the error and got Vonda. Probably Dixie, too."

"That's a shame. Nice girls. How does Marcus Jarrett fit into all this?"

"I really can't say. I'm sure there're two separate agendas. He may have been killed to protect Zach Chastang. Not by Waldo, since he couldn't have made it all the way to Jarrett's house at the time of death."

"He could have ordered it done."

"No. He's … not the sort."

"Uh-huh. Will you use that reasoning on Lieutenant Trainer."

Amy suppressed a grin and shook her head. "No. I'd use something else. His background and training, for one thing. Waldo is real good, according to what you found out. He was part of a front-line infiltration unit and I know what that means. He's a planner, all about strategy. I can't see him sending in a flunkie to sit down with Jarrett over a beer, and then shoot him with a .32 caliber revolver. But that same night, decide to tail Chastang. Then watch the sting with no idea what was happening and follow me back to your place. It wouldn't make sense."

Frank studied her for a moment, then said. "Impressive. Any other reason?"

"He doesn't come across as someone who would order a hit on an innocent man to protect an asshole like Zach Chastang."

"I hear what you're saying and I'm inclined to agree. Stating the obvious—it's conjecture, not evidence. You *like* him."

Amy was taken aback. "Excuse me?"

Frank laughed. "C'mon. Admit it. Waldo interests you."

"He's … *all right*. Never mind that. Let's take a step back and look at the big picture. If I'm right and those drugs were planted in Marcus Jarrett's bedroom, then someone was manipulating our impression of him."

"I'll buy that. We'd be looking for someone who killed a date-rapist, not a successful businessman."

"Yes. And whoever it was, may have wanted to take the focus off Zach Chastang. Of course, they wouldn't have known Chastang would be killed the next day."

"Sure. Although, let's not forget the other possible scenario. That the murders are totally unrelated. Somebody just flat-out wanted Marcus Jarrett dead and killed him."

"Yeah. Then, it probably wouldn't be an ally of Chastang."

"Right," Frank said. "I got a hunch this all circles back to Gilbert Kyser. He was at the party when Dixie was raped. Weeks later, Cruz sees Kyser meet Vonda in the park but we're not sure what it's all about. Now Kyser suddenly ditches his car and bags work. Plus, he's been paying off Corky Buck, your standard dirtball-for-hire. Kyser and Buck have something cooking."

"Yes. And now that you mention it—what about Joyce Kyser, his wife? Maybe she's up to no good. I mean, besides the *adultery*."

"Ouch," Frank said with a laugh. "Nice *dig* you stuck in there."

"Oh, c'mon. These cases are getting to me. You know I don't really give a damn. I'm not exactly a prude."

"Ahhh, how well I know. I've met a few of your friends. I've heard about those school days of yours."

"Hey! Give it a rest. That was college—a one-time thing on vacation."

Frank paused and a smile spread across his face. "I was talking about high school— the senior prank."

"Oh! Um, right. You heard about that, huh?"

"Yeah. Getting your boyfriend to weld the school's front and back doors shut. Clever. So, no one could get in the building on the last day of classes."

Amy shrugged and gave a nod.

"And you never got in trouble?"

"No." Amy sighed. "A few friends know the truth. And rumors fly around. But we got away with it."

"I appreciate the simplicity. I have to admit that's damn good!"

"Well, thanks. Just … don't tell my mother!"

"I'll take it to my grave. So—what happened on vacation?"

Amy replied promptly. "Nothing … really. Silly thing at the beach."

"Sure, sure. You're not a prude. But you definitely like to pick on Cruz."

Amy exhaled. "Yeah. I guess I do."

"Why is that?"

"I'm not really sure. But you have to admit this thing looks damned suspicious. Joyce hired Cruz because she thought her husband was cheating. Now suddenly she's having an affair with Cruz. It doesn't follow."

"Like maybe Joyce Kyser has an agenda? You're saying she got Cruz emotionally involved for some scheme in all this?"

"Wouldn't be the first time we've seen it."

"Cruz is too sharp for that."

Amy scoffed and was considering a snappy come-back when the phone on her desk jingled. She picked up and listened for a minute, then thanked the call-er. Turning to Frank, she said, "Nancy was checking something for me. Get this. A white Kia Optima is missing from the Oxford Circle area. The family is away and a neighbor says it disappeared yesterday. Nancy ran search parameters for any connections with all our suspects, witnesses, everything. It's not much, but Corky Buck grew up on the same block of Algon Avenue—just four houses down. His mother, Louann Rekito Buck, lived there until she died in 2014."

"Mmmm." Frank ruminated for a moment. "Okay. That means Buck knows the neighborhood, maybe keeps in contact with a few old pals around there. If he wanted to steal a car, it makes sense that he'd do a little homework. A vacationing family is a good mark. You think Buck boosted the car and used it to follow Waldo to Friar Tuck's?"

"It makes sense somehow. Gilbert Kyser works with Waldo and we know Kyser is paying off Buck for some-thing. Buck has to be the one who tied up Adrienne in the van and stole the equipment."

"It's not enough to charge him. Not yet. Unless we can connect him to the stolen Kia."

"We got enough to question Kyser. We both think he's involved. Plus, Joyce Kyser hired Cruz to follow him and that puts them both right in the middle of all this."

"True enough." Frank grinned. "The good thing is—Kyser's fancy car was towed and is in police custody. Sooner or later, he'll want it back and will come to *us*."

CHAPTER 23

Cruz watched from the Astro van as Mindy Lyons pulled up to the Kyser home and parked her big SUV in the driveway. Stepping out, he had to admire the view. Long legs and a lean figure in a tan sheath dress—businesslike, but very sleek. She knocked and Joyce opened up right away, admitting her with a quick hug. Okay. Mindy was expected. Cruz leaned back and flicked a switch, glad that he'd finally decided to have both eyes and ears on the situation inside. Chosen to be inconspicuous, the camera was small, brown, and securely hidden under a shelf. Unless someone bent down and looked close, it would be nearly invisible. There were risks, of course. If Joyce ever found out about that he had bugged her home, and now included video surveillance, sure, she might be pissed. But it was for her own good.

Cruz adjusted the monitor and waited until the women appeared from the kitchen with glasses of wine and a small snack tray. They settled on the couch and began some small talk. Joyce looked so cute and tiny next to her friend. Both were blonde, but Mindy was tall, larger framed, and had curly hair in a puffy style that came to her shoulders. This was just a social call, so Cruz leaned back, getting comfortable. One thing about stakeouts and surveillance, you quickly learned patience and how to accept that hours might pass before one scrap of useful information unfolded. This was probably a waste of time, so he'd half-pay attention while reading a Linda Howard novel.

"Oh, Mindy. I don't know where to begin. It's a long story."

"It always is."

"I really don't know what Gilbert's up to. I guess I haven't for quite some time."

"You still think he's whacked out on drugs?"

"I'm sure of it. As you know … I have proof. Well, a kind of proof."

"Yes. I remember. Did you ever have all those different pills analyzed? I mean, to really know what kind of addiction it is."

"No. I never did. They're gone. I don't know where he hid them now. So, I decided to hire a private detective to follow him."

"You did?"

"Yes. I just felt I needed to know what's happening. It turns out he's been paying off some creep. It must be for drugs. I mean, what else could it be for?"

"Well, I really couldn't say. You know him better than anyone. Where's Gilbert now?"

"That's the thing. I don't know. He left his car in a parking lot at a shopping center downtown but hasn't gone back to it."

"This private investigator told you that?"

"Yes. That was yesterday and he hasn't been home."

"My goodness, Joyce. You poor dear."

"Well. There's more. This private investigator ... I've started seeing him."

"Started seeing him? As in ... Well, you're thinking of getting intimate? Or is it like, well, you know—" --"

"We had sex on Sunday. And a few times since then."

Mindy laughed out loud. "Oh, my God."

"For the first time in my life I feel like things are out of control. I'm really at a loss."

"This private eye ... Is he a decent guy?"

"Yes. He's sweet. It's not like he started hitting on me. There was ... chemistry. I didn't give him any choice."

"Oh, my."

Joyce sighed. "Yep."

"Well then, what will you do about Gilbert?"

"I'm honestly not sure what to do. I don't think I love Gilbert anymore. But I care what happens to him. Oh, my. I'm supposed to go to lunch."

"With ... him? The P.I.?"

Joyce laughed weakly. "No, not hardly. Sylvia Jarrett. Just something informal at her place."

"I haven't seen Sylvia for a while. Not much since, well ... you know. She's very nice."

"Would you like to come? Might be fun."

"She wouldn't mind?"

"Not at all. Just between us, she always felt you and Marcus were a great match."

"Really? That's nice. I didn't know. Although she's always been sweet to me."

"Please come. I think she's having crab cakes. Very summery. I'm sure we could get the help to mix us up a few margaritas."

"You know, that sounds great. I'd like to tag along."

Cruz was fully listening and had put down the novel several minutes ago. He watched as Joyce and Mindy prepared to leave, then headed for the front door. They took separate cars, with Mindy following Joyce north on Corinthian Avenue.

Shaking his head, he tried to get a handle on that conversation. *What the hell was all that about?* Why would Joyce admit their affair? And the really odd thing—drugs? Cruz distinctly remembered Joyce saying her husband was not into drugs. Yet, now she was discussing Gilbert's ongoing drug issue with Mindy. And apparently, she showed Mindy a secret stash at some earlier time. *Why wouldn't Joyce just explain if Gilbert had a drug problem? Was she embarrassed? Afraid?* Maybe she didn't want Gilbert in rehab or in jail and not making the big bucks. Stranger things happened. However, he'd need to get the real story out of her if they were going to solve this mess. At least he knew Joyce would be safe and having a nice time at the big Jarrett mansion. For now, he'd get back to figuring out Gilbert Kyser.

Amy hung up the phone, glanced at her watch—1:23 pm—and jotted a few notes as she started to jump up to go find Frank. Since he'd come up behind her with his usual silent approach, she had to stop halfway out of her chair. "Damn it!"

"Woah, what's the rush?"

"We just got this from the switchboard. The Jarrett family maid called in. She's worried about Sylvia; says she was acting strangely."

Frank shrugged. "All rich people seem nuts. How can she tell?"

"Apparently this is out of the ordinary. Sylvia was having lunch with two other ladies. Then they were all just gone."

"They probably went out."

"The maid says that Sylvia Jarrett wouldn't leave the premises without telling anyone or giving instructions. Plus, she found Sylvia's necklace on the floor of the patio. It's valuable."

"Okay. Sounds a little weird. Why don't they send a patrol car by?"

Amy smiled. "Lieutenant Trainer said to send *us*."

"Uh-huh. Two plainclothes detectives. Because … it's the rich and powerful Sylvia Jarrett?"

Shutting down her computer, Amy said, "Something like that."

More than likely, there was nothing amiss in the Jarrett's home. She and her friends may have gone shopping or to some other function, and just hadn't informed the maid. Sylvia may have shown the necklace to the other women and it simply got knocked on the floor as they left. Any number of logical explanations were possible. An attack or adduction from within a huge mansion in the middle of Chestnut Hill was unlikely. But the woman's stepson was recently murdered and Philly PD would want to coddle a VIP in the aftermath, particularly since the crime was yet unsolved.

This was an odd wrinkle, Amy thought, as they climbed into their unmarked Stratus. Frank drove and looked a little out of sorts—things to do with Sylvia Jarrett seemed to have that effect on men. Or was it something else? Frank wasn't talking or listening to music. The Phillies beat the Braves two nights in a row and he hadn't even brought it up.

"You okay over there?"

Frank appeared aloof. "Why do you ask?"

"Well, you're a little quiet. Normally we're discussing the case. Either that, or you're tapping the steering wheel to something really distracting like Foghorn or Thin Lizzy."

"That's Fog-*hat*. True enough, I guess. I have stuff on my mind."

"Stuff?"

"Yeah. Stuff. I guess you might call it … I don't know—*woman problems*."

Amy tried not to look amused. "Women problems," Amy said casually. "As in a relationship?"

"Mmmm. Yeah. Or maybe lack thereof. You know that long term stuff is kinda rare for me."

"To say *the least.*"

"You know, you're really getting a razor tongue lately."

"From hanging around you, no doubt."

"Probably. Anyway, my parents were asking me … remember last week when I went up there … and this is way out of character for them … about my plans."

"Your plans?"

"Yeah. Like serious plans. Women plans. Things to come. That stuff."

"It's normal to talk about family matters with parents."

"Not with *mine.*"

Amy was amazed. Whatever cosmic forces may have converged to get his parents to bring up this issue, it had to be somewhat expected—and maybe a decade or so overdue. "What do you think brought it on now?"

Frank shrugged. "I'm not sure. See, I realize they've always hoped I would settle down. They got married and had my brother right out of high school. He was almost nine years older than me. You know he died in combat, right?" Amy nodded sadly, and he continued. "I'm basically all they have. You know, to carry on the family name and all that. I'm just not sure I'm the type. I mean, I don't have anything against the idea, but I'm set in my ways."

"Doesn't mean you can't change. You know, consider a new direction."

"I guess. Sure. Okay, here we are. Hey—thanks a lot for talking."

Amy's mouth dropped open a little. She looked around at the Jarrett mansion as Frank negotiated the cobblestone driveway. *Was that it?* Thanks a lot for talking … *Is he serious?* She hadn't gotten a chance to elaborate about one damn thing. Just like a man. He presented the subject matter, outlined the major issues, and finished up without ever getting to the point.

Amy noticed a familiar Dodge Challenger out front in the extended driveway, no other cars. She'd seen it before at Cruz's place and knew it belonged to Joyce Kyser. A woman had the front door open before they'd even climbed the stairs. Her name was Janie Roland, a mid-fifties picture of efficiency, complete with formal maid's attire and silvery hair tied in a neat bun. She answered their questions and told essentially the same story they'd heard from her prior call. Ms. Jarrett was dinning in the sunroom shortly after noon with two other ladies; when Janie came back to check on them, they were gone. She identified the women as Joyce Kyser and Mindy Lyons, both of whom had been to the Jarrett home on previous occasions.

"Did the two visitors drive here together?" Amy asked.

"I couldn't say for sure, Detective, but they arrived around the same time."

Janie led them out to the sunroom where they'd first spoken to Sylvia Jarrett days ago. On the table were three place settings with partially consumed food and what looked like two lemonades about half to two-thirds full. A similar drinking glass was sideways on the floor. The carpet was wet underneath. No other signs of a struggle or disarray. It appeared that the diners suddenly stopped eating and simply walked away. Off to the far side of the table was a jewel-covered necklace with a decorative series of gold leaves, clearly a sophisticated piece.

"What were they having?" Frank asked.

"Lump crab cakes with a salad of goat cheese, roasted grape tomatoes, arugula, and red onions."

"Do you prepare it?"

"Yes, I did."

"Sounds tasty. You found this necklace here?"

"No," Janie admitted, pointing at the floor. "It was right there. I picked it up and placed it on the table. I didn't move anything else."

"It's real, right?" Frank asked. "I mean, expensive?"

"It was a gift to Ms. Jarrett from Mr. Bradley Jarrett a number of years ago. Victorian Revival from the mid-nineteen twenties. My duties include household inventory so I keep track of all valuables. That is Ms. Jarrett's favorite but she only wears it on formal special occasions. Gold and platinum, six carats of emeralds and a total of over two hundred carats in diamonds."

"What do you think it might be worth?"

"I believe Mr. Jarrett paid $97,000."

"Wow. No shit?"

"No sir."

"Why was it in this room?"

"I couldn't say. I didn't know it was out of the jewelry safe until I saw it."

Amy jotted a few notes as Frank started to look around. She understood the maid's concern, probably a woman who was loyal, well-schooled, and well paid. Sylvia Jarrett was a person who liked being in charge and thought things through. *Why would they all jump up in middle of a quiet luncheon? Why would Sylvia have an exquisite necklace out unless she was just showing it to the others? How could they not notice it on the floor?* Sure, it could be something like they all decided to go shopping and one of their handbags brushed it off the table as they left. As logical as that seemed, Amy didn't think it was so. She trusted a professional housekeeper's instincts that enough inconsistencies existed to demand a closer look.

Amy said, "Does Sylvia Jarrett have a cell phone?"

"Yes," Janie answered. "It's programmed with two lines, one personal and one for business. I tried both and each went to voicemail. I left urgent messages."

"Does Sylvia have her own car?"

"Yes. Three. She mostly prefers to drive herself and uses a chauffeur only on occasion. Her Mercedes SL, Tesla Model X, and Bentley Continental are all in the garage."

"Amy!" Frank called out from nearby.

To the maid, she said, "Thank you. Please don't touch anything for now," and went to join her partner. The next room over was kind of a secondary living room, a bit more stuffy than the sunroom, with high-end furniture. The room was purposely old-fashioned and had no TV, electronics, or other signs of the 21st century.

"Check this," Frank said, pointing to a waist-high antique curio with an assortment of photographs in exquisite 5 by 7 and 8 by 10 frames. She looked at a few before one caught her eye. It was an informal shot of a couple—both smiling—Marcus Jarrett with his arm around ... *umm* . . .

"I know that woman from somewhere," Amy finally said.

"It took me a minute, too. I think she's the babe in one of the photos Cruz took."

Amy nodded. "Yes, of course. The woman leaving the Kyser home." She pulled out her notebook and flipped back a few pages. "Right. The hair is shorter here but I remember the face. It's Mindy Lyons, head of PR at Pierce Brothers."

"Got it. So according to the maid, that's the other lady here for lunch."

"Yes. She's also the one who put us onto Kurt Waldo in the first place—from the conversation Cruz overhead."

"Looks steamy. She and Marcus must've been an item at one time. And she's here when Sylvia Jarrett vanishes. Let's face it—something is screwy."

Amy left the room and returned a minute later with Janie. She pointed. "What can you tell us about this photograph?"

"I haven't seen that one for a while. From back when Mr. Marcus was dating Miss Lyons."

"How long ago was that?"

Janie thought about it for a moment. "I don't think I can say exactly. They first dated maybe four years ago and it seemed to be periodic. From appearances, Mr. Marcus may have fully ended the relationship last year."

"Did Mindy take it hard?"

"I am not privy to the details. From what I understand of the matter—yes. She called and came by on a number of occasions after the breakup."

"Trying to patch things up?"

"I suppose that would be my understanding. Also, she seemed to maintain a sporadic social connection with Mrs. Jarrett."

"Thank you. Please do a check of the residence and tell us if anything is missing."

Janie nodded and left the room as Frank and Amy considered the very odd turn of events while staring at the photo.

"A three-year romance," Frank finally said. "Nice pose, two lovebirds."

"Yes. And it's easy to figure that Marcus broke it off with Mindy for good right around the time he started seeing Vonda Cantu."

"This is a shitstorm. We've got three unrelated deaths all connected somehow. Vonda and Dixie are missing. Now Sylvia Jarrett vanishes from her house. We need to get back to the Roundhouse and bring Lieutenant Trainer up to speed."

"You think we've been following the wrong trail all along?"

"I don't know and we have to find out fast. And we need put out a BOLO for Mindy Lyons."

"You handle that," Amy said. "I'm getting gloves and an evidence kit from the car. There's a few things I want to take with us."

CHAPTER 24

No one spoke as Lieutenant Norman Trainer processed the information imparted by his two detectives. With quiet intensity, he paced back and forth for a moment and then took a seat behind his desk. Amy was trying to sense his thoughts. The case was like a giant puzzle with oddly shaped pieces that didn't seem to fit no matter how they were positioned. From all she'd heard, Trainer had a reputation for unravelling just those kinds of cases. Like Frank, he was a great strategist and had a knack for reading people, but the resemblance ended there. Frank liked the streets, shunned political correctness, and never tried for promotions. Trainer supervised a number of detectives, checked mountains of paperwork, dealt directly with the higher brass, and routinely handled an overzealous press, all while maintaining an enviable family life.

"Let me see if I've got this right," he finally said. "You're telling me that Sylvia Jarrett, the owner of one of our biggest companies and widow of a decorated veteran, has been kidnapped by the deranged ex-girlfriend of her murdered stepson?"

"That," Frank said, "is the way it shapes up."

"You don't know for sure?"

"Not yet."

Amy noticed the big veins in Lieutenant Trainer's neck and forehead were bulging. She had some ideas but might wait for a direct question. None of this was their fault. They'd done everything by the book for a tricky situation since it was only supposition pointing them in Mindy's direction. A BOLO had been initiated for her car, a silver 2018 Volvo XC90, although it hadn't been spotted yet. There was no activity on any credit cards used by Sylvia Jarrett, Joyce Kyser, or Mindy Lyons. Their cellphones were all off or out of range so triangulation was impossible. Mindy's home, office, and known associates had already been checked out. Her background was now top priority and currently under evaluation by researchers who would scrutinize relatives, friends, phone records, properties, hobbies, and bank transactions. These were trained analysts who could conjure up places she'd go, people she'd turn to, or a pattern that would intimate her next move. The basic problem—it all took time.

The fact was, no credible information showed that Sylvia Jarrett was compromised or in any real danger. There were no witnesses to an abduction or any ransom demands. There'd been no 911 calls or crime reported. Mindy Lyons had no criminal record or history of aberrant behavior. Raising the alarm and alerting media could be disastrous if it turned out Sylvia Jarrett was in a private business meeting or simply out shopping.

"So," Trainer said, "what's your take on this? I want some assessment. It's just us in here, off the record. Give me something."

Frank nodded. "All right. Mindy is Marcus Jarrett's ex-girlfriend. He dumped her around the end of last year, probably to date Vonda Cantu."

"The one who's missing."

"Yeah. There's no trail. We're sure Vonda and Dixie left the apartment complex in Vonda's SUV, but it hasn't surfaced."

"What's the link between Zachary Chastang's death and Jarrett's?"

Amy couldn't hold back anymore and chimed in. "We think there're several agendas at work here, sir." She turned to Frank, who gave no objection, and continued. "Vonda Cantu is a possible suspect for the Zachary Chastang shooting. We don't believe she's guilty but there's strong motive from the rape of her friend. There's a chance that Cameron Chastang may have had Vonda killed."

"Is there evidence to support that?"

"Nothing substantial. We haven't been able to question him since his people claim he's unavailable. We expect him to surface for Zachary's funeral."

"So that situation may be unrelated to what's happening now?"

"Yes, sir, but it's unclear. I went over Vonda Cantu's diary. It was helpful with background, but unfortunately, Vonda stopped writing just over a month ago when Dixie's rape occurred. It's clear that Marcus broke it off totally with Mindy right around the time he started dating Vonda. Mindy also may have killed Vonda or helped plan it. We know there's a connection to the ex-con, Corky Buck. It's possible that he killed Dolores Griego by mistake at Birch Tree Apartments, then went after Vonda Cantu."

"It's also possible that Kurt Waldo is involved. He's the head of security for Cameron Chastang and works with Mindy Lyons. Is he on your suspect list?"

"Not really. Not at this time."

"For any reasons I'd agree with?"

"I like to think so, sir."

Trainer appraised her for a moment, then let out a grunt. "We'll come back to that another time. Why do you think Mindy Lyons would abduct Sylvia Jarrett?"

"We took drinking glasses from the Jarrett place when we left. From the housekeeper, we know where Mindy was sitting at the table, and that she had lemonade. A partial print on her glass is a match to one found on a bag of date-rape drugs in Marcus Jarrett's drawer. Her fingerprints were not on file."

"That would make her a prime suspect in his murder."

"Yes. We believe she planted the drugs. And Sylvia Jarrett may know something that can prove it. We just found out that Mindy Lyons used to work for

Jarrett Enterprises up until a few years ago. Mindy resigned and took the position she still has with Pierce Brothers."

Lieutenant Trainer was silent for a moment. He had that way about him—stern, calm, and collected, with a lot of smarts bubbling just beneath the surface. "When was that, precisely?"

"Umm." Amy frowned. "When was what, sir?"

"When exactly did Mindy Lyons leave Jarrett Enterprises?"

Amy leafed through a folder for about ten seconds before finding the answer. "Three years ago on August 30th."

"I see. Tell me the date that Bradley Jarrett died?"

Again, Amy had to ruffle through some reports to find that particular data. "October 5th, same year."

"Approximately five weeks later. Anything there?"

Amy looked over at Frank who shrugged and then returned her attention forward. "What are you suggesting, Lieutenant?"

"Just that you both need to consider alternatives. Don't look at the power structure of the company now, look at it when Bradley was still in the driver's scat. Was Mindy Lyons let go with a push from Bradley Jarrett? Or possibly Sylvia? Is there animosity between the two? And why? Or perhaps something else is going on there. You're both proceeding as though the rape of Dixie Newberry was the beginning of all this. I'm merely saying that you may need to dig deeper."

"Of course. Thank you, sir."

"Just one more thing. Sylvia Jarrett is a prominent and highly visible presence in this city. Meeting in one hour. Let's dig faster and use bigger shovels."

Alvin Cruz heard the ring and flipped open his cell phone. He was still using a flip phone and couldn't take the idea of going to a smartphone yet. "Yeah."

"Cruz. This is Dewey, impound lot on Bath Street. McGrail told us the basics and said to give you a heads up."

"What've you got?"

"Gilbert Kyser picked up his Lexus, just now pulling out. We noticed your tracker in the wheel well but left it in place."

"He alone?"

"Yep. Came walking in off the street. Weird. Didn't see anybody else."

"Appreciate the help. Thanks." Cruz ended the call, tried Joyce's number and it still went directly to voicemail—he'd left two messages earlier and she hadn't called back yet. He took a big swig of Arizona iced tea and set the bottle in the cup holder before pulling out of the Wawa parking lot. Flipping on the GPS tracking device, he tapped one button and a screen popped up with a colorful map that represented about a twenty square block section of the city with Kyser's Lexus—as a tiny pulsating red indicator—smack in the middle. The impound lot was over near the river; it would take only a few minutes of watching his movements to determine if Kyser was headed home, to the office, or somewhere else. Glancing at his watch, Cruz noticed it was a little after 6 PM. Nice out, probably low 70s. Knowing Kyser as he did by now, the guy might head straight for the nearest place with hot wings or pizzas for a pre-dinner snack.

Cruz flipped open his cell and pressed a speed dial number.

"McGrail."

"It's me. Dewey called. Kyser picked up his car alone.. Corky Buck may have dropped him off up the street. He'd know to avoid any security cameras."

"Makes sense. Where's Kyser headed?"

"Can't tell yet. I'm a few blocks away on Richmond. I'll be right on him whichever way he goes."

"All right. Keep me posted."

Cruz disconnected, tried Joyce's number once more, then flipped the phone closed and tossed it on the passenger seat when again it went to voicemail without ringing. No one was behind him so he sat idling at the edge of the lot and watched the screen. Soon Kyser's car veered off East Allegheny Avenue to a spot that Cruz recognized. He wasn't even surprised to see it was the NewDaze Pizza Palace. This could definitely take a while. Kyser was a strange guy—but his eating habits were plain as day. Cruz drove to within half a block and saw Kyser head inside. No choice now but to sit tight. With modern electronics on his side, this was the easy part. Cruz reached to the cooler behind the front seat and grabbed an energy drink and a Chunky.

The hard part was figuring out his own feelings for Joyce and what he was going to do about it. The whole thing was so very wrong in many ways but it felt so damned good being with her. In the sack, she was as passionate a woman as he'd been with in a long time, maybe ever. There was definitely a strong attraction. Okay, he could admit it to himself—he was hung up on her. Did Joyce feel the same? He hoped so. And yes, having what amounted to an affair with a married client was against his normal code of personal conduct. He hated to admit it, but the thought of Gilbert Kyser going to jail was a relief of sorts, a black mark on the man's character while effectively getting him out of the way. Cruz knew he would never manufacture evidence or railroad an innocent guy into prison. It just so happened in this case, that Kyser's actions probably called for incarceration. The plain truth was that whatever he and Buck were into had to be against the law—it was the only thing that could possibly bring those two together. Whether it was drug-related, money laundering, corporate-level shenanigans or a cover-up for other crimes, Cruz could only guess. It very well could have something to do with Marcus Jarrett's murder and the disappearance of Vonda Cantu and Dixie Newberry. Either way, Joyce could be in danger and the notion of a "hit" still floated in the back of his mind. At the very least, her marriage, reputation, home life, and financial situation could change drastically by whatever her husband and Corky Buck were cooking up.

Somehow, he would find a way to intervene.

Amy leaned on an old wooden table in Nancy's computer alcove, the only area large enough for everyone to congregate. Stacks of case files were everywhere and few bare surfaces existed. Even the file cabinets had piles of paper on top. A corkboard on one wall had a selection of notices, memos, photos, and the obligatory 'wanted' posters. Nancy, the police researcher, was next to Frank at her desk. Then came Jim "Turkey" Carver and Kristi Yadao, detectives with a solid reputation in the department. Turk was a former college football player and still maintained the sturdy build of a running back through exercise. His smooth dark skin belied his 42 years. Kristi, 37, was tall and lean with straight black hair and a perpetual tan. A good detective, her recent engagement to a local well-known defense attorney brought relentless jokes and ribbing. Two other veteran detectives, Kyle Trombley, age 39, and Joshua Harvey, age 51, rounded out the hand-picked task force for this operation.

Lieutenant Trainer's appearance, the last to arrive, squelched any horseplay. He stood, ramrod straight and looked over the group. "I'll make this quick. You all know the basics. Sylvia Jarrett and her friend, Joyce Kyser, have most likely been abducted by Mindy

Lyons, a Public Relations executive at Pierce Brothers. We'll have an agent here soon from the local FBI field office, but we need to move on this now. The evidence suggests that the suspect Lyons may also have murdered Marcus Jarrett, her former boyfriend and Sylvia Jarrett's stepson. Lyons has a clean record but we have no data on her current mental state or intentions. Consider her armed and dangerous. I'm sure I don't need to remind anyone that Sylvia Jarrett is a respected member of our business community and Joyce Kyser is the wife of Gilbert Kyser, a senior executive at Pierce Brothers, another highly-visible company." He nodded to Frank and then stepped aside.

Nancy tapped a keypad that displayed images on her monitor. Along with the rest, Amy leaned, turned, or tilted her head for a better look. Frank relayed physical descriptions and known characteristics of Sylvia, Joyce, and Mindy, as each of their photos appeared. In any rescue operation that could quickly become a hostage situation, all responding officers needed to know each of the participants at a glance when possible. Photos of Vonda Cantu, Dixie Newberry, and Gilbert Kyser were also presented in an effort to be thorough, although Amy didn't expect they would be involved in whatever came next. Mug shots of Corky Buck and the best views of him from Cruz's recent surveillance photos were shown as Frank outlined his peripheral involvement. An overview of the murder,

Vonda Cantu's disappearance, and Mindy's possible motivations was concise.

"There is no trace of the three women," Frank continued. "Or Mindy's SUV, a silver Volvo. There's nothing at her apartment. We have officers at the Jarrett mansion, phones are tapped. So far, no ransom demand or any contact. Nancy has come up with two locations that Mindy might use. Go in easy. Harvey and Trom, take the Lyons family home on Boulder Road in Plymouth Meeting. Mindy's mother is supposed to still live there so keep that in mind. Yadao and Turk are with Amy and me. We'll take the college friend, Leslie Madonna—lives in a rural home, Delaware County. Mindy stays in touch and there are routine text messages and four calls to and from Leslie's phone in recent weeks. Okay, that's it. Time is important. Questions?"

Kristi Yadao said, "I understand this woman's motive for Marcus Jarrett's murder. Sounds like jealousy. What would she hope to gain by taking Sylvia Jarrett?"

"We can't be sure," Amy answered. "Although it may be a panic move. Mindy dated Marcus Jarrett for over three years and has maintained a social friendship with Sylvia since they broke up. No one suspected her of killing Marcus. It's possible that during lunch, Mindy inadvertently slipped up, said something to tip off Sylvia Jarrett. She may have put it together and accused Mindy directly. Sylvia Jarrett could be a hostage in the hope to collect a ransom."

"So, Mindy hopes to vanish?"

"That's our takeaway. It's also been confirmed from Jarrett's housekeeper that jewelry is missing. Expensive pieces, which might make them difficult to fence."

Kyle Trombley spoke next. "This Buck sounds like a real shitbag. Is he working for Mindy on this?"

"He might be," Frank said. "We're pretty sure he went after Vonda Cantu and ran a very large icepick through the wrong woman. Then Vonda and her friend both fell off the earth."

"Damn. I really hope I come across the guy."

"You and me both." Frank looked out over the group. "All right, folks? Let's move."

As everyone headed away with a minimum of idle chatter, Amy closed up some paperwork. To Frank, she said, "I've got to stop by my desk. I'll meet you at the car."

Frank thought the briefing went well. Everything was in place to mount an organized search for Sylvia Jarrett and Joyce Kyser, both in the clutches of Marcus Jarrett's crazed ex-lover. Strange how things worked out. The last twenty-four hours had produced so many unexpected revelations, it was hard to keep track. Supposedly, Kurt Waldo was the good guy, apart from breaking into a police detective's house and attacking another. As much as he'd like to give the benefit of the doubt to a fellow U.S. serviceman, Waldo could still be involved in either murder or possibly covering up after the fact. He trusted Amy's hunches but knew that Waldo had an effect on her. Despite claims of wanting to date doctors and accountants, she was more attracted to the strong and suave. She took pride in pulling her weight and earning her own living, but still appreciated a man who opened a car door for her or showed up with a bouquet of flowers. Charming, with just-enough confident sex appeal. Having watched and discussed both old and recent movies with Amy, he knew she never leaned toward sensitive, fluffy heroes. From the previous era, she liked Steve McQueen, Sean Connery, and Clint Eastwood—the kind of guys who could kick ass and have fun doing it. Her favorite newer films seemed to have action and she thought Vin Diesel, Jason Statham, and Daniel Craig were particularly intriguing. Whether she knew it or not, Kurt Waldo was her type right down his biceps.

The best part was how Amy had thwarted the 6-foot-3 fiend and sent him on the run. The next morning, she mentioned the guy was really big and she was right. On the mock date with Chastang, Amy would have been decked out nice and sexy. He'd just bet that Waldo was impressed, since the former Delta Force Sergeant would be expecting to easily overpower a standard party gal and extract some answers. Inwardly, he laughed—she must have surprised the hell out of him. As Amy's friend, he found that pretty cool. As always, her gender and good looks never held her back, it was just a part of doing the job well.

Now it was time to wrap things up. He gathered up some files and noticed Kristi Yadao hanging back. A moment later, they were the only two still present. The child of a native Philippine father and a California-bred U.S. servicewoman, Kristi wore the gray women's business suit like a supermodel. Usually cool and collected, she seemed anxious, a little more twitchy than usual. She walked towards him slowly—definitely something was on her mind.

"Frank," she said quietly, "I know you … Well, you don't always go strictly by the book."

"Okay." He grinned. "I just don't know yet if that's a *compliment.*"

Kristi laughed. "It is—sort of. I have something … Not much, really. I doubt if it's really important."

"It's information that you can neither confirm nor deny?"

"Yes. I think that's it."

Frank shrugged. "How could you have told me since this conversation never took place?"

Kristi thought for a moment and then nodded. "You know my fiancé is a junior partner with Whitlow and Hamilton … Well, I may have heard something I shouldn't have."

Frank waited for a moment, then said, "Not to rush you, but we've got a rich lady to save from a kidnapper."

"Yes, I'm sorry. All right. Like I said, I shouldn't be aware of this. Marcus Jarrett was *married.*"

Frank was stunned; he hadn't seen that one coming. "Seriously?"

"Yes. Last month. He and Vonda Cantu flew to Vegas but didn't tell anyone. Marcus amended his will shortly after that. His trust fund, too."

"Sylvia Jarrett never mentioned any of this to us."

"Maybe she wasn't aware. Marcus and Sylvia had issues. Recently, I believe she was told for legal reasons, but I don't know exactly when."

One word sprang to mind: motive. Frank mentally catalogued the information but wasn't sure if it made a difference in the case. Marcus and Vonda eloped to Vegas—a happy occasion. Taking the timeline into account, Dixie's rape would have occurred right after that, probably the following weekend. It made sense that Marcus and Vonda postponed any announcement or big celebration for a while. Mindy Lyons, the jealous ex, may have found out about the marriage and it sent her over the edge. In a rage, she killed Marcus and had Vonda murdered. It added up.

Kristi said, "It's probably not even worth worrying about. I couldn't keep it to myself, just in case."

Frank took her hand and gave it a little squeeze. "You did the right thing. For now, it means we need to hurry and stop Mindy Lyons from killing anyone else."

CHAPTER 25

In the passenger seat, Amy read over their intel on Leslie Madonna. Her home was west of the city on a country road in the Glen Riddle area. From the information they were able to gather, Leslie, age 35, an only child, lived on the family property in an impressive seven-bedroom house. The owners, Leslie's parents, were apparently spending a few months on Malta in the Mediterranean. The product of several generations of oil speculators and wise investors, all three were comfortable and no one had a police record.

Research had turned up one interesting fact—there was a Leslie Madonna presently listed on a Silversea Cruise ship that was approaching New Zealand. If Leslie was out of the country, her secluded home might make an ideal hideout for Mindy Lyons, a close friend in a world of trouble.

"It's just off Bortondale Road. Another two miles, then turn left," Amy said. "All residential properties along there."

Frank nodded. "Got that. So, what's on your mind?"

"What makes you think there's something more?"

"I sense the wheels turning."

"Okay. Well, that little something Kristi told you—about Marcus Jarrett and Vonda being married . . ."

"What about it?"

"You think it makes sense? I mean that it made Mindy want to kill Marcus."

"Possible. The jilted ex-lover. It's reasonable motive, no doubt about that."

"I was thinking—it's going to change things for Sylvia Jarrett."

"Things?" Frank scowled. "Like what?"

"Well, assuming for the moment that Vonda is still alive … For starters, Vonda might inherit everything belonging to Marcus. That would have to be substantial."

"I suppose. Sylvia would still to have money to burn."

"True. I mean, it's just that . . ." Amy paused for a moment collecting her thoughts and perused the neighborhood. It was a stunningly beautiful area, plenty of tall trees, shrubs, hedges, wildflowers, and forsythia. Nothing seemed intricately landscaped or prudently arranged, and nothing was cluttered or overgrown. The houses varied greatly in architecture, size, and distance from the street. They were getting close to their target. She finally said, "I guess I'm still bothered by the anonymous call that came in on Marcus Jarrett."

"Okay, yeah. That's a mystery. My guess—it's a woman who came across the body and got freaked out. Didn't know what to do, so she called it in and made up a story about shouting and gunshots. It's somebody who couldn't tell the guy was dead since the night before."

"Why wouldn't she ID herself?"

"Mmmm. Two reasons. One, she didn't want to get involved but couldn't just walk away. Or two, she was afraid for some reason. It might not matter. Has to be someone not involved in the murder itself." Frank waited a moment and said, "Maybe Sylvia Jarrett."

"No, definitely not."

Frank grinned. "Why is that?"

"Doesn't fit. She wouldn't be squeamish about being involved and she's not afraid of anything."

Frank laughed. "Geez. You really don't like that woman, do you? She has a solid alibi for the TOD so we know she didn't kill Marcus. Tell me you're not suggesting that Sylvia Jarrett has something to do with Vonda's disappearance."

"Well, I'm open to ideas. You always told me not to jump on board with pet theories. It's just that when we first interviewed Sylvia, she didn't mention that Marcus once dated Mindy Lyons seriously. Also, she claimed that Marcus didn't have a steady girlfriend."

Frank grinned. "That all sounds nice and logical. But down deep, I think you just want to poke the bear."

"What?"

"You heard me. The rich-bitch Sylvia Jarrett has been in your crosshairs since this started."

"Well, her actions are suspicious. You have to think she'd be shocked to find out Marcus got married."

"A surprise, sure. I can't imagine her getting too wound up over it. She's filthy rich by any standard. Although … Trust funds, company rules, and wills can be tricky. I suppose it couldn't hurt to find out how all the legal shit unfolds."

"Yeah," Amy said sadly. "Or would have unfolded if Vonda were alive. All along, we thought Vonda might be in danger as a suspect in Chastang's death."

"I see where you're headed. She could've been targeted for a different reason."

"Yes." Amy checked the GPS and then looked to see that Kristi and Turk were right behind them. "We've got less than a mile to go."

The landscape shifted to a more rural setting. To the right of the winding road, there was a drop in elevation with a short guard rail at the edge. Roofs and upper levels of secluded homes could be seen through the trees. To the left, the land continued its upward slope. The driveways were uphill and pretty far apart indicating large properties. The Madonna's had 8.5 acres.

"This next one," she said. Amy knew in this instance they would never just drive up and knock on the front door. The plan was to cruise on past, get a feel for the layout, and decide on a covert approach. Frank slowed just a little by the entrance and then pulled off on the shoulder that was wide enough to park. The driveway was paved and had a tapering stone wall on either side with old-fashioned lamps on each. As expected, the house was not in view. Checking in all directions, Amy was glad they were in a favorable spot and would be unobserved. It was helpful for detectives when they weren't being watched by people on porches and looking out windows.

Kristi and Turk pulled in behind and joined them as Frank spread a printout across the hood of their unmarked. A satellite view of the house and grounds had soft but useful detail. Amy gave out palm-sized handheld communicators that had a five-mile range, multiple channels, and good clarity. All were set to the same secure frequency.

"Big place," Frank said. "Most of their property is wooded but it looks like lawn for about sixty or so feet all around the house. We'll go in quiet and quick. Keep it low profile. Remember, we don't know that a crime is being committed or that Mindy is even here. Or anyone. The place could be deserted." He pointed to areas on their map. "Amy and I will walk straight up the driveway to the front door. You two follow behind, then peel off about the halfway point. Stay out of sight. Looks like a big detached garage on the left. Kristi, you go around it and come towards the back of the house. Turk, you go right, sweep wide, and come around the far side. Amy and I will knock and just ask a few questions—they'll never know you two are out there. If no one's home, we'll all spread out and look around."

Kristi asked, "Did anyone try calling?"

"Yep. Twice. Got an answering machine both times. A female voice said, 'you've got the Madonna's, leave a message, blah, blah.' Then it said, 'If you really need to find me, call on my cell." We have it so we did and got voicemail. Makes me think Leslie is really on that damn cruise in the south Pacific. Remember, these folks are well off. They might have perimeter alarms or six rottweilers. There could be live-in maids, groundskeepers, or houseguests. It's almost five o'clock so if somebody's home, they might be making dinner."

Turk looked around. "You're right about this place. Out here would make a good hideout."

"It would," Frank agreed. "And we got word from Trom and Harvey. They're in Plymouth Meeting now. No sign of Mindy at the family home. The mother swears she hasn't seen her since last week. That makes this place our only good lead. Let's be sure. Keep in touch. Questions?" When no one spoke, he said, "Move."

All four went up the driveway; Kristi and Turk veered left and right, disappearing in the underbrush. Amy trailed ten feet behind Frank and soon, the garage and house came into view. It was a sprawling rancher in a log-cabin design that was nicely harmonious with the surrounding forest land. Clearly this was modern construction intended to look old-fashioned.

The lawn was weed-free with neatly trimmed shrubs and several flower beds. The four-car garage had a similar style to the house.

"Everything is so gorgeous," Amy whispered.

"For sure." Frank slowed up and took a peek in the garage windows. "Son of a bitch. These people have a GTO, a '65, I think. Looks like Cragar SS mags. Damn nice. And an Audi Q7." He paused and held up his hand. "Oh, shit!"

"What?"

Frank waited until Amy came alongside. "Take a look."

She stood on tiptoes, blocked the glare with her hand and peered inside. "Big silver Volvo! Damn it— that's *Mindy's!*"

Frank flattened himself against the garage as he thumbed his communicator, keeping his voice to a whisper. "Mindy's car is here. Repeat, Mindy Lyons's car in the garage. Switch to Plan B. Kristi, what have you got?"

Her voice was low and controlled. *"Moving in closer. I'm on the porch in back of the house now. Can't see inside, curtain's closed ... All quiet ... I just pushed the sliding glass door a little—it's unlocked."*

"Keep checking the perimeter," Frank said. "Turk, come back."

"Turk here. Far side of the home. I see movement through a window near a door up a short flight of steps. Might be the kitchen. No curtains. Can't look in without being seen."

"Keep checking. Out."

"Frank," Kristi's voice was low, with forced control. *"Window in the back. I see one victim in a bedroom. A blonde. Looks like … Joyce Kyser. She's tied to a chair. I think she's okay."*

"Stand by." Frank looked over at Amy who had already drawn her Sig-Sauer. "I think we need to move in. Any thoughts?"

"Mindy is desperate and we know there's at least one victim alive."

"My feeling, too. How about this: You cover me while I slip up to the main door. If it's locked, we'll head around back and go through the patio. With any luck we can get inside quiet."

Amy nodded. "That works. Tell them to go in—"

A gunshot rang out and was followed by three more shots.

Frank sprinted across the walkway, fired once at the knob, and hit the side door at full speed. Wood splintered as it flew open and Frank stumbled in. Amy caught up and followed him into a foyer and panned right as Frank went left. She moved swift and silent through a spacious dining room until she heard a voice. It was Kristi Yadao calling out up ahead but the words were indistinct. Amy stepped through a tall archway that led into a living room just as Frank came around from the other side.

"Anything?" he asked.

"Nothing."

"Kristi, Turk," he whispered into the communicator. With no replay, he said, "Dammit."

Both detectives moved along a wide hallway. Their first objective would be to protect civilians.

Under his breath, Frank muttered, "This house is fucking huge."

A door appeared on the left. Frank turned the knob, pushed through and turned left, allowing Amy to shift right in a practiced procedure. Sylvia Jarrett was disheveled but very much alive as she knelt beside Joyce, tugging on the ropes.

"Oh, thank God," Sylvia cried out. She leaped up and ran to Frank, giving him a fierce hug. She released him and turned to Amy, touching her shoulder. "Thank you both so much."

Kristi came running in and paused long enough to sum up the situation. "We're okay," she said. "Turk got clipped. He's all right. One unknown male suspect is down. Mindy Lyons, too." Frank's eyes widened and she added, "Wasn't us. She was dead when we got here."

"I think ... I think they turned on each other," Sylvia said, breathlessly. "That big man wanted all the money."

The victims were safe, that was very good news. Frank went to Joyce and finished untying her as Kristi led Sylvia from the room. Amy looked around, making a mental image of things. A bedroom, large, about 20 by 30 feet, with distinctive feminine décor and coloring. Bookshelves, desk and an open area where a laptop would sit. Bureau with large round mirror on top. Poster of Blink 182 on one wall, an impressive landscape painting on the other, a few big tapestries with brightly-colored zodiac images. Overall, a comfortable bedroom for a well-to-do woman—probably Leslie, Mindy's friend. In addition to the chair that held Joyce, a second chair near the desk had rope tangled around it and more on the floor nearby. Amy went out and through the hall, arriving in a beautiful kitchen done in bricks, complete with large center island and an impressive selection of cookware hanging from above. They even had a steel-door baking oven. On the floor of elegant stone tile was a tall, burly man in a flannel shirt with the sleeves cut off at the shoulders. His chest had two bloody bullet wounds and another in the shoulder. She was surprised that it was *not* Corky Buck—this guy was bigger and younger. Turk leaned on the sink, his powerful hand clutching his side.

"Just a graze," he said. "Missed the vest. This guy shot first. I guess my aim was better."

Amy smiled at him. "It's a good thing."

CHAPTER 26

About damn time …

A Kyser finally emerged from the pizza place. His car started moving, doglegged through the immediate area, then soon turned on Aramingo Avenue. Cruz pulled out, deciding to catch up and leisurely move into position about a block behind. He continued the tail for about ten minutes when the display indicated the car had veered off the road and stopped in the Port Richmond section between I-95 and the river. The area was zoned for industrial properties and populated with large-scale businesses. There were no homes, or retail stores and had limited foot traffic. He was generally familiar with that part of town but rarely ventured in unless a case took him there. He was quickly approaching the spot where Kyser's car would be seen and tried to decide on a course of action. Kyser wouldn't know his Sunfire and from a distance, might not recognize him. Up close, Kyser would surely remember the annoying—and bogus—insurance agent from yesterday's visit. Taking such chances was not wise at this point and he wouldn't underestimate any adversary, not even one as incompetent as Kyser.

Cruz grabbed a pair of wraparound sunglasses from the glove compartment, slipped on a red Phillies baseball cap, and checked his image in the rearview mirror. *Not bad.* If Kyser was up to no good, it was better if he continued that course. Suspicion and disruptions could easily make Kyser overly cautious or cease his activities altogether. Cruz needed to leave him comfortable and proceeding forward since amateur criminals were the toughest to analyze. Kyser, the uptown professional, would be unpredictable on the streets.

The indicator showed that Kyser's car was roughly a football field or so away. To the right was a fenced area that surrounded a large unmarked building, maybe a warehouse. There was no break in the fence and no parking lot so he knew this was the rear of a huge property that extended to the adjacent street; Kyser couldn't be in there. On the left were several smaller buildings in a row, older construction that were probably storage facilities, wholesale outlets, or manufacturing structures. Luckily, limited security. Almost everything had fencing around the perimeters but many front gates were wide open. Activity was sparse except for a few slow-moving tow motors loaded with bundles of pipe, far behind the facilities—Kyser would be somewhere closer. Cruz figured to just drive on past for now, try to get an idea about what was going on and then decide what to do next.

He spotted Kyser's Lexus parked towards the very back of a small one-story building, maybe for offices. No one appeared to be in the car. To the left was a much larger structure, some type of storage facility. Maybe forty feet high, it was all a dull slate blue with a few tiny windows. A sign read Canzoneri & Stokes which didn't seem familiar. The front door was closed but one of the wide bay doors to the left was about halfway up. The interior seemed dark but possibly only in contrast to the outside since there was still a little daylight left. He rolled on past, scanning ahead for a place to park when a thought occurred to him.

Was Kyser in trouble?

At first, Cruz had thought this to be a rendez-vous, probably with Buck or some other hoodlum that hadn't surfaced yet. Now he wasn't so sure. Kyser certainly hadn't been driving like he was in a hurry. But he'd then pulled his car into a secluded spot that was out of sight unless you happened to be looking for it. Didn't quite make sense. Unless Kyser spotted the tail and made a panic move … *Or could someone else be after him?*

Cruz turned hard to the left, drove onto the grounds, and pulled to the right side of the main building. No other cars in the lot; workers had gone home for the day. Not exactly a hotbed of activity this late so no one would be paying him any attention. He reached into the glove compartment for his Smith & Wesson M&P, attached the clip-on holster to his belt and adjusted his shirt to cover it. Jumping out, he crossed in front of the structure, scanning the small building and seeing no lights or movement. A quick check of the Lexus brought no helpful data. There was no damage, nothing suspicious, and no sign of Kyser.

Cruz moved slowly towards the front of the building along the wall, hearing no hums of machinery or voices. He considered turning around and bagging this whole idea but then decided to press on. He might blow his cover or at the very least, get questioned by a nervous guard. One thing was certain—he wasn't about to let anything happen to Gilbert Kyser. Joyce had hired him to watch her husband and that's what he'd do. Part of that responsibility was keeping him alive and in one piece, regardless of the man's questionable pursuits and possible drug habit. There'd be time later to sort out his feelings for Joyce and determine the best legal course of action for Kyser.

Cruz rounded the building and came to the wide bay door that was partway up. He slipped off the sunglasses and peered down, but couldn't see much of anything. Crouching, he was able to easily scoot inside. The air was slightly cooler and a little damp and seemed to smell of grease and sawdust. The area was large, maybe eighty feet across and at least a hundred feet deep. The light from outside brightened things a little towards the front. A few of the long fluorescent tubes on the high ceiling were lit, bathing the rest of the place in an eerie glow with deep shadows. Sitting idle throughout were an assortment of excavating machinery, a few Bobcats, Cub Cadet tractors, back-hoes, scrapers, and a cherry picker. All of it showed dings and wear, but seemed clean and maintained. Probably for sale or rent. Cruz slowly made his way forward, keeping silent and listening for any peculiar sounds. He gradually worked his way further in, figuring to make a sweep of the premises. A network of shelves along the far wall held tools, cartons, and other equipment. There was a small office to the right but the windows were dark. As far as he could tell, the place was deserted.

So where could Kyser be? Five minutes ago, the damn guy was driving his car which was now just outside. He supposed it was possible Kyser went around back, maybe in another door. Or he might not be here at all. This just seemed most likely since he'd apparently moved fast. Somehow, that guess was wrong.

In his peripheral vision, Cruz thought he noticed movement to the left near the bucket of an excavator and tried not to react suddenly. He couldn't be sure. As his right hand slid slowly towards his sidearm, he heard the unmistakable click of a hammer being pulled back.

A calm voice came from the darkness. "Don't try it, dick-face."

Damn, Cruz cursed inwardly. *Careless…* He turned slowly as the man stood up, still in shadows. Wasn't Kyser; taller and not pudgy. Probably security or a worker tending equipment, so there might be an easy way out of this mess.

"Yo," Cruz said, raising his arms to appear non-threatening. "Didn't mean to scare anybody. Just need to rent a tractor, friend." The man didn't move or reply but Cruz could see a glint of light from the distinct shape of a handgun. He needed to make the guy relax. "Something sturdy, like maybe the 4000 series with a front loader. Cash in advance. Do you rent by the week or month?"

The man remained still and silent which was a little baffling. Cruz needed to get going but didn't want to startle some jumpy maintenance man into shooting him. "Look, can we get down to business? I need a tractor and you got 'em—"

"I don't think you're here for a fucking tractor." The man stepped past the framework of the earth-mover and into the light. The revolver was steady in his hand. "I think you're Alvin Cruz, a nosy prick with some fancy gadgets."

Son of a bitch. How does he know who I am? Cruz gave up on the pretense when he suddenly realized the man's identity. Inwardly, he shuttered at the implications of a silencer on the end of the barrel. "What's this supposed to be?"

"It's the end of the road for you." Corky Buck maintained a safe distance from his target. "Two fingers. Take it out slow and drop it on the floor."

Cruz cursed his mistake and reluctantly complied. "Look, let's not—"

"Shut up, asshole. I figured you might be followin' Kyser."

"Uh-huh. So, where is he?" *Keep him talking,* Cruz said to himself. Need time to think.

"Back room. You don't have to worry about him."

"Okay. So here we are. Let's talk. Maybe we can help each other."

Buck raised his voice. "No way. You're with the goddamn cops. I *hate cops.*"

"I hate cops, too. I'm private. I just—"

"You're friends with cops."

"Okay, yeah," Cruz said. "They work with me sometimes. It's a means to an end. I'm here to help Gilbert Kyser. I just want to be sure—"

Buck snorted. "You want to help Kyser?"

"Exactly. I'm kind of looking out for him."

"Yeah? You're full o' shit. Aren't you fucking his wife?"

Cruz swallowed hard. *Well, yes. But how the hell would Buck know that?* The distance between them favored the shooter—close enough that he wouldn't miss and not close enough for a slick move on Cruz's part. Despite the nifty evasive measures used by James Bond and Batman, that stuff didn't work against bullets in real life. He switched into panic mode—*think!* There were no possibilities for a distraction. His own gun was too far out of reach. The closest machinery to hide behind was a good twenty feet away. The look on Buck's face was matter-of-fact and he held the gun as though born with it. That, plus the way he carried himself. No compromise, no apologies, just business. An adversary's life or death didn't really matter to him; it was all in a day's work. Cruz knew he'd get hit at the first step in any direction. "Well, that's complicated. It's awkward for me, too. You see, Gilbert Kyser and his wife have some serious issues that—"

"Fuck that shit, man. I couldn't care less. Kyser was a loser."

Was … a loser? More bad news. "Hey, I'm just doing a job. C'mon. Let's work together."

For the first time, Corky Buck smiled, just a little. "You don't get it, fuck-wad. You showin' up right after Kyser is like Christmas fucking day. This is my cousin's place who owes me a few favors. Nobody around. Plenty of tools, an incinerator, and lots of drains in the floor for cleanin' shit up. Bleed all ya want—they'll ever find either body."

Either body? Fuck! "Don't do it, man. We can work this out."

"Can't." Buck took aim. "I'd kill you for free, but I'm glad I'm getting' paid for it."

CHAPTER 27

Amy, Frank, Kristi, and Turk arrived to a standing ovation around 9 PM that evening at Sal's Doghouse. The old building, formerly a delicatessen, became a local watering hole for law enforcement personal in 2007, when it was purchased and remodeled by a retired officer. Attractive barmaids, inexpensive pitchers of beer, and a digital audio system in the guise of an old-fashioned jukebox, went a long way to establishing success. A quieter adjacent room had two pool tables, two foosball tables, a shuffleboard table, and three dart boards. Amy knew the reasonable assortment of bottled craft brews was a concession to modern times, but they sold a fair amount of Budweiser, Michelob, and Genesee Cream Ale. Coors and Miller Lite were on tap.

Word had gotten around about Frank McGrail's team and their operation to locate Sylvia Jarrett, a well-known business leader whose status evoked local royalty. She had already given a brief statement to the press on her abduction, even as medics treated the rope burns on her wrists and ankles. In typical fashion, she'd been shaken, but undaunted, and overly flattering in her assessment of Philly detectives for an investigation that uncovered her stepson's killer and provided a flawless rescue of herself and a friend from armed kidnappers.

Some conclusions came from the evidence, some came from deductive reasoning, and the blanks were filled in by Sylvia Jarrett and Joyce Kyser—summarized from Mindy's sporadic confessions, perhaps cathartic in nature, as revealed during the ordeal. Though Amy was still fuzzy on some details, the way it laid out: The bitter ex-girlfriend of Marcus Jarrett admitted to killing him in a rage from their breakup. As suspicions rose and the truth was about to be revealed, she took Sylvia and Joyce hostage during lunch. With stolen jewelry, and by extorting money, Mindy hoped to finance an escape and new identity. Unfortunately, the troubled young woman was betrayed and murdered by her own accomplice, Luke Chappelle, who also met his fate during the police incursion of the hideout. The Philly-born miscreant spotted Detective Turk Carver on approach and got off one shot from the kitchen before the officer returned fire. Chappelle was pronounced dead at the scene. Turk was treated and released for a graze to his side.

Glasses clinked as the crowd reminisced, laughed, and told jokes on the wave of an all-too infrequent success. As the only one wounded, Turk received more than his share of attention, dutifully showing his bandages a few times. Pretty soon, things died down and Frank and Amy settled on barstools away from the remaining partiers.

Frank took a swig and said, "I've come to a major decision and I have you to thank for it."

"Really? About what?"

"I'm going to ask Lindsay to marry me."

Amy was aghast. "Jesus, Frank. I mean, are you sure that's what you want? And also, um, which one is Lindsay?"

"You know … Lindsay Cresmont. Her nickname is Krinkles. She's the dog groomer, works at Planetary Pet."

"Um, the redhead?"

"Nah, that's Jasmine. Or could be Melanie. But you remember Lindsay. We stopped by her birthday party after work a few months ago."

"We did?"

"Yeah. Tall blonde. She's got a parrot and a big dog named Barker."

Amy's eyes widened. "Okay. I remember now. She was wearing pink sweatpants with *you're following too close* across her ass. Half of her hair is lavender."

"That's the one."

"I see. You know, there's sort of a … Well, what I mean is—she's not your usual type. This is really what you want?"

"Yeah, pretty sure it is."

"There's an … *age difference* to consider."

"You're saying she's too young for me."

"Well, you may want to … Frank, is she pregnant?"

"Um, well, that's the other thing . . ."

"You got her pregnant? Oh my God, Frank. That's insane. How old is she? Thirty? C'mon. How old?"

Frank exhaled. "Twenty-four."

"Oh, good God. Do you realize this is a monumental decision? It's not a shift in direction, it's a whole … Wait a minute! Me? You said you have me to thank? How did I have anything to do with this decision?"

"The other day when we talked in the car on the way to the Jarrett Estate. You got me thinking about stuff and I realized I needed to make a change. Give up the single life. So, I just want to say thanks."

"*Me?*" Amy shook her head. "No way! You got that from what I said? I hardly even spoke. And I certainly never meant anything of the sort. I've seen you grow, seen you change. And now you pick the youngest girl I've ever seen you with. You're a better judge of character than anyone … I … never—" Amy's speed-talking came to a halt as Frank started laughing. "What the hell is so funny?"

"That look on your face." Frank relaxed, still chuckling. "We don't date. I'm just fucking with you. Not pregnant. No romance. Lindsay moved down to Philly from my hometown three years ago. As a favor to her parents, I check up on her from time to time."

"Oh, damn it." Amy stewed for a minute, not sure if she was more mad or relieved. It was definitely some of both. "You are a real shithead sometimes."

"Sorry. I just couldn't resist messing."

"Yeah, sure." Okay. Frank was just razzing her. Apparently, relief and overall joy were greater than the need to stay pissed at an asshole. "Try harder next time."

"Duly noted," he said and held out a bottle of spring water.

Amy tapped hers against it in tacit salute. "Fair enough." She sipped her water and tried to let the day wind down, although her mind was still piecing things together. There was a strange sense of loss with the death of Mindy Lyons. She would have loved the opportunity to question her and put a few murky issues to rest.

Although the chain of events seemed unequivocal, each aspect of Sylvia Jarrett's abduction had quickly been checked in an effort to be thorough. Phone company records showed that at precisely 3:35 PM, Sylvia Jarrett made a call to her maid, Janie Roland. Under duress, she ordered Ms. Roland to take all the household money and additional jewelry from the safe, place it in a cloth shopping bag and put it in the bushes near the edge of the Jarrett property. Ms. Roland did so and told no one in an effort to protect her employer's life. When questioned, she verified the story and the bag was recovered intact. After the fact, they could only deduce that Mindy planned to use the ransom to finance her flight from the law. Eventually, Chappelle killed Mindy, intending to keep the money for himself. The cell phone used by Sylvia to make the call was found on Chappelle, further corroborating Sylvia Jarrett and Joyce Kyser's account, which brought the investigation to a conclusion.

Later as the crowd dwindled, Frank and Amy took a few good-natured bows and left amidst protests. Once in the parking lot, they climbed into Amy's Mustang and drove away in oddly subdued silence.

So, this was victory … With such a boost to her career, Amy thought she should feel ecstatic. The perps were dead, the victims were safe, and Marcus Jarrett's murder was solved. Turk's injury was superficial. Every article and every newscast would be favorable. They were heroes all the way around—to the department, the public, and the press. She was thriving in her chosen profession.

And yet … It wasn't that the dots weren't connecting. They were. It was the way they connected so well, conveniently leaving out a lot of nagging variables.

"Frank," she finally said. "I told Nancy to go back fifteen or more years and take a close look at the whole Bradley Jarrett empire, including his relationship with Sylvia."

Surprising her, he said only, "And . . .?"

"She found nothing. No scandals, no missing funds, no unusual lawsuits, nothing suspicious."

"Uh-huh." He waited a moment, then said, "But . . .?"

"Well, there was one little thing. Bradley Jarrett died of a heart attack. About a week after the funeral … One of the guys in the ME's bio-science lab was killed in a hit and run."

"I remember that. Yeah. An okay guy, as I recall. I think his name was Freddy something. Anything there?"

"Frederick Plank. No. No red flags. Not really. Except that it was never solved. He was a forensic serologist."

"I'm not sure where you're headed with this."

"He ran the blood tests for anomalies from Bradley Jarrett's autopsy."

"Were there any?"

Amy shrugged. "None."

"And this means what?"

"I have no idea. But today at the house—when we first came into that back bedroom, Joyce Kyser was tied up and Sylvia was kneeling beside her."

"Huh? This has to do with *blood tests?*"

"No. Something else."

"Okay. Switching tracks, but let's see … Yep. Sylvia was trying to untie Joyce."

"Right. Across the room there was another chair and some rope on the floor. However—stop and think how it went down. We were by the garage. Kristi was to the rear of the house and reported looking in a window. Remember, she told us about Joyce Kyser but never mentioned Sylvia."

Frank frowned. "Maybe Kristi couldn't tell—"

"No. I checked with her a little while ago. Kristi is pretty tall, saw Joyce tied up and no one else. She's positive Sylvia was not in the other chair. So—Joyce was alone in the room. Right then, you and I heard shots and moved in. It would have been maybe sixty seconds later when we burst in there. Where'd Sylvia come from all of a sudden?"

"Mmmm. I have to admit, that's a fair question. Maybe Mindy or Chappelle separated them earlier."

"Then she would have been tied up somewhere else and escaped. I don't remember any evidence of that, like rope lying around in another room."

Frank had to ponder for a moment. "Maybe Chappelle untied Sylvia to use the bathroom. Then when we arrived, he was distracted—Sylvia would've gone back to help Joyce."

"At that *exact* moment? Sylvia didn't mention anything like that." Begrudgingly, she mumbled, "Yeah, it's possible, I guess."

"Sylvia definitely had rope marks on her wrists. I get your point. We'll have a look over the crime scene photos, see if we missed anything."

"Does it bother you that Corky Buck never surfaced?"

Frank looked at her askance. "Does Buck have something to do with Sylvia Jarrett not being tied up?"

"No."

Frank laughed. "Okay. I'll be honest here. I'm not thrilled with this case either. I mean, sure, I came off as a damn genius. The Chief is ready to throw us a parade. Lieutenant Trainer will stay out of our hair for the next month. Overall, though … Some things are bothering me."

"Me, too. I feel like we've been in the middle of one big deception all along. Corky Buck is an ex-con in the shadows of this whole case. When we finally solve it, he's nowhere around and some other hoodlum gets killed. There's another thing. Luke Chappelle measures six foot five, two-seventy. He's way too big to be the masked man who tied up Adrienne in the van and stole the equipment."

"So, there's still a missing bad guy somewhere. Maybe Buck."

"Exactly. He's five eleven. And I stand by my other theory—that Corky Buck killed Dolores Griego by mistake, thinking it was Vonda."

Frank nodded. "I can see that. It's a spiderweb. We know Kyser and Buck have been cooking up something. Cruz called earlier—started tailing Kyser from the impound lot, but now I can't reach him. Jesus."

"What do you think became of Vonda Cantu and Dixie Newberry? I mean, I have to believe they're dead. They vanished at least four days ago."

"We'll find them. They seemed like nice women. I'd like to see they get a proper burial. If Buck killed them, we'll nail that prick for it—even if I have to do it on my own time."

"I'm with you on that," Amy said. "And I can see the jealous angle. Marcus told Vonda about his prior relationship with Mindy—Vonda mentions it in her diary. Mindy dated Marcus Jarrett for over three years—on again, off again, it seems. Remember what Lt. Trainer said about studying the company? I did, and one thing stands out—Bradley Jarrett was ex-military and reportedly a stickler for rules. He had a policy banning romances within management and office personnel. He took it seriously, I checked. Looking it over, I think Mindy resigned from Jarrett Enterprises and took a job elsewhere to avoid conflict. She was free to pursue a relationship with Marcus."

"Makes sense. And it worked; they were together for a while. Maybe things cooled down. Then Vonda Cantu comes along and *wham-o*—Marcus falls in love. By then, Bradley Jarrett is long dead and times have changed. Must have pissed Mindy off."

"Right. I checked that, too. The rule still exists, but isn't actively enforced these days. Maybe Mindy got crazy jealous and let's assume Chappelle was working for her. Why would he mistakenly kill Dolores Griego and let her drop right in the bushes? Then afterwards kill Dixie and the real Vonda, going to the trouble of stashing the bodies and Vonda's car? Efficiently, too, since they haven't turned up. It doesn't make sense."

Frank nodded. "Point well taken. Another oddball thing. The phones were all tapped in the Jarrett mansion. But Sylvia Jarrett called the maid's personal cell phone about ransom demands. Why in the hell do that? The maid has her own business cell, supplied by the family. If Sylvia had called that one, or any of three damn house lines, our people would have recorded the call and been on top of it."

"Mmm, you're right. That is weird."

They drove along for several minutes. Turned to a low volume, Australia, by the Shins, played in the background. Amy knew there had to be parallel series of events coinciding and the investigation had steered them on only one. It was nearly impossible to see the whole thing because there was so much in it.

"So … You want to tell me what happened on that vacation?"

Amy grunted. "Not particularly."

"C'mon. We're partners."

"Why do you need to know about my personal life?"

Frank shrugged. "We're friends, too. You've heard a lot of stuff about me."

"And not all good, either." Amy sighed. "Fine. It's really not a big deal, anyway. I was a senior in college. Six of us pitched in on expenses and went to Daytona for spring break in this guy's big van. Three girls, three guys. None of us were dating each other, just hung out in the same crowd. We had a great time. Well, right before heading home, we realized there was hardly any money left between us. Not enough for gas, much less food."

"That happens. So … you … robbed a liquor store?"

Amy laughed. "Not hardly. No. That night we drove around checking out nightclubs. Then we picked the best one. A huge place. My friends kind of talked me into it. We all went in and I … sort of … entered the *wet t-shirt* contest."

Frank's eyes grew wide. "Seriously?"

"Very serious. Won seventy-five bucks."

"Oh, wow. And that was your gas money. First place?"

Amy shrugged. "Second."

"How many, um, contestants were there?"

"Fifteen, at least. Maybe eighteen."

"Wow. I've seen a few wet t-shirt contests. You win by *applause*. You wouldn't get the big yells unless … Well, you know. Did you flash the crowd?"

Amy rolled her eyes. "Yes, I flashed the crowd."

Frank grinned. "I understand. It was for a good cause. Sorry I missed it."

"Well, big news. There are photos. When I graduated there were blowups on the wall of at least two frat houses."

Frank laughed out loud. "Oh, geez. One of your friends took pictures."

Amy sighed. "Actually … I think all of them took pictures … and maybe some video." As Frank roared with more laughter, she yelled, "Just don't tell my mother."

After a minute, Frank composed himself and said, "Thanks for telling me."

"Don't mention it. Besides, you would've kept bugging me."

"True enough."

"You know," Amy said. "I still keep going back to Zachary Chastang. We're sure he raped Dixie at Marcus's birthday party. From the bruising the doctor observed, we know two people carried her from the bathroom to the bed."

"Some scumbag joined in. Or a partier was told she got drunk and passed out in the tub."

"My bet is on a second rapist. We were thinking the murder was about revenge for some woman he assaulted. Possibly that's not what happened. What if he was killed to keep him silent? Maybe by the other rapist. Someone who thought Chastang was getting careless. Who we might have figured was Marcus Jarrett."

"Sure. Because of drugs in his drawer and Chastang's fingerprints on some beer bottles. Now we know Mindy planted the drugs when she killed him. It's her fingerprint on the bag."

"You really think Mindy did it? Killed Marcus, I mean?"

Frank tilted his head and gave it a shake. "I'd love to hear an alternate theory. Mainly 'cause I don't like the one we've got. But you're forgetting that Mindy confessed to Sylvia and Joyce. While she had them held hostage, I might add."

Amy drove in silence for a moment. Under her breath she muttered, "So they *say*."

Frank stared at her. "I see what you're getting at. But Mindy did have the revolver that killed Marcus in her pocket."

"It appears that way. What's the basic rule you always tell me?"

"Never trust a man who doesn't like The Three Stooges."

"Well, yeah. What's another one?"

"Always be suspicious of … *convenience.*"

Amy nodded. "Exactly. Remember the scene at the mansion? A tumbler on its side. The only other disarray is one piece of crazy-expensive jewelry on the floor—which alerted the housekeeper. Mindy and Marcus in a cutesy photo that tipped us off to the prior relationship. Think about it. Marcus fell in love with Vonda while he still lived in the mansion—he would never have left a framed shot of him and Mindy on display."

"Okay. Plus, I seem to remember the housekeeper said she hadn't seen it for a while."

"Right. So maybe it was just put there again—for *our* benefit. After that, it all happened at high speed. Mindy Lyons and Chappelle are now dead. Marcus Jarrett is dead. His wife Vonda, who would be his heir, has vanished. Gilbert Kyser is staying out of sight. Corky Buck, the only known offender we've been looking for, is in the wind. And the only one left to tell the story is Sylvia Jarrett—who has a lot to gain."

Frank was silent for a moment, then said, "Dammit."

"What?"

"I hate it when you make sense."

Amy laughed. "Okay. Am I … on to something?"

"Yeah," Frank conceded. "I knew it felt off. Did you see the ME's report on Mindy Lyons?"

"No."

"Dead at least one hour before we got there. Maybe a little longer. So, let's say Chappelle killed her. What the hell was he waiting for? He would've been sitting around on his ass for that hour with a dead body and two hostages he didn't need anymore."

Amy shrugged. "Sure. By then, the money was waiting. The housekeeper didn't tell anyone. He could have killed Sylvia and Joyce, then just left. The problem is—these are suppositions, not evidence. You know what Lieutenant Trainer will say. We need more, a lot more."

"You're right about that. But here's something else. I can't get my head wrapped around Mindy spearheading this whole deal. Or killing Marcus. How would she have recruited Luke Chappelle for this mess? He was mainly a knuckle-buster with a few robbery and assault convictions. Dumb as a toaster from what I hear. Adding it all up—Mindy's MO was basically for shit. Like picking a hideout we found in a matter of hours. Did you know she had a 146 IQ?"

Amy was surprised. "You checked her background?"

"Yeah. A few hours ago. Honor student, University of Michigan on a scholarship. Spoke fluent French and Spanish. She did a year after college overseas in the Peace Corps as a business advisor."

Before Amy could respond, her cell phone began ringing. Resting on the console, the caller's name glowed: K WALDO.

Frank looked down and smiled. "Well, well. It's pretty late. Must be a booty call."

Ignoring him, Amy reached down and tapped the screen. "You're on speakerphone with Detectives Lepone and, um, McGrail."

"Where are you?"

"Well, hello to you, too." Amy answered. "We're … in the car."

"Where at?"

"Well, if you must know—Frankford Avenue, Kensington area."

"Close. Going anywhere urgent?"

Frank grinned and Amy rolled her eyes. "Not really."

"Good. I'm texting you an address. Not far from your position. I need you to come now. Both of you. See you soon."

Amy frowned as the call ended. "What the hell?"

Frank let out a hoot of laughter. "Does he do that often?"

"What? No, of course not. I've only spoken to him on the phone twice."

"Well, you're driving. So, the obvious question is—are we going?"

Amy pondered momentarily. She didn't know the man all that well. Not really. But if early impressions meant anything, then Kurt Waldo was not the whimsical or impulsive type. She tapped the screen and read the text. "Well, I suppose so. Over by the river, maybe ten minutes away."

"I understand completely."

"You do, really?"

"Sure." With a wide grin, he said, "However, I have to advise caution. Of course, I realize a three-way is a big chick-fantasy thing. A sick, twisted fantasy, that is. I'm just not sure I can approve this behavior."

Amy turned her head long enough for a disgusted glare. "A threesome … That's what you think this is about?"

"Sure. And I understand the appeal. Now, I'm not saying *yes* and I'm not saying *no*. The problem is—I'm not sure you can handle me and Waldo at the same time."

Amy snorted and shook her head. "Get real. I could turn you *both* into Jell-O. But pull your mind out of the gutter—that's not what this is about. Whatever's going on will be case-related."

Frank raised an eyebrow. "Case-related? Ha. At this time of night?"

"Are you coming along? Or can I drop you somewhere?"

Frank eased back in his seat. "Wouldn't miss this for the world."

CHAPTER 28

I t was after dark as Amy drove along the Delaware
River just east of I-95. There were a lot of wide-open
spaces interspersed with businesses that included natural gas, petroleum, construction, steel, and many
others. Buildings varied greatly in size, shape, and
material. Some had large systems of pipes that came
out of the ground and fed into the structure. Others
had vast metallic framework that could be tall, wide,
circular, or rectangular. The purpose of it all was
inconclusive. No homes, fast food, or tourist stops,
but she knew there was a nightclub or two tucked
among the unadorned concrete, stucco, and old brick
structures. This was truly the unheeded nuts and bolts
hub of Philly. Few signs guided visitors within the
area. Those who came this way already knew where
they were going.

"Should be right up here."

Frank's voice jolted Amy from her thoughts. A
small sign came into view that said only Canzoneri
and Stokes. From a quick internet search, they'd determined it was a rental place for motorized equipment.

The structure was huge, like a warehouse, with a smaller one-story building off to the right, probably for offices and customer service. Windows in both were dark. A Ford F-150 and Cruz's Sunfire where in the lot, both off to the side, as though they were parked to stay out of sight.

"That's Cruz's car there."

Frank nodded. "I also caught a glimpse of a car straight back by the other building. Looks like maybe a Lexus. The pickup is Waldo's."

"He drives a Land Rover."

"He owns this truck, too."

"Really? You checked him out?"

Frank gave her a crooked smile. "Military records are one thing. I went deep. Hobbies, pets, allergies, hat size. Played first base in little league. Sectional wrestling champ in high school. Hell, yeah, I checked him out."

Amy had to smile. *Okay, she couldn't blame him.* "What's he allergic to."

Frank shrugged. "Nothing. But you may be interested to know he also has a 2012 Harley-Davidson Street Glide."

"What else did you find out?"

"Can we play twenty questions later? I'd like to see what the hell is going on here."

Amy grumbled. "Fine."

The property had a formidable-looking fence surrounding the property, yet the gate at the front was wide open. She just wasn't sure if that was good or bad. She killed the headlights and slowly drove into the lot, easing toward a rollup door in front that was partly open. A large floodlight up above brightened the immediate area.

Amy pulled up close and turned off the ignition. "How do we play this?"

Frank opened the door and stepped out; Amy did, too. The building across the street was in darkness. No movement, no other people. She watched her partner as he surveyed the situation, looking up, down, back and forth, quickly taking everything in. Frank's thought processes functioned in 360 degrees.

"We'll do it by the book," Frank said quietly. "Whatever's going on, they surely know we're here. We'll just ID ourselves—"

A booming voice from inside called out. "Come on in, you two. It's safe."

Amy knew immediately. "That's Waldo."

"Yeah," Frank said. "Go in left, I'll go right."

Amy needed to duck down only slightly and slipped inside, hand on the Sig 9mm by her hip. Even in gloom, she saw the room was enormous. Tractors, backhoes, and other large devices were abundant, probably for excavating, most of which she couldn't put names to. The only real glow was straight back. Nearby, were groups of generators, compressors, pumps, and various landscaping equipment. Chain saws, reciprocating saws, sanders, and the like sat on shelves or hung on the far wall. She eased forward, with Frank about twelve feet to her right, and noticed an oddly relaxed setting by the light from a single desk lamp.

Standing to the left of a long wooden workstation, Alvin Cruz leaned on his elbows. Kurt Waldo sat comfortably on a wooden bench, a neutral expression on his face. The big surprise was over to the right. An average-sized man with long, disheveled hair was tied to a folding chair. It was hard to make out his face amidst dried blood and duct tape, but she was pretty sure that was Corky Buck.

Waldo stood as they approached. "Look around if you want. But it's clear. Back door locked and no one else in the building."

Now that she could see Cruz up close, he had the look of a lost puppy caught out in the rain. Atypical, to say the least. Waldo was calm, collected, and definitely in charge. Buck … Well, he looked like he'd been mugged, hit by a bus, then kidnapped. She was anxious to hear what happened for him to end up in that condition. Not ready to let her guard down, Amy looked left and right, quickly surveying the premises. Quiet, still. No sense of impending trouble or attack. According to regulations, Amy knew they should go through and clear the place themselves. Her instincts were telling her this was no scam or trap. It was where she needed to be.

She stepped closer and saw two clear plastic bags on the workbench. One held a revolver, the other, a peculiar metal shaft, tapered, with a thick handle.

On it, appeared to be … Amy pointed. "Is that blood on the … *thing?*"

"Indeed it is," Waldo said.

Frank asked, "You had evidence bags with you?"

Waldo shrugged. "Sure. Always."

"Interesting." Frank exhaled loudly. "Do we need to call in EMTs?"

"No. We can't help the guy missing the blood."

"Is he here?"

"What's left of him. In the back room."

Frank turned to Cruz. "You okay?"

"Barely. Yeah, I'm in one piece."

Amy's mind was racing, trying to put it all together. A gun. A dead body, apparently, in back. A bloody weapon. A prisoner. How would this all lay out for the district attorney? She and Frank weren't even here for whatever went down—yet somehow it would all be their fault. Then there was the issue of Cruz and Waldo working together … Tough to figure how that came about. She couldn't piece it together yet, but felt they'd stumbled upon the lynchpin needed for filling in all the blanks.

Frank looked around and shook his head. "We've got a fucking mess here. I've got to call this in. Our superior is gonna shit a sailboat."

"Maybe so." Waldo grinned slightly. "But there's good news to go with the bad."

By the following morning, the kidnap and rescue of Philly's leading businesswoman had blossomed into a sensation that was the talk of the town. Amy had watched TV earlier as Sylvia Jarrett gave a gracious press update from her front lawn. It would be shown on all local stations and was expected to generate a certain amount of national attention.

Frank and Amy arrived in their unmarked Stratus at the splendid Jarrett home in Chestnut Hill. Still a hotbed of activity, she counted five news vans, three police cars, and many other vehicles clogging the street. At least twenty reporters continued a vigil hoping for photo opportunities, quotes, or even a mere few sound bytes. Dozens of onlookers turned and cameras clicked as the crowd parted for Frank and Amy as they stepped around the police barricades. A round of applause erupted for the hero-detectives—their photos and video clips had made the news. Voices immediately called out their names as they crossed the walkway.

"Detective McGrail," a reporter shouted, "how does it feel to have saved one of our city's business leaders?"

Frank slowed and gave a little wave. "Well, I'd have to say—it feels pretty darn good."

Everyone laughed and another voice said, "Is Ms. Jarrett in protective custody?"

Frank replied, "Only from all of *you*."

More laughter and the voices overlapped, coming more rapidly. "Why are you here now? Was Mindy Lyons a suspect all along? Are you still investigating?"

"Just finishing up. That's about it."

Amy was glad that Frank turned and headed towards the house, now ignoring the clamor of bombarding questions. It could easily get drawn out and they had work to do. "This should be interesting," she whispered.

Frank replied, "To say the least."

A uniformed patrol officer stood just inside the front door and nodded hello as Janie Roland greeted Frank and Amy. The housekeeper was all smiles as she led them through the stately home and into the now-familiar sunroom. Sylvia Jarrett was seated at the round table in the center, Joyce Kyser to her left. Close by on the couch was Warren Hamilton. Sylvia leaped up, gave quick hugs, and offered beverages with just the right mix of humility and hospitality. The men quickly stood and handshakes went around.

She was shrewd and classy, Amy wouldn't deny her that. It was as if a public relations expert had briefed her on the most expedient way to look and act in this situation—which, for someone like her, was a real possibility. The hair was brushed but not styled, and the make-up faint. In a loose-fitting peach jumpsuit, she appeared neither pampered nor disheveled, radiating the shaken but triumphant spirit of a brave victim. She made smooth introductions, glossing over the credentials of a well-known attorney. She didn't need to mention he was from the biggest firm in town. The message was clear: Sylvia Jarrett was a survivor and still in command. Her interests were protected—just a formality since she didn't need protecting. Joyce, a friend and fellow victim, was by her side showing fortitude and respect. Amy was more than perturbed and ready for this next scene to play out.

"We need to talk to Mrs. Kyser," Frank said. "If there's a place we could go in private."

Joyce looked solemn, her lower lip quivering as though she expected bad news. "If it's all the same to you, I'd like to be with my friend right now."

"Of course," Frank said. "First, I need to know— have you heard from Alvin Cruz?"

"Not since Tuesday evening." Joyce seemed to think it over. "Mmm. Yes, that's when I saw you detectives at Mr. Cruz's home. To be honest, he's been checking on my husband for me."

"May I ask why?"

"Well, I thought he might be cheating on me. It turns out Mr. Cruz found no proof of that. I'm relieved, of course. What does this have to do with anything?"

Frank exhaled. "It's just that Alvin Cruz seems to have disappeared. We're afraid he may be caught up in this whole thing somehow."

"Oh my." Sylvia leaned forward. "As you know, I also hired him to investigate Marcus's murder. I felt I owed it to my late husband to have an independent look at his son's death. No offense to the police department, of course."

Frank nodded. "None taken."

"Thank you, Detective. In my last talk with Mr. Cruz, he hadn't uncovered anything substantial. I hope he's all right."

"So do I." Frank turned back to Joyce. "I'd like to know about your relationship with Mr. Cruz."

Joyce looked insulted. "I resent that implication, Detective. There is no *relationship*. He's been keeping an eye on my husband and that's all. Completely professional."

"I see. Well, we'll keep you informed. And tell us if he contacts you. Now I have very unpleasant news. I'm terribly sorry to inform you, and there's no easy way to say it. Your husband, Gilbert, has been found dead."

Joyce trembled and then burst into tears. Sylvia came up from her chair and embraced her friend. The two held on momentarily until the sobs subsided.

"May I ask," Joyce said with a shiver, "what happened? I mean, how could he ... How did he . . .?"

"He was murdered, Mrs. Kyser. It's under investigation, I assure you."

"I ... I ... just can't believe it."

"Our sincere condolences for your loss, Mrs. Kyser. And we're sorry to bring up the other matters at this time but there is a connection. In your account of yesterday's ordeal, you both mentioned that Mindy said something about planting drugs in Marcus Jarrett's home. Is that correct?"

Sylvia and Joyce nodded in unison. "Yes," Sylvia said. "We didn't really understand what she meant."

Frank nodded. "A bag of illegal drugs *was* found in Marcus's drawer but the information was not released. There was a partial fingerprint on the bag that was not on file. We know now it belonged to Mindy Lyons."

Sylvia sat back down in her chair. "It's true, then. So, she must have intended to stain Marcus's character. My goodness. I had no idea. The woman was positively deranged."

"That's exactly what we thought—*originally.*"

Sylvia looked quizzical. "I beg your pardon?"

"Yes." Amy stepped forward. "Some anomalies have caused us to look closer. The first of many is that all three of you had homemade lemonade with lunch. From fingerprints, we know who drank from each of the glasses. Mindy's glass fell to the floor and spilled out. But I used a special device that works like a sponge to collect enough of the liquid for examination. Oddly, there were traces of sedative. None in either of your glasses."

Sylvia Jarrett shrugged. "I'm not sure what you're suggesting, Detective."

Amy smiled. "Fairly simple. It means someone slipped her a knockout drug then dumped out the remainder so it wouldn't be discovered."

"Well," Sylvia said, "I have no idea about that."

"It will be clear in a few minutes since other information has come to light. The evening of Marcus's murder, neighbors heard a noise that sounded like a car backfire. Within minutes, a blonde woman came out of Marcus's house and got in a car in the driveway. They watched it start up and drive away."

"So," Sylvia supplied, "they witnessed Mindy leaving."

"Actually, no. Mindy Lyons was nearly six feet tall with curly hair. Both witnesses describe a short woman with *straight* hair." Amy turned. "They saw you, Mrs. Kyser."

"What?"

Amy watched closely as Joyce stammered while trying to decide what to do next. There was shock in her eyes but also a little outrage. Clearly by now, she expected to get away with it.

"I … I … How dare you say these things. I just heard about my husband. I'm grieving, damn you."

Warren Hamilton spoke up. "I must interject here that a witness popping up suddenly is confutative."

"Not really. These neighbors were never inter-viewed because they had been away, camping on Chincoteague Island. But they were home the night of the murder packing suitcases. After putting put their children to bed around nine, they relaxed qui-etly in deck chairs out front, kccping lights off to avoid insects."

Sylvia looked at Joyce with disbelief, shot a glance to Warren Hamilton and then jumped to her feet. "Just what's going on here? Joyce is a trusted friend. Why would she be involved in Marcus's murder? Obviously those people are mistaken."

"I'm afraid not." Amy stood before Joyce and carefully spoke the Miranda Warning as used during arrests in the United States since 1966. She watched with interest as odd glances between Joyce, Sylvia, and Warren Hamilton went back and forth that seemed to include unspoken questions, instructions, and confusion. For the police, it was both curse and blessing that a lawyer was present. Amy couldn't afford to make mistakes but then any jury might feel the suspect's rights were protected from the start.

Hamilton stepped forward. "I have not been formally retained in this matter," he said. "Obviously, I represent the Jarrett family and want Marcus's killer brought to justice. However, I am familiar with his new place of residence. The homes are large and quite far apart. A lot of trees and shrubbery. I recall the time of death was established at around 10 PM. Any adjacent neighbors would be far enough away to consider this a tenuous identification in the dark."

"Possibly," Amy said. "However, their verandah lines up directly across from Marcus's driveway. I checked the weather. That night had clear skies and nearly a full moon. These neighbors clearly recall the departing vehicle had a distinctive low rumble, describing it as a sports car, dark in color. Mindy drove a large silver SUV. They saw your car, Mrs. Kyser, with a 5.7-liter, V-8 engine. The man even mentioned he thought it was a newer-model Dodge Challenger."

Joyce turned to Sylvia Jarrett. "Please tell them— this is outrageous."

Warren Harington said, "It would be best if neither of you speak right now."

"They don't need to speak," Amy said, suppressing a grin. "We know the handgun discovered in Mindy Lyons's pocket was the murder weapon used on Marcus. Her fingerprints were on it—one shot had been fired. That makes Mindy look quite guilty. However, identical .32 caliber ammunition was found in a leather carryall near Gilbert Kyser's body in a facility across town. That box contained exactly forty-four rounds out of fifty. And Joyce, *your* prints are on the box. That means *you* handled the same bullets that were loaded into the gun that killed Marcus Jarrett."

Confusion crossed Joyce's face and then it quickly changed to fear. Turning to Sylvia she said, "How could that box be with Gilbert?"

"Shut up, Joyce."

"Just tell me what the fuck's going on."

Warren Hamilton held up a hand. "I advise both of you to not say another word."

"No one has to talk to us. The evidence speaks for itself." Amy nodded to Frank who handcuffed Joyce behind her back. She continued by saying, "We're very sorry to inform you Mrs. Jarrett, but Joyce Kyser killed your stepson. She's under arrest for murder and for conspiracy to commit murder in the case of her husband."

Joyce looked at Sylvia and shouted. "I'm not getting fucked over here. No way."

Sylvia shook her head. "You're not. Just calm down. I'll get the firm on this right away."

"I get it." Joyce's eyes widened and she screamed. "You set me up. You bitch. How could those bullets be with Gilbert? Buck wouldn't have left them there. You told—"

Sylvia lunged and slapped the much smaller woman hard across the face. Frank grabbed a stunned Joyce by the shoulders to prevent her from falling down.

"That's enough, Mrs. Jarrett," Amy snapped and stepped between them.

"She *wanted me* to kill him." Joyce was mumbling while regaining her senses and then yelled as Frank shuffled her out the door. "She knew all about it. I want a *deal!*"

Warren Hamilton stepped in front of Sylvia. "Mrs. Jarrett has nothing to say at this time."

Amy returned a thin smile, knowing this would work out in favor of the good guys.

Late last night, Kurt Waldo had intervened at the last second and prevented Corky Buck from killing Alvin Cruz. Unfortunately, he'd been too late to help Gilbert Kyser, who was lying dead in a back room, killed by the tapered weapon that was now being examined in the crime lab. She'd bet a week's pay their techs would prove it was also the weapon used on Dolores Griego. Whatever threats or pressure Waldo applied on Buck was unclear—but he was cooperating. Mindy Lyons may have still loved Marcus Jarrett but it was her only real involvement.

According to Buck, it was planned out in advance. Pretending to be worried, Joyce showed a baggie of her husband's drugs to Mindy that she briefly handled. Then later, Joyce placed that bag in a drawer at Marcus's home after killing him. Also, in a search of Buck's residence, a manila folder was found. Inside, was printed material that showed Marcus had been secretly investigating Sylvia Jarrett, his father's will, and his father's death. Some detailed notes and theories were written in longhand. The best part, in addition to Marcus's and Buck's fingerprints on the folder, it also had Joyce Kyser's. It all made sense and tied up a lot of loose ends. Marcus's computers, however, showed no such research. It was possible he had concern about Sylvia's guile and indomitable skills. As such, he could have compiled it all from a remote computer with no ties to Jarrett Enterprises. "That's just fine, counselor. She's under arrest, anyway."

"You can't mean that, Detective. Joyce Kyser is clearly under extreme stress right now. Her statements will be declared inadmissible in any—"

Two men in dark suits stepped in to the room that seemed to startle him. Amy knew he would recognize them as detectives for the DA's office. One of the men handed Hamilton a folded paper.

"Her statements aren't the only thing we're going on. That's a warrant to search the premises." Amy nodded to the second man who handcuffed Sylvia Jarrett as Hamilton quickly scanned the document. He'd be wondering how they managed to produce a warrant so soon—but not for long. Three more detectives came through the living room and deployed in all directions. Amy began reciting the Miranda warning for the second time that day, speaking clearly and never varying from the proper format. Sylvia tried to interrupt with, "This is ridiculous," and Hamilton scolded with, "Don't speak."

"I suggest you follow your lawyer's advice, Mrs. Jarrett," Amy said when finished. "You don't have to tell us anything." She smiled and added, "Corky Buck is in custody, by the way. He's been telling a long interesting story since we picked him up last night."

Sylvia laughed nervously. "I never heard of him."

"Don't speak," Hamilton said.

Amy ignored the attorney. "Really? That's funny. Because at 5:22 yesterday afternoon, Buck sent a text message on his cell phone that said, 'it's done.' At 5:35 he got a reply that said, 'good – clean up, no mistakes.' There are other texts, too."

Sylvia shrugged. "So?"

"He claims those were to and from *you*—the person paying him and giving orders."

"He's lying."

"Shut up," Hamilton said loudly.

"Those must have been to Mindy," Sylvia blurted. "Or maybe it was to Joyce. You said she murdered Marcus. They could have been working together."

"Stop talking *now!*" Hamilton shouted.

"No, they weren't." Amy stood her ground in front of the rich and powerful widow of Bradley Jarrett. There was no denying she was beautiful, smart, and had a head for business. Computers, charts, graphs, statistics, payrolls, investments, interest rates, tax deductions—they were all second nature. She was used to commanding respect, being in charge, and overcoming pecuniary rivals. In the board room, she had an aura of authority and a reputation as unflappable. In the criminal world, she faced a whole different set of rules and they'd caught her off guard. At this point, Sylvia didn't know what Buck told them or what deal he might make to offset maximum jail time. She would also be shaken by Joyce Kyser's sense of betrayal—manipulated, of course, by arresting and removing her first. Joyce, clearly the weak link, would surely open up in exchange for leniency. Flustered now, Sylvia was in a state of panic—a situation to which she was unaccustomed.

"Those messages were to you, Mrs. Jarrett," Amy continued. "The usage has been tracked. We also know that a burner cell phone received those texts at the Madonna home where you were rescued. We didn't find it inside the house or on the bodies of Mindy Lyons or Luke Chappelle. That means it left there with *you*. And we also know that very phone is in this house right now. Trust me, our team will find it. Also, Corky Buck has something to back up his story. He stole high-tech recording equipment from a police van on Tuesday evening. He's actually quite savvy and used it yesterday to record some interesting conversation. An analysis verifies that it's your voice giving explicit instructions. It's time coded and he's described the circumstances that it was made." Amy paused for effect and gave a friendly smile. "To put this all very simply—you're under arrest for kidnapping, fraud, and three counts of conspiracy to commit murder."

Sylvia Jarrett, in handcuffs, lost a few shades of color in her face as she was led outside by two burly detectives. Warren Hamilton fell in behind, looking none too happy at the coming upheaval. Amy was thinking about all those reporters and onlookers out front who were about to get the surprise of their lives. Videos of the next two minutes would quickly get hits by the thousands on the internet and the event would be relentlessly tweeted. She could imagine the headlines now: SYLVIA JARRETT IN KIDNAPPING HOAX. SYLVIA JARRETT ARRESTED IN MURDER PROBE. SYLVIA JARRETT MASTERMINDED HER STEPSON'S MURDER. With a deep breath and a sigh of satisfaction, Amy followed.

CHAPTER 29

Amy drove along, reviewing the rest of a day that had become a blur of meetings, debriefing, reports, and paperwork. She remembered her big grin when word came through that a prepaid cell phone had been recovered in the Jarrett residence, complete with Sylvia's fingerprints and the incriminating text messages still intact. That kind of evidence would suggest a slam-dunk. Of course, the rich widow would try every trick in the book—maybe a few that weren't. They'd been able to sneak up on her once but wouldn't get that chance again. The DA's team would need to carefully prepare the case for court—the beginning of the end for Sylvia Jarrett. Hopefully . . .

Corky Buck was booked for the murder of Gilbert Kyser and remained a suspect in the murder of Dolores Griego, pending further developments and lab test results. Joyce Kyser was booked for the murder of Marcus Jarrett. Her testimony, as well as Buck's, along with mounting physical evidence, would send Sylvia Jarrett to prison for decades. Amy knew they might never be sure who pulled the trigger to kill

Mindy Lyons, but at the very least, Sylvia Jarrett was a conspirator, as well as for the murders of Marcus Jarrett and Gilbert Kyser.

In the coming days, Amy planned to review the untimely death of Bradley Jarrett and determine if Sylvia may have been complicit in what was, at the time, considered to be of natural causes. In conjunction, they would also reopen the case of Frederick Plank, a lab tech who died in an unsolved hit and run less than a week after performing key forensic tests for Bradley Jarrett's autopsy. Amy was betting on more charges against Sylvia.

By the time she arrived at Frank's place, Goggles, Gigi, and Alvin Cruz sat on the couch drinking beer and watching a Phillies game on Frank's big screen TV. Layla jumped up, danced in circles, and ran back and forth as though she just couldn't decide who would provide the most attention.

"Well, well," Frank said, emerging from the kitchen and looking Amy over. "Now it's a party."

"Wow," Goggles said. You're all decked out."

Cruz let out a whistle. "My, my, my!"

Amy knew that was coming—she had changed into medium-heeled white sandals and a vibrant-blue off the shoulder cocktail dress. And did her makeup. And used a curling iron to put a little flip in her hair. For something later, but she wasn't going to mention that yet. "I stopped home and changed," she said with a shrug. "No big deal."

Frank said, "Well, you're just in time. We're about to order pizzas."

"Oh," Amy said, "don't think I'm in a pizza mood."

"Stromboli?"

Amy frowned. "Not for me. But go ahead and get whatever you want."

Cruz laughed and said, "You know, Amy—you look like you've got a hot date."

Dammit, Amy thought, and hoped she didn't blush. Leave it to Cruz hit the nail on the head while trying to be funny. "It's just—I'd been in my work clothes for twelve hours."

"So, she doesn't live in jeans and sneakers," Frank said, glaring at Cruz, "Like you're the fashion plate around here. All this is from a guy who got sucked into an affair with a married client—who also turned out to be the killer."

"Hey! That's not cool. When you put it that way, I sound like an *idiot*."

"You *are* an idiot."

"It wasn't my fault. Besides, I thought Kyser wanted Joyce dead. And I swear, Sylvia Jarrett said to spare no expense. You should've heard her. She practically demanded that I find Marcus's killer."

Frank grunted. "Of course, she did. That was for show, Genius! Because she already planned to have *you* killed."

"Oh … Right."

"Besides, Joyce is a con artist. Not to mention she knew about her husband's fucked up hobby and just let it go on. Probably so she'd have something to shift focus away from her when she got rid of him."

"Yeah, we know that *now*." Cruz looked around like he expected support, but none was forthcoming. "Okay, fine. I admit it. I got sucked in. One thing you have to admit—Joyce Kyser is a major cutie-pie."

Frank stared at him for a moment. "So, that makes it all okay? You're invoking the *hot-babe* defense."

They were all laughing and Amy was glad for a distraction that had effectively dropped the subject of her wardrobe. The reason would be clear soon enough.

Gigi leaned forward with a huge smile. "I suppose, we all remember my insightful report on the Marcus Jarrett crime scene. Someone short. How tall is Joyce Kyser?

Frank exhaled. "Just over five feet. We'll give you that one. Seems obvious now that Gilbert Kyser and Zach Chastang were date-rape buddies. Those ass-holes are the ones who raped Dixie and carried her to the tub afterwards."

Amy nodded. "Right. And we know Chastang was getting more and more reckless. He grew up rich, thinking he was above it all. And Kyser was just the opposite. He was paranoid and worried about getting caught."

"So, he decided to have Chastang taken out. Buck did the job and then put the cash and ammo in Vonda Cantu's place to frame her. But mistakenly killed Dolores Griego instead. *Scumbag!*"

"That's how I see it, too," Amy said. "Gilbert Kyser hired Corky Buck for his dirty work. At some point, Sylvia Jarrett slipped in and took over, making it all part of her big plan. A guy like Buck would've been just fine switching sides for a price. And a little while ago, Kristi gave me a new tidbit from her fiancé."

Goggles asked, "That's the lawyer, correct?"

"Yep. It seems that according to the company's bylaws, Sylvia will have to step down from her position while defending herself. That goes for any capital case. Assuming she's found guilty—which I'm pretty certain of—she'd lose all authority. But that might not even matter. The collusion and felonies in this situation violate a prenuptial agreement that Sylvia signed."

Frank said, "A double whammy."

"Yes. It means forfeiture of assets. If Vonda Cantu was still alive, or I guess I should say Vonda Cantu *Jarrett,* she would have inherited the mansion, a serious fortune, and the top spot in the company as Marcus's widow."

"That's a shame," Frank said. "Vonda seemed like a sharp cookie. I'll bet she would've done Marcus proud."

"I liked Dixie, too," Amy said. "We'll figure out what happened to them. Buck won't talk about it. I think he wants more cards to play as things move forward."

"Could be. For now, we got nothing on him for that. Besides, somebody else could've done it—like

Chappelle, who's in the morgue. Or some other scumball we don't know about yet. If the bodies were dumped in a remote area or they're in Vonda's car at the bottom of a damn lake someplace … Shit! With no leads, it might be years before they're found."

"Well, you're right. I'm going to keep at it, anyway."

Frank nodded to his partner. "Yeah. Me too."

She knew what Frank was feeling because she was feeling it, too. Sometimes, a particular case or victim would get under your skin a little more than others. Down deep she just wanted to scream. Vonda and Dixie just seemed like good people. She would really like to see to it that those young women could rest in peace.

"I did find out that Marcus Jarrett's body has been released," Amy said. "I heard the company has taken over planning the burial."

"Apparently a good guy," Frank said, turning toward Cruz. "And it seems like you owe Kurt Waldo a really big thanks."

"Yeah. I got careless. Wandered in the door of that damn tractor place and started snooping around. I wondered what Kyser was up to. Buck had already killed him when he got the drop on me. Thank God for Waldo. He tailed me trying to figure out what *I* was doing."

"A good thing," Frank said.

"You got *that* right. Buck's plan was to use the heavy-duty tools in that place to dispose of Kyser's body. If not for Waldo . . ."

380

"You and Kyser might have vanished without a trace."

"That's about it.."

Everyone took slugs of beer and munched on chips until a knock on the door drew their attention. Amy was closest, checked the peephole and opened up. Kurt Waldo stepped inside wearing a stylish dress shirt and sport coat. Amy looked him over quickly, nodded a little hello, and thought *wow!* Cruz stood, walked up to him, and vigorously shook hands, then formally introduced the man to Goggles and Gigi.

Waldo said, "I hope I'm not intruding."

Frank waved him in. "C'mon and join us. Besides, it's not like you to wait for an invitation."

Waldo froze. "Am I … welcome?"

"Sure," Frank said, walking over to shake his hand, too. "We definitely owe you a few beers. Follow me."

Gigi looked at Amy and mouthed the word: "Wow."

Amy was relieved. They all knew that Waldo was the one who broke into the house, then dove out Frank's living room window. But in the end, he helped solve the case and saved Cruz's life. That would be enough to put him on their list of friends.

"I'll take one. Thanks." Waldo turned to Amy. "You look stunning, Detective."

Amy rolled her eyes. That seemed to come up a lot. "Thanks, Kurt."

Moments later, they were all seated except for Cruz, who was wide-eyed and on his feet. "It was unbelievable. I was about to get shot. I mean, my life passed before my eyes and all that stuff. This guy came out of nowhere and took Buck down like Jason Bourne against a fourth-grader."

"That's quite a rescue," Frank said, turning toward Waldo. "But I'm curious about something. According to Cruz, when Corky Buck came to, for the first ten minutes, all he would say is 'lawyer.' Later, when we questioned him, he laid out the whole shebang. And I understand before me and Amy got there, you spent some time alone with Buck—in a maintenance room full of power tools."

"Yeah," Waldo said with a thin smile. "We had a chat and I explained some things. You know the value of life and how a person can do some good in this world, or they just might fade away. Figuratively, of course."

Frank nodded. "I suppose he had a change of heart."

"Yep," Waldo said, and finished off his beer. "Must be it." He rose to his feet and looked around. "This has been great and I appreciate the hospitality. Now I think Amy and I should get going and leave you to enjoy your evening."

All eyes turned to Amy who definitely knew she blushed this time. Gigi winked and gave her two thumbs up. "Uh, yes. I guess we should. Kurt and I are going out for a late snack."

Everyone stood and said good-byes, then listened as Cruz thanked Waldo again for saving his life, praising his fighting skills with comparisons to Jackie Chan and including a more detailed account of disarming Buck with ease.

Frank took the time to pull Amy aside near the door. With a huge grin, he kept his voice low and said, "So—you and Waldo are having dinner."

"Yes, we are. He asked me, and I accepted."

"Do you date all guys that attack you in dark hallways, or just certain ones?"

"That's not funny." Amy smirked. "Okay, it's a *little* funny."

"Where are you headed?"

Amy didn't reply for a moment, then said, "La Travita."

"Ahh. Good choice. Not big and splashy. He's going for ambiance. Great menu. The lobster risotto is terrific."

"Of course, you'd know the place. So, what are you saying? Kurt Waldo is a classy guy?"

Frank scoffed. "Not exactly. Just that he's springing for an expensive meal. Drinks. Nice subdued atmosphere. Some caution is in order. I know men and I have to warn you—he might think he's getting lucky tonight."

Amy curved her index finger, making a little motion. Frank bent down and she whispered in his ear. "He's *definitely* getting lucky tonight."

CHAPTER 30

The surprise and confusion surrounding the arrest of Sylvia Jarrett and the related murders of Marcus Jarrett, Gilbert Kyser, Mindy Lyons, and Luke Chappelle, had, predictably, whipped the media into a frenzy. The story drew headlines, dominated local news, sparked internet chat, and jammed the call-in lines of local talk-radio shows. Amy had received requests for interviews which she abruptly declined. Such things rarely worked out favorably and were taboo while the case was pending. She was thankful when Saturday came, a welcome day off, and Amy met Frank to head out for Marcus Jarrett's services.

In the interest of loyalty to their founder and his victimized son, the company executives took charge in planning a fitting and dignified funeral. The private services were held before a selected group of family, friends, and longtime employees at an undisclosed church in the suburbs. Four of the company's management staff, two of Marcus's fraternity brothers, and one cousin all recounted his upbeat personality, superior work ethic, and many accolades. Sylvia Jarrett, in police custody, did not attend.

The burial afterwards attracted a smattering of onlookers and various bloggers and reporters who had the good sense to remain unobtrusive. The quiet ceremony took place at a local memorial park where two previous generations of the Jarrett family had been laid to rest. There were no tombstones throughout, only small plaques to mark the sites. Gently rolling hills, tidy landscaping, and judiciously placed trees and shrubs provided picturesque surroundings. It was a beautiful day in the high seventies as the time came to place flowers on the ornate casket. Amy and Frank watched the proceedings from a position well behind the main group of mourners.

"I think I figured something out," Amy said quietly as Frank leaned closer. "I'm guessing Mindy to be the mystery 9-1-1 call that morning. She still cared for Marcus and probably came by to talk. When she found him dead, she wouldn't have been able to just leave him there."

"Why wouldn't she just ID herself?"

"Hard to say. People panic sometimes. Fear of getting involved. Fear that she'd be blamed as the jealous ex-girlfriend."

Frank nodded. "Makes sense. Another guess, she suspected Kurt Waldo of his murder."

"That follows, too. She knew about Dixie's rape and how Marcus was devastated that it happened at his birthday party. I'm sure Mindy connected that up and figured it's why Marcus was killed. Plus, we know she overheard Zachary asking a VP to send Waldo to stop Marcus."

"Yeah. And that's the kicker. That sad mess had nothing to do with his death."

"True. Mindy was misled. Sylvia and Joyce were supposed to be her friends. She was looking for an explanation into the murder that made sense. And she didn't know Kurt very well."

Frank grinned. "Well, not nearly as well as *you*, that's for sure."

Amy winced and held her tongue for a moment. It was only a matter of time before he started in on *that* subject. Finally, she said, "You just couldn't resist, could you?"

"Aww, c'mon. This is the first time I mentioned it. I held out as long as I could."

Amy nodded. "Yeah, I guess you did." She motioned them forward to pay respects. Amy picked up a white carnation from a small table then stepped aside to allow others through.

"So," Frank said softly. "What kind of man is he?"

Amy rolled her eyes and whispered back. "Do we have to do this now?"

"I just mean the basics. You know … Generous lover? Technique? For instance, does he have—"

"Frank—it's a funeral. Respect!"

"Fine, fine. You can tell me all about it later."

Amy mumbled, "Yeah, right. Don't hold your breath."

The detectives turned solemn once again as the service continued until finally, the casket began lowering. A low rumble of sobs and moans floated through the crowd, some of whom began to disperse. Frank was looking off to one side and appeared to be concentrating on something. Amy went up on her toes but still couldn't see a damn thing.

"What's up?"

"I think I saw … Not sure." Frank raised himself up a little to allow a better view over the people, then started to move. "C'mon."

"I wanted to place this flower on the coffin."

"It can wait," he said and motioned her along. "You're not gonna believe what I see."

"What is it?"

"Not *what!*"

Amy followed close behind as Frank led them around the gravesite and away from the main crowd toward a shady spot under a big dogwood. Two young women were standing alone and watching the proceedings from a distance. She was incredulous as recognition hit. "You're right," she said to Frank. "*I don't* believe it."

Vonda Cantu and Dixie Newberry were dressed in subdued dark clothing and openly crying. They seemed to be almost leaning on each other for support.

"Hi," Vonda said quietly as they approached. With some difficulty, she composed herself. "I, um, remember … You're the detectives. I'm sorry, but I forget your names."

"McGrail and Lepone," Frank said. "Our condolences. I'm very glad to see you. Amazed, in fact."

"Thank you both for coming. I think they did a nice job with this. I was hoping they would. It's weird—I haven't seen Sylvia Jarrett yet. Dixie and I didn't make it to the service. Was she there?

"Um, no. She wasn't."

"I can't understand how she would miss this."

Frank drew a breath. "We can explain that. First—may I ask where you two have been for the last week?"

"Sure," Vonda said with some waver in her voice. "With what's happened, we decided to get away from it all. Camping up in Tioga County, Pine Creek Gorge."

"Camping?" Amy said in disbelief. "You went camping?"

Vonda nodded. "We got back just this morning, heard on the news about the funeral, and called for details. All they would tell us is the location of the burial."

"But," Amy said, "why would you leave during the investigation?"

"Well, I don't know." Vonda's face was unsettled. "The investigation? It had nothing to do with me. Besides, Sylvia Jarrett is the only one the authorities seem to care about. They were treating her like the queen."

Amy said, "You are Marcus Jarrett's *widow.*"

Vonda nodded, pleased. "Yes. I didn't realize anyone knew that. I wasn't going to bring it up now since people might think it was some kind of stunt.

Especially Sylvia Jarrett. She'll never accept me. Besides, I wanted to grieve in my own way and I don't want a media circus. Marcus deserves better."

"All right." *So far, so good.* Amy took a deep breath. "We have a few other things to clear up. We know that you met with Gilbert Kyser, an exec from Pierce Brothers, in Tacony Creek Park around midnight almost two weeks ago."

Vonda seemed surprised. "He told you?"

"We'd like to know why you met and what was discussed."

"Well," Vonda said sadly, "I was asking around about that party when Dixie … Well, you know." Amy nodded and she continued. "All the men who were there claimed not to know anything. But then Mr. Kyser came forward. He was the only one who would talk to me. But he wanted to meet discreetly. He hadn't seen anything suspicious that night, but heard rumors afterwards. He said that he was sure Zachary Chastang had done it."

"Is that all?"

"Also, he said Zachary was a menace, and had been for a long time, but was protected by the company's money and power. He felt really bad about everything."

"I'm sure. Okay. I have another question. You gave me your diary. In it, you wrote that Marcus was looking at Sylvia Jarrett for possibly tampering with his father's will. You even mention he had theories about how it was done. Also, that he had collected some telling evidence. But here's the problem. His home and work computers showed no trace of any research along those lines."

Vonda nodded. "Oh, there wouldn't be. Marcus never really liked her or trusted her. However, he knew how smart she is. Sylvia Jarrett is like a super-hacker when it comes to computers. Also, she has a lot of resources. We didn't even talk openly about those things. He was always wary of her finding out what he was doing. He was even afraid she may have bugged his home. Marcus was certain that his father revised the will months before he died. He even told Marcus that. But somehow, that version vanished, like it never existed. Also, he never believed his father died from a simple heart attack. Marcus's research was done completely away from work and home. It was all in one of those manila folders." Vonda let out several sobs. "But … It's gone. I don't know what happened to it. It's just … *gone.*"

"Tell me—what was on the outside of the folder?"

Vonda thought about it for only a second, then looked Amy straight in the eye as she answered. "Just one word: Dad."

Amy shared a quick glance with Frank—it all rang true. Vonda and Dixie were alive and well because Corky Buck never got to them. Perhaps they unknowingly spared their own lives simply by being out of town. Just when hope had faded to despair, the extraordinary happened. "All right. I want you to know

Marcus's efforts are safe. That folder is in police custody now. The truth will come out, I promise."

"Oh, my goodness. Thank you, thank you." Vonda looked at Dixie and the two friends quickly hugged.

"So, you've both been out of touch with the outside world since you left?"

Dixie nodded. "Pretty much. We did some hiking. Only one cellphone charger between us. No signal there so it didn't matter much."

"There's another reason, too, why we got away." Vonda paused to draw a breath. "I'm … pregnant. I thought I might be." She sobbed a few times, then composed herself. "I never even told Marcus. I was waiting to be certain before I … Now I … I wish . . ." She cried again and Dixie hugged her. Moments later, they all began a slow walk towards the long line of vehicles that stretched through the cemetery.

"I understand," Frank said. "That's very big news. Congratulations. Just so you're aware, the police department has been looking for both of you. There's been some new developments."

Vonda perked up a bit. "You caught Marcus's killer?"

"Yes, we did." Frank winced. "And we're sorry to hit you with all of it now. This is going to come as a shock. He was killed by Joyce Kyser."

"Dear God. Joyce?" Vonda stopped walking and a tear streaked down her face. "That's—Gilbert's wife. I've met her socially. Oh, my God. Why would she? Were she and Marcus—"

"No," Amy stepped forward. "You were right to believe in Marcus. The whole story is rather convoluted. He was definitely a good man victimized by some very ruthless people."

"I don't understand any of this. But I never doubted Marcus. Down deep, I knew him."

They all stood in silence for a moment. Amy twirled the white carnation while searching for a way to begin the dreadfully intricate story.

Vonda finally said, "You were going to explain why Sylvia Jarrett isn't here. I was sure she'd at least say a few kind words."

Frank nodded. "Right. Well, she's pretty busy and not saying many words at all. That situation will need more explaining. For now, let's just say there's been some surprises concerning leadership of the Jarrett empire. In fact, you're going to be at the center of them."

Vonda glanced at Dixie, then turned back to Frank. "I'm not sure what you mean."

"Marcus amended his own will after you two got married. Between the company bylaws and you being his heir, you're in a unique position. There'll be a lot of red tape. You'll be sorting it out around a big conference table with a bunch of lawyers, I'm sure. Overall, though, I think Marcus would've approved these coming changes. Wouldn't you agree, partner?"

Amy nodded and handed the flower to Vonda. With a sad smile and a tear in her eye, she said, "Yes, I believe he'd be very pleased."

Thanks for reading Root of Deception.

This is the first in a planned series of
Amy & Frank murder mysteries.

I appreciate comments, questions, and critiques.
Email me at amylepone_mysteries@yahoo.com